The Dedalus Book of Greek Fantasy

Edited and translated by David Connolly

Dedalus

Dedalus would like to thank the Greek Ministry of Culture in Athens and The Hellenic Foundation in London for their assistance in producing this book.

Published in the UK by Dedalus Ltd,
Langford Lodge, St Judith's Lane, Sawtry, Cambs, PE28 5XE
email: DedalusLimited@compuserve.com
www: dedalusbooks.com

ISBN 1 873982 84 4

Dedalus is distributed in the United States by SCB Distributors,
15608 South New Century Drive, Gardena, California 90248
email: info@scbdistributors.com web site: www.scbdistributors.com

Dedalus is distributed in Australia & New Zealand by Peribo Pty Ltd,
58 Beaumont Road, Mount Kuring-gai N.S.W. 2080
email: peribo@bigpond.com

Dedalus is distributed in Canada by Marginal Distribution,
695, Westney Road South, Suite 14 Ajax, Ontario, LI6 6M9
email: marginal@marginalbook.com web site: www.marginalbook.com

First published by Dedalus in 2004

Printed in Finland by WS Bookwell
Typeset by RefineCatch Limited, Bungay, Suffolk

A C.I.P. listing for this book is available on request.

THE EDITOR/TRANSLATOR

David Connolly (1954–) was born in Sheffield, England. He studied Ancient Greek at the University of Lancaster, Medieval and Modern Greek Literature at Trinity College, Oxford, and received his doctoral degree for a thesis on the theory and practice of Literary Translation from the University of East Anglia. A naturalized Greek, he has lived in Greece since 1979 and has taught translation at undergraduate and post-graduate level for many years at a number of university institutions in Greece. He has written extensively on the theory and practice of literary translation and on Greek Literature in general and has published some twenty books of translations featuring works by major Greek poets and novelists. His translations have received awards in Greece, the UK, and the USA. His translation of *Eroticon* by Yoryis Yatromanolakis was published by Dedalus in 1999.

Contents

Introduction

Fantasy literature as we understand the term today has not really been cultivated as a literary genre in Greece until quite recently. Few, if any, Greek writers in the two centuries covered by this collection have devoted themselves systematically to the genre and those who have belong almost exclusively to a new generation of young writers. The appearance of these writers perhaps reflects the fact that (or explains why?) fantasy literature has begun to interest a wider readership in Greece only in the last couple of decades. During this period, numerous works by foreign authors of fantasy fiction have been translated and published in Greece. This same period has also seen the appearance of several anthologies of Greek fantasy literature and all its subgenres. The most notable of these is the four-volume anthology of fantasy short stories (published between 1987 and 1998) covering works mainly from the nineteenth and twentieth centuries and edited by Makis Panorios, who, single-handedly, has done more than anyone to promote fantasy literature in Greece. Roughly half the stories translated for this collection have been taken from his anthology.

The fact that fantasy literature has not been systematically cultivated in Greece is perhaps surprising given that all the constituent elements of fantasy literature exist in the Greek literary tradition from antiquity right up to the birth of the modern Greek State in the first half of the nineteenth century. As Panorios points out, Greek mythology contains almost all those themes found in modern fantasy literature: super heroes, fabulous beasts, the living dead, spirits, magic, journeys in space and fantasy worlds. And these same elements are also present throughout ancient Greek literature. In the *Iliad* and the *Odyssey*, we have numerous instances of divine intervention, clashes with demons, voyages to other worlds, descents to the netherworld, spirits of the dead, magical objects, transformations, and the appearance of gods and demons. Similar elements are present in ancient tragedy – superhuman beings, mysterious beasts, flying chariots, ghosts, the return of the dead, fantastic places, witches, magical objects – and even in Attic comedy, notably in the works of Aristophanes, we find cities suspended in the sky, talking animals, sprites, satyrs, journeys to Hades, etc. And it should not be forgotten that in Plato we have the first reference to Atlantis and the motif of the lost submerged world. In the later Hellenistic period, these same fantasy elements are abundantly in evidence in Apollonius' *Argonautica*, which contains perhaps the first literary reference to a robot in the shape of Talos, the bronze giant, and also in pseudo-Callisthenes' *Romance of Alexander the Great*, which contains perhaps the first literary reference to a submarine in the form of the 'glass ark' in which Alexander travels under the sea. However, the most striking example of fantasy literature in the 2nd century AD is provided by Lucian in his novels *Icaromenippus* and the *True Story*, in which we find journeys to the moon by ship or on an eagle's wings, cosmic battles, giant beings, strange beasts, transformations of people into animals and the workings of magic.

Yet, even in the medieval and modern era, fantasy elements are prevalent in the Greek literary tradition beginning with the 11th-century epic of *Diyenis Akritas*, who has superhuman power, fights with beasts and Amazons and duels with the personification of death in the figure of Charon. During the following centuries, there is a multitude of romances and tales of chivalry almost all with elements of fairytale, the supernatural and magic, including motifs such as enchanted palaces, dragons and magic rings. After the fall of Constantinople in 1453 and during almost 400 years of Turkish rule, the only outlet for these elements was in the living oral tradition of the folk song. Here again, we find phantoms, people who return from the dead, haunted bridges, dragons, magic rings, talking animals, fantastic places; in short, a dream world freed from rationalism or, put another way, a poetic rationalization of an irrational world.

Coming at the end of this period of subjugation, the most notable literary work of fantasy is provided by the national poet, Dionysios Solomos, in his *Woman of Zakythos* (1825). This is a text characterized by a dream-like atmosphere, with the presence of phantoms and eerie visions, and in which the story is narrated by a hieromonk who, though invisible, is physically present and witness to all taking place.

Following the 1821 Greek War of Independence and in the century after the birth of the modern Greek State, Greek literature tends either to be influenced by foreign models or dominated by the depiction of Greek manners and customs, culminating in writing characterised by a search for national identity, by the search for Greekness. Fantasy literature during this period is marginalized and relegated to the realm of non-serious literature. If these factors partly help to explain the break with the fantasy tradition of the past and why the genre has not been systematically cultivated in Greece in the past two centuries, Panorios' anthology shows, nevertheless, that it is possible to find numerous works of fantasy written during this period by authors who would not normally be associated with fantasy fiction, and herein lies one of the main interests in the present collection and one of the basic criteria for the choice of the authors included. So, for example, the collection contains prose works of fantasy by C.P. Cavafy and other Greek poets such as Achilleus Paraschos, Napoleon Lapathiotis and Tassos Leivaditis. It also contains fantasy works by modern classic authors such as Alexandros Papadiamantis, Andreas Karkavitsas and Yorgos Theotokas, and similar 'forays' into the world of fantasy literature by contemporary authors better known for their work in other genres, such as Petros Ambatzoglou, Yoryis Yatromanolakis, Demosthenes Kourtovik and Aris Marangopoulos.

A further criterion for the choice of works to be included was the attempt to provide examples of fantasy writing from the whole period in question and, within this period, to provide examples of all the sub-genres within fantasy literature, defined in its broadest sense as referring to events which depart from what is possible or plausible in reality or which take place in that area where the rational and irrational worlds overlap and often clash. Of the thirty stories anthologized, roughly a quarter were written and published in the nineteenth century, a quarter in the first seventy-five years of the twentieth century and half were published in the last twenty-five years, which is indicative of the growing interest in fantasy literature in recent years. The themes in this anthology include inter-planetary travel (Lascaratos and Grigoriadis), vampires (Paraschos, Ambatzoglou), encounters with the devil (Cavafy, Theotokas), fairytale (Roïdis, Papadiamantis, Karkavitsas), haunted places (Kourtovik), the accursed hero (Kontoglou), the macabre and grotesque (Episkopopoulos, Gonatas), the surreal (Embiricos, Valaoritis), the bizarre and absurd (Leivaditis, Houliaras) and so on. The collection also features works by authors who have systematically cultivated the genre: namely, Tassos Roussos (who describes the quest of a latter-day alchemist) and Makis Panorios (who puts his actor in the position of having to decide whether he will agree to perform on another planet).

Despite this attempt to make the collection as representative as possible, both historically and thematically, it is never possible in any anthology to exclude the criterion of personal taste and I make no apology for this. It is also for reasons of personal taste that the collection is limited to short stories and does not include extracts from longer works or novels, which rarely, in my experience, do justice to the original. So, some notable Greek fantasy novels and novellas such as Demosthenes Voutyras' *From Earth to Mars* (1929); Yorgos Dendrinos' *Ichor* (1936); Alexandros Schinas' *Before the Machine Gunner* (1960); Renos Apostolidis' *Anthyli* (1973) and Tassos Roussos' *The Manuscripts of Manuel Salinas* (1987) are not represented in this anthology. Nor would it have been feasible to include extracts from the substantial number of fantasy novels published in the last ten to fifteen years by at least a dozen younger writers.

It is evident from the fantasy literature being produced today in Greece that its devotees are keen to establish it as a serious literary genre and to create a tradition for that genre. For example, a number of recent anthologies devoted to science fiction and horror contain specifically commissioned works by established writers better known for their work in other genres. Similarly, by looking for fantasy elements in works of writers of the past, it is possible to produce large anthologies of fantasy writing, even though the fantasy elements may be extraneous to the author's main purpose, which may be satire or didacticism or humour or social criticism or whatever. And, just as the surrealists attempted to establish a tradition by claiming authors of the past as surrealists, so, in Greece, the devotees of fantasy literature may choose to appropriate many of the authors whose works are presented in this anthology as precursors of their own fantasy works. And in this sense, the works in the present anthology should be seen not as a selection from the best of Greek fantasy writing of the past, but as possible foundations on which to build the future of Greek fantasy.

Journey to the Planet Jupiter

Andreas Lascaratos

It was a bright clear summer evening and, reclining in my deckchair, full of arrogance, I was gazing at the stars, lost in my own metaphysical reflections.

Full of arrogance because Earth and sea and everything they contain are all man's playthings. And I, being a man, regarded myself as Master of the Universe.

The heavens had been created for me; to receive me in my consummation after death. And the shining celestial bodies to enchant me during my existence here. Coming down to my own person – I was the centre of the infinite and the purpose of Creation!

Jupiter was the star that above all caught my eye. A huge and splendid star! A world twelve hundred times the size of ours, so our astronomers tell us!

If that planet, I thought to myself, were inhabited by animate beings, these beings, whether human or otherwise, would naturally be huge, corresponding to the size of their planet; and perhaps correspondingly intelligent. Nevertheless, my vanity would not permit me to accept other beings more intelligent than us, and all I was left with was a burning curiosity to find out what was up there.

Why, I said to myself, can we not communicate with them? There was so much we might learn! So much perhaps that we might misconstrue!

The sight of this Star enchanted me. I was unable to turn my gaze from it; and my desire to explore it brought me closer to it and almost carried me there.

Dante went on longer journeys, while living, for he went to Hell and to Purgatory and to Paradise, leaving no stone unturned in those unearthly abodes. You'll say that he, *tanto era pien di sonno in su quel punto*, that he may have seen them in his sleep. Yet Voltaire's heroes were clever and went from world to world with the greatest of ease and left us in their journals a precise record of all they saw in those worlds and the manner in which they went there. And as,

> the steps of the first
> are a bridge for the second,

I too resolved upon my journey, planned it, bided my time, and when the sun's rays, passing over the surface of our Earth, fell upon the planet Jupiter, I grabbed hold of one, mounted it, and in the wink of an eye, I found myself on my beloved star.

Cast down amidst a huge forest on another planet, everything was for me an object of marvel and surprise. The trees were so tall that their tops, which appeared to touch the sky, were almost beyond reach of my vision; their trunks and branches corresponded to their size. The greens . . . O the greens! One cabbage leaf would have feasted numerous families on earth.

I was quite beside myself when I saw it growing dark around me. I raised my eyes and beheld the strangest of sights. Without doubt, it was a man, but a man a thousand times bigger than me, who was bending over me and looking at the ground through what was evidently a magnifying glass.

I straightaway concealed myself behind a leaf equal in size to one of our bed sheets; and from there I leaned forward, full of fear, to see what this remarkable man was doing.

In his right hand, he was holding a pair of pincers, the two arms of which were wrapped in cotton, and he was out catching insects, which he placed inside a glass container. Needless to say that the insects he had were such that, if brought to one of our slaughter-houses, butchered and skinned, they would be sold by the pound; that his small pincers were an enormous instrument and that the glass container for the insects was equal to a huge rotunda for us, given that everything was of a corresponding size.

And so, searching among the leaves and thanks to the power

of his magnifying glass, he wasn't long in uncovering me and immediately brought his pincers to bear on me. I then set off running as fast as I could, trying to escape, hiding from leaf to leaf and from cabbage to cabbage; but the distances that I covered were for him like the distances that our insects cover; in other words, everything was in his sight and within his reach, without his having to move to catch me. Thus, it wasn't long before he had me in his pincers. He placed me in his palm and looked at me with great wonder; then he emptied out all the insects in his container and put me inside, since he feared, justifiably so, that if he put me with the other insects, they would eat me.

Then, this enormous man, not wishing to go on with his hunting, put me in his pouch and set off straightaway for the town.

About this town, or any other town of theirs for that matter, I can tell you nothing, for having fallen into the hands of the entomologist, I ceased to be a human being and became an insect. On arriving at his home, my entomologist-captor put me under a glass bell jar on his desk. He sat beside me and, taking a piece of paper (a piece as big as a large bed sheet for us), began to write.

'To the editor of . . . Please include in your daily newspaper the following amazing news:

Mr X . . ., an imperial entomologist, wishes to announce to the capital's entomologists that while combing the aristocratic country gardens today, he discovered in the grass an insect hitherto unknown and truly amazing, for it possesses the shape and form of a man. He invites his scientific colleagues tomorrow morning at eleven o'clock to examine this unique insect together with him.'

Believing that my natural food was the grass in which he had found me, he had brought a root with him and put it under the glass bell jar for me. Being hungry, I sampled the grass, but it had an unpleasant taste and I was unable to eat it.

I am not going to go into any more details concerning my sojourn under the bell jar as they are of little interest and I shall come straight to the gathering of the entomologists.

The next day, eight entomologists from the capital presented themselves at the residence of the imperial entomologist, Mr X . . . Then this gentleman took hold of me, still inside the glass bell jar, and carried me into another room, where his colleagues were waiting around a table; all of them armed with magnifying glasses.

I am not relating here every single thing in all its glory as this would continually interrupt the narrative and would be tiresome for you and would perhaps even be unnecessary for you, since being aware that this Planet is twelve hundred or fourteen hundred times bigger than our own Planet, you may easily imagine that, correspondingly, everything there is more or less twelve hundred or fourteen hundred times bigger than it is here.

So, just imagine what sort of men these were! What sort of room that was! What sort of table it was around which they were standing! And what a sight I presented before them . . .! Such a sight that they needed magnifying glasses to see me! They passed me from hand to hand, and each of them examined me through his magnifying glass, marvelled at me and at the same time marvelled at the power of the Almighty for having endowed nature with even anthropomorphic insects.

Of course, they said, there has to be more than one of them. There must be others like this, and God in his Greatness has placed these in nature in order to curb our arrogance, by giving our human form to insects.

I listened to all they said as, to my great good fortune, they spoke Greek! I have to admit that though at first their size frightened me, the sound of their language filled me with joy and so heartened me that I gladly came close to them and desired to communicate with them.

There is nothing more heartening in a foreign Land than hearing the sound of your own language. 'I too speak as you do,' I shouted, without being able to restrain myself. They stared at each other and exclaimed: 'It can talk!' And they gazed at me with merriment and compassion and repeated 'It can talk like us! We can learn from it directly whatever we want to know about it and about its kind.'

The sound of his voice fell upon me like thunder; and I imagine my own voice barely reached his ears, even though I shouted as loudly as I could; for they too, on hearing me speak their language, gladly picked me up in their pincers and held me close to their ears in order to hear my reply.

'Are there more like you in the cabbages where you were found?' This was their first question.

'No,' I told them. And I related to them whence and how I had come to their world. They no longer had any doubt that my wondrous coming was the work of God, in order to curb their human arrogance, showing them that they should not take such pride in their supposedly superior human form, since even insects possess it.

Next, they desired to learn from me about our World. And I considered telling them about Epirus and Thessaly and how we hoped before long to liberate Ioannina, too, from the Turkish yoke. But to my great surprise, I saw that they understood nothing of what I was saying. All they were interested in was the sound of my voice, which, so they said, was just like that of one of their mosquitoes! Strange, I thought to myself, such people yet they know nothing of geography! Shame on them and their size!

They wanted to learn whether we had any idea concerning the existence of God. And I told them that we were familiar with the one true God, the Creator and Legislator of the boundless universe.

They seemed pleased by this and marvelled that the knowledge of God's existence should reach as far even as insects. And if I had left it at that, I would have come out of it with honour in their eyes. But heartened by my immediate success, I thought I would reap further laurels, by outlining our entire theology.

I told them, therefore, that God deigned to send His Angel to Earth to visit one of our women and to announce that she would bear God's son, which is in fact what happened.

'Which means that God is your in-law!' one of them said, jokingly.

I was shocked by his irony, but I continued, saying that this

Son is also God of all, and consequently their God too; together with his father and a third person known as the Spirit. And these Three are not really Three, but One; nor are they One, but Three, and again not Three but One. And I told him how we baptised him the Son of God and how one of our kind was his godfather. At which the previous man spoke up again:

'Well, so you've become godfathers to God too . . .!'

I simply turned my back on him and related to the others various aspects of our Orthodox doctrine.

Smiling, they thanked me, telling me they knew nothing of what God did on our clod (by clod, they meant, of course, our Earth!).

I was about to continue, but a peal of thunder caused by their irreverent laughter long held back, made me shake with fear . . .!

'What a strange idea,' they said, laughing irreverently, 'that God should wish to have a son!!! And by one of His own creatures . . .! And by an insect . . .! And one coming from that insignificant clod of earth . . .! And given that these insects fashioned an insect god in their own image and likeness, it's hardly surprising that as his attributes they gave him their own needs and desires and habits. See how God gave a human form to these insects, but did not give them a human soul, or a mind and spirit worthy of their human form, so that they might come to know the true God, the Creator of All, and their Creator.

And, jokingly, one of them said to me: 'Is it not strange that God never revealed to us anything of what he did with you on your clod of earth? Never revealed to us that we have a Successor? Is it perhaps that he wishes only to be God of your clod of earth and not God of All? Why is it that he is so involved with you whereas he's never had anything to say to us . . .?

And when he arranged his marriage on your clod of earth, and likewise when his son was born, shouldn't he have made all this known to us too? And, indeed, to all the Solar Systems of the Universe, since the whole of Creation everywhere would be equally interested in such matters . . .? And shouldn't he have sent copies of your Doctrine throughout the Firmament to be used everywhere as theological instruction . . .? A necessary step, without which, only you have the privilege of knowing the nature of the Divine hypostasis, whereas the whole of Creation remains in the dark concerning true knowledge of God . . .!'

And one of the others, addressing his fellows, said: 'I am afraid that this insect is putting together an amusing collage of a religion all his own. As I once remember reading in ancient chronicles of ours, three thousand years ago another insect from the same clod of earth came to our Planet, also in human form, and told our ancestors that on their clod they worshipped a God named Zeus, if I'm not mistaken. And it said that this God was in the habit of coming down to their Earth in some guise – I don't recall whether it was that of an angel or some other – and of enjoying himself with their female insects. So, it's quite easy now for this insect here in his semi-ignorance to come up with a pastiche of the two doctrines. For, of course, I am sure that the insects of this clod today, though still insects, must have undergone some spiritual development so as not to attribute to the true God what their forefathers three thousand years ago attributed to the then God, Zeus.'

Another one of them, but with a kind and earnest expression, leaned over and said to me: 'Can't you see, my dear chap, that this doctrine of yours is insulting to God? Can't you see that you've made him an insect the same as you, that in your imagination you've fashioned him in your own image and likeness, that as his attributes you give him your own desires and vices, that you have made him adulterous, slandering him, with one of your married women, whereas he laid down for you, as you say, the commandment *Thou shall not commit adultery*? You have even made him incestuous by having a child with one of his own creatures! And not only this, but as usually is the case with all those who deceive women, you made him abandon the woman, exposing her to the public, together with the child he had cast into your world, and to the harshness of their fellows! Can you not see that you have created Gods for yourselves unworthy even of insects, given that those insects have human form? Gods who are comical, being created from two different natures? Gods . . .'

Angrily, I cut him short: 'So you don't believe . . .'

'No!' he retorted, 'the sublime idea that we have concerning God does not allow us to believe in things that insult His sublime nature.'

Afterwards, one of them said, and the others agreed: 'Let's not get annoyed with these wretches, they're insects; we mustn't ask too much of them simply on account of the fact that they share our human form. It is not the form alone that makes the human. Their soul, as we have seen, corresponds to their microscopic body and they are not open to development of such a kind to enable them to elevate their spirit to the true God. And urged simply by the natural instinct to seek the Divine everywhere, they have fashioned for themselves a God of a kind that their intellectual abilities will allow them.'

The different beliefs of this other World, supported by the unquestionable superiority of its inhabitants, put me to shame. Nevertheless, I was hungry and called my captor, who put me back beneath the glass bell jar, took me with him and carried me back to the cabbages in which he had found me so that I might choose to eat whatever was most suited to me, while he stood there, watching me unceasingly, and with his pincers ready in his hand.

But I had planned my escape well. Thus, at around dusk, when the setting sun began to withdraw its rays from that Planet, I grabbed and held onto one of those rays that had to pass by our Earth and before my fine entomologist had realised it, I was back in our own World among you,

Hale and hearty by God's grace,
And I wrote this story about that place.

Original title: 'Taxidi ston planiti Dia'. Translated here from the text anthologised in Makis Panorios (ed.), *To Elliniko Fantastiko Diiyima* [The Greek Fantasy Short Story], Athens: Aiolos, 1987, pp. 177–182.

Blossom*

Emmanouil Roïdis

And Jesus said, 'Suffer little children to come unto me'.

(Luke 18, 16)

In a village in Magna Graecia, there once lived a little girl who was so kind and pretty that everyone loved her. Though she wasn't rich, she always found a way to help the poor. She shared with them whatever she was given, and when her hands were empty, her heart and mouth were always full of kind sentiments and kind words to comfort them. And it wasn't only the people and domestic animals that loved her, but also the birds of the forest. Whenever they saw her passing, they would come down from the trees and follow after her like little dogs, so that she would share her bread with them.

She was called Blossom, because they had found her one April morning beneath an apple tree, covered in white blossom that had been blown from the tree during the night.

The old couple who had adopted her were so poor that what they earned from the old woman's knitting and the old man's woodcutting was only just enough to keep them from going hungry. Blossom, too, did all she could to help them. She would gather wild strawberries, violets and other flowers from the woods and offer them to passers-by with such a sweet smile that it was rare for anyone to deny her a few coppers; at least those who had any money to give. For there weren't many of those in that poor village, and the bread and chestnuts that the old man and woman ate were never enough to satisfy their hunger, and Blossom's portion was even less, as she shared it with the poor and the birds.

* I would often hear this fairytale during the years of my childhood in Italy; the bare story, that is, and not the detailed episodes. I wrote it without any claim or pretension to extreme demoticism.

Blossom was seventeen years old when, one night, she heard the old man say to his wife:

'I don't know what will become of us unless God works a miracle to help us. The wood that I can carry on my aged back is getting less each day and, as for you, you now need five days, instead of three, to knit one sock. Blossom doesn't eat much, but she loves the poor and the birds and shares her bread with them. I'm wondering what will happen when we have closed our eyes. If she were a couple of years older, I'd send her to settle in the town. Sensible and hard-working as she is, she'd easily find a good position and she wouldn't forget the poor people who had raised her, when, that is, I no longer have the strength to cut wood nor you the fingers to knit.'

Blossom pretended not to have heard anything. The next morning, however, she rose before dawn; made a bundle of her few possessions, hardened her heart, wiped her eyes, that were running like a tap, and went to say goodbye to the old couple. They wept too, but then reflected that it was a sign of God's Will that, that very same night, Blossom had thought exactly what they had been thinking. So they let her go, after giving her a great many kisses, their blessing and a pie to eat on the way.

The entire village came out to accompany her on her way as far as Krya Vrysi. Even a blind man led by his dog and two cripples on crutches followed her that far. She was also accompanied by goats, sheep, hens, geese, ducks, turkeys and crows because people and animals alike loved her and all were sad at her leaving.

As long as she could still see the old couple in the distance waving their handkerchieves in farewell, Blossom tried to be brave; but when she could no longer see them, she felt that she was all alone in the world for the first time and she was overcome by sorrow and her eyes again filled with tears. She walked all day, without stopping even to take a bite of her pie. Heartache fills the empty stomachs of the miserable like bread.

After walking ten whole hours, she sat down beneath a chestnut tree to rest. She had barely sat down, however, when she was startled by two gunshots and the husky barking of a dog. She turned to see what was happening and saw a cloud of birds flying away in fear.

'Come over here,' she shouted, 'come quickly and hide in this thicket. Don't be afraid, I'll help you escape, providing the hunter doesn't kill me too and the dog doesn't eat me.'

The birds recognised her voice, gathered around her and rushed to hide in the undergrowth, huddled next to each other, and Blossom could hear their hundred tiny hearts beating ticktock like the clocks in the clockmaker's workshop.

At that moment, the hunter appeared together with his dog, a terrible beast with yellow hair, sharp teeth and red eyes that shone like burning coals.

'Little girl,' he asked her, 'have you seen any birds or other game pass by this way? I've been hunting since this morning and I still haven't killed anything. I'll give you this silver coin if you point me in the right direction.'

While the hunter was speaking, the dog continued to bark and the hearts of the birds to pound and the red sunset made the silver coin glitter as if it were gold.

'You were right to ask me,' Blossom replied. 'Only a moment or two before you came, I saw a flock of partridges flying north, two hares running opposite, a roe setting off eastwards and a brace of pheasants westwards. All you have to do is choose, but you don't have any time to waste, if you want to catch up with them.'

The hunter gave her the coin and set off eastwards, but the dog seemed reluctant to go; it obstinately remained, sniffing among the twigs, growling and baring its terrifying teeth. It was then that Blossom thought of giving it her pie in order to pacify it; its master also gave it a kick and only then did the evil animal decide to follow him, albeit disgruntled and continuing to bark, as if to say to the hunter that it was shameful that a little girl should thus fool a full-grown man.

When the hunter had disappeared far into the woods and the dog's barking could no longer be heard, the birds came out of their hiding-place and couldn't do enough to show their gratitude to Blossom. They perched on her shoulder, sang their thanks in her ear, fanned her with their wings and playfully pecked her hands, lips, cheeks and neck. The chaffinches and wrens went off to bring her cherries, jujubes, blackberries and gooseberries, while the sparrows and robins prepared a soft bed of chestnut leaves, mint and lavender for her to sleep on. When she had said her prayers and lain down on this fragrant mattress, they covered her with fern so she wouldn't be cold and then settled in the surrounding trees to watch over her.

In the morning, the lark's cry woke her up and the other birds came to bid her good morning. When all the singing was over, that most melodious of orators, the nightingale, took the floor (so to speak) and said to her in bird-language, which Blossom understood and even spoke a little:

'Yesterday, you told us that you were on your way to the capital to seek your fortune, and this morning we learned from a magpie that a unique opportunity has arisen that you should grab by the tail. Since becoming a widower last year, the king has grown weary of splendour, glory, riches and everything else for which the world envies him. His boredom and melancholy is such that he has had recourse to offering half his kingdom to anyone managing to help him pass just one hour without yawning and sighing. Many have come from all over to try. The contest will take place this evening and it is only five hours' walk to the capital. Rise up, then, Blossom, and adorn yourself in order to go to the palace and win the prize. I will accompany you together with some of the other birds and I'll whisper in your ear what you have to do.'

'My beloved birds,' Blossom answered, 'you are all so kind, yet you lack good sense. You ask me to adorn myself without reflecting that it is only you that God has seen fit to adorn with fine feathers. I have nothing to wear but this old dress I have on. Surely you don't expect me to go in this to stand before the court and the king?'

'Birds are not as silly as people think,' replied the nightingale. 'I wouldn't have told you to adorn yourself if we hadn't taken care to prepare the fineries. We are friends with the silkworms and we set them to work all through the night to make you this dress, which is second to none in the whole world.'

And then they brought a gown of pure white satin, embroidered with all the flowers of spring and all the stars of the sky.

'I searched all night,' said the bee-eater, 'to find you this white rose to put in your hair.'

'And I collected drops of dew,' said the wren, 'and I have made you this necklace that sparkles more than any diamonds.'

'And I've brought you this fan,' said the wagtail, 'for which each bird gave its finest feathers.'

After putting on all these precious fineries, Blossom looked so beautiful that all the birds together began to sing in praise of her abundant charms. She alone continued to be worried and pensive.

'What will become of me,' she said, 'when the king addresses me and realises from my words that I am a peasant girl from the hills who knows nothing of the world?'

'Don't worry,' replied the nightingale. 'My friend the crow, who you see beside me, has had her nest on the palace roof for a hundred and twenty years and knows everything, including all the secrets. I have brought her here on purpose, in order to instruct you. In one hour, she will teach you so much that you will know more about the king than he knows himself.'

With the hunter's coin, Blossom hired an elegant coach for the evening and at the appointed time of nine o'clock, she presented herself in the great hall of the palace. The impression created by the beauty of her face and the splendour of her dress was such that all the women not wearing make-up turned green with envy, and from that evening it was known which of them daubed themselves and which did not.

The king stepped down from his throne and went over to receive her; a thing he never did, save only at the visit of the Empress of the Levant. Without any thought for formality, he took her by the hand and made her sit beside him, asking from which realm she had come, or if she were heaven-sent, as he could not believe that the earth could have given birth to such a beautiful woman.

Blossom blushed and answered with great modesty and charm that she was a humble peasant-girl who had come to compete with the others for the prize.

'You should be aware,' the king told her, 'that I am so sick and tired of all entertainment and amusement that nothing pleases me any more. It's been many years since I last laughed. Everything seems dull, insipid, tame and tedious. And your beauty has dazzled me, though without curing the weariness and boredom in my heart. I hope that your ability to amuse is as great as your beauty.'

And having said this, he ordered that the contest begin.

His words frightened Blossom, who had no idea how she would manage to make this sullen king laugh. She would have lost her nerve if, at that moment, the nightingale hadn't come to sing in her ear: 'don't worry, the birds have prepared everything.'

The first contestant to appear was a famous foreign conjuror or legerdemainist, as the erudite might say, who was so dextrous that he had been taken for a wizard and had been forced to leave his country, where they were then in the habit of burning wizards. He guessed the card, the ace of spades, that the king was thinking of, fried eggs in the Lord Chamberlain's hat and sent the blond wig of the Grande Dame to cover the groom's bald patch. Then, he succeeded in removing a gallows rope from the nose of the Minister of Justice and a shy little hare from the pocket of the Field-Marshal. Everything was going well, only the king still hadn't laughed. In the hope of achieving this too, he found a means to conjure away the royal crown, which he used to crown the head of a boar that was set in the centre of the dinner table. It seems, however, that the king was not in good spirits. Instead of laughing, he found the prank tasteless and ordered that the prankster be thrown out with a good kick to the part of his body that is located below the back.

The second contestant was a serious, white-bearded philosopher from the region of Holland. He had with him a strange contraption, which had a kind of glass cauldron on top. He opened it and tossed some coal dust inside, a spoonful of mercury, a handful of blue vitriol, a twig of rosemary and a pinch of ammoniac salt. He stirred it with a gold spoon and the mixture immediately grew hot, glowed red, flared up, then cooled, and the cauldron was found to be full of diamonds as big as a pigeon's eggs. All the courtiers were ecstatic and all the ladies reached out to take one of the diamonds that the Dutch sage had begun to hand out. But, once again, the king was angry and ordered the ladies to give back whatever they had taken and, addressing the alchemist, said angrily: 'Did you not consider, foolish man, that if diamonds become as common as pebbles, then mine, which are the finest in the land, will lose all their value, and if I should ever need money, how will I sell them for as much as I want? Get out of here, and if you ever again fashion any diamonds, I will smash your contraption and your head with it.'

The third contestant was the leading scientist of a new world, discovered by someone called Columbus, across the great mass of water known as the Atlantic. After many studies and tests, this man from the new world had succeeded in enclosing the sun's rays inside small pear-shaped bottles so bright that the king and all the courtiers were dazzled and blinked their eyes like bats beset by the morning sun before they have had time to dart inside their caves. After almost blinding everyone, the scientist started to explain that these bright pears were a new form of lighting, and that for half the expense, they would produce ten times more light than oil, the price of which would, therefore, fall to one tenth of what it was, since it would no longer be used except for frying and for salads.

'Are you not aware, vile wretch,' the king broke in, red with rage, 'that the estates in my kingdom, both mine and my people's, are covered with olive groves, yet you come here to make the price of oil fall! Get out of my sight, and if tomorrow you are still in my realm, I will have you doused in oil and burnt alive.'

Now it was the turn of Blossom, who was shaking from head to foot on seeing how riled the king was. But the nightingale again sang something to her to give her courage. Everyone's eyes were fixed on her and the silence was such that you could hear an insect flying or a blade of grass growing.

Blossom then gave the order for them to open the twenty windows in the hall. And straightaway little birds of every kind and description flew inside: yellow bee-eaters, redwings, silvery kingfishers, blackbirds, fine-feathered thrushes, pied goldfinches, linnets, lapwings, wagtails, marsh birds, blue tits, swifts, larks, whitetails, woodpeckers and jays. After fluttering to and fro for a few minutes around the lamps and the chandeliers like the mad birds that they were, they formed a large circle. The nightingale stood in the middle, beating the rhythm with his wings like a maestro, and such a sweet symphony was heard that you would have thought it had been composed by the hymnographer of Paradise, Saint Cecilia. Of all the pieces, the one most liked was a languorous quartet by the linnets that moved everyone to tears, together with the magpie's comic song, which had such a bouncy and lively rhythm that all the courtiers began to twitch and tap their feet as if their leggings had filled with ants.

'Now dance, my birds,' Blossom commanded.

Twenty pairs of canaries then began to dance an extraordinary and unprecedented waltz. Each pair of birds held onto each other by one wing and flew with the other. The couples whirled like spinning-wheels and did the round of the hall ten times. Then the hoopoes danced a lively quadrille on the floor, and the cotillion, with all its changes of step, went down even better. Everyone shrieked with laughter at the coquetry of a haughty goldfinch who liked none of the ten dancers that presented themselves to her; she looked at them with scorn and shook her head. She happened to like the eleventh, and to prove it to him, she gave him a fly she had caught. He swallowed it, then took hold of his partner and they began to twirl with incomparable grace and art.

I'd never finish if I were to endeavour to recount everything. The entertainment ended with a shower of rare flowers that the swallows had brought from foreign parts. The rarest of all was a blue lotus from the upper Nile that Blossom offered to the king.

He was now full of life and joy. The blood raced through him and lent colour to his pale countenance, and his eyes sparkled. Without giving any thought to his grandeur or his noble line, or to what the princes, dukes, generals, ministers and bishops watching might say, he bent and kissed Blossom on her forehead, both cheeks and her chin. This cross of kisses, so they say, was tantamount to an official betrothal in Magna Graecia at that time. I cannot say whether this betrothal was pleasing to all the courtiers or to one woman in particular. Yet, whether they liked it or not, they were all obliged to shout: Long live our queen! The birds shouted the same thing in their language, and on seeing that Blossom wept as she bade them farewell, they promised to come and visit her often.

The wedding took place the following week, with great pomp and ceremony. And among the guests invited, of course, were Blossom's foster parents, the old man and woman, whose joy made them look ten years younger.

So that his beloved wife might have them near her, the king ordered that they be given a public position in his capital. Seeing that the old woman was prudent, thrifty, diligent and moderate in her needs, he made her minister of finance. It was a little more difficult to find a position for the old man. He didn't even know how to read or write. The king was wracking his brains to find some way of accommodating him when the minister of public education happened to die. There not being any other position available, he put the old man in the position vacated by the deceased, and from that time on, it has been the custom, and still is in many parts, to give the ministry of education to whoever is the most illiterate in the land.

Original title: 'I Milia'. First published in 1895 in the Christmas edition of the newspaper *Acropolis*. Translated here from the text anthologised in Makis Panorios (ed.), *To Elliniko Fantastiko Diiyima* [The Greek Fantasy Short Story] vol. 4, Athens: Aiolos, 1997, pp. 147–153.

The Vampire's Son

Achilleus Paraschos

In Leivadia, during the years of Turkish Rule, there lived an old midwife, ma-Rene, who was renowned for her professional skill, not only in the town itself but throughout the neighbouring region, even as far as Thebes.

One wintry Saturday night, around midnight, while ma-Rene was sleeping, she heard three knocks at her door and a voice calling her by name to open up quickly.

For a midwife and, particularly, one like her, a visit of this kind was nothing strange. And so ma-Rene got up straightaway and, calling to her visitor to wait a little, she hurriedly got dressed and went to open the door. Facing her was a man she'd never seen before. He was a young man, dressed all in black, with gleaming black eyes, long shiny hair falling over his shoulders, a thin, twirling moustache and a long, well-kempt beard. Despite the gleam in his eyes, however, his face was white and drawn, like the faces of the dead. On the whole, however, his appearance was impressive and imposing; the look of a man not to be refused.

This stranger, then, stood for a moment on the doorstep and said to the midwife:

'Two horses await us. Make haste, old woman, for my wife is suffering and in the pangs of labour . . . Come . . . Tonight, your fortune is to be made. But don't dally . . . Make haste.'

'I'm ready, fine sir,' stammered the old woman. 'Though I don't think we'll be needing the horses. For surely we're not going far.'

The stranger smiled; and pointing to the two horses standing nearby, he asked ma-Rene to choose which of the two she wanted to ride.

'Don't be afraid,' he added. 'They're both as meek as lambs. Besides, I can't believe it's the first time you've ever ridden a horse . . .'

And while ma-Rene was somewhat at a loss and unable to think straight, the stranger went up to her and, taking her in his strong arms, lifted her up and sat her on the first horse. Then, with cat-like agility, he leapt onto the second horse and thus they set off together, side by side.

During the course of the journey through the town's deserted streets, the stranger replied laconically, though with the utmost politeness, to the old woman's hesitant questions. Meanwhile, on seeing them pass by, the dogs let out a plaintive howl and cowered in fear, with their tails between their legs.

Every so often, the horses whinnied and then, like an echo, came an owl's hoot in reply.

Once they were outside the town, the stranger spurred on his horse. The old woman tried to hold hers back, but, uncontrollable, it followed the other one.

The two of them now galloped side by side in the darkness.

It was a gloomy night. Not a single star shone in the sky. You couldn't see a hand in front of you. And yet the horses raced unhindered as if it were day, jumping over bushes and ditches, turning this way and that, galloping up and down slopes with uncommon assuredness and agility. And – what was really strange – throughout this mad dash, the old woman felt neither unsettled, nor stunned, nor dizzy. She kept on galloping beside her strange escort, without being able to see anything of him in the pitch blackness.

At one point, feeling scared, she asked him where they were and where they were going and begged him to stop a while. But he answered her curtly:

'Keep going and don't ask!'

The old woman felt even more scared and tried to halt her horse. But in vain.

After another hour of non-stop galloping, they spied a faint light flickering in the distance. Whinnying and galloping even faster, the horses made straight for this spot.

In a few minutes, the two riders found themselves before a cave, the entrance to which was covered by thick bushes and thorns. A lamp was shining within. The man dismounted first and, after helping the old woman down, patted the rumps of the horses, which, whinnying one last time, vanished like smoke.

'Listen, old woman,' said the stranger to ma-Rene, 'if my wife gives birth to a male child tonight, your fortune will be made, as I told you. But woe betide you if the child is a girl or if it dies in your hands. Now follow me . . .'

Unable to do anything else, the poor midwife followed him, speechless and terrified.

The cave they entered was deep and was lit by candles placed here and there. The mysterious stranger suddenly stood before an upright gravestone attached to the wall and, pushing it with his foot, opened it like a door flap. Behind this was a stone stairway leading deeper into the cave and lit by a huge funereal lamp. The man turned round, looked imperiously at the midwife, and then slowly and formally began to descend the steps. This was a silent command to the poor woman, who, willingly or otherwise, followed him with fear in her heart. Trembling, she walked down thirteen steps and found herself once again in front of a large door. This door opened onto a marble passageway leading to a large brightly-lit chamber, in which there was nothing save for a round table with a candelabra and a dish of sugared wheat, an offering for funeral mourners.

The mysterious stranger sat down, or rather sank wearily into the only armchair, which was set beside the table, and reached out to take from the dish.

'I'm hungry!' he said.

And taking a handful of sugared wheat, he greedily gulped it down.

Then, turning to the midwife who was standing there terrified and cowering, he said commandingly:

'You'll go through that door at the end and you'll enter an empty chamber, and then another, till you get to my wife, who is in labour in her bed. See to it that the child born is male . . .! Go, and if this be so, your fortune will be made. I shall sit here and eat my sugared wheat.'

The old woman, urged on by a higher power, by the power of this stranger's commanding presence, walked towards the door he had shown her and entered a brightly-lit chamber that recalled a Sultan's harem. Suddenly, she heard a loud groan coming from the adjacent chamber. Trembling, she went in and found herself before a woman lying on her bed. She was a beautiful woman with long fair hair, yet so thin and with such a look of pain on her wan face that, on setting eyes on her, the old woman shuddered and took a step backwards.

'Who brought you here, poor woman?' asked the pale woman, beckoning to her to go and sit beside her.

The old woman recounted everything that had happened and asked what all this meant and where she was.

The young woman shook her head sorrowfully.

'And where have you left him?' she asked.

But at that moment, excruciating pains wracked her, making her groan loudly.

For an hour the labour pains tormented her, causing her spasms of great agony. Finally, with one last groan, the baby came out into the world.

Trembling, the old midwife took the baby in her arms and immediately jumped for joy on seeing that it was a boy. Yet while she was arranging the swaddling clothes to wrap the newborn, she saw him suddenly open his large round eyes and stare straight at her. And before the old woman had recovered from her surprise, this frightful babe opened his mouth, armed with its fangs, not to cry but to let out loud and horrific peals of laughter.

Shuddering in horror, the old midwife threw this monster onto the bed and began crossing herself.

Then, the young mother turned to her and, sighing, said:

'Suffocate it, my poor woman, suffocate it! It's the Devil's spawn, a child of the Vampire.'

Pale, speechless, stunned and at her wits' end, the old woman listened while the young mother went on imploring her:

'Oh, dear woman, if you love life and your soul, then go; go far away from this infernal place. The man who brought you here is a Vampire! He is my husband . . . He has been dead for a great many years. He could find no rest on his own and one night he snatched me and brought me here . . .'

She went on to relate how the newborn was the fruit of her horrific union with him, with a Vampire, and how she suffered indescribable torments living with him, though she wanted for nothing; she led a princely life.

'. . . For three whole years,' she added, 'I have been living this infernal life with my Vampire husband. For three whole years he has kept me as his slave and his queen. I have never once heard him speak to me. With his eyes alone – with those terrible eyes – he expresses his desires to me. He sits beside me at our plentiful table and eats in silence. Then, he sleeps all night with me and leaves in terror at the squawking of the first bird. He leaves and goes into the great parlour and sits in his armchair next to the round table with the sugared wheat. During the day, this armchair becomes a coffin; his coffin. Every Friday at midnight, I lose him from my sight and I see him again on Saturday at midnight . . . Only three times a year, on Christmas night, on Twelfth Night and throughout Holy Week, he vanishes completely . . . I've often tried to get away from here, to escape, but each time I try, a giant snake comes and wraps itself around my legs and binds me like rope. I think that this huge snake is the Vampire himself. Can you see this tiny spot on my neck? It's from a wound that he made. Once a year on All Souls' Night, he sinks his teeth into my neck here and sucks my blood . . . But go, poor woman, go quickly from here, if you value your life and your soul!'

There was still more she wanted to say, but the sound of heavy footsteps in the passageway caused her to fall silent and feign sleep. And before long the Vampire appeared. He grimly walked up to his wife's bed, glanced at the baby and, on seeing that it was a boy, broke into a ghastly smile of joy. Then, he took the child in his arms and, opening a tiny hole in its neck with his teeth, no bigger than the hole made by the weasel in the hen's head, he put his lips to it and began sucking the infant's blood. At the same time, however, the newborn did precisely the same thing to his father's neck. And thus, father and son, entwined in a monstrous union, drank each other's blood . . .!

When, eventually, they had slaked their thirst, the Vampire motioned to the old woman to follow him. And so with him leading the way, they walked along the passageway, crossed the large empty chamber, ascended the thirteen steps of the stairway, trod over the damp ground in the cave and emerged at the entrance covered with brambles and thorns. It was still the middle of the night and pitch black. There, the Vampire halted and, in a resounding voice, said to the old woman:

'I'm thirsty . . .! You have living blood in your veins. You whet my appetite. But because you helped my wife to give birth, I shall not harm you . . . If the child born this night lives, you and your kin shall live happily. Woe betide you and yours, however, should he die! Now, go and be on your way . . .'

With these words, the Vampire vanished, as if the earth had opened up and swallowed him.

Trembling, the poor old woman crossed herself and, reciting prayers under her breath, set off in the night to get as far away as she could from that god-forsaken place. She walked until daybreak over rough paths, groped her way between rocks and tree-trunks, stumbled in ditches, clambered up slopes and when, after indescribable hardships and frights, she finally reached her home, she collapsed in exhaustion, almost swooning, onto her bed.

A few good neighbours came to her aid, helped her, brought the priest to bless her, and when she had recovered somewhat, she sat and related to them everything about her terrible ordeal of the previous night.

Time passed quickly after that and the tale was almost forgotten. But exactly a year later, on the anniversary of that terrible night, the old midwife opened a drawer in her chest and found it full of florins! The largest of these florins, on the top of the pile, bore the image of the newborn child on one of its faces.

The old woman immediately realised where the florins had come from and closed the drawer in terror, without ever spending even one florin, even though she often found herself in great need.

The same thing happened regularly every year. On exactly the same day every year, a new drawer in her chest was found full of money, with the only difference that the florin on top with the child's image was doubled.

In the fourth year, however, the old midwife found only one florin in the fourth drawer of her chest with the image of a dead four-year-old child. She opened the other drawers and, instead of finding the money there untouched, she found only piles of human bones.

The poor old woman realised at once that the Vampire's child had died and guessed the fate awaiting her. So she ran to a priest and confessed in order to take communion, for, as she said, she wouldn't have long to live.

And a few days later, one Saturday night, she saw the Vampire in her sleep, staring at her with his fearful eyes, and heard him say to her:

'I kept my word in what I promised you. While my child lived, I showered you with florins, making you the richest woman hereabouts. But now that my son is dead, you and your kin will die too . . .'

The next day, the old woman called a few neighbours and, after telling them of her dream and asking them to forgive her, she crossed herself and died.

And a year later, all her kin were dead. Wiped out, every last one of them!

This tale was told to me by an old woman from Leivadia.

Original title: 'O yios tou vrikolaka'. Translated here from the text anthologised in Makis Panorios (ed.), *To Elliniko Fantastiko Diiyima* [The Greek Fantasy Short Story] vol. 2, Athens: Aiolos, 1993, pp. 185–189.

Flower of the Shore

Alexandros Papadiamantis

For many nights in a row, Koronios' boy, Manos, had been staring from the spot where he tied up his boat each evening, close to Kotronia on the east side of the shore, between two high rocks and down from an old, abandoned and ruined cottage. It was here that he spread his cape over the prow of the boat and was rocked and lulled to sleep, three feet above the waves, while gazing at the stars and contemplating the Pleiades and all the sky's mysteries. He had been staring, as I said, out to sea, beyond the two grassy islets that like sentinels guarded the mouth of the harbour, at a single sorrowful light – a lamp, beacon, candle or fallen star – flickering far off in the depths of the blackness, atop the waves, and remaining there for hours, seemingly floating and unmoving.

Manos, boatman and fisherman, was feeble-minded just like all mortals. It was already enough that he tied his boat there each evening, beside the two blackened rocks, below the abandoned cabin, a looming, lifeless phantom, which, as rumour had it, was haunted. It was commonly known as 'Rosebud's Cabin'. Why? No one knew. Or, if there were still a few old 'washerwomen' or one or two old-timers who knew the ancient tales of the place, Manos hadn't had any opportunity to ask them.

He'd been staring for several evenings now at that strange light as it flickered and glowed far out to sea, knowing full well that there was no beacon out there. The Government hadn't bothered to take care of such matters in small places where there were no powerful parliamentary representatives.

So, what could the light be? And because, almost every day, he sailed his boat through that passage between the two grassy islets and saw no sign of anything during the day that could explain the presence of that light at night, he felt a great desire to put out in the middle of the night, foregoing his blessed sleep and his contemplation of the stars and the Pleiades, and go there to see what it was and, if necessary, chase after that mysterious glow. Whereupon, Manos, being a feeble fellow as we said, a young twenty-year-old, sought the help of Fafana's grandson, Yalis, who was ten years his senior, telling him of the nocturnal sight and asking him to accompany him on this unusual venture.

⋆ ⋆ ⋆

They put out one night, when the moon was nine days old and would set at around one in the morning. The light could be clearly seen, motionless almost fixed, while the fiery truncated disk slowly sank in the west and was about to disappear behind the mountain. The further they sailed in their boat, the further away the mysterious flame grew, though without visibly moving. They heaved hard at the oars, breaking their backs. The light became ever more distant, seemed even further away. It was unreachable. In the end, it vanished from their sight.

Manos and Yalis crossed themselves several times and exchanged a few words:

'It's not a lamp, it's not a fishing boat, no.'

'So what is it?'

'It's . . .'

Yalis didn't know what to say.

On the night of the third day, and again a couple of days later, the two seamen undertook the venture once more. They saw the mysterious light dancing on the waves. Then, the closer they came, the further away the sight became, till it finally vanished. What could it be?

⋆ ⋆ ⋆

Only one neighbour had noticed the two friends' repeated nocturnal venture in the boat. Libos Kokoïas, a fifty-year-old man, had read many old books thanks to his rudimentary schooling and he'd talked with many knowledgeable old women no longer alive. He sat up awake all night, beside his window, looking out to sea, and it was then that he read his books, that he gazed at the stars and the waves. His cottage, where he lived alone and isolated, was situated a few rocks beyond Rosebud's cabin, where Manos tied his boat, and between the cottages of Rayas' girl, Vasso, and Gavaloyina.

One night, Koronios' boy and Fafana's grandson were preparing to untie the boat, and take to the oars, for the fourth time, to chase after their still uncaught prey.

Libos Kokoïas saw them, emerged from his cottage wearing a white cap and a long robe, as was his custom in the house, clambered over two or three rocks and came to a point just above where the two friends were.

'Where, in God's name, are you off to?' he called to them. 'One or two evenings of late you've been scurrying outside the harbour, without casting lines, without lighting any lamp – and we've not seen you coming back with any fish. Have you both had a vision and you're off somewhere digging for treasure?'

Manos asked Kokoïas to come down and talk more quietly. Then he lost no time in recounting what he'd seen.

Libos listened attentively. Then he laughed:

'Of course, how would you young people know of such matters,' he said, vigorously shaking his head. 'In older times, Manos, things like those you've seen could be seen by all as were pure, now they're seen only by those as are fey. I can't see anything! . . . Can Yalis see the same thing that you say you see?'

Yalis was obliged, with a shyness unbecoming to his age, to admit that he himself couldn't see the light in question but had been convinced of its existence by Manos, who said that he saw it.

Whereupon, Kokoïas began to recount his tale:

'Listen close, young lads. I'm old enough to have known ol' ma Koerano Rayas, the great-grandma of Vasso, my neighbour, and I also knew Gavaloyina's old mother and other old women. They told me many things of long ago, of times long past, like this that I'm about to tell you.

You see that ruin, Rosebud's cabin, that they say is haunted? In times past, there lived there a maiden, Rosebud, so called because of her beauty – when the sun shone she shone too – together with her father, old Therias (or, more properly, Thereus), who hunted Dragons and Spirits with his silver arrows and poisoned darts. A Prince from foreign parts fell in love with the beautiful Rosebud. He gave her his ring and set off to go to war, swearing an oath to her that, once he'd conquered the barbarians, he'd come back to wed her on the day of Christ's birth.

The Prince left. Rosebud remained, casting her tears into the waves, sending her sighs into the air and her prayers to the heavens that the Prince might be victorious, that the day of Christ's birth might come, and that her betrothed might return and wed her.

The day of Christ's birth came. The Blessed Virgin, her face shining, without pain, without help, gave birth to her Infant in the stable. She lifted him, wrapped him in swaddling clothes and laid him in a manger to let him sleep. An ox and an ass joined their breath over the manger and blew softly to keep the Holy Infant warm. There, now the Prince will surely come to take his Rosebud!

Then came the shepherds, two old men with long white hair, holding their crooks, and a shepherd boy with his flute, all three astounded and astonished, and they fell on their knees to worship the Holy Infant. They had seen the Angel, resplendent with glittering white wings; they had heard the cherubim singing: 'Glory to God in the highest!' They remained kneeling for a long time beside the manger, their eyes filled with amazement, avidly worshipping the heavenly marvel. There, now the Prince will surely come to take his Rosebud!

Then the Three Wise Men arrived, riding on their camels. They had gold mitres on their heads and wore furs tinged with deep crimson. And the star, a shining golden star, came down and rested over the roof of the stable, and shone with a sweet celestial light that swept aside the night's darkness. The three aged kings dismounted from their camels, went inside the stable and fell to their knees to worship the Child. They opened their rich saddlebags and took out gifts: gold, frankincense and myrrh.

There, now the Prince will surely come to take his Rosebud!

Christmas passed, the miracle happened, the saviour was born, but the Prince didn't come to take his Rosebud! The barbarians had enslaved the Prince. His armies had been victorious at first, his standards had flown atop the barbarians' castles to the sound of loud cheers. The Prince had attacked with impetuous rashness amidst the ferment and intoxication of victory. The barbarians had captured him by trickery!

The maiden's tears turned bitter in the sea's waves, her sighs dissolved in the air and her prayers fell back to earth, without reaching the throne of the Almighty. Unseen, between these two rocks, sprouted a tiny fragrant flower, known as the Flower of the Shore, and invisible to the eye. And the Prince, who had fallen into the hands of the barbarians, prayed to become a Spark, a flame on the sea, in order to arrive in time, on the day of Christ's birth, so as to keep the oath he had sworn to Rosebud.

Some say that the Flower of the Shore is the flower of the waves' foam. And the Spark, the flame that you saw out at sea, Manos, is the soul of the Prince, who languished and died in the chains of slavery, and no one sees it any more other than those as were pure in times gone by and those as are fey in our days.'

Original title: 'Anthos tou yalou'. First published in the newspaper *Hestia* (24 December 1906). Translated here from the text anthologised in Alexandros Papadiamantis, *Skoteina paramythia* [Dark Tales], selected, edited and introduced by Stratis Pascalis, Athens: Metaichmio, 2001, pp. 121–127.

In the Light of Day

Constantine Cavafy

One evening after supper I was sitting at the San Stefano Casino in Ramleh. My friend, Alexander A., who was staying at the Casino, had invited me and another young man, a close friend of ours, to dine with him. As there was no music that evening, very few people had come, and my two friends and I had the whole place to ourselves.

We talked about various things and, as we weren't the richest of people, the conversation turned quite naturally to the question of money, to the independence it offers and to the pleasures it brings.

One of my friends said that he wished he had three million francs and began describing what he would do and, above all, what he would cease to do if he had such a large amount.

Being more frugal myself, I would have been content with an income of twenty thousand francs a year.

Alexander A. said:

'Had I wanted, I could have been a millionaire many times over – but I lacked the courage.'

His words seemed strange to us. We were more than familiar with the life of our friend, A., and we did not recall his ever being presented with the opportunity of becoming a millionaire many times over, so we assumed he was not being serious and that this was the prelude to some joke. Yet our friend's face showed him to be extremely serious and we asked him to explain his enigmatic remark.

He hesitated for a moment – before saying: 'If I were in any other company – especially among so-called "progressive people" – I wouldn't even try to explain, because they would laugh at me. But we are a little ahead of these so-called "progressive people", in other words, our thorough intellectual cultivation has led us back to simplicity, yet simplicity without ignorance. We have come full circle. And so we have naturally returned to our point of departure. The others have remained midway. They neither know, nor can they even imagine, where the path ends.'

These words did not surprise us in the least. Each of us had the highest regard for himself and for the other two.

'Yes,' Alexander repeated, 'If I hadn't lacked the courage, I would have been a multimillionaire – but I was afraid.

It was ten years ago that it happened. I didn't have much money then – just as now – or rather I had no money at all, but in one way or another I was making progress and lived reasonably well. I was living in Rue Cherif Pasha, in a house owned by an Italian widow. I had three well-furnished rooms and a personal servant, apart from the services of the landlady, who was at my disposal.

One evening I had gone to Rossini's and after having listened to more than a little nonsense, I decided halfway through to return home to bed, since the next day I had to get up early, having been invited to Aboukir on an outing.

Once back in my room, I began in my accustomed way to pace up and down and reflect on the day's events. However, as nothing of great interest had happened that day, I grew sleepy and got into bed.

I must have slept for about one and a half or two hours, without dreaming, as I recall that at around one o'clock I was awoken by a noise from the street and I could not remember any dream. I must have fallen asleep again at around one-thirty. Whereupon, I had the impression that a man of medium height and aged around forty had entered my room. He was wearing rather old black clothes and a boater. On his left hand he wore an extremely large emerald ring. This seemed to me out of place given the way he was dressed. He had a black beard with numerous white whiskers, and there was something strange about his eyes; he had a look which was at once derisive and sorrowful. Generally speaking, however, he was a rather average type. The kind of person you meet often. I asked him what he wanted of me. He didn't reply immediately but stared at me for a few minutes as if in suspicion or as if examining me to make sure he was not making a mistake. Then, he said – in a tone of voice that was humble and servile:

"You are poor, I know. I came to tell you of a way to become rich. Near to Pompey's Column, I know a place where a great treasure lies hidden. Myself, I want none of the treasure – all I want is a small iron box lying at the bottom. Everything else will be yours."

"And of what does this great treasure consist?" I enquired.

"Of gold coins," he said, "and above all of precious stones. There are ten or twelve gold chests filled with diamonds, pearls and, I believe," he said as if trying to recall, "of sapphires."

I wondered why he didn't go himself and get what he wanted and why he had need of me. He didn't give me time to voice my question. "I know what you're thinking. Why, you wonder, don't I go myself and get what I want. There is a reason, which I am unable to reveal to you, which prevents me. There are some things that even I cannot do." When he said "even I", it was as if a light shot from his eyes and an awful grandeur transformed him for an instant. Immediately, however, he returned to his humble manner. "So you would be doing me a great service were you to come with me. I definitely need someone and I choose you, because I have your interests at heart. Meet me tomorrow. I'll be waiting for you from midday until four o'clock in the Petite Place, at the café next to the iron-monger's."

With these words, he vanished.

The next day when I awoke, the dream had completely gone from my mind. But after I had washed and sat down to breakfast, it came back to me and I thought it exceedingly strange. "Would that it were true," I said, and then I forgot about it.

I left for the country outing and enjoyed myself tremendously. There were rather a lot of us – approximately thirty men and women. We were in exceptional spirits; but I will refrain from recounting the details as this has no bearing on the matter in hand.'

At this point, my friend, D., remarked: 'And there is no need. Because I, at least, know all the details. If I'm not mistaken, I too was on that outing.'

'Were you? I don't recall you.'

'Wasn't that the outing organised by Marcos G. . . . before he left for England?'

'Yes, that's right. So you recall what a good time we had. Happy days. Or, rather, days long gone. It's all the same. But to get back to my story – I returned from the celebrations rather tired and it was already quite late. I only just had time to change my clothes and eat before going to the house of friends where an evening of cards had been organised and where I stayed playing till around two-thirty in the morning. I won a hundred and fifty francs and returned home jubilant. I went to bed free of all cares and immediately fell asleep after such a tiring day.

As soon as I was asleep, however, a strange thing occurred. I saw that there was a light in the room, and was wondering why I hadn't turned it off before lying down when I saw coming from the other end of the room – it was quite a big room – the end where the door was, a man whom I immediately recognised. He was wearing the same black clothes and the same old boater. But he looked displeased and said: "I waited for you at the café yesterday afternoon from midday until four o'clock. Why didn't you come? I'm offering you an opportunity to make your fortune yet you appear to be in no hurry. I'll wait for you again at the café this afternoon from midday until four o'clock. Be sure to come." Then he vanished just as on the previous occasion.

But this time I awoke in terror. The room was dark. I turned on the light. The dream was so real, so vivid that I was alarmed and shaken. I couldn't help going over to see whether the door was locked. It was locked as always. I looked at the clock; it was three-thirty. I had gone to bed at three.

I can tell you, and I'm by no means ashamed, that I was terrified. I was afraid to shut my eyes lest I fell asleep again and once more set eyes on my phantom visitor. My nerves on edge, I sat down in a chair. At around five o'clock, it began to get light. I opened the window and watched the street slowly coming to life. Some doors had already opened and the early milkmen and first bakers' carts were passing by. The light reassured me somewhat and I went back to bed and slept until nine o'clock.

At nine o'clock when I woke up and recalled my alarm of the previous night, the events began to lose something of their intensity. In fact, I was at a loss to understand why I had been so upset. Everyone has cauchemars and I had had plenty in my life. Besides, this was hardly a cauchemar. It was true that I had had the same dream twice. But what of it? And was it sure that I had had it twice? Perhaps I'd only dreamt that I'd seen the same man previously? Yet, sifting through my memories, I rejected that idea. It was certain that I had had the dream the night before. Even so, what was strange about that? It seems the first dream had been so vivid that it had left a great impression on me and this would account for the fact that I had had it again. Yet here my logic faltered somewhat. For I couldn't recall the first dream having left much of an impression on me. Throughout the previous day, I hadn't given it a thought. During the outing and the evening's gathering, I had thought of anything but the dream. Yet what of it? Doesn't it often happen that we dream of people whom we haven't seen for many years and about whom we haven't thought for many years. It seems that their memory remains etched somewhere in our minds and suddenly reappears in our dreams. So where was the strangeness in my having dreamt again of something that had happened only twenty-four hours before, even if during the course of the day I hadn't thought about it at all? Then again I wondered whether I had read somewhere about a hidden treasure and that this had secretly acted upon my memory, though however much I racked my brains, I couldn't recall reading any such thing.

Eventually, I grew tired of thinking and began to get dressed. I had to go to a wedding and my haste and choice of what to wear quickly drove the dream from my thoughts without further ado. Then I sat down to my breakfast and, to pass an hour or so, I picked up and read a periodical published in Germany – *Hesperus*, I think it was called.

I went to the wedding, where all the high society of the city had congregated. I knew a lot of people then and so I had to repeat countless times after the service that the bride was beautiful albeit a touch pale, and that the groom was a fine young man and had money and so on and so forth. The wedding was over at around eleven-thirty and afterwards I went to the Bulkeley Station to look at a house that had been recommended to me and that I was going to rent for a German family from Cairo, who intended to spend the summer in Alexandria. The house was indeed airy and well laid-out, though not as big as I had been led to believe. Nevertheless, I promised the landlady to recommend the house as being suitable. The landlady couldn't thank me enough and, in order to win my sympathy, told me of all her hardships, how and when her late husband had died, how she had seen Europe, that she wasn't the kind of woman to rent her house and that her father had been doctor to I don't remember which Pasha, etc. Having performed this obligation, I went back to town. I arrived home at one o'clock and ate heartily. After finishing my meal and drinking my coffee, I went out to visit a friend of mine who was staying at a hotel close to the Café "Paradiso", so as to arrange something for the evening. It was the month of August and the sun was scorching. I strolled slowly down Rue Cherif Pasha so as not to break into a sweat. The street, as always at that time of day, was deserted. My only encounter was with a lawyer with whom I had business concerning the sale of a small lot in Moharrem Bey. This was the last piece of quite a large plot which I had been selling bit by bit in order to partly cover my expenses. The lawyer was an honest man and this is why I had chosen him. But he was talkative. I would have preferred him to swindle me a little rather than make me dizzy with his jabbering. He would begin an endless discussion at the slightest pretext – he'd come out with commercial law, Roman law, bring Justinian into it, refer to former lawsuits of his in Smyrna, praise himself, explain a thousand things to me, all of them irrelevant, and hold on to my clothes, which I hate. I had to endure the fool's chatter, as every so often when the flow of his babbling dried up, I would endeavour to find out about the sale, which, for me, was of vital concern. These endeavours took me out of my way but I followed him. We walked along the pavement by the Stock Exchange in the Place des Consuls, along the short street joining the Grande and Petite Places, and by the time we finally reached the middle of the Petite Place, I had got all the information I wanted and the lawyer left me, remembering that he had to visit a client living there. I stood for a moment and watched him walking away, cursing his chatter, which had caused me, in all that heat and sun, to go out of my way.

I was preparing to retrace my steps and to head for the street where the Café "Paradiso" was situated, when suddenly the thought that I was in the Petite Place struck me as odd. I asked myself why and I remembered my dream. "This is where the famous possessor of the treasure made an appointment with me," I said to myself and smiled, mechanically turning my head in the direction of the ironmongers' shops.

What horror! He was sitting there in a small café. My first reaction was a feeling of dizziness and I thought I would faint. I steadied myself against a stall and looked at him again. The same black clothes, the same boater, the same features, the same look. And he had his eyes fixed on me. My nerves grew taut; I felt as if molten iron were running through me. The thought that it was broad daylight, that people were passing by indifferent and unaware that anything unusual was happening and that I, and only I, was aware that such an outrageous thing was happening, that a phantom was sitting there, who knows with what powers and from what unknown realm – from what Hell, from what Erebus – paralysed me and I began to shake. The phantom didn't remove his gaze from me. Then I was seized by the fear that he may get up and come over to me – may speak to me – may take me with him, and what human power would be able to help me against him! I jumped into a carriage and gave the driver an address far away, I don't recall where.

When I had calmed down a little, I saw that I was almost at Sidi Gabir. I was somewhat more composed and began to rationalise the matter. I ordered the driver to go back to town. "I'm quite mad," I thought. "I was undoubtedly mistaken. It must have been someone who resembled the man in my dream. I must go back and make sure. He's quite probably gone and that will be proof that it's not the same man, because he told me that he would wait for me until four o'clock."

With these thoughts in my head, I had already reached the Zizinia Theatre; and, summoning all my courage, I ordered the driver to take me to the Petite Place. As I drew nearer to the café, my heart was pounding so fast that I thought it would break. When only a short distance away, I made the driver stop. I tugged at his arm so hard that he almost fell from his seat, because I saw him getting very close to the café and because the phantom was still there.

Then I set to scrutinising him carefully in an effort to find some dissimilarity with the man in my dream, as if the fact that I was sitting in the carriage and scrutinising him carefully – which anyone else might easily misconstrue and demand an explanation for – was not sufficient to convince me that it was him. On the contrary, he responded to my gaze with an equally scrutinising gaze and with an expression full of anxiety concerning the decision I would take. He seemed to know my thoughts, just as he'd known them in my dream, and in order to remove any doubt I might have concerning his identity, he held out his left hand towards me, showing me, so clearly that I was afraid lest the driver notice, the emerald ring which had so impressed me in my first dream.

I let out a cry of terror and told the driver, who by now had started to worry about his passenger's state of health, to go to Ramleh Boulevard. My only aim was to get as far away as possible. When we reached Ramleh Boulevard, I told him to head for San Stefano, but when I saw that the driver hesitated and mumbled something, I got out and paid him. I hailed another carriage and asked to go to San Stefano.

I arrived here in a terrible state. I entered the main hall of the Casino and jumped when I saw myself in the mirror. I was as pale as a corpse. Fortunately, the hall was empty. I collapsed onto a couch and began to consider what I should do. Going home was unthinkable. Going back again to that room where that supernatural Shade had appeared in the night, that same creature whom I had just previously seen sitting in a common café in the form of an ordinary man, was out of the question. I was being irrational, because of course he had the power to come and find me anywhere. Yet for some time now I had been thinking incoherently.

Eventually, I came to a decision. I would have recourse to my friend, G.V., who was living then in Moharrem Bey.'

'Which G.V.,' I asked, 'that eccentric who concerns himself with the study of magic?'

'The same – and this is why I chose him. How I got the train, how I reached Moharrem Bey, how I looked to left and right like a madman lest the phantom appear before me once again, how I stumbled into G.V.'s room are things I remember only vaguely and confusedly. The only thing I remember clearly is that when I found myself next to him, I began to cry hysterically and shake all over and recount my awful experience. G.V. reassured me and, half-jokingly, half-seriously, told me there was nothing to be afraid of; that the phantom would not dare enter his house, and that if he did, he would drive it away immediately. He knew, he said, this kind of supernatural presence and knew how to exorcise it. Moreover, he persuaded me that I no longer had any reason to be afraid, because the phantom had come to me with a specific purpose: the acquisition of the iron box, which he was unable to obtain, it seemed, without the presence and help of a human being. He hadn't succeeded in this purpose; and he must have already realised from my fear that there was no longer any hope of his succeeding. Without doubt, he would go and try to persuade someone else. V. simply regretted the fact that I hadn't informed him earlier so that he might go himself to see and talk to the phantom, for, he added, in the History of Phantoms, the appearance of these spirits and demons in the light of day was very uncommon. Nevertheless, all this failed to reassure me. I spent a very restless night and I awoke the next day with a raging temperature. The doctor's ignorance and the heightened state of my nervous system led to a brain fever from which I very nearly died. When I recovered a little, I asked what date it was. I had fallen ill on the 3rd of August and I imagined that it must have been the 7th or 8th. It was the 2nd of September.

A brief trip to an Aegean island helped me to make a speedy recovery. During the entire length of my illness I was at the home of my friend, V., who cared for me with that kindheartedness that you both know. He was annoyed with himself, however, for not having had the strength of character to dismiss the doctor and treat me with magical means, which I too believe, in this case at least, would have cured me as quickly as the doctor did.

So this, my friends, is the opportunity I had to become a millionaire – but I lacked the courage. I lacked the courage, but I have no regrets.'

At this point Alexander stopped. The conviction and simplicity with which he had related his story didn't allow us to comment. Besides the time was twenty-seven minutes past midnight. And since that last train back to town left at twelve-thirty, we were obliged to bid him goodnight and leave in a hurry.

Original title: 'Eis to phos tis imeras' (1895/6). First published in the Italian translation of Renata Lavagnini (University of Palermo, 1979). Original Greek text presented by Mario Vitti in the newspaper *To Vima* (27 April, 1980). Subsequently published as an independent booklet (Athens: Agra, Phylladio 1, 1982). Previously translated into English by James Merrill as 'In Broad Daylight' in *Grand Street* 2, No. 3 (Spring 1983), pp. 99–107 and reprinted in *Aegean Review* 1 (Fall/Winter 1986), pp. 8–15. Also translated into English by Nicholas Kostis as 'In Broad Daylight' in *Modern Greek Short Stories*, Athens: Odysseus Publications, 1993, pp. 69–78.

The Mermaid

Andreas Karkavitsas

I was aboard captain Farasis' brig, sailing through the straits that night. And what a rare night it was! The first and last such night in my life, I could say. What was our cargo? What else but grain. Where were we bound? Where else but Piraeus. I'd done the same thing at least twenty times. But that night, I felt such a weight in my heart that I was in danger of passing out. I don't know what the reason was. Whether it was the calm sea, the bright sky or the burning heat, I can't say. But my heart was so heavy and life seemed so full of nonsense, that if someone had grabbed hold of me to throw me into the sea, I would have made no murmur.

The sun was long set. The golden-red clouds that had accompanied its setting climbed in places like large puffs of black smoke. The evening star shone amid the darkness like crystalline snow. One by one, the constellations appeared overhead. The water below took on that gleaming black colour, the coldness and allure of steel. The ship's boy lit the lamps; the captain went below to sleep; Boulberis took the helm. Our dog, Brachamis, curled up at the foot of the capstan to get some rest too.

Myself, I could find no rest. Sleep was far from me. I tried striking up a conversation with the helmsman, but it was so insipid that it soon burnt itself out like a fire lit with damp wood. I went over to play with Brachamis, but he just pushed his snout further between his legs and wearily whined, as if to say: 'Leave me alone, I'm not in the mood!' So, weary myself, I went and lay face down with my hands covering my eyes. I didn't want to see anything, didn't want to feel even that I was alive. And little by little, I almost managed it. I felt something faint, like a dim candle, inside me and my body merging and being assimilated into the deck's lifeless timbers.

How long I stayed like that I've no idea. What came into my mind, if anything, I can't recall. Suddenly, however, I began to quiver, as if a magnet were exciting my nerves, just as humidity makes the birds chatter. And immediately, a crimson wave poured over me. I thought I was swimming in blood. And just as someone sleeping in a dark room automatically wakes up at the bright light of day, I too opened my eyes. Opened or closed them, I don't recall. All I recall is that I remained still. My first thought was that I'd woken up inside the belly of a fish that had swallowed our ship. But it wasn't the belly of a fish. The sky was above and the sea below. But everything, above and below, was clad in a deep red, undulating garment that bathed even the very rim of our vessel in a delicate glow. Somewhere at the ends of the earth, a fire had tossed its flame up high and was shooting out terrible tentacles here and there. But where was the blaze and where was its smoke? Both were missing.

Below in the distant north, a violet cloud spread and shrouded the stars in blue, concealing them beneath its thick veil. And above, a pale yellow aurora spread and flooded the sky with dark rivers and green rivers, golden red and blue as if wanting to colour the whole firmament. And the aurora, moving like a windswept curtain, shook its fringes forward, spread its gossamer laces and advanced, as the tide advances and covers the sand with foam and watery tongues. These rivers in the air raced quickly and swelled and rolled ever dark or green, golden red and blue, and scattered glowing rays everywhere like huge, inexhaustible electric beams. The motionless sea reflected all the colours and everything appeared startled in such radiance. But I was even more startled. I didn't know what to do or suppose. I thought the end of the world had come. Yet such an end would please anyone. The earth wants to die in the rosy waves . . .!

Suddenly, I shuddered. Below in the distance, from within

the violet cloud, I saw an enormous shadow approaching. Its thick build, its towering head loomed like Mount Athos. Its two eyes formed luminous circles and haughtily gazed upon the World before hurling it to destruction. There he is, I thought, the angel sent from God, the destroyer and redeemer! I watched him, trembling in my heart. At any moment, I expected the terrible blow to fall like a hammer. This was the end of the Earth and its fruits, the end of the sea and its vessels. No more songs or voyages or kisses!

But I didn't hear the blow. The shadow advanced through the water with fiery strides. And the quicker it advanced, the smaller it became in build. And suddenly, the terrifying mass stood before me, a ravishingly beautiful girl. She wore a diamond-studded crown on her head and her thick hair, a blue mane, cascaded down over her back to the waves below. Her wide forehead, her almond-shaped eyes, her coral lips radiated an immortal glow and a royal demeanour all around. From her crystal neck a golden scaly breastplate hung down and hugged her body and in her left hand she held a shield and in her right the Macedonian javelin.

I hadn't recovered from my surprise when I heard a sweet, gentle and soft voice saying to me:

'Sailor, goodly sailor, is Alexander the Great alive?'

'Alexander the Great!' I murmured with even greater bewilderment. 'How can King Alexander still be alive?' I didn't know what kind of a question this was or how to answer. The voice asked a second time:

'Sailor, goodly sailor, is Alexander the Great alive?'

'After so long, my Lady!' I replied without thinking. 'After so long, Alexander the Great! Not even the earth covering him still exists.'

Alas! That was my undoing! In an instant, the beautiful girl became a horrid abomination. A cyclops emerged from the waves, revealing a body covered half in scales. Her silken hair became live snakes that rose this way and that, shooting out their tongues and poisonous barbs and hissing terrifyingly. Her plated breast and virginal face changed at once, as if she were the Gorgon of fairytale. Now I knew only too well with whom I was dealing! It wasn't the Earth's Charon, the destroying and redeeming angel. It was the Mermaid, Alexander's sister, who had stolen the water of life and roamed alive and all-powerful. It was the Glory of the great ruler of the world, ageless and eternal on land and sea. And it was just for Her coming that the Pole had revealed its Aurora, filling the sky with its crimson colours. Of course, she wasn't asking about the perishable body, but about her lord's memory. And now in response to my imprudent reply, she had placed her hairy and heavy hand on the ship's gunwale and, in her fury, was swinging her tail to right and left turning the calm Sea into an Ocean.

'No, my Lady, it's not true . . .!' I shouted as my legs buckled.

She stared at me grimly and in a trembling voice asked once more:

'Sailor, goodly sailor, is Alexander the Great alive?'

'He's alive and well,' I answered immediately. 'He's alive and well, and ruler of the world.'

She listened carefully to my words. As if my voice had poured the water of life into her veins, the monster immediately altered aspect, once again becoming the beautiful maiden. She removed her lily-white hand from the gunwale and smiled, scattering rose-petals from her lips. And suddenly the crimson air was filled with the strains of a war song, as if at that moment the Macedonian army was returning from the lands of the Ganges and the Euphrates.

I looked up and saw the sky's rivers, the dark and green ones, the golden-red and blue ones, merging in the sky and forming a giant Corona. Was it an effect of the weather or perhaps a response to the immortal girl's question? Who knows? But slowly the rays began to dim and fade one after the other, as if the Mermaid were taking the beauty away with her into the sea's abyss.

Now, neither Corona nor Aurora could be seen anywhere. Here and there, some scattered clouds remained, ashen and pale; and in my heart the dull and faded crimson of my homeland.

I was aboard captain Farasis' brig, sailing through the straits that night.

Original title: 'I gorgona'. First published in 1899. Translated here from the text published in Andreas Karkavitsas, *Loyia tis ploris* [Tales From The Prow], Athens: Hestia, 2000, pp. 181–186.

The Phantom Never Seen Again

Menos Philintas

It was April then, I recall – so many years have passed now. As many as a hundred people swore that they'd seen the phantom with their own eyes, down by the river, a quarter of an hour's walk outside the village, clad all in white and toweringly tall. It roamed the area around the river and wailed as if in torment, and amid the wailing, they distinguished the words: Andrias! Andrias!

Fear and terror had taken hold of the village; it was harvest time and yet the vineyard-workers left off work in the afternoon; doors were locked early, mothers fearfully guarded their children, all night long the dogs howled so wildly that it made people's flesh creep and there was talk of nothing else. The older ones recounted past tales of ghosts and spectres; grandmothers made their grandchildren shudder with their stories about spirits and sprites. It was the same time that down by the river, without laments or prayers, they had buried a girl who had upped and drowned herself, and no doubt it was she who had returned as a ghost. Everyone knew that the cause of the evil was Andrias, who'd loved the girl and then deserted her.

Listen to the tale:

Many years ago, at the end of May, on Saint Constantine's Day, we organised a celebration, as was the custom, beneath the willows of the monastery, just beyond the river. The whole village was there. Andrias then would have been a twelve- or thirteen-year-old lad. A dozen or so youngsters, boys and girls, were playing beside the river, at some distance from the groups of people. While playing, it seems, no one knows, one girl slipped and fell into the river. The other youngsters were frightened and began screaming. But Andrias lost no time; he threw off his coat and jumped in after the girl. The youngsters' cries alarmed us and we all ran in their direction. And then we saw Andrias coming out of the river and carrying Zapheiritsa in his arms. Her fair hair had been swept back by the water and the noonday brilliance adorned her little, round head with a bright garland. In the same way, the sun reflected on the dripping boy and bathed him in splendour, so that it was like looking at an archangel carrying a pure soul up to Heaven.

And how am I to tell, now, of all the congratulations and praise showered on Andrias then? We all talked of nothing else, of his bravery, his daring, how he'd acted in keeping with his name; while he basked in all this glory. The parents of both youngsters even agreed to match them when they came of age. And from that day, even the two young scamps looked at each other differently, and as they grew day by day, so their love for each other increased, and we all took it for granted that they would wed once they came of age.

They lived like that for four years, as though betrothed, and they were the pride and joy of their parents. They then decided to send the lad abroad to study, to see the world and become a man. It was a shame that such a fine young lad should remain idle in the village. And so they separated with longing and with anticipation. The years passed and Zapheiritsa grew into a lovely and charming girl, who waited with longing for her sweetheart to return from abroad, handsome and learned and mature, so as to enchant him with her beauty.

The poor girl; how could she ever have imagined that he would forget her!

Well! He studied, saw the world, heard much, read much; how was he to remember that little village girl? So what if he did save her from the river? Was he obliged to marry her, too? And all the more when so many wealthy and cultivated girls were making such sweet eyes at him here in this land! It's true what they say: 'Out of sight, out of mind'. He stopped writing letters and sending greetings. And before long, a crafty little minx had him well and truly ensnared through her wiles and so he became betrothed to her. Meanwhile, his father died, and so he decided to return to the village in order to sell all he had, and then to go back and get married. And so our fine young lad returned to the village after six long years; but the news had arrived there ahead of him. When Zapheiritsa saw his indifference, when she learned that he was betrothed to another, when she saw her fair dreams disappear and all her sweet hopes fade in an instant, those same sweet hopes that she'd nurtured while waiting for him with such love and longing, while he was now so cool and distant, she fell into deep contemplation and the more she contemplated it, the more terrible it seemed to her. And so one night, who knows, her gaze darkened, her mind clouded and she secretly went and threw herself into the river, at the very same spot, and the poor wretch drowned. She had, you see, sweet memories of that river and it was with these that she wanted to end her life.

This bad business caused a great stir in our village as such things were unheard-of, and everyone said that the cause of it was Andrias, for though she had loved him so deeply, he had deserted her so callously.

Meanwhile, something even worse was to shake the village. Because they'd buried her there beside the river, without any prayers, she had returned as a ghost and came out at night. There were at least a hundred people who, during those days, had seen a toweringly tall phantom, clad all in white. It roamed around the river and wailed as if in torment, and amid the wailing, they distinguished the words: Andrias! Andrias!

In any other situation, Andrias would have taken all this with a pinch of salt and laughed at the villagers' stuff and nonsense because those with any brains don't believe in phantoms and ghosts and the like.

But now these events caused him to sink into a wretched mental state.

It was as if he were drowning in the blood of the poor dead girl and every day you could see him, alone, walking up and down the sandy riverbank like a lost soul. It was as if he wanted at all costs to encounter the phantom. He'd go there and sit on the sand by the mouth of the river and reflect. His conscience stirred and he remembered the years of his childhood, innocent, golden years, and he brought to mind that same old story in which he'd once saved the young girl from this very same river and he wondered why his fate should have dictated that he save her when later he would behave so unfairly to the poor girl, who had spent so many happy days with him, who had loved him so faithfully and sincerely, when later he would drown the hapless girl himself through his unfaithfulness, his shallowness and his lack of conscience. Thus, his heart broke, his head swam, his ears buzzed, his gaze darkened and his pulse beat faster; and, in a frenzy, he shouted out:

'Come out so I can see you! Come out so I can speak to you!'

And he waited to hear and expected to see; but he saw nothing, nor heard any voice other than the wailing of the wind and the murmur of the river.

Phantoms don't appear during the day.

And he shouted out again:

'Come out and cast your black curse upon my head! Come out and blast your faithless Andrias! Andrias!'

And again frightened by the sound of his own voice, he leapt up like a madman and returned as quickly as he could to the village and shut himself in his room, silent and speechless, and there was no one he wanted to see and no one he wanted to hear.

It was April then, as we said. One Sunday evening, as we were about to go home and lock our doors, we saw Andrias coming towards us with a strange boldness and a forced smile.

'Well, lads,' he said to us, 'which of you dares come with me tonight, to go and pay a visit on the phantom?'

We all looked at each other in astonishment. 'Now, what's got into him? Has he gone mad?'

The poor wretch hadn't gone mad yet, but for sure he wasn't in his right mind. The thought of his sin so burdened him that he'd resolved to go and find the phantom at night, perhaps to ask forgiveness, who knows?

And just as in every case there's always someone foolhardy enough to attempt even the most ludicrous things, so now too there was one, Mitros Kazilis was his name, who said: 'Let's go, boss, I'm with you.'

'All health to you, Mitros, my fine, strapping friend! Inn-keeper, pour us a drink!'

The inn-keeper brought out the glasses filled with mastic and we all drank to Kazilis' good health. We ribbed the crack-pot about his courage and teased him.

And since two people had been found to go and face the phantom, we were ashamed to go and lock ourselves inside our homes, as we usually did. So we stayed there, under the wooden awning of the inn, until the time that they would set off.

Andrias said nothing; but you felt that something was on his mind. He kept ordering drinks:

'Same again, inn-keeper.'

'Same again.'

We drank and talked till it grew dark. An April night; the sky was cloudy in places; the moon almost full and blood red that night; it appeared and disappeared behind the clouds. There was a chill breeze blowing and the ripples lapped upon the shore. Andrias took out his watch and turned to Kazilis:

'It's time, Mitros.'

He shuddered. But now it was a question of pride!

'Ready, boss,' he said; and he got up.

Then we all got up.

'Come on, lads, enough of the joking.'

'What joking?' Mitsos replied. 'We'll grab it and bring it back to you all trussed up; no ghost has arms like these, now does it?'

'Hark at you!' said the others, laughing at him, 'it's only air, what need does it have of your strong arms?'

The hush of the night that at times was made to seem even more eerie by the distant hooting of an owl was now shattered by the howling of some mangy cur close by us.

'Hearken, lads,' said old man Tsalis, 'it's a bad omen; some great evil is going to befall our village.'

'Keep your thoughts to yourself, old man Tsalis,' we all cried.

'Come on, Mitros. Don't pay any attention to these villagers,' said Andrias boldly, 'let's go.'

'Let's go, boss.'

'Aren't you going to take a lamp with you?' said one.

'Eh, the phantom's eyes shoot flames; they'll light our way!' said Mitros Kazilis, forcing a laugh to hide the fear that was beginning to take hold of him.

Yet, on he went with Andrias and we watched them go till they left the village behind and disappeared among the reeds.

'Let's go, lads, let's all go to our homes for it's unwise to play around with demons,' said the old man, and we were all of like mind.

Before long, there was not a soul outside.

It was a wild and terrifying night. From time to time, we stuck our heads out of our windows and stared. We fancied we heard lamenting and plaintive cries; we fancied the stars were falling from the sky and fading. The moon grew redder and redder and huge shadows flitted over the sea as if the spirits were chasing each other.

This terror, this struggle lasted into the middle of the night, till the first cockcrow; and not one of us closed an eye till then. But when the cock crowed in the middle of the night, everything began to grow calm; the lamenting was no longer heard, nor did the stars fall any more.

The moon became bright gold again and the shadows on the sea sank into the waters' depths. It was then that we too were at last able to get to sleep.

In the morning – and who will ever forget that ill-fated morning! – we all gathered at first light under the same wooden awning and enquired of each other; no one knew what had happened. But before long, there, coming towards us, was Mitros Kazilis.

'What happened, then,' we all asked him with one voice.

'Evil and unpleasant things,' he replied.

'Out with it, let's hear.'

'When I saw it rising out of the river, toweringly tall and clad all in white and with shining eyes, I began to tremble and without keeping to anything I'd said, I took to my heels.'

'And Andrias?'

'In my terror, I had no time to think about him. As I ran off, I thought I heard wailing and voices behind me, who knows?'

'Why don't some of you go, lads, and see what's happened? You'll be doing an act of kindness,' said old man Tsalis.

Cold feet again! And who had the heart for such a task after all we'd heard? While we were all standing there at a loss, we suddenly saw Andrias emerging from the reeds; he was coming hastily towards us, barefoot, his hair dishevelled and his clothes in shreds.

When he came close to us, we were all gripped by horror at his appearance; his face was yellow like sulphur and his eyes strangely bulging. And he was screaming in a hoarse voice.

'So then! She got what she wanted. She robbed me of my wits. Are you happy now? Are you happy?'

We all looked at each other with a hidden fear and plainly sad at the sufferings of this poor young stalwart!

'Poor Andrias! What a miserable thing man is,' I said.

'I'm cursed! I'm cursed! I'm cursed!' he cried at the top of his voice, and making a noise like a horse whinnying, he headed towards the hill with a rush.

From that day on, the phantom was neither seen nor heard ever again.

Original title: 'To phantasma pou den xanaphanike'. Published in the periodical *Ebdomas* 164 (1930). Translated here from the text anthologised in Makis Panorios (ed.), *To Elliniko Fantastiko Diiyima* [The Greek Fantasy Short Story] vol. 2, Athens: Aiolos, 1993, pp. 217–221.

The Three Tests

Demosthenes Voutyras

'I'm telling you, don't take it tonight!' my pharmacist friend, Mavroeidis, told me. 'Bring it to me tomorrow so I can have a look at it and see what kind of concoction that sleeping draught is, because Dogalis may be an eminent botanist, but he's well on his way to becoming an eminent madman. Now he's started playing the astrologer. That's the result of his going to his hometown, no doubt.'

'I'm going to take it,' I replied. 'What do you think? Will it poison me? Just joking. I've been waiting for him to come, like I would the Saviour. All he said was that it's very strong. As for the other one, I took it only once, then I dropped the bottle, and where was I to find him? He'd gone back to his hometown. What do you think? The good thing about the draught is that it doesn't bring with it a world of non-existence, but of dreams. Do you remember what I told you then, about the dream I had . . .? I was working on a case, pages of it, and I'd almost forgotten it. It was as if someone had taken this case in my dream and had applied it to me, making me the protagonist, so that I went through no end of things. And with all these things, I didn't wake up! I woke up late, the next day, after the show was over . . .'

I left. I went home and, after the meal, I took the draught and went to bed.

There was a strong wind blowing; it was whistling. It was as if it had taken hold of me and was sweeping me along. Yet, now, I thought I saw a horse's head before me.

I started to come round. I must have fallen asleep. And how was it that I hadn't fallen from the horse! Ah, that wine I'd drunk at the inn was very strong, too heavy. Fortunately the horse, the black steed . . . It was jet-black with red reins. I saw the crest it had on the top of its head. This too was of red feathers.

It was a fine horse. I saw passers-by stop and stare at it. But they weren't only gazing at the horse; they were staring at me. And I, too, stared at myself, at how I was dressed. I was wearing black velvet clothes, a red cape with black braid, boots stretching above my knees, a handsome sword dangling on my left side and a dagger on my right.

I wanted to know where I was going and why, but I had no answer.

'What's wrong with me? Something's wrong! Something . . .,' I reflected.

I was suddenly seized by fright and looked to see whether I had any money. I felt relief to find my purse full of gold coins.

At that moment, I heard:

'There's Baron Olf, riding on his warhorse!'

'Do they mean me?'

There was a soldier and he was pointing at me amid a crowd of soldiers and civilians. It was me he was referring to, there was no other horseman around.

'Olf? I'm Olf! No, he must be making a mistake. But who am I then? Who am I?'

I tried to recall anything, to prove I wasn't Olf, but I couldn't. There was darkness behind me, before me, everywhere, as if out of this I had become what I was, as if there on that black horse, I had been created in an instant. And nothing else, nothing. Mother, father, kinfolk, home . . .

And again I heard:

'There's Baron Olf, our valiant warrior.'

'I must be Baron Olf!' I thought. 'And something must have happened to me. I've had a spell put on me and I've forgotten everything, everything! What else can it be? Who am I? Who? I have gold, a warhorse, everyone knows it! But what else? They've done something to me and I've forgotten everything.'

I saw how I was shaking. And my horse must have suffered the same thing because he leapt, suddenly trying to break free. I held him back.

A crowd had gathered and was staring. Again I heard:

'Baron Olf, the valiant Olf!'

'That's who I am! That's me! I'll come round, the spell will wear off. Just be calm . . .'

And I put my arm on my waist. And as though understanding everything, the black horse, arching its neck, began prancing as if playing on the street.

'You'll come round,' I thought to myself: 'Patience and care is what's required.'

Everyone had stopped and was staring at us, and my name was continually on their lips.

And there, suddenly, was a fine sedan, carried by two strong and sturdy men. It was decorated with a coat of arms.

From its window a beautiful rose appeared and gazed at us. The sedan halted. And the rose spoke in a voice that I thought only nightingales possessed.

'Baron Olf! Welcome!'

I removed my small, black velvet cap with its large white feather and greeted her. My black horse was standing erect.

'But when did you arrive?' asked the sweet voice coming from the rose's mouth.

'Today, my lady!'

'Today, indeed! Yet we were told that you were seen yesterday at the "Black Lion" Inn.'

'And where is that? For I never recall the names of inns.'

'On the outskirts of the town.'

'Ah, so you see. It was today that I entered the town.'

'Quite right. We wondered why you had not come to see us.'

'To see you?'

'Naturally . . .'

And the sedan moved forward once again after a few more brief words.

'How beautiful she is! And she is well acquainted with Olf; it's plain she loves him. And I, who am I? I can't recall, I've lost my memory. Oh, oh! And who is she? Where does she dwell? And I told her I would go . . . Where? Ah, the coat of arms. I recall it. On, my black steed, on!'

I hadn't gone very far, however, when I heard:

'Greetings Baron Olf! At last, you've left your castle and come to us! What, is it only to go to battle that you leave your castles?'

It was an old man with a long beard. But his sword was girded to his waist.

We exchanged a few words and parted.

'He said I have a castle . . . But of course, I wouldn't be without one, would I? Oh, what's happened to me? And am I a bachelor or married? I must be a bachelor, because no one has asked me about my wife . . .' he reflected.

That made me feel somewhat relieved.

As I went on, the number of people on the way increased. But where was I going? Where would I stop? I saw a river. There, a horseman appeared coming over the bridge. His horse must have been a mare, because my black steed whinnied. But when the horseman saw me, he halted his horse and shouted:

'O, Olf! My dear friend! How are you, old friend, how are you?'

I returned his kind words. I told him, however, that I was not too well because of the strong wine I'd drunk. That I couldn't even see where I was going.

Another rider appeared charging over the bridge.

'Are you still here, Dinak?' he said to my friend, restraining his horse.

And when he saw me:

'Well, well, it's Olf! How are you, dear friend? You must have come for the celebration. But I have to be on my way, I'm carrying messages. We'll meet at the palace, all right? I'm going now. Farewell!'

And he left, lashing his horse.

'What celebration is he talking about, Dinak?' I asked my friend.

'But I wrote to you about it.'

And coming over towards my horse:

'For the Protestants. In four or five days. Never mind the night of Saint Bartho . . . Not a hair will be left of them! It's an order from the Pope.'

'Then we'll have plenty of fine work. I won't leave even half the papists . . .'

'What are you talking about?' he said, laughing.

'I got it back to front . . .'

'It's all the same. Well, we'll see each other presently. I, too, have to be going.'

He, too, left.

I crossed the river, saw an imposing building, and went towards it. There, numerous men awaited me, took my horse to the stables and led me into the palace. And all this time, I kept hearing: 'Olf, valiant Olf!'

I entered one chamber and there were many men inside surrounding one man in black, a proud man, who was saying something to them. I realised who it was, and when he saw me, he said:

'Welcome Olf, welcome! You of all people should not be absent from the celebrations. Now we're going to test a new weapon; a new invention! I myself am about to test it. They say it's accurate. You'll see how good a shot I am. Louis, open the window!'

King Charles Valois picked up a rifle from the table in the middle of the room. His eyes glared. And he searched outside with his gaze.

At that moment, a man was passing by, hurrying over the bridge.

A loud bang was heard and the man crumpled to the ground . . .

We were passing between some very tall bushes and couldn't see what was going on beside us. And this was after a terribly tiring trek through a large, thick and dark forest. My three companions and I are the last of the armed men. Following behind us were black bearers carrying our provisions and supplies on their heads. We were drawn out in a long line. Fortunately, I'd heard that we would soon arrive at the sultanate where we were heading.

However, it was just as though I'd woken up or been freed from something which had forced me to do things without my wanting to. What am I saying! There was a time when I wanted it. For I wanted to become a missionary, to roam through savage lands and try to confuse the illiterate peoples there even more!

Now, as I walked, I muttered:

'Whatever possessed me to become an explorer?'

I must have been beset by that which takes hold of me sometimes, when I do things that I don't want to do, as if someone else is driving me; as if someone else is in control of my being.

And now I was accompanying those explorers. Though it's a good thing I'd found them because, no doubt, I would have got lost in that huge African forest.

They were English and were taking gifts, so I understood, to the Sultanate of Uganda; gifts consisting of fine rifles of the latest type.

Why did I suddenly think of an old saying? I'd either heard it or read it somewhere: 'Beware of Greeks bearing gifts!'

At that same moment, I heard cries of joy. And rifle-shots too.

We'd arrived. There were no longer any tall bushes, and we saw a wide river with fast-flowing waters.

On its opposite shore, however, we saw numerous blacks preparing boats and other means to take us across the river. And so we crossed it. Then, escorted by the blacks, we entered the capital and went to the Sultan's palace.

He received us, sitting down. The Englishmen bowed and scraped. They're skilled at such things. Not being skilled myself, I put my hand to my empty stomach and forced a bow. Following this, they presented the two weapons to the monarch. On seeing them, his eyes gleamed and he leapt up.

They showed him how to fire them.

The Sultan quickly got the hang of it and, with the rifle in his hand, looked outside, searching for something.

Someone was passing by, laden with wood. The Sultan aimed at him and fired. The man crumpled to the ground.

The Sultan's gaze fell on someone else. He saw a young man leaning against a tree, looking at the man who had just crumpled to the ground.

The Sultan aimed at him too and fired. The young man crumpled to the ground . . .

I was muttering to myself:

'What was I thinking of to board this huge plane! What was I thinking of! And where are we going? Into the unknown?

And sea below, sea, sea everywhere! Land, where's the land? Has it vanished and has everything turned into sea?'

'Tell me,' I heard a voice asking, 'what are you mumbling about all the time?'

I saw a red-haired man coming over to me. It was he who was asking me.

'Sea, sea everywhere . . .' I replied.

'It's nice like that. But that, too, will end after the show.'

'What show?' I asked.

'Come on, now, don't you know? What show! The show that's about to start!'

I didn't speak. I knew nothing about it.

'Your English is not very good. Where are you from?'

'I don't know,' I replied, 'from somewhere and nowhere.'

'I respect your secrecy. I see that you must be one of those volunteers who conceal their name and country. Who only reveal these things when necessary. As they do in my country, in the Foreign Legion. Their past bothers them and . . .'

'I have no past or future!' I said, cutting him short.

The red-haired man moved away. He went and sat with some others, who were engaged in a long discussion. They were speaking English. Now he didn't understand a word.

I left the spot and went elsewhere. Yet, there was the red-haired man again! And he said to me:

'The majority in here are mad! They want us to go closer than all the others so that we can see. We'll get ourselves killed in other words . . . And the show's beginning!'

There was a terrible bang. Our plane almost turned over. I fell to the floor.

The red-haired man appeared:

'Look, look!'

I rushed to the telescope, somewhere in the distance a volcano had erupted, had shot up. Flames, blackness, terrible smoke, flashes.

Just like when the earth was being formed and flames shot from its womb and terrible cries leapt from its breast . . .

It was as if my mind opened up at the sight. And I heard a voice saying:

'Not a hair will be left!'

I remembered that I'd heard those words somewhere before.

A small-built man with large glasses appeared:

'Hiroshima has gone the way of the lost worlds!' he said, 'it no longer exists!' And, nervily waving his right arm:

'Here now, science has had its say! Our test was a success . . .'

Original title: 'I treis dokimes'. First published in 1954. Translated here from the text anthologised in Makis Panorios (ed.), *To Elliniko Fantastiko Diiyima* [The Greek Fantasy Short Story], Athens: Aiolos, 1987, pp. 25–29.

Nightmare

Nikolaos Episkopopoulos

The table had for some time been strangely spinning and the lamp drawing luminous circles, and the walls were maliciously getting closer as if about to clash, when Petros decided to leave the pothouse.

It was the eve of a big feast day and the hour was well after midnight. Besides, he lived a way long off and had to pass through the whole of the forest in order to reach his home.

Not even he could remember how much wine he'd drunk and how much tobacco he'd smoked in a long dirty pipe that gave out intolerable clouds of smoke. All he could remember was the strange thirst he'd felt after the first few drinks; an immeasurable thirst, which he had in vain sought to quench. Of course, it must have been the first time he had ever been drunk in his life. He was always so downcast and weary after finishing work at the slaughterhouse and selling the meat to the butcher that he would generally go straight home. Tonight, however, he had allowed himself to get carried away. After a long day of exhausting and quite hideous work, he had gone with his friends to the pothouse. He had eaten, drunk one glass, had been stood another, had felt thirsty again, had drunk a fourth, had smoked a great deal though unaccustomed to it, and was now leaving, his steps faltering and his head spinning.

He bade goodnight to his friends, who in vain tried to keep him there, and he went out into the street.

From the heat and stifling atmosphere of the pothouse, he now came out into the cool, fresh air. The whirling in his head eased a little and he began to walk more steadily.

The countryside stretched out vast before him, without the eye being able to see virtually anything amidst the darkness.

The rows of trees seemed like enormous blots of India ink in a boundless world of shadows and shapes, the outline or kind of which it was impossible to discern.

Darkness down below, darkness and black shapes in the surrounding hills, darkness in the sky, which was, for the most part, filled with clouds. It was like being inside a huge abyss enclosed by giant walls and sealed above by the black sky, which the man found strangely stifling, as if it were pressing down on his chest.

The cool air brought with it the restless breath of nature's hidden and mysterious life, and there arose a whisper, terrifying in its subtlety, and the entire forest of trees came to life as though living phantoms.

To Petros' eyes, everything seemed to be in motion; the tree-tops were swaying calmly and lugubriously, the shadows were dancing fantastically and even the hills seemed to be moving.

A sudden noise sowed terror in his heart; a strange noise, like cloth tearing and the dull scratching of shavings on metal and glass shattering.

Then, overhead, an eerie sound was heard; the trees shook, a shower of dry leaves fell mournfully on his head, and a swarm of black birds flew up and disappeared, dryly beating the air with their wings.

Afraid, he penetrated deeper into the thick masses of trees, as if he were entering a dark tunnel, and he saw the trees above him like huge shadows, like monstrous parasols, with their branches passionately entwined in a wild embrace.

As he passed beneath the young trees, his nostrils were filled with the fresh smell of sap, a disagreeable smell like raw albumen, a smell of bestial orgasm, which made him feel nauseous, reminding him of the other smell that was always in his nostrils; that of the fresh blood and dismembered carcasses at the butcher's shop.

And he reflected on his entire evening, and all his tiring and frightful work on the eve of a feast day.

All the savage slaughter of the cows and sheep and pigs, with the squirting blood, and the heavy choppers, and the wild bellowing and the desperate looks, and the last spasms of death, and all the steamy vapours from the blood and the innards, with its characteristic membraneous smell, and then the carving up of the flesh and the hanging pieces with the reeking fat and the drops of blood frozen like stalactites appeared before his eyes, illumined by the reddish light of the big fat-burning lamps with their large wicks emitting smoke with a disgusting stench from the burning fat, beneath the enormous blackened pillars in the slaughterhouse, with the darting shadows inside and the oscillating movement of the light, as if it were being shaken by the departing souls of the victims.

On the tiled floor, he saw piles of flesh and rivers of red and disembowelled carcasses with their legs in the air in shameful positions, with their limbs bare, with their tissue dangling, ribbed with blue veins, and the warm and bluish innards pouring out of their cavities.

And his impression, disgusting and mournful, as if from a battlefield or cemetery, came back to him; his head felt now even more confused, his heart was pounding and rapid flashes rent the pupils of his eyes.

For an instant, he was overcome by a great terror and looked around him with his pupils dilated, ready to break into a run, but his feet were stuck to the spot, floating in some liquid, the warmth of which he felt reaching up to his shins.

And his nostrils filled with a strong whiff of life, a disagreeable and horrid smell, just as he experienced it over the large tubs into which the blood from the slaughtered animals flowed, remaining there before it separated into a white mass with yellow-brown liquids floating upon it.

It was blood, warm blood, living blood, flowing round his feet and soaking his shins.

He felt as if an iron hand had seized hold of his heart. He looked down and saw, red and black in the darkness, an entire river coming like an inundation from afar, and swelling and rising, and from its red reflection, the sky overhead shone with a faint crimson hue.

Terrified, he looked ahead, his face completely distorted with fear.

In the depths of the black horizon, the trees were moving even more, coming together and getting ever closer.

And he felt his whole body shudder on seeing thousands of flashing eyes and a multitude of heads appearing, swept along by the red current.

They were the heads of cows with their huge glassy eyes staring menacingly, their gaping snouts, their necks dripping blood, and in the bloody reflections were a flock of white sheep and other flocks of animals with tragic expressions, with their contorted faces and frightening looks.

And he saw the blank, innocent eyes of the sheep looking at him with a fixed irony, and the heads of the pigs coming towards him dripping blood, with their tiny eyes closed, blind, threatening only through the force of their coming. And he turned round and saw another flood of animals with little heads, with small insolent eyes, glaring eyes, with their throats cut and held by thin tissue, with their arteries convulsively gushing blood.

Before him and behind him, the eternal convulsion of death was suffocating him and ghostly looks came from all directions and he could hear bellowing, the bellowing of the cows at the first strike of the chopper, the bellowing of imploring, of threatening, terribly magnificent, as life departed forcefully, and the mournful bleating of sheep and the squeals and grunts and cries of animals of all kinds.

And now the warm blood was covering him, coming up to his knees and belly and even up to his chest, and the torrents of animals swimming in this were getting closer and he shuddered at the first warm drops of liquid to splash his face amidst the agony of the convulsions.

The air filled with an overpowering stench and with lives departing and it was as if it too were alive, as if it too were letting out a groan of agony.

He felt the fair silky hair of the cattle smelling of the wild and the wool of the sheep reeking of old, rancid milk, and the pigs' muddy, rough hair against his flesh, and in that infinite jostling he breathed their poisonous exhalations as if of decomposing bodies.

And the billowing waves of blood now reached up to his neck, and as far as his chin and before long he had that brackish taste in his mouth.

He tossed his head back and saw the pitch-black sky, glittering with thousands of animal eyes, which were looking at him furiously, and the whole atmosphere was inundated with the blood's wet vapours, thickly covering the horizon like a red mist.

Shudders ran through his body and he opened his mouth to cry out, but his throat had closed and his hair stood on end and he felt the blood stop flowing in his veins. His hands were grabbed by thousands of sharp and hungry teeth, and on his brow he felt rough, sharp tongues like files licking him, and the cattle's horns and the hens' beaks piercing him, and his blood gushing out from thousands of wounds and it was as if all the hordes were bellowing their demand for fiendish revenge.

Then, the blood covered his face and eyes; he could no longer see, his teeth were chattering, he was unable to get his breath, a groan of agony rent his breast and he collapsed unconscious into the forest's muddy torrent, into which he had strayed.

Original title: 'Ephialtis'. First published in the newspaper *Asty* (12 May 1894). Translated here from the text anthologised in Nikolaos Episkopopoulos, *Trella diiyimata* [Mad Tales], Athens: Nefeli, 1989, pp. 23–29.

A Very Odd Case

Napoleon Lapathiotis

I have to admit that I wasn't at all surprised, when, just a few days ago, I learned of the death of my friend N.D. I knew that he would no doubt kill himself one day. In fact, I'd even begun to grow concerned at the delay with which this happened. I'd heard his confession, and I was genuinely at a loss as to how he managed to go on living, given the strange illness that made his life a torment . . . It was inevitable that this strange illness – one of the oddest illnesses I've ever heard of – should close every door to him and deprive him of every source of happiness! Anyone else in his position would most likely have found some way of profiting from it – perhaps even trying to exploit this exceptional case for their own personal gain. Nikos, however, was a sensitive man and it was not in his nature to use it to his advantage . . . And I fully understand his desperate act: he was unable to endure it any longer . . .

I'd heard his confession one evening – a warm autumnal evening – last year, if I recall correctly. We'd been to the cinema and, on leaving there, had gone to an 'all-night' club. We'd been drinking wine and we were in rather good spirits. This gave me the courage to ask him in confidence about the notable change I'd seen in his character. He was no longer the person I had once known.

This benign, kind-hearted, tender and charming friend had radically changed during the previous two years – and, specifically, following his discharge from the hospital, where he'd been for I don't know how long, because of a wound to his head, a remnant from the horrid war. He had become sullen, suspicious, averse to contact with his friends – he had become a veritable misanthrope . . . And yet, he was completely cured – the doctors had assured us of this – despite the ordeal he had been through. That old wound to his skull had not harmed any vital organ, and the wound itself had healed. His mind functioned just as it always had. He had also completely recovered from the nervous breakdown that followed his ordeal and which was naturally attributed to the shock he'd suffered during the war, as was the case with so many others. He had recovered from all this, yet it was from this time that the change in him began. He had shut himself up inside his house and refused to see anyone. From that time on, a great many rumours went around concerning his situation. And that evening, I wanted to find out if there was any truth in them.

He seemed shaken by my questions. As he walked with short steps and held on to my arm, I realised that his hand was trembling. I regretted my interrogation of him and tried to change the tone of it. He, however, didn't say a word. He knew very well how much I loved him – in fact, *he knew it extremely well, more than I could have imagined* – and I felt sure he wasn't annoyed. And something else too: I noticed that before I'd even asked him, his countenance had darkened *as if he knew what I was going to say . . .*

I was able to give an explanation to all this later, when he revealed to me his secret suffering. It was the first time he'd disclosed it to anyone. Even his voice was trembling. He held on to my arm more tightly, with a vacant look in his eyes. At first, he said nothing. He seemed to be hesitant about revealing it to me – or perhaps he was searching for the right words. But, at the same time, I sensed his great need, the need tormenting him, to tell someone, to find relief . . . I sensed that this secret, which rendered me speechless when I heard it, was waiting for an opportunity in order to be revealed . . . And no greater or better opportunity than the one given to him now would ever present itself. I was his dearest friend. Twenty years of genuine friendship was no small precedent. And, besides, he *knew* how much I loved him and how my question stemmed from a deep, honest and unselfish concern . . .

So he began to confide in me, in a low, hesitant, frightened voice at first – he was frightened that I wouldn't believe him, or that I'd take him for a madman – then in a strong, vibrant, feverish one, full of anxiety!

'First of all, promise me,' he said, 'that you won't think I'm mad. It's the one thing I couldn't bear from you, the one thing that could hurt me! I prefer you to tell me I'm lying! But even if you think I'm mad, I have a way to dispel your delusion . . . I have the *proof* with me! Then you will be immediately convinced that I have all my wits about me! How I've managed to keep them, even I don't know . . . Perhaps because of the evil nature of my fate, that I might be tormented even more . . .

. . . Before that wound I received in the war, I would never have imagined it! I, too, was just like everyone else! I believed in love and kindness, I fashioned dreams, *I lived under a delusion* . . . Since then, I no longer believe in anything . . .

. . . I can't explain what happened to me: what changes took place inside my brain, what cells grew unexpectedly stronger so that I acquired this ability, I am unable to tell you . . . I am, now, this incredible phenomenon – unique in the world – and instead of my becoming the happiest of men as a result of this, I have become the most wretched . . .

. . . The first time that I realised what had happened was during my convalescence. One day while I was talking to a nurse, I noticed that before she even spoke to me, *I could clearly read her thoughts*; before even her lips moved, *I knew what she wanted to say to me*! This aroused my curiosity. I experimented on others. I experimented on my doctor, on my friends who stood by me, on my sister who came every day and kept me company for a few hours . . . And I experimented on you, too, each time you came to visit me!

. . . I was dumbfounded! *I could read people's thoughts just like reading a book*! At first, this terrified me in a way that, unfortunately, I haven't the words to make you understand . . . I felt that I'd acquired a mysterious ability that surpassed all imagination! I knew all about mind-reading, that strange ability that allows certain people, with a little effort, to guess other people's thoughts. But I could see their thoughts moving, as if their brows were made of glass, and *without any effort at all* . . . I could see the beginning of their thoughts, the course they took and their slightest movements in a way that was truly amazing . . . Nothing escaped me . . .

. . . When I came out of the hospital, the situation continued. It hounded me like a nightmare. I realised I'd go mad . . . I distanced myself from people, I didn't dare speak to anyone! I found solace in the company of animals – because, *though I could read their thoughts too*, these thoughts were so basic, so guileless and natural, that they couldn't hurt me! They had none of the wickedness, incredible secretiveness or outrageous selfishness of people's innermost thoughts . . . I could endure no one but my sister, because in her *I read* her love for me and her kindness towards others. I had cut myself off from all my friends so as not to read anything unpleasant, any terrible thought about me . . .

. . . I had shut my door to people. The very thought of them tormented me! I sensed it, slimy and indescribable, circulating in the air and destroying my hopes, like a sly and insatiable snake trying to wrap itself around me . . . I knew what they were thinking about me, I knew what they felt about me, their wickedness and hypocrisy, the terrible and incredible gap that exists, at every moment, between their words and their thoughts – and this knowledge I found unbearable . . .

. . . I could neither love nor associate with anyone anymore. I couldn't stand to have anyone beside me, certainly not any woman – for none of them bears any kindness – and I believed in nothing but kindness, I sought nothing but kindness, I longed for nothing but kindness . . .

. . . I told no one of my secret. I buried it deep inside my soul and I lived with it for many years . . . I didn't dare reveal it: because either they'd take me for a madman or they'd believe me and leave of their own accord, run away in fear lest I learn their hidden reflections, lest I discover their wickedness, their ulterior motives, all their secrets . . . One way or another, I'd end up alone again . . .

. . . Gradually, however, I grew used to seeing all this, too. Their sight no longer has any effect on me, nor does it disgust me as much as it did at first . . . Though I took care in my personal relationships to associate only with those who loved me . . . And I've now learned to forgive the infernal and hidden passions, the moral perversions and terrible desires that I read in these too; all I want is that they love me – how much doesn't concern me – and do not wish me ill . . .'

He stopped for a moment and put his hand to his brow.

I was about to speak to him, to comfort him.

He reached out his other hand and squeezed my shoulder:

'That's all right, *I know* what you'll say! Thank you . . . I know you love me and that's precisely why I've revealed my amazing secret to you . . . *I knew* you were curious to learn it . . . And what I've done, I don't mind telling you, was a great relief for me . . .'

Then, he suddenly steadied himself before me, and convulsively taking hold of my hands, in an insane and desperate manner, he cried out in a heart-rending voice:

'And now, how will I live, HOW WILL I LIVE? How will I dare face people, how will I warm to them, how will I look at them? Every thought they don't voice hurts me; every lie they tell hurts even more . . . They either terrify me or disgust me . . . I have cut off all social contact, all dealings with them! I live alone, like a recluse, surrounded by my cats and by their innocent and primitive thoughts, which I've at least grown accustomed to and which neither frighten nor upset me . . . Wouldn't it have been better if I'd died in the hospital or if I'd been killed in the war instead of living with this anxiety, with this monstrous nightmare that kills my every hope and forbids me any love – that shuts me up in my room like a condemned creature with no possibility of deliverance . . .?'

After that night, I never saw him again. And when, the other day, I heard of his death, I grieved for a moment as a friend – but I immediately found comfort in the thought that he had found deliverance . . .

Original title: 'Mia poly paradoxi periptosi'. First published in the magazine *Bouketo*, issue 470 (March 1933). Translated here from the text anthologised in Makis Panorios (ed.), *To Elliniko Fantastiko Diiyima* [The Greek Fantasy Short Story] vol. 2, Athens: Aiolos, 1993, pp. 95–98.

Pedro Cazas

Fotis Kontoglou

I was still young when my father died. I'd met none of his family though I know that there were no more of them than there were on my mother's side. At the time I was born, her household numbered six people in all: her father, her two brothers, her two sisters and her – of all of them the only one who was married. My father, a profligate, married at an advanced age; for a while it seemed he had succumbed to home life or to his age; but about the time that my mother had me in her belly, he suddenly took up his previous dissolute life again and he became irascible, unbearably so . . . It was amidst this misfortune that I came into the world, wrinkled and with mousy wisps of hair.

Before very long, my father left home – after quarrelling with my uncle . . . I was five years old when one day we learned that he had died of a heart-attack during a drinking bout in Lisbon.

There's little more I know about him . . . When we were small, we often cried together with our mother; but because of the tears she shed when she remembered him, and not because we were fatherless.

I was born in Goa. It seems that my mother's family was a very old one – over three hundred years old . . . The wife of the first of our ancestors whom I was able to drag up from the depths of time is recorded under the name of Almagro; the vague tradition that came down to me had clearly lost its historical truth; I definitely had it from the mouth of my uncle that the Almagro family was none other than the family of the widely-travelled companion of Francisco Pizarro. Yet, even if one regards as false the claim that a little blood dripped from the heart of the Spanish adventurer into the Portuguese family, nevertheless many on their purely paternal side share the same characteristics with him. The oldest is a certain Sidonio, a close friend of Paira, whom he accompanied on the foolhardy voyage to India. Following Paira's murder and after incredible ordeals, he and a couple of companions who had escaped came upon Covilham's expedition, which was about to set sail for the Red Sea. In 1497, a grave illness kept him from the voyage made by Vasco da Gama. Ten years later, however, he was captaining one of Albuquerque's ships. In a naval battle with the Egyptian armada, he lost his arm, at the shoulder, and later he was left with only one eye. Though maimed in this way, he maintained his indefatigable vivacity till the last; he had the habit of always supporting himself on a stick made of Ceylon cinnamon-wood – which he would pare and make a present of. It was with this stick that, from Porto, he would often threaten the King of Abyssinia, who prevented the Portuguese from implementing their satanic plan to destroy Egypt by diverting the course of the Nile . . .

Even in my days, there was still a painting, dating from 1500, of another of my ancestors from that period: he was known as Leocadio and was renowned for his travels to the farthest places to which the Europeans were driven by their curiosity and their thirst for gold in those times. His head was large and his gaze dark from within his swollen eyes, which had black pouches beneath their sockets; his thick lips and even thicker nose, together with the wispy beard that framed his face, invested him with a strange fierceness. In his right hand, he held a small box adorned with many precious stones . . .

Around 1650, the short-lived friendship linking the Portuguese and the Dutch led the Sidonio family to acquire a little northern blood.

The line unfolding after 1700 shows no signs of worry in its prudent commercial ventures. The new century exerts an evident constraint on this mad generation; nevertheless, the idiosyncrasies of the previous generations remain and there was always some dreamer who came along and broke with the new ways. My nearest ancestors were fond of solitude, virtually misanthropes, and with a severe austerity in matters of morality; more than ten monks are buried in the monasteries of Estremadoura and around Guarda . . .

By the end of the 1700s, we were the possessors of a fortune of sorts in India – which, happily for me, survived down to my days, albeit somewhat reduced as a result of total indifference to either increasing or even maintaining it . . . After all this, one might easily conclude that the asceticism and misanthropy characterising the last of our ancestors were the signs of a generation that had grown old. It has not been many years since my elder brother died, after living a life akin to his father's. Of the three of us, it was he who had taken my mother's family name, with the aim of saving it from extinction; but fate played a harsh trick on him, for he never married. My other brother died very young. And so, today, the last drops of blood of my father and his wife are slowly running through my weary body. Death caresses my soul with an inexpressible calm. How weary I am! Only eternal rest becomes the weariness I feel . . .

From a very young age, I displayed a great hunger for learning. And fortune left me no cause for complaint, as I was able to enter *Bombay University* – which had opened not too many years before, in 1857.

Note: Thus far, I have informed the reader of matters which are of no significance to anyone but me. Yet, let him be patient! For later he will realise how these relate to the strange events which I am about to tell. You see, I can't get it out of my head that: *I wouldn't have seen or heard what I saw and heard if I hadn't been the last remaining descendant of the line of Leocadio Calvo*!

Only God knows if I'm right. This is why I thought it prudent to make the reader aware of my family history . . . And there's also another reason: the events I mentioned, being unnatural, would end up being totally unbelievable – even supposing it were possible for them to become any more unbelievable – in a tale from which life's common details would be absent. Thus, I have tried to offset the strength of this wine, which is not for mortals, by deliberately mixing it with a little water from the earth. Everyday life or, as I might put it, the *positive* events, served my benumbed mind as an anchor which held it firm in the maelstrom which mercilessly beset it . . . These events through which, with no small effort, I regained my belief in my senses at crucial moments, and which held together my wits – which were ready to take flight like a feather in an indescribable whirlwind – will no doubt have a similar effect on the soul reading this . . .

I spoke above of the University in Bombay . . . I spent some miserable days during the final year because of a strange nervous anxiety that took hold of me without any cause. I couldn't stay still! Virtually all day, and most nights, I paced about without getting any rest. I thought of leaving for Europe! Then, I don't know how it came to me to write an *Ode on the bones of Camoens*, which was printed in four hundred copies – which drew more attention to me than even Camoens himself deserves . . . I had intended to read it over his grave – when I returned to Goa . . . My sole companions were a few books and my own thoughts. Yet there were very few books that contained what I was looking for. And the more rare those that quenched my thirst were, the more precious they seemed to me, just like everything that is hard to come by. I recall how my joy was beyond expression when, after much effort, I found a Dutch pipe, a whole yard long! Just see what happened to me as a result of this pipe.

One evening, before turning in, I sat at the open window, resting my pipe on the rail. The moon was in its first quarter and as the smoke rose in a thin column in the pale light, my reveries began to transport me far from the earth . . . It must have been midnight – when I suddenly leapt up in alarm! The moon had hidden itself and I was surrounded by darkness . . . At first, I couldn't understand what was happening and simply stood there with my mouth open – from which, unwilled by me, came the word: *Kavna! . . . Kavna!* I broke out in a cold sweat! My ears heard this strange word as if it were not coming from the lips of the same body! I dragged my legs in the darkness, with arms outstretched striving to grab hold of something and, confused, I tumbled into my chair! Before very long, when I came round, I realised that I'd fallen asleep – and that I'd been awakened by the pipe falling out of the window . . . I shut it and lit a candle. I walked past the mirror with my head turned in the other direction, and collapsed fully-dressed onto the bed . . .

The next day, when I awoke, I realised that it was raining very heavily outside.

I stayed inside the entire miserable day; I was beset by a great weariness.

Whatever I did, I couldn't recall the word that had come out of my mouth the previous night . . .

Towards evening, banging my fist down, I cried out in a loud voice:

'*Kavna!* . . . yes, *Kavna!*'

I don't know why, right from the start, I took it for the name of some state – and I jotted it down so that I wouldn't forget it . . .

Those who knew me in Bombay and Goa were of the opinion that I was mad; and moreover, they made sure I was aware of it; yet I know that deep down they were puzzled as to why I was so indifferent and not the slightest concerned to prove to them that my mind was in no way impaired. . .

Imagine, mad! What odd ideas pass through people's heads! May God forgive me for having often laughed at his creatures . . .

Whatever the case, I soon left India; and if I still feel a certain bitterness at my fate, this is not because of the bad name I acquired, but because it went through people's minds that I hastened to bid them farewell because of being unable to endure this bad reputation. Nonetheless, I never saw them again! The truth is that I didn't waste my time with all this hot air; I spent most of my days at the boatyards and in the teak forest at Malabar. Meanwhile, my countrymen were waiting for me to read my *Ode* over Camoens' ashes, while I wasted my time, as I said above, leaving my studies at Bombay University in the middle, burning as many books as I could.

Of the few things I gained from there, the most notable was the friendship of an English gentleman, Sir Corke. May God grant him eternal rest!

In the meantime, I passed by Goa on one occasion for two months and on another for twenty days. The second time, I found only my aunt alive; I wanted to take her with me to Lisbon, but she wouldn't agree and she died in India a few months later.

On returning from Europe, after selling everything I had in Goa (worth roughly 150.000 pesetas), I boarded a ship and headed for Macao. (Till then, I had always signed using my father's name; after that, I don't know why, I decided to change it and use my mother's – yet I no longer recall putting my signature to anything . . .)

The next ten years found me either in the Sonta islands or in Micronesia – as far as Touamotou . . . I couldn't stay anywhere for longer than two or three months – at the very most! My hotheadedness was enough to make me set out barefoot, with a cane stick, to go in search of Eldorado!

I remained in Mindanao several months because of sickness, at the start of a journey that I'd set out on with Corke. Nevertheless, before long, we were out of God's eye: in the Christmas Islands! We spent roughly two years together on the Great Ocean. In 1868, we parted in Sydney, from where Corke set out for the Transvaal, after I'd promised to go and find him there some time towards the end of the same year . . .

Though I liked Sydney, during my second month there, I decided to leave in a hurry for India . . . Quite unexpectedly, a few days later, I found Corke in Calcutta – he had just disembarked! He explained that serious matters had obliged him to return to India, and we agreed to leave for Natal together, as soon as he had finished his business . . . I forgot to say that he was something of a fanatical hunter and always I felt I could see Death's bony hand stroking his fine wavy hair – so fired was he by danger! Africa appealed to him more than India; perhaps because it was unknown to him, and it was around this magical centre that his simple heart turned, drunk with longing . . . As for me, I was unable once again to find any purpose in the journey, in the same way that I had spent my entire life without purpose; though, to be fair, I mustn't hide the fact that I wasn't wholly indifferent; I didn't fall short of my friend in anything, even though hunting would never inspire me or give me an aim in life.

It wasn't until 1870 that we were able to get to Natal. I was then thirty-three years old. From the very first day, we both fell ill, as though fate wanted to warn us of the sad end, which was not long in coming. Corke's horse died of a bite from a poisonous Tsetse fly! Ten days later, he himself was killed, hunting a female elephant on foot!

In a daze, I crossed into Mozambique . . . There was no doubt that the power governing the world did not look upon me favourably.

The Portuguese in Sofala were the worst I've seen; they mercilessly beat the Negroes and stole from each other! After so many years, I still recall a small tavern outside the town, near the sea. It was owned by a Spaniard without a hair on his head or face, and it was frequented by two Negroes, who wore baggy white trousers and had large bows, also white, on their shoes. They had a mouth organ and, every time, before starting to sing and dance like madmen, they began by getting into a quarrel with the tavern-keeper, though the festivities always ended in all-round good spirits amidst a cloud of flies . . .

From Sofala, I returned to Natal, with the intention of taking ship for Tananariva, and from there for the Seychelles, from where I planned to head once again for Sydney, following the course that goes down from Aden. But in Durban, I changed my mind and boarded a schooner that was headed for Fagoua . . .

This island is a stop for the boats that fish in the South Seas; they put in there for the winter and attend to what needs to be done, before sailing out to sea again in spring.

The ship I boarded was loaded with timber for the boatyard, where I found three brigs waiting in line . . .

Note: the Foo-i-maa (or Moses) group was discovered in 1661 by a Portuguese ship that came across it by chance during a storm that blew it off its course for India. Its out-of-the-way location at the southern end of the Indian Ocean and the lack of any significance that its deserted islands held for people fired by the thirst for gold meant that it remained, even after its discovery, virtually unknown, given that, till 1700, only the need for water obliged the odd ship to enter its dangerous waters. In 1755, in Fagoua, the largest island in the group, a small settlement was established, consisting of a hundred souls, victims of the earthquake that destroyed Lisbon at that time. When I went there, I found a small village, very prettily built and quite prosperous . . . Apart from the trade in animals, cattle, sheep and pigs, as a result of the boats, the land is fertile, and for it to render its fruits (renowned vegetables and a thick grain like that of the Transvaal), all it required was toil and perseverance, things lacked by the adventurers in former times, who were accustomed to seizing the ready wealth amassed by foreign peoples.

Fagoua is located at 41° south and 52° east.

Two people made an impression on me in Fagoua . . .

But first of all, I ought to say a few words about this island, which is so far from all the centres of the civilised world.

It is a very low yellow piece of land, consisting entirely of earth, surrounded by a strip of sand with a width of at most half a mile. From ten miles away, the land is invisible save for a dark rock, some hundred metres tall, which suddenly rises up from the sea's wastes . . . Its shores are divided by neither cove nor mound. An inexpressible melancholy grips man's soul when a ship passes alongside the land . . . Here and there, a few clumps of thorns or a flock of gulls glimmer amid the desolation . . . Yet, when you set eyes on the houses and harbour close to the mountain, the impression changes in an instant! Here, the sight is as pleasant as anyone could hope to see: the little houses – most of them white – spread out over a sandy stretch. Clearly visible on the seafront is the harbour-master's office and the few shops, scattered over the clean sand – each with a large weathervane on its roof. The shipyard is at the foot of the rock, which sinks into the waters of the harbour, and a little further off are two huts where the timber is stored.

Nowhere else have I seen so many seabirds! They have their nests on the rock and all day long squawk so loudly that it's difficult for the one person to hear what the other is saying. I saw some birds there that were smaller than the gulls and that can't be found in any other part of the Ocean. The inhabitants of Fagoua call them cohalos.

Now I'll return to the people I mentioned above . . . No matter how much I want to pass quickly over everything unrelated to my tale, I can't resist the temptation to say a few words about one individual . . . But what am I saying! Now that I've thought more carefully about it, I see that this person definitely has his place in my tale! So here's to Tin Tin's fat lips! And here's to that precious smile of Tin Tin, who has to devour half a pound of meat in order to reveal a thin line of white teeth! Nature poured him into a special mould. *Rara avis*! You wonder on hearing of a *Tin Tin*, that rings like crystal in the air, coming from the folded cushion before you! We know where we have to go to find rare animals; but who could tell us where Tin Tin spread his canvas? Thus, my meeting with him was purely a piece of good fortune.

One day, while I was walking with my head full of dark thoughts, apart from dark people, I saw him sitting on the blade of an anchor that was lying close to the boatyard. From the very first, he showed a great desire for company – an unlikely thing as he was surrounded by sinister tales. In fact, no one could expect anything from him different to what I'd heard said about his person. His beastliness went beyond all limits. His walk was like that of an ape in the way that he tossed his arms forward. If he were to pick his teeth, no doubt he would pull out a piece of human flesh! He looked at you with tired and bleary eyes, circled by a red ring formed by his outward-turning eyelids . . . I was amazed by how he passed, in an instant, from good spirits into a rage! At such times, he was like the devil! So, despite all the good will he showed towards me, I never ceased to be wary of him. Strange how, right to the end, he seemed peaceful to me; and not only that, but more real than all the inhabitants of Fagoua! The scoundrel! He drank so much that if he squeezed his nose, it would come out with a litre of spirit! Now and then, he'd spit out a word in a tongue that I didn't understand – from his homeland, it seems. And sometimes, he'd mumble a couple of words from an old English song: *I've lost my head . . . I've lost my head* . . . He'd get up, stiff as he was, and do a couple of turns, stumbling on his long legs that ended in two feet stretching all the way from here to there . . .

His gull, a greasy creature, worthy of his master, would join him in his festivities! While ever Tin Tin remained quiet, this accursed bird stood before the flap of the tent with a sobriety worthy of Scipio; and every so often, it would simply let out an endless caw – with its head low to the ground; but as soon as it saw its master dancing, it was gripped by a nervous rush; it ran up and down in the tent, wild-eyed, and tried to take flight, took a few pecks at the canvas, and eventually began to whirl between the nigger's legs in a Bacchic frenzy!

Outside the harbour were two deserted islets. Sometimes, when the sea wasn't rough, Tin Tin got into a boat and spent all day on those islands . . . Who knows what he got up to! One day, I saw him coming back with someone else; he seemed very happy. I asked him when we could go together to the islets. 'Whenever you want!' he replied.

We went a few days later . . . I saw nothing in those rocks, on which you can't even walk . . .

My companion fished, while I slept. When I woke, I clambered up onto a high rock and, to the south, saw a couple of islands that gleamed like icebergs in the dark waters. 'I'd like to go over there,' I said to Tin Tin.

We hoisted sail and went back to the harbour.

How strange that those two white islands should take such a hold of my mind! Tin Tin was unable to give me any more information, other than that there were four of them: three small ones close together and a large one called Zato.

Within a few days, I'd managed to discover the whole history of these islands from the beginning of time. There wasn't much to tell. To be more exact, no one would have had anything to say about these islands if it hadn't been for a strange man, known to the seafarers as 'Osso' – Spanish for 'Bear'! He was a caulker and fisherman, a helmsman, carpenter and even a miller! He switched from one job to the other depending on what fortune brought, but only God knows why he hardly ever spoke! When he wasn't working, he never even came into contact with anyone else. He lived in an old warehouse, half an hour outside the village, where they used to store fish oil, dried fish and sealskins. He'd often wander alone at the other side of the island, either with a long staff on his shoulder – no one knows why – or with a large sailor's knife tucked into a leather belt (more madness, since there are no wild animals on Fagoua). There was a rumour that he was skilled with weapons, but none of those I met knew whether this was true. But his favourite walk was on the white islands I referred to previously. He'd spend two and three weeks there. (Often, they thought he'd drowned.) He'd take an old launch – that was always tied up in front of Tin Tin's tent – and would set out! Even in a rough sea.

Within a few days, I too was able to set foot on Zato. There were three of us. The other two were a captain from the Philippines, now working as a merchant, and one of those lost Englishmen, widely-travelled and feckless, that you find in the farthest parts of the world . . . As soon as we had moored, the skipper and I leapt out . . . The Englishman remained in the boat and fell asleep; just like all his kind, he had not the slightest curiosity . . .

We walked for about half an hour along the shore . . . The merchant was sleepy, too, and kept on yawning like a sheep! In the end, he said he was sorry and lay down in a small creek . . . I continued on my way and reflected on how I spent my days always searching, urged on by that sleepless viper, curiosity, while others spent their lives in a state of total indifference . . .

I stopped and looked around me . . . The sun was scorching . . . A few trails of foam danced here and there out at sea. The roar of the waves echoed from one end of the sand to the other, hollow and subterranean, as if someone were digging beneath my feet. The seaweed moved on the flat shore as if it were alive, hounded by the slight breezes still ranging over the sea . . . I felt the desolation oppressing me and, for a moment, thought I was dreaming . . . Bustling India! (I felt sleepy . . . why the hell was I so sleepy?) Without realising what I was doing, I took off my clothes to go for a swim – pondering on the thought that somewhere in the world was Bombay, and that poor Corke was rotting where I'd left him. In fact, as I was pulling the shirt over my head, I clearly saw my uncle putting on his spectacles with their long, black cord! Then a thousand things passed like lightning through my mind – ending with a lame Jew and an old Chinaman called Til, with whom I was playing cards in Calcutta . . .

I stayed for over half an hour in the sea. Then I ate something, and fell asleep . . .

I awoke after something like three hours. I was in very good spirits – almost verging on merriment . . .

I went on walking, like a man who knows where he's going. Apart from the seabirds, I saw no other living creature. It was with some relief that, after a while, my eye fell upon some rocks atop a small hill, whose ridge was uneven, just like the back of a cow lying on its side. On reaching the spot, I remained astounded before a world of rocks resting on top of each other in an indescribable disorder! It was as if I'd come upon them at the very moment that they had begun to tumble. On its other side, the hill swept smoothly down to the waters of a tiny bay, which was closed in on all sides . . . Good Lord! What heavenly peace filled me at the sight of that forgotten stretch of sea! From where I was standing, I could make out beneath the clear water the stones and green shadows of the bottom. My heart immediately filled with delight; the heavens opened above my head and God rained down his blessings . . .

The land, which was dry and low, enclosed the sea on all sides, as I said, and ended in a tongue of sand, which stretched out at a short distance from the hill on which I was standing, just leaving between them a narrow neck of sea, no wider than half a mile . . . At that time, there was a strong current going out to sea, just like a large blue ribbon, between the two yellow sides of the channel. I went down and stood on the narrow shore . . . An idea passed through my mind, and other things which were not ideas, so it seems . . . Nevertheless, I was in a strange state . . . *As if that place were familiar to me*! If I hadn't felt embarrassed, I'd have said that it was something I'd seen in my dreams! Before long, since we all know that a thousand things hover like infernal shadows in such fathomless depths that, even to the end of the world, not one pale ray of reason will ever reach them, I sat down and, in my imagination, designed a small house, low and blackened, and with a fence around it to make it more compact, with a low door which you would have to stoop to go through. A man, wrapped in warm clothes, comes up to the house, looks at it with pride, rubs his hands and goes inside, followed by a dog. From a small chimney visible on the hut's roof, a billow of smoke cheerfully emerges in the midst of the wilderness. Two small windows are open towards the sea and through these you can see the seabirds gleaming in flocks on the water, and the large fish. And even a black shadow on the opposite beach, which you take for a man, even though you know it's only a rock . . . And you give praise to God that the devil's wickedness doesn't reach this far. You think: I'm happy! The sun shines on my island for me alone, for the seabirds and for the seals; and in the evening I'll eat my supper with a soul filled with peace . . . It's been a good many years since I thought of other men . . . I recall the myth of Pythagoras, who from a philosopher became a king, woman, horse, fish, frog, hedgehog and, finally, on being transformed into a cockerel, saw that man is the most wretched of all creatures . . . The big cities sometimes pass through my mind like dreams, but they soon disappear and I go outside to listen to the seals barking . . . I expect nothing tomorrow, or the next week, which would cause me concern. Time seems not to pass, neither flying nor stopping. I have no sense of it at all, because nothing obliges me to think about it . . . I am aware that the most stupid people in the world might laugh at me as they would at a child for becoming so simplistic. Sometimes, I cry at the most insignificant things, which is not at all becoming, such as when I see the straight and simple line where the Ocean ends, or when my dog becomes wild with delight and shows me more gratitude than is warranted . . .

We returned to Fagoua by moonlight . . . My two companions fell out with me. They'd realised, they said, that I was a person who spent hours reflecting on Paradise like the monks of Toledo . . . I let them go on. I said that the most stupid people in the world might laugh at me as they would at a child for becoming so simplistic . . .

I forgot all about Osso . . . What nonsense for this man, too, to carry a staff around with him for no reason!

I was unconscious for twenty-four hours from getting drunk! I'd been drinking all day with the nigger. With us was a captain who, without doubt, as I realised, owed his body to the nigger, just as he owed his soul to the devil. He kept his eyes constantly shut – as though he didn't have need of them! His mouth was warped! When he spoke, you expected him to spew up his lungs from the rasping! Like a water-powered saw!

During all this time, I was sitting in a cloud of smoke, through which I could see nothing save Tin Tin's head, which shone like glass. I still recall that I reached out my hand and grabbed a large knife that the nigger had in his yellow belt . . .

But why am I relating things of no importance? Do I owe anyone anything? And why supposedly? Is it easy to take the knife from around the waist of a drunk? And then, I had an idea: I want to show that it's not my style to hide the kind of people I mixed with, and that I'm not ashamed of what I did . . . And furthermore, I don't mind your learning that my name is Vaca Cavro! To hell with the madness that grips me, lest people say that I'm vainglorious. Why shouldn't I be when my nerves are playing me? Then again, why should I conceal my name, as there's no one left in my family to feel shame? After all, my name has nothing to gain by it; the tale seems to me to be written by a blockhead!

I drank for a whole week, non-stop! Then it was as if I were dead. Weariness and languor . . . This world is suffocating me! People work like maniacs and screech all day like hens in a coop! It bothers me, I grow irritated! As if they were asking me to observe what they're doing, and I cry out: 'To hell with you all!' Then, I calm down, my mind sinks into a cool light and my heart swims in a deep green lake . . .

I lie down on the earth and gaze at the insects carrying tiny bits of wheat. Then, I get up, I look at the endless sea, and weep with joy that I'm alone!

Osso with his long staff often comes into my mind, as if I wanted to get used to him and not to laugh at him . . .

I rummage in my pockets and something cools my throat. I open my hand and look inside . . . I reflect: what's stopping me from spending whatever days I have left on Zato? What I have in my hand is gold! For the first time in my life I realised how wretched I would be if I were without it! Poor Osso can't stay more than a week on Zato – and perhaps he spends half the days hungry! No doubt, where I stopped, close to the narrow shore, he, too, plans his house, identical to mine, with two little windows overlooking the sea and a chimney that smokes in the wilderness!

I came across him in the old warehouse where he lived . . . Damn and blast! What an odd man . . . He stared at me indifferently, as if expecting such an unhoped-for thing! (Who would expect such a miracle! No one else would believe their ears, he'd jump with joy after such a love affair with the white, rocky islands of Zato!) I said to him: '. . . I have as much money as you want for us to live alone during the years we have left!' He half-concealed himself behind the door-flap, and in no more than a few words led me to understand that he *agreed* to share the wilderness on Zato with me . . .

That he *agreed*! From that day, I no longer feel like laughing when he comes into my mind, burdened with the long staff he carries with him . . .

We cut rocks from the hill . . . Osso took me and showed me a stream that welled up some five hundred metres from our hut!

The little house was a picture! So lovely! I felt intoxicated! May your foundations be blessed! May peace embrace you . . . Here, beside you, I'll find my rest one day!

We built a large hut, with a small cellar attached to it on the side where the sun set. On the side facing the hill, the wall was so low that the roof hid it beneath its overhang, as it almost touched the ground. On the side of the sea, it was high, almost three metres, with two single windows. The door was in the section of the wall left uncovered by the storeroom, which blocked only half of it, forming a right-angle on the side facing the hill. The storeroom, too, had a small door facing the sea. We divided the large hut into two; each part had its own window. In one part was the front door I mentioned and another, smaller one, that led into the storeroom. The second partition was our living room. Up above, the thick beams of the roof were blackened. Below, I covered the floor with a black carpet and threw lots of skins on top of this, which left it showing only in a few places. In front of my wooden bed, I had spread a black Japanese bearskin, which still had the head and claws. Beneath the window was a small couch and in front of this a little round table, invisible under its crimson table-cloth, which spread like a big jellyfish over the floor. In one corner, I fixed a black shelf for a good few books, which I never read, and beside it a table on which you could see a bronze inkwell, always closed, and a few sheets of paper held down by a piece of that *andalusite* that the geologists call *silicate* . . .

I gathered up whatever I found on the shore; a whole world of pebbles and shells and coloured stones . . . And I used all these as decorations! It impressed me more than anything in the world. I stood for hours gazing at it all. I'd get up and look out of the window at the hills and the sea, and I listened pensively to the wooden clock – that I'd set going just for the ticktock, without its showing the time . . .

It often seemed to me that I was entering the world *at that moment*; as if a light were passing before my soul, and I was *amazed*; it was as though I were seeing the hills and the sea *for the first time*! Then, I would turn my gaze to the walls as if mentally counting two paintings, a pistol, a rifle and a barometer in carved wood, hanging over my table. I'd rub my hands with delight and button my jacket – as if wanting to shut it all inside my clothes! Outside, the gulls were circling the trough, swimming with their white wings in the light of a clear day!

Note: Henceforth, my tale is interspersed with one or two entries taken from the journal I kept while my life was running smoothly . . . These days were the best days of my life . . . So, apart from the fact that these notes reveal the state of my soul at the time, now that I re-read them, it's as if they were once again adding a little cheer to the bitter days I am living now, old as I am and surrounded by uncouth people . . .

. . . Osso is busy cooking a plump fowl and he's filled the kitchen with smoke. He's kept company by a dirty cat without whiskers because of old age. We have three goats and seven geese; we'd also have had *Prince*, our dog, if he hadn't died during the first days, of what I don't know.

We also have a sailing boat. We moor it in front of our hut, and its mast sticks out above the roof like a thin line with a narrow red flag at the top. Often during the day, I lean out of my window to look at it. When the weather is not too bad, I take it and wander all day in the channel, measuring the water with the plumb-line. Often, I moor somewhere on the opposite shore and I scour the beach, as I like to, for some unusual shell. From there, I look at our house and the hill overlooking it. I can see Osso moving around . . . The goats, grazing up above, seem as if they're hanging there, because from afar the hill looks completely vertical . . .

A white pebble on the sand, a bit of wood lying on the shore, attract my attention. The most insignificant things here seem full of interest to me. In these expanses, nature is simple and primitive, desolate, without the prodigal spawn of human beings. Life is rare and sparse – and vanishes into the chaos that we call *Earth* and *Water* . . .

I see things straight, without my impression being injured by what I've come to understand till now when uttering those two words: *Water* and *Earth* . . . Here, even without names, the things themselves fall upon my soul with their full significance, wild and indifferent, stripped of the friendly disposition that the human tongue gives them in our eyes . . .

I can speak no more, nor any better, of these things. Once, I felt, with some relief, a *sense of humanity* – let's call it that – taking hold of me at the sight of these simple things I mentioned above . . . It often happened that I would carry an insignificant stone back to the hut – from two miles away! – in order to throw it from the window, puzzled as to why I'd picked it up. The hut, and everything testifying to a human hand, brought me back to myself . . . I go out and stand shivering in the shade stretching over the ground. Then, I clamber up the hill and sit on a rock as if surprised. My eye falls from above on the hut and my heart pounds . . .

Beyond, the sandy shore is pale, desolate and plain . . . Occasionally, a seal crawls out slowly, like an oiled goatskin, and suns itself . . .

I can make out the three white islands . . . They seem to me as if they are hanging in the chaos that begins at my feet and vanishes into the horizon, mixed with the sky . . . When it rains, they turn pale and can't be seen clearly . . . particularly after midday. But whenever the weather is dry, they become lily white, adorned with numerous red dots.

I say to myself: *They're lying in silence and waiting for the end of the world* . . . What a thought! But it's not really what I mean . . . When I see them, I recall the words written by Ritsiolis beneath the map of the moon: 'Here, no people live, not even the shades of the dead ever come . . .'

I mutter to myself: 'What's happening, I wonder, at this very moment on the Ocean floor?'

I sit for some time like a fool – as if my mind has gone numb.

In winter, we shut ourselves inside for many days. Our provisions were plentiful in everything. For bread, we ate hardtack . . . When the geese wanted to go out, we opened the door of the storeroom and they flew to the sea; they'd fly for two or three days and graze together with the other seabirds; but they'd regularly come back to the hut and when they arrived outside, they'd call and we'd open for them! Till the very end, not one was lost.

I can say that not one cloud ever appears without my noticing it from my window and my feeling a deep contentment as it rolls on, sailing through the sky . . . A bird caws as it flies over the roof and I go outside to look at it . . . I hear for a moment its powerful wings as it flaps them hurriedly, and then it vanishes like a miracle! I remain lost in thought . . . Often, after just such an insignificant event, I say a prayer . . . The heavens are wide-open! In the deep waters are thousands of fish and monsters . . .

April: the weather is chilly. Today, the fifth day of the month, the seven heavens opened like cascades!

In the channel, the water is dark from the churned-up earth!

10: This evening, just before the sun went down, I thought of people. Perhaps the reason for this was the blood-red colour of the sun, that sets and casts long shadows over everything . . . It brings to mind the coloured glass of the churches in Goa, during the years of my childhood! I still recall the flies chasing each other in the air and twinkling like stars!

Very rarely, a silent shadow passes through my mind . . . It reels as though drunk and then fades like the shadow of my pipe-smoke on the wall, as if it understands that I'm in no mood to become acquainted with it . . .

And it's true that I have no wish to let them trouble my head . . . Even love on the part of my fellows would be an intolerable burden to me . . .

This, more or less, is what I think, as I stand beside my window . . .

Beneath my eyes, the foam leaps, reddened by the sun, between the rocks . . .

Osso comes over to me and we stand like that for a long time, without opening our mouths . . .

3 August: Today is the fifth week that an accursed wind has been assailing us without respite! I've never before seen such rage! Its fury has changed the appearance of the earth to such an extent that it's difficult for us to recognise the very spot before our eyes! We're embroiled in complete chaos . . .

At this moment, the sea has nothing to offer the human eye . . .

This morning, the storm seemed as if it would let up and, till noon, the wind played its role so well that it fooled us; suddenly, however, it unbridled itself after turning a few degrees eastwards. It changed from a southerly into a sou'wester . . . In the harbour, the sea bubbled like water in a cauldron! The tiny waves are thick and race quickly, producing a hollow whistling; they don't foam at all, just some big bubbles, thin and opaque, leap up everywhere from the water . . .

Our sailing boat has sunk; though it's still tied to its anchor. The ocean can be seen only at the spot where the land opposite becomes low, or better, all we can see is a thick haze, through which a glimpse of light appears every now and again.

The desolation blocks the throat and deadens all thought. The daylight is yellowy and dull, as if we were looking through the coloured glass of a bottle . . . As if it were the world's last day . . . Not so much as a feather is visible in the sky . . .

In the hut, everything is peaceful. The fire's burning and Osso is carving a pipe. The cat is sitting next to him, huddled up on the firewood, and every so often it opens its eyes and looks at Osso as if to ask him what's going on . . .

As for me, I listen to the roar with the same feeling that you experience when you stick your head under the bedcovers to escape from ghosts . . .

As I was getting ready to go to bed, a gust of wind blew down the chimney roaring like a canon; as if demolishing it! God help us tonight.

11: I was thunderstruck this afternoon when I saw Osso coming in with a human skull in his huge hands. He told me that it belonged to some Englishman from a ship that had been wrecked on the island many years back. Of the three who had been saved, one had died. The other two had been rescued by Frenchies who had come to the island looking for seals . . . He'd discovered the bones on a previous occasion when he'd spent a few days on Zato . . .

We killed our last goose! Osso is happy and is whistling as he plucks it . . . I watch him. His nose is running and his eyes show that his mind is wandering in distant parts . . .

An iron fist grips my heart as it flashes through my mind that I have no one else in the world but him . . . Poor Osso! He can't show his love for me enough! When we're at the table, he keeps getting up to bring me whatever he thinks I might need. He brings me ten times more than I want. He fills my plate with the choice morsels and keeps the scraps for himself. He makes me sit beside the fire while he sits with his back to the window, through which comes the cold night air . . . He's always asking me: are you cold? He gets up with his mouth still full and pokes the fire . . . then he sits back down again, silently fixes his deep eyes on a spot in front of him and continues to eat slowly, with the couple of teeth he has left, without raising his head . . .

His words are few and far between. He rarely opens his mouth other than to reply; and he replies briefly, though with great willingness. It's as if he were saying: 'It's your fault for making me talk so much.' He endears himself to me with that strict silence of his, because I know that behind that iron door lies a hugely tempestuous life. For me, his words are like precious stones scattered on a table covered with black felt . . . We close our eyes and then we can see countless rubies shining in a dark and vast valley . . .

No man I've ever met has left a deeper impression on me with his words than Osso did with his silence; and, again, I can recall nothing that resembled his voice: a heavy plumb-line that went down further than anything from the upper world could reach! No one knows where he was born, and I often ask forgiveness of his savage soul if I upset him by recording the place where he died.

During the whole time I lived with him, he said nothing about other people. You would wager that he knew nothing of their existence . . . He had about him the indifference of the elements that break our backbones. He was silent, like all great things; like God and Hades. Nothing had the power to take him out of his resounding apathy . . .

I knew that he was widely-travelled . . . He'd crossed the Indian Ocean, covering it from end to end, like the prisoner the floors of his cell in every direction; he'd roamed for many years through the countless islands of the Great Ocean; he'd been shipwrecked aboard a Japanese ship in Ouroup, and again in Tiocoa in Polynesia, in Balouk in Foo-i-maa . . .

Once, he gave in to my curiosity and came out with a couple of words; but he never said more than what my question demanded. His narration had nothing of the fictional style that I so loved; he paid no attention to what he was relating. His expression was just like that of an animal that we admire through the bars of a cage, without its caring a jot for our foolishness . . .

He showed a great interest in cooking – though he was no big-eater.

In general, he was blessed with great ease in whatever required skill. In Fagoua, I heard them talk of his great skill with weapons – above all, of his technique at swordplay. Whenever we went hunting, he would buckle on a huge sailor's sword, of a kind much heavier and larger than any I've ever seen. It seemed so submissive in his hands that he might easily be compared with Pierson, the Norwegian corsair, who sheared the ears off seven hundred captives, without letting his blade touch the shoulder of even one of them . . .

He'd often talk to the cat, but would never touch it with his hands.

Yet I could never explain his habit of imitating the sound of gulls and seals; he'd often mix these sounds with his words, without his eyes showing any signs of mirth. His expression, stony as always, prevented anyone from taking this peculiar habit as a sign of mirth – so much so that the impression was more terrifying than anyone could imagine.

As to his external appearance, disproportion has rarely made such sport of the eternal proportions of human architecture. His arms were short, but his huge fists, always hanging far from his sides, reached more or less down to the level of his knees, and were bare below the elbow. His right shoulder sagged, perhaps from the weight of his right hand, which was thicker than his left one, though it was missing a finger shorn at the root. His belly was tucked in, which made the breadth of his chest even more terrifying. His rib-cage was so immense that I reckoned it could hold two pairs of lungs!

He had the open walk of one used to a ship's deck. His feet completely lacked arches and his soles had become flat like those of a bear – and so hard that whenever I heard him walking over the stone slabs, it sounded as if he were wearing clogs.

His head was huge and bare, and two slight protrusions on his brow gave his skull a square shape. His face was riddled with pockmarks, which in many places were as thick and deep as the holes in a cork! A truly Gordian knot of wrinkles covered his forehead, above his left eyebrow. His mouth was divided by a knife-cut, which flayed out on his right cheek – just like cracks in a pane of glass.

His eyes were deeply set, more so than I could believe in a living being. To put it better, I never saw more than a tiny star in the depths of his sockets; sometimes he'd rub them, when the smoke from the fire bothered him, and I saw how his big finger disappeared completely as if into the empty sockets of a skull . . .

I'd be hard pressed to put an age to him . . . though, I'd never have said he was less than sixty years old, and, then again, I often reflected that he must have come into the world a couple of centuries before me . . . Thus, letting my thoughts carry me along, I tried in vain to imagine the kind of family he'd been born into or the place where he'd first crawled and played. The desolate Ocean stretched out wild before me . . .

One evening, a strange thing befell me: I don't recall what it was I needed; the cellar-door was half closed and only a strip of light from the kitchen fell onto the opposite wall. On entering, I saw Osso sitting and looking intently at that strip of light . . .

He seemed annoyed when I pushed open the door and hastily regulated the door flap in such a way that it formed that bright line, just as it was before . . .

Then, he turned again to stone, gazing at the wall . . .

The seabirds squawk all day long in the channel. There must be thousands of them and of all kinds; even many of those cohalos that I'd first seen in Fagoua.

One day, I noticed that these birds always congregated close to the mouth of the channel. Their preference for these waters seemed strange to me as they had to struggle ceaselessly in order to maintain their position in the face of the strong current sweeping them along. But there you are: what I couldn't understand was that their movements showed that they were all struggling to reach the same point, and it was around this that they all congregated, like bees around a beehive, filling the air with a polyphony of cries.

My surprise at the motivation prevailing in the flock was further increased by the thought that these birds are peace-loving, and constitute a notable exception among all the Ocean's winged creatures, which are the most irritable and insatiable creatures in the whole of creation. You could observe them for days on end without hearing anything more than a melancholic and monotonous cawing – by which they express their contentment at fishing . . . They always distance themselves from the battles waged by the insatiable harpies of the water, as soon as day breaks. They are the only species always absent from these symposia, which include all the greedy birds of the Ocean: from the bloated albatrosses to the tiny sea-swallows.

When I asked Osso, he told me that they struggle to drink from a stream of fresh water that comes up from the sea, no longer daring to come anywhere near the water that we drink, as we often set traps for them there.

One night in winter, Osso had said to me, in rather strange words, that it would be worth our effort, when the good weather came, to dig a well so as to have water close by.

I was surprised, as it was the first time he'd ever expressed an opinion on anything, without my asking him. I was even more astounded by the spiritedness of his words; in fact, I even thought I'd noticed a shadow of alarm upon him . . .

But, everything about this strange man (supposing that he were no other kind of creature) rebelled against the laws governing us, and often I'd find nothing in his expression that corresponded in any way to what all people have in common: in the end, seeing that no doubt I had before me a creature who obeyed unknown powers, or none at all, I stopped trying to fathom everything I noticed about him, at least at those times when you wouldn't take him for a human . . .

Nevertheless, in a few days – it was then the middle of October – his manners acquired such a pronounced irritability that it was clear to me that I had to be *careful* . . .

He no longer spoke at all! A shade from Hades would have been less silent! I could see it; he strove in vain to smile. He passed by me and I shuddered! Most nights, I lay awake . . . He never closed his eyes for a moment!

At times, I couldn't hold back my tears. (Not for twenty-five years had my eyes filled with tears.)

To the north of our hut, before the open sea, was a level piece of land between the shore and a series of rocks that left only a narrow passage in-between. Once or twice I'd found

Osso sitting there, lost in thought . . . On another occasion, I saw him coming from there in alarm, as if something were chasing him . . .

After this, when he indicated to me that this was the place where we would dig for water, it flashed through my mind that perhaps he was keen to uncover some treasure. Such a thing held no excitement for me at all and, by the bones of Adam, I was surprised at the agitation provoked by the love for gold in a man whom I'd taken to be of stone . . .

The earth was soft and it was covered by sparse weeds and a few bushes laden with small black berries, rather like grapes. Some of these bushes had climbed up to the highest part of the rock, and when the wind blew, their cold rustling suddenly disturbed the silence of the tomb below. There, the echo was louder than the repeating sound. My ear grasped the palest shade of sound and I shuddered whenever a dry leaf fell from above. At times, I felt that the slightest noise would crack my skull.

I had gone hunting. I sat beside the channel to rest . . . Suddenly, I thought I heard a lot of bellowing all together. As if a whole herd of buffalo were lowing! It sounded muffled to my ears as if it were coming out of the sea . . .

I stayed where I was for quite some time, but without hearing it again . . .

Setting out for the hut, I happened to turn my head and I saw Osso coming towards me like a drunk . . . I said nothing to him . . . I've grown afraid of him . . . But he came up to me in desperation and shouted in my ear, in a loud and wild voice:

'We have to begin digging tomorrow, Vaca Cavro! *I can't do it without you*!'

Then he clenched his fist and mumbled something that I was unable to make out . . .

His flung his head back nervily, like a horse bitten on the neck by flies . . . His mouth hung open . . . The veins in his neck, thicker than my finger, bulged as if he were having a fit . . .

What in God's name should anyone make of all this?

We began digging on 27 October, 1873.

Osso had suddenly got better a couple of days before; in fact, he was in good spirits that morning . . .

When we arrived at the spot I mentioned previously, and entered through the only pass, he proceeded to the right, and came to a sudden halt at the base of the rock, carrying a spade, a pick and a rope. He threw the rope down, still in a coil as it was, and stuck the pick into the middle of the circle formed on the ground, sighing slightly. Then he bent down and drew a circle, a wide circumference, and we immediately set to work, with great enthusiasm . . . The earth was soft and free of stones, being of rock sediment amassed by the rainwater, and we proceeded so quickly that by the evening of the same day, we saw that in the morning it would be necessary to set up a winch for the earth.

A little before midnight, a strong wind got up; in the morning we found the door of the store-room on the ground; we set about securing it straightaway. It was after midday by the time we'd finished. Then we set up the winch over the well and as a result, we did no digging that day.

The next day, the wind blew with the same fury. Occupied with other tasks, it was three in the afternoon before we lifted our picks.

Because of all the wind, the sun burned in the dry air. As we went down to the shore, the spray hit us in the face like a jet, at a distance of two hundred metres from the sea!

I followed behind Osso, and I watched him walking, leaning into the wind so as to form an angle of no more than fifty degrees with the ground . . . His stout legs kicked up a cloud of small stones, some of which hit my face and arms . . .

I stood beside the winch and he set to digging. Neither of us spoke . . . About half an hour must have gone by when I heard him shout. I jumped, thinking that he'd called me to raise the bucket with the earth.

I found him with his back resting against the wall of the well and with his hands on his knees . . . He was shaking from head to toe and his head hung over his chest . . . His lips were pale and thick beads of sweat were running from his brow . . .

I leapt down beside him and, taking hold of him by the shoulders, I asked him what was wrong . . . My hands, resting on him, shook with him; and for a moment, a powerful spasm ran through my entire body, as if I'd touched an electric pole! The sweat was pouring from his brow and falling to the ground, hitting the fine dust like molten metal . . .

At that moment, a swirling wind passed over us and I got a pile of dust in my eyes . . . Without opening them, I clambered out, cursing, and steadied myself against a tree so as not to fall . . .

My head was swimming. I rested it on my knees, keeping my eyes closed. For a moment, I heard the roar of the sea and then I sank into a black vortex! My senses deserted me and my impression of everything around me grew ever more hazy – till it became as dark as the tomb . . .

When I began to come round, I stopped as if on the threshold of life, with my senses confused and dulled – no more acute than those of someone about to fall asleep . . .

I don't know how long I remained in that state . . . Eventually, I began to distinguish, from the fathomless depths where I found myself, the regular sound made by the blood beating against the temples and, together with this, a faint impression was created that something was floating in my head . . .

Before long, my skull was humming with a vortex consisting of thousands of tiny patterns which never managed to crystallize into a thought, as they flickered and faded at an incredible speed . . .

All I could determine was a persistent attempt on my part to think, but without being able to produce a single thought. I'd say it was like a kind of sneeze that continually stops on the brink, that never bursts, bringing a mortal desire to grasp something that is continually out of reach . . . Finally, my mind went numb with a sudden jolt – and I let myself once again tumble into the abyss. When I returned to the world above, I was no longer sitting in my original place, but was lying face down on the earth and the chill night air was raking my shoulders . . .

This time my soul returned with a jolt so sudden that my ears were still ringing with the barking of one of Tartarus' hydras . . .

Yet, there were voices coming from somewhere just a few feet away from me, mingled with the sorrowful rustling coming from the wild trees!

It was the voice of neither animal nor man; it lacked all expression, whether of sorrow, pain or joy; yet it was terrifying, more terrifying than any voice ever heard by man!

Yes! . . . Now I see how bereft I am of words that I might give to my fellow kind even the faintest idea of the voice I heard. (Nevertheless, I always maintained an innocent belief in the human tongue, as long as I kept my mouth closed. What a strange delusion, when faced with events, for us to feel this conviction more deeply the more vivid the impression and, one day, for us to see that all this remains terribly far from the human tongue!)

After growing louder a couple of times, in such a frightful way that I felt my courage deserting me, it gradually began to grow silent, and finally became a few interrupted growls . . . Then, all I heard was the sorrowful roar of the wind amidst the chaos of the rocks – as if it were falling upon the last flames of a dying fire . . .

I waited, without moving from my place . . . Before long, however, I found myself calmer, and I attempted to stand up on my feet; but as soon as I put my hands on the ground, I was again gripped by fear – and it was impossible for me to stop my teeth chattering . . .

Then the sound of many voices reached my ears, as if coming from a mile away. It seemed as if they were rising from the depths of the earth, precisely beneath the spot where I was lying . . .

After a while, they faded . . . And then, that indescribable voice that I had heard at first howled again: 'Owoo . . . owoo!' continuously, like a dog that's had its leg broken . . .

When it ceased, there was a brief silence . . . and then I clearly heard a sorrowful voice, a human voice . . . I recognised Osso's voice – though it was greatly distorted . . . For he was weeping! Lord above! Osso was pleading! He kept repeating: 'give me peace, senhor Leocadio! Senhor Leocadio . . .' Then he began uttering frightful cries – and before long leapt out and stood with his legs sunk into the earth!

I don't know how I didn't die of fright! The scant light of day still remaining was enough to allow me to see him: he had a wound on his forehead, around the hairline, and the blood was trickling from his nose . . . But what really horrified me was his open mouth: his lower jaw was drooping, as if unlocked, and his enormous tongue was hanging over his lips (which were black, like a bear's), while the froth streamed continually from his mouth . . .

I just had time to look at him before he jumped once again into the well, shouting: 'Senhor Leocadio! Senhor Leocadio!'

This was followed by indescribable mayhem and, trembling, I dragged myself away from that accursed place . . .

The wind was raging and a pale sliver of light revealed that the clouds were flying extremely low . . . I immediately took the path back to the house; but before long, I saw that I had to pass beside some dark rocks, and this idea made me make a large circle between the bushes that stood out here and there in the darkness.

On arriving at the hut, I collapsed inside . . . All night long, from my bed, I listened to the wind that howled with savage fury . . . Towards dawn, I fell asleep – and this kept me all day far from the torments of the earth.

When I woke, I saw that night was coming on, and that the storm hadn't let up at all . . .

The next day, I remained inside . . . By three in the afternoon, the light was so dim that I lit a candle.

The storm is thundering with even more fury than yesterday and the doors are rattling continuously . . .

I sat for hours on end, with the candle before me, which

went on burning without the slightest movement. At one moment, it seemed to me to be a delusion that I was still living in a world in which I remembered I had once been born; the very candle sat there before my eyes *unfamiliar* and *incomprehensible* . . .

It wasn't long before I was ill . . .

I had a bad night. Towards dawn I got up exhausted and began cursing. This unpleasant habit had left me from the time that I had cut myself off from my fellows, and it was as if the wild earth on which I was walking was quaking beneath my feet . . . I took it into my head to go outside and howl together with the wind and roam along the deserted shores, where there was not so much as a single creature . . . The candle was about to go out and its flame, which had suddenly taken on a vivid blue colour, drew my attention. I reflected that perhaps it was the devil who was keeping me company . . . Before long, I extinguished it and lay down on my bed, wondering whether everything that had befallen us might be caused by a lost spirit roaming the desolate place where we were . . .

The night seemed as if it would never end . . . I ran out of patience and got up to go outside. For I'd made up my mind to go and find Osso!

And, in fact, on going outside I saw a shadow moving beside the open kitchen door and I stopped in alarm . . .

I called out his name many times, but seeing that he made no reply, I decided to wait till dawn . . .

Would that that day had never dawned, because the marrow froze in my bones, and a black shadow lay heavily over my soul throughout the days that followed. I didn't know that for the man with whom Satan keeps company, the night has no way of guarding his life until daybreak . . .

Two days later, I killed Osso with my own hands, as that was the day I broke his leg!

I said that I was waiting for day to break; I've no idea why or what I would do when it did. I can't deny, this once, that I was in the grip of great evil . . .

Dawn brought me some relief. I lit a lamp and could make him out, hunched beside a barrel with his head against the wall. Half his back was bare; his thick neck seemed scratched – as if he'd spent the night in the devil's embrace . . .

Before I'd had time to take a closer look, I stumbled and fell! I felt as if my nose had been sliced off and a stream of blood was spurting from my open nostrils! The lamp shattered at my feet . . . When it stopped rolling, the silence of the tomb prevailed in the darkness . . .

I slowly dragged myself outside . . . My nose was still in its place . . . I didn't see even one droplet of blood on me . . .

Towards noon, the wind suddenly abated. A few clouds, like sparse smoke, hung over the island. Behind the line of the sea, an enormous mass of white vapour stood motionless – as if it were foam continually swelling . . . The silence gripped me!

I don't know if anyone else suffers as I do. I felt an irritation in my nose and squeezed my eyes shut to stop them filling with tears.

I can't deny that this is a bad constitution for a man; my soul is innocent like the bird on the shore that seeks its food among the tiny rocks when the tide goes out . . .

An iron hand gripped my heart . . . I went over and leaned against the door of the storeroom and softly called his name.

He didn't speak at all, didn't move at all . . .

After a short while, I did the same . . . this time he lunged and grabbed hold of the cat that was sleeping in there, put its legs on the barrel and cut them off with an axe he was holding! The animal leapt like a ball into the air. A lash whistled across my cheek, together with a spray of warm blood!

I took the pistol down from the wall and let fly at him!

I missed him.

He seemed as if he'd heard nothing! He went and stood in the middle, with his knees bent and his chin resting on his chest . . .

Without wasting any time, I aimed at him again.

This time, I hit him in the leg! He grabbed hold of it with his huge hand as if wanting to rend it! That moment remains ever clear in my mind. It's certain that in no other being in the whole of creation can you see such savagery . . .

Towards evening, a sudden storm blew up.

The moon rose late . . .

I shut myself inside and spent all night leaning against the window . . . My gaze wandered in the dark squalls of wind that raced over the desolate sea . . .

Once or twice, I heard him groaning . . .

In the morning I was so exhausted that I thought I would die.

My teeth were chattering.

I saw that all I could do was to give him peace and get myself out of that unbearable situation . . . I was living with a wounded wolf. I had to finish him off! His clothes were filthy; the stone slabs stank from the excrement.

I took my pistol . . .

He'd wrapped his leg in a fleece.

When he saw me, he lunged at me; but his leg prevented him.

My bullet, it seemed, had passed through his side!

For an instant, he stood erect on his toes, stretched – and fell on his back! (His one leg was still shaking . . .). I bent over him . . .

Though he was lying in the dark, I could still make out a wild glint in his eyes. He was drenched in sweat – as though he were going through the throes of death of a thousand people at the same time!

Then, as I was leaning over him, over his open mouth, my ears picked up a sound, faint and faded, carried on a breath of air:

Kavna . . .

I was struck numb! It was coming from the ends of the earth! I had the impression that my head turned right round, behind my back! My mind became unhinged – it seems I'd gone mad! I was mad, raving mad!

I dragged the lifeless body to the door . . . A wild fury was raging inside me. Perhaps he was the devil! I felt like breaking his ribs with a club, to make him crawl, before he expired, outside the hut where I'd bury him. (The cat with its chopped-off legs flashed through my mind . . . Lord! What a state I was in! I was mad, raving mad!)

I ripped his shirt to shreds – to what end? To measure his chest, to see whether I could embrace it! I was beset by this weird curiosity . . .

It was covered all the way down to his navel with designs and letters. Drawn between his nipples was a topmast – divided in the middle by the name:

Pedro Cazas
1530

His one side was full of letters almost all faded; all I could make out was the word: Pavo.

1530! I had before me a man who had lived over three hundred years – or was it perhaps one who had returned from Hell?

No doubt, if I hadn't been mad, I would have died of fright!

Yes, mad! Through a single blow, my mind had rejected the laws governing it. An unprecedented earthquake had shaken the foundations of my very being. My judgement no longer had any difficulty in accepting things that were beyond the limits of human belief! I was swimming in an ocean where no child of the earth had ever been baptised!

After a while, I went to look at him again . . .

His face had a vivid colour . . . His firm chin was now in its place – keeping his mouth tight shut . . .

That night, I left him with his head resting on the doorstep of the storeroom.

It was no longer any problem at all for me to pass by him, however many times, in the middle of the night . . .

I didn't sleep at all, for about five days and nights . . .

I had gone down to the channel . . . I remember that it was a clear day and around noon . . .

That morning, I'd suddenly felt a sharp pain in my side . . .

I remember that I was exhausted and my legs would hardly support me . . .

Without realising, I found myself below the rocks and I proceeded towards the well.

When I saw where I was, I felt no fear in my heart at all. But, when I bent down, I saw a skeleton inside looking up!

The skull was still attached to the neck!

All its teeth, big and white, were in place!

Shining around the thighs and the forearms were what looked like iron shackles! I jumped inside. That was it!

I noticed that it had another two irons around each ankle . . .

The body was fixed in the earth and presented a horrid contortion of agony . . .

The neck was stretched – like a bird being dragged by its wings . . .

The stony earth, between its ribs and its joints, was the thing that held it in one piece and prevented the bones from scattering.

Around the skeleton, the earth had been carefully cleaned away.

This man had been *buried alive*!

I leaned against the wall of the well and examined the reddish bones for a good while . . .

In the end, I took hold of the rope to climb up.

It was then that my gaze fell upon a long sword in its scabbard, half-buried, and I bent down and picked it up. The scabbard fell to pieces from the rust; I cleaned it off and when only the blade was left, I saw the stamp on the sword: *two iron fists clenched together*! The stamp was that of the renowned Gata, who made the finest swords in Lisbon around 1500 . . .

On the other side, I read clearly, exceptionally clearly, the name:

Leocadio Calvo

God must have felt pity for my poor mind! This shackled man was no other than Leocadio Calvo himself, one of my ancestors, who, dying, had left a legend behind him!

I knelt beside those lifeless bones, and my eyes ran over his bare ribs, without being able to understand what was happening.

I still recall his thin arms – and his elbow, which was pushed into the earth as if he wanted to pull himself up . . .

The rust had stained the bones beneath the shackles.

The pelvis was a hard lump of earth . . .

The skull had a hole in the top – through which passed a mournful ray of light that escaped through the jaws . . .

Original title: 'Pedro Cazas'. First published in 1919. Translated here from the text anthologised in Makis Panorios (ed.), *To Elliniko Fantastiko Diiyima* [The Greek Fantasy Short Story], Athens: Aiolos, 1987, pp. 123–147.

Oedipus Rex

Andreas Embiricos

For Maria Bonaparte

The time has come for people to learn the truth. And the one to tell it to you is a simple man of the woods, of Pan and the Hamadryads born and bred.

On leaving Boeotia and after much wandering in the region of Athens, King Oedipus and I, Habrius the huntsman, finally arrived at Colonus. Panting and downcast, with his eyes still dripping blood, the blind ruler of Thebes supported himself on my shoulder and walked behind me with the help of a staff, groaning from the pain of his physical and mental anguish.

Our journey had taken two days and two nights and now, early in the morning of the third day, in the wonderful Attic light, I was able to make out the shrine of the Furies not far away. I helped Oedipus as best I could, holding him up by the arms, but despite his superhuman efforts the wretched king could barely drag himself along. Apart from all his other torments, his feet had swollen up again.

Rest assured that everything I say here is said reliably in order that the truth may become known, for several matters relating to the Theban king's last moments alive are completely inaccurate as recorded by the historians and tragedians. I am in a position to testify to the truth and I will proclaim it in a loud voice, for, as you will hear, I witnessed these dramatic events with my own eyes.

Oedipus was not led to Colonus by his daughter, Antigone. His beautiful daughter had taken him as far as Cithaeron where she encountered me returning from hunting with my three dogs, and she begged me to lead her flagging father to Attica because, fearful lest the old man take his own life before much longer, she wished to arrive first at the shrine to have time to propitiate the Furies and so ease as much as possible the king's life after death. I agreed to take Antigone's place at her father's side, and the beautiful girl, making haste for Colonus with one of my three hounds, my good dog Mersyas (whom I ordered to accompany her to protect her along the way), arrived at the place, which lies close to Athens, many hours ahead of us.

I shall never forget the painful journey of the blind wretch, who dragged himself along at my side. When, bewailing his fate, he recounted to me the tragedy that had broken his spirit, I, simple man of the woods that I am and having Pan as my chief god and protector, repeatedly tried to comfort him, saying that the fact that he had lain with Jocasta, his mother, did not seem to me to be particularly terrible, and I added that I too would have done the same and that had I had daughters by her or any other woman, I would quite happily have lain with them too and, no matter how tender their age, without the least remorse. To add strength to my arguments, I referred to the Gods of Olympus who almost every day engage in similar amorous couplings.

But the tormented king anguishedly rejected my arguments, showering curses and imprecations upon himself for all that had happened in the bosom of his family. Then, I once more opened my mouth and restated my beliefs.

'My dear lord,' I said, 'don't distress yourself so . . . Take heed of what I say; I'm telling you the truth . . . Even today, most people are mad . . . It is not becoming, however, for a great king like you to trouble your mind with such simple matters . . . You have punished yourself to no avail and you torment yourself unjustly . . . A day will come when incest will be regarded as being as natural as all other kinds of love and then, given that the son will no longer fear his father, he will feel no need to kill him. People and love will at last be free, just like we simple and healthy people of the woods . . .'

At that point, I wanted to add: 'Only those who wilfully turn a blind eye do not see it this way.' Thinking though that it might be taken by the blind king as mockery, I refrained from voicing this thought.

Nevertheless, once Oedipus had heard all I had to say to him before I fell silent, he was overcome by even greater distress, by untold distress, and beating his breast, he once again began showering curses upon himself.

On seeing that what I said as an honest and truthful man not only did nothing to alleviate the king's distress and grief, but that, on the contrary, it only deepened his mental anguish, I abandoned the discussion and fell silent, for the wretch was in no position to talk of anything else.

Finally, after much wandering (I should say here that I did not know the land beyond Cithaeron), we arrived at Colonus.

Here, it befell me to witness a scene that I will remember all the days of my life with revulsion and horror. Ah! . . . If only Oedipus had had the strength to listen to me! He'd still be alive today, happy and strong.

Antigone, who was not only a very beautiful girl, but good as well, and who loved her father and her brothers, was waiting for us at the entrance to the shrine. As soon as she set eyes on us, she ran towards us full of joy, with my good dog Mersyas at her side.

'Father! My dear Habrius!' she cried and, after embracing the king who was barely able to stand on his feet, added: 'Father, I've succeeded in propitiating the Furies! . . . They will be merciful . . .'

Full of delight and optimism, I handed Oedipus over to his daughter and withdrew for a short while, explaining that I wished to rest. The truth of the matter is that the lovely young Athenian girls I'd encountered on the way had completely charmed me. Not having any of the compunctions of the Theban king, I resolved to win one or two of these and, taking my dogs with me, I went off into the countryside.

My hunt was crowned with complete success. My amorous prey (two young girls working in Attica's boundless olive grove) proved magnificent, and two hours later and overjoyed, I returned to Colonus.

Alas! A horrid spectacle awaited me there. The three Furies

had deceived Antigone, her father and me! At the gates to the shrine, lying sprawled on the paving, Oedipus, the blind king of Thebes, was screaming in agony. And while Antigone, on her knees and with her breasts bared, wailed and tore her garments, the detestable Furies, clearly possessed by an unholy madness, were engaged in a hideous and unmentionable act beneath the splendid Attic light. With horrible faces and eerie cries, Alecto and Megaera were holding the hapless wretch down, while Tisiphone, laughing like a hyena, was biting off the man's genitals.

Then I, Habrius, a simple huntsman of the Boeotian woods yet skilled archer, becoming the world's conscience and avenger and executioner, hastily removed the bow hanging from my back and, taking three sharp arrows from my quiver, quickly and repeatedly released the string and slaughtered the three Furies.

Sadly, though, the castration had already been carried out and before very long Oedipus expired. Later, the familiar tragedies were enacted. Yet, if nothing else, three of this world's fiends no longer existed and my good dog, Mersyas, together with my other two dogs tore the Furies' bodies to pieces and erased them from the face of the earth.

And all this in order that the truth may become known. For hitherto, in this matter – that is, in whatever concerns king Oedipus' last moments – the historians and poets, either in error or in bad faith, have talked without rhyme or reason.

Original title: 'Oidipous Rex'. First published in 1960. Translated here from the text published in Andreas Embiricos, *Grapta i prosopiki mythologia 1936–1946* [Writings or A Personal Mythology 1936–1946], Athens: Agra, 1980, pp. 145–152.

Westminster

Yorgos Theotokas

All this happened in a carriage on the London Underground when I was coming back from the cinema with Sylvia one evening.

I was feeling tired and restless as I wasn't accustomed to the climate or the life. An invisible clamp was continually pressing against my temples. Sun! Sun! I needed sun, pines, blue seas and a hot sandy beach, to feel the light on my brow and the Aegean breeze in order to recover. Sylvia said I ought to take an aspirin before going to bed, but I couldn't be bothered chasing around in the evening fog to find a chemist's. We talked about it for some time.

'I don't want an aspirin,' I said at last. 'I want to sleep.'

'Do as you like!' Sylvia replied.

She always made a grimace when she came out with that phrase, knitting her eyebrows and stubbornly pursing her lips, then she'd lower her gaze and fall silent. But before long, she would again begin her charming chatter and talk on and on without stopping.

'Do you like horses?' she asked, out of the blue. 'I like horses very much. As much as I like dogs. I'd like to marry a gentleman with a large estate in the country with lots of horses and lots of dogs. All with fine pedigrees. I'm very fond of life in the country. I'd come to London every so often to go to the cinema. There are no cinemas in the country . . .'

Everything leapt in my memory with each jolt of the train, muddled, hazy, unclear, incomprehensible and impenetrable. Everything rolled into one – the endless flood of houses, people, lights, engines, legends, the black river and the unfrequented, wet parks, the palaces, the old castles, the Gothic towers, the banks, the marble, the gold, the coal – and above everything Nelson, unyielding, imperishable, in stone, guarding the Empire with teeth gritted. Nelson atop his column, like a taut bow in the grey sky of the proud island. We were surging through the bowels of London, well ensconced in what seemed like a shell. The endless, dream-like city was teeming with life amidst the fog.

'Where are we going, Sylvia, where?'

Our carriage was full of silent people, open newspapers, dripping umbrellas, cigarette smoke, muddy shoes. The harsh electric lighting bothered my eyes. I looked out of the window and the blackness bothered me.

'It's cold,' said Sylvia.

She covered her legs as much as she could, tucked her hands under her arms, and huddled up to me, shivering. Her face was fresh like a childhood dream. My gaze found an ideal refuge in the blue infinity of her eyes. My heart beat faster because of her.

'I'm very fond of you,' I said in a soft voice.

'Now's not the time,' she replied plainly and looked away.

Yet she seemed pleased.

I forgot to say that sitting opposite us was an apparently well-to-do gentleman, wearing a dress-coat and top hat. He was exceedingly thin and lanky, all skin and bone. He held his umbrella tight between his knees and was tenderly caressing its wooden handle as if it were a living creature. He looked first at Sylvia then at me with beady eyes that were restless, drawn and bloodshot; eyes that gleamed mysteriously. I didn't very much like his expression or manner, though, as I said, he seemed very well-to-do, and I avoided looking at him so as not to encourage him.

When Sylvia noticed him and realised that he was watching us, she turned to whisper something in my ear.

'Do you know him?' she asked.

I shook my head.

'I wonder,' she continued in the same tone, 'whether he might be mad.'

To overcome her fear, she giggled nervously. Her forced laughter increased my concern. Suddenly, without knowing why, I felt an overpowering need to forget where I was and, above all, to forget the presence of that strange man sitting opposite me.

'Sing something,' I said to her.

'You want me to sing?'

My request seemed so strange to her that she stopped laughing at once and fixed her deep, grave eyes on me, as if trying to understand what had come over me.

'It's not the place,' she continued.

I persisted as gently as I could.

'You'd be doing me a great favour,' I said. 'Sing something softly, so that no one else will hear, just for me . . .'

She didn't want to. I persisted. Eventually, with a look of resolve, she agreed to the favour I'd asked. She leaned over close to my ear and quietly sang a simple melody from an American student opera that we'd seen together just the previous week:

Stars belong to everyone,
flowers belong to everyone
and love belongs to everyone.
The best things in life are free . . .

The soft words and the song's childlike rhythm poured into me like soothing balm. For a moment, I did, in fact, forget what I wanted to forget. I felt myself completely carefree, light, filled with a joyous and relaxing sense of total ease. The world was beautiful, pleasant and simple. And it was all mine. I'd reach out my hand and I'd have whatever my heart desired, I'd reach out my other hand and I'd cast away all care. The best things in life are free . . . I was swimming free, in the starlight, in a mythical lake that was warm and fragrant, amidst a multitude of ethereal, nymph-like shades, to the sound of an invisible flute that gently lulled my soul. Stars, flowers, love, the joy of birds and insects, a bubbling of life . . . A sweet thrill! Sylvia's cheek close to mine, chaste, vibrant, fresh, like the first day of God's creation . . . O the joy of life!

A strange event came to rob me of my euphoria. The communicating door between the carriages suddenly opened and in walked a train attendant with gold buttons, erect, flawlessly attired, like all the attendants in Great Britain, but with something wild about his appearance and with eyes bloodshot and gleaming, like the stranger sitting opposite me.

'Westminster!' he shouted. 'Westminster! We're passing under Westminster!'

At the very same moment, I felt the train's speed rapidly increasing. I instinctively jumped up.

'Why isn't it stopping?' I asked.

But the attendant slammed the door and disappeared without answering, without even paying any attention to me.

None of the passengers showed the slightest interest in all this. They all remained in the same position as before, with the same expression, and continued reading their newspapers or staring blankly at the floor. Only the stranger in the dress coat grinned tauntingly at seeing my alarm, and his eyes gleamed so intensely that I was forced to shut mine momentarily, unable as I was to withstand their brilliance. I felt the skin on my face tightening and a cold air enveloping me.

'We're passing under Westminster,' Sylvia sang softly.

'But why didn't they stop?' I asked again in a broken voice.

'They won't be stopping anywhere,' the stranger hissed.

His hissing wrapped itself around me like a snake. My limbs were paralysed, incapable of even the slightest movement, and I could breathe only with difficulty. I felt myself choking. Westminster, the awesome Westminster was above us, suffocating us with its dark stone, as if it were blocking our exit and air on all sides.

'Where are we going, Sylvia, where?'

But without hearing either the stranger's hissing or my own voice, she mechanically removed her bonnet, rested her head on my shoulder and closed her eyes. Her hair, golden and glistening like wheat in the noon-day sun, spread over my cheek, gently caressing me.

'Stars belong to everyone,' she murmured one last time.

And immediately I heard the rhythmic breathing of her sleep and sensed a happy smile blossoming on her half-open lips. Her fresh little soul was already soaring into the infinite blue expanse of her girlish dreams.

I too closed my eyes without looking again at the stranger. I sensed that he alone knew what was going on. But I didn't have the nerve to ask him in order to find out. At that particular moment, I didn't even have the strength to endure his look again. I tried once more to forget it.

The train was travelling at a demonic speed through the darkness in the tunnels. I'd surrendered myself without any physical resistance to the crazy rhythm of the engine, assailed on all sides by its continuous jolting. My head was bursting. I could no longer see anything in my imagination other than raging steel that rattled in the darkness and flowed all around me like a torrent. An unstoppable current of metal violently swept me along, broken and helpless as I was . . .

I was awoken by that same wild cry:

'Westminster! We're passing under Westminster again!'

For a brief moment I managed to see the attendant's frenzied expression before he quickly closed the door and disappeared again. The bloodshot eyes of the stranger in the dress coat were still gleaming with the same intensity. With some difficulty, I mustered what was left of my strength and spoke to him for the first time.

'Excuse me, sir,' I stammered in a faltering voice, 'whoever you are, can you please tell me what's going on?'

'Don't you know what's happened?' asked the stranger in a most natural manner, as if it were all very simple (his eyes had suddenly become quite human, almost soft). 'Let me explain. All the attendants on the train have gone mad and they don't want to stop anywhere. That's what the problem is.'

I was, so it seems, expecting to hear something strange and so this information didn't have the same impact on me as it would have done under different circumstances. Besides, I was so exhausted that I no longer had recourse to my reason. I tried, nonetheless, to continue the discussion in order to find out more.

'But how did it happen that they all went mad together?' I asked.

'Who knows! Perhaps they were drugged.'

'Who by?'

'By someone who wanted some fun, I imagine.' We remained silent for a few moments.

'I wasn't aware, sir,' I mumbled as some sort of a reply, 'that there were potions or powders or tablets and such like that make train attendants go mad so that they no longer want to stop the train.'

'I'm not certain, myself,' he replied. 'I said it as a possible explanation.'

He stared at me calmly with a gentle smile of ironic forbearance.

'At least be so kind as to tell me,' I continued, 'why they keep shouting every so often that we're passing under Westminster.'

'We're going round and round in circles beneath London,' said the stranger, 'and they're using Westminster as a mark to know how long it takes them to go round each time. That's why they shout it out. Even the mad, you see, have their own form of logic.'

It was then that I suddenly realised that the stranger and I were now alone in the carriage, apart from Sylvia, who was asleep. The other passengers had disappeared without trace, simply gone up in smoke. I shuddered so violently that my whole body jumped and I felt my eyes leap out of their sockets. A loud, inarticulate cry of terror rose up from my breast and stuck in my throat, unable to reach my lips; it stirred my innards, gripped me, almost choked me.

'Where's everyone else?' I whispered with trembling lips. 'The others, sir, where are the others?'

'They don't exist,' he said.

I rested my head on Sylvia's hair, completely defeated. I again heard her rhythmic breathing and felt her heart beating calmly and softly next to mine. Her beauty, her childlike abandon, the untainted health of her body warmed the blood in my veins for a moment. A tiny, fleeting recollection of joy fluttered in my mind. A wave of tenderness and compassion welled up inside me, two tears ran down my cheeks.

'Let's not wake her!' I begged the stranger. 'Let's let her sleep, so she'll never know – never – because if she knew, she'd be terrified.'

'There's no reason to frighten her,' he said.

His eyes again gleamed with the same intensity, but this time, I didn't close mine. I kept staring at him, captivated, magnetised, unable to avert my gaze. Suddenly, his nails began to grow unnaturally and from between his legs emerged a headless red serpent, like a large pig's tail. His ears had become pointed.

I watched all these sudden changes to his appearance with the firm resolve of a condemned convict and with a kind of cold admiration.

I whispered:

'Are you . . .'

But I didn't dare utter the frightful name.

'It's not important,' he said.

'It's a great honour, Your Highness,' I murmured, 'truly, a great honour.'

It was at that moment, I think, that the electric lighting went off and we were plunged into darkness.

The deadly voice echoed once again in the night:

'Westminster! Westminster!'

But I didn't care about anything anymore.

'You see, they're not stopping,' hissed the stranger for the last time. 'I told you, there's no stopping.'

I no longer cared.

I surrendered my soul completely to the violent jolting of the engine and to the endless lure of the tunnels and I forgot myself there, with the feel of Sylvia's hair on my cheek and with my gaze fixed on the stranger's gleaming eyes, the only lights amid the darkness . . .

Original title: 'Westminster'. First published in Yorgos Theotokas, *Evripidis Pentozalis ke alles istories* [Evripidis Pentozalis and Other Stories] (1937). Translated here from the text anthologised in Makis Panorios (ed.), *To Elliniko Fantastiko Diiyima* [The Greek Fantasy Short Story] vol. 4, Athens: Aiolos, 1997, pp. 71–76. Previously translated into English by Themi Vasils in *The Charioteer. An Annual Review of Modern Greek Culture* 19 (1977), pp. 88–94.

The Daily Myth or The Headless Man

Nanos Valaoritis

CHAPTER 1. WORKS AND DAYS

One morning, Mr Talmudes, David Ioacheimoglou Talmudes, woke up without a head. He wracked his brains trying to remember where he'd left his head. It was no use. 'They must have beheaded me while I was sleeping,' he muttered to himself – and he got up to rinse his face and brush his teeth. He'd forgotten that he had neither, no teeth or face. 'To hell with it,' he thought, 'lousy thing, habit.' On the stairs, he bumped into the maid who, on seeing him, fainted on the spot without so much as a murmur. 'This is too much,' thought Talmudes, 'I have to do something about it.' But he didn't know what to do. Finally, he decided that the best thing he could do was to go to the doctor's, to get his advice. So he went out to get the bus to the doctor's. On the bus, no one dared say anything as they all thought they'd gone crazy. When he asked for a ticket, the conductor gave him one without taking any money – because of his shock.

On seeing him getting off the bus, a woman about to get on let out a scream and fell flat on her back. She was an old spinster, who all her life had dreamt of beheading a man. She suffered such a fright that they had to fan her for a whole hour before she recovered.

CHAPTER 2

Meanwhile, Mr Talmudes arrived at the doctor's. 'There's no surgery today,' the nurse told him, in no way perplexed. She was, you see, accustomed to such things. 'Damn,' Mr Talmudes muttered under his breath, 'now what will I do?' 'You could go to the lost property office and tell them you've lost your head. If that's why you've come, the doctor can't do anything for you. There's obviously a woman involved somewhere,' she added, 'and she's the reason you've lost your head.' While going down the stairs, Mr Talmudes reflected that the nurse had been extremely rude and impertinent in making remarks about his personal life, and he went back up to tell her to mind her own business next time. But before he could open his mouth – besides, he no longer had one – the nurse, who was young and attractive, sealed it for him with a kiss saying that she would help him 'to get his head back again', and she made an appointment with him at eight that same evening so they could go and search for it together. And so Mr Talmudes was well satisfied with his visit to the doctor's.

CHAPTER 3

Mr Talmudes hated innuendoes. One and one make two, that's what he liked. And that's why, before losing his head, he never mixed with shady customers who spend all day sitting in cafés. In fact, he bought a newspaper and tried to read. But how could he when he no longer had any eyes? He tried to support his glasses on his non-existent nose and ears, but to no avail. In the end, he was forced to hold them in his hand and soon set aside his reading for some other time. He ordered a ham sandwich from the waiter, who thought he was dreaming and kept rubbing his eyes to make sure he was awake. When the sandwich came, however, he realised he had no teeth to chew it with and had to throw it down his throat as it was. He found that very annoying and, for a long time, could feel the sandwich in his stomach. He swore never again to put anything solid in his mouth before first finding his head.

CHAPTER 4

When Mrs Margarita Ioacheimoglou Talmudes – née Kastales – returned home after a visit to her cousin's in the country, she was worried at not finding her husband, David Ioacheimoglou Talmudes. 'Strange,' she thought to herself, 'something must have happened, because he never goes out in the morning. He's obviously lost his head again.'

Her long experience of married life meant that Margarita Talmudes could guess her husband's every move even before he thought of it himself. And naturally, after searching a little, she found his head under the bed. She popped it into a basket and put it in the fridge to keep it fresh, then waited for her husband to return. It wasn't the first time he'd lost his head, and so Mrs Talmudes began to knit some socks for her son who, at that time, was in the army, doing his military service.

CHAPTER 5

Mr Talmudes was convinced that he was a major thinker, just as others are major industrialists or major ship-owners. He was sure that newspapers throughout the world carried reports on it and published his photo, even if no one believed it. Now that they'd read that he was the only Headless man in the whole world, things would undoubtedly go very well. He waited impatiently for the evening newspaper in case it had anything about him. *The Evening Star* said nothing – nor *The Midday Man* nor *The Night Light*. He had just one hope left: *The Hearth* wouldn't let a 'mishap' like that go by unreported. He opened it with trembling hands and read. 'Rumours are again circulating that the Headless man has appeared for the second time this year in our town. Those who spread this nonsense have obviously themselves lost their heads a long time ago and haven't realised it yet. Stupidity is lopping off more and more heads every day and gullibility is cutting down the populace with the reaper's sickle. We say it again once and for all. The Headless man does not exist, never existed nor will ever exist, unless by this specious figure-phantom certain people are referring to Kazan = (the) Hearth.'

He immediately decided to write a reply:

He ordered paper and pen and began:

Dear 'Hearth'

I exist!

The Headless man

'If you have any doubts, send one of your reporters tomorrow to "THE GREAT PRETENCE" café. I'll be there for him to interview. Please have a photographer there as well.

H.M.

He folded it, sealed the envelope with water from the glass, and posted it.

CHAPTER 6

The nurse showed up at around eight.

'Haven't you found it yet?' she asked him.

'No,' he said, 'I was waiting for you.'

'Where shall we look?'

'I've no idea.'

'So why did you want to meet me?'

'To take you to the theatre!'

'What's on?'

'We could see the new play at the "Idea Theatre": *The cat went to the ball, but didn't dance at all, so they cut its tail small.*'

'Great idea! Let's go . . .'

'Do you feel like eating first?'

'Let's get a bite first!'

They ate till they were bursting, chicken, fish, lobster, caviar. Mr Talmudes had decided to live it up. Besides, he hadn't eaten since the morning.

When they arrived at the theatre, it was closed.

'Tuesday today,' said Mr Talmudes resignedly, 'I'd forgotten.'

'What'll we do now?' asked the nurse.

'Go to my studio for a drink,' said Mr Talmudes.

'Never in a million years,' replied the nurse, pretending to be shocked – though from the very beginning, she knew that that's where they'd end up.

'Okay,' said Mr Talmudes indifferently, 'some other time.'

'Not some other time, now or never.'

'How can I persuade you?'

'Persuade me, take me by force.'

'But if you don't want . . .'

'I make out I don't want to, stupid. Deep down, I'm dying to go, but I can't show it. I'm ashamed, what will you tell your friends about me afterwards?'

'I have no friends,' said Mr Talmudes. 'I have a wife, a son and a daughter.'

They went, but what they did will remain a secret. The taxi driver demanded double the fare because the passenger didn't have a head.

'Mind you don't lose your head one day for some pretty little thing like I lost mine today,' Talmudes told him.

'Who cares, pal, what's a head, anyway. I buy and sell them, myself.'

'How much?' Talmudes asked.

'What do you mean how much?'

'How much do you buy them for? Because if you buy them, tell me where they sell them so I can go and buy one.'

'I wasn't being serious,' the driver retorted, 'did you believe me? You can't make a joke these days without it being taken the wrong way. What a lousy world!' He snorted and drove off after pocketing double the fare.

When Talmudes returned home that evening, his wife stared at him long and hard.

'You look pale,' she said, 'what have you been up to again? Monkey business?'

'N-n-no,' stammered Talmudes, 'N-n-nothing.' He always stammered a little in front of his wife.

Mrs Talmudes wagged her finger.

'Where've you been to lose your head again?'

'I don't know w-w-where,' answered Mr Talmudes like a whimpering child.

'I don't know what you'd do if I weren't here to find it for you.'

She presented him with his head in the basket.

'Put it back quickly before anyone sees you,' she told him.

With his tail between his legs, Talmudes put his head on his body like others put their hat on.

'Oh Lord,' he thought 'tomorrow, the *Hearth* will triumph again at my expense.'

For now that he'd found his head, he'd have to wait a long time before losing it again. Since no one ever loses his head willingly.

Such things always happen 'against our will'.

Original title: 'O kathimerinos mythos i o akephalos anthropos'. First published in Nanos Valaoritis, *O omilon pithikos* [The Talking Ape] (1986). Translated here from the text published in *Paramythologia* [Paramythology], Athens: Nefeli, 1996, pp. 237–244.

A Day Like Any Other

Tassos Leivaditis

Waking up fully dressed in bed, in a room you've never seen before, is, of course, a bad omen for the day about to begin. But not being able to remember how you came to be in this unknown house is something of a nightmare. 'Did they find me drunk last night and take me in?' I wondered. It happened sometimes. Yet my mouth was fine, without that coarse and sour taste of wine drunk the night before. And my head was quite clear.

I looked around the room, trying to remember. It was spacious, almost boringly spacious, with a high ceiling, rather like the rooms in those old, crumbling mansions that you sometimes see tucked away in distant parts of the city. The only furniture in it was the bed on which I was lying, this too ancient, wide, with a black iron bedstead, and, in an alcove in the wall, there was a tarnished washbasin, like those you find in cheap neighbourhood hotels. The weirdest thing of all was a window close to the ceiling. But a window that wasn't mine; I mean, it didn't belong to the room I was in. The window belonged to the house next door and the shutters opened outwards, overlooking me. 'Has reconstruction in the city reached such a level,' I thought, 'that the windows of one house now look into the other?' Behind the windowpane, a featureless man pretended to be on the phone, while watching my every move out of the corner of his eye. I was about to engage in a series of reflections concerning town planning and the population explosion when the door opened and an old, bent man with thin white hair entered, carrying a tray. His face seemed familiar, though I couldn't be sure.

'It's already evening,' he said, in a somewhat tired voice, and he put the tray with the cup on the bed beside me.

Before I had time to ask him where I was, he'd already left, closing the door behind him. 'It's most likely a hotel; I was right,' and I gazed again at the tarnished washbasin. 'This is the last time. I've had enough of this irresponsible way of living, disgusting more like, hanging round pothouses and hotels. Besides – I'm not young any more.' These healthy resolutions gave me heart and I felt quite cheerful when I turned to pick up the cup. But the cup was empty. Very nice! 'Could it have been spilled?' I stooped to look on the floor. Not a drop. I'd already opened my mouth to start shouting and give that old fool of a hotel-keeper a piece of my mind, when I suddenly had a reassuring thought. 'Perhaps it's for the best. Who knows how long he brewed the coffee, and what if he left it in the kitchen and some cat had messed in it? He might very well have pulled a cockroach or even a whole rat out of it before bringing it to me. I know his kind only too well. In short, you're better off when they don't offer you anything, because you can be certain that there's always some risk involved in taking what they give you.'

In fact, I was surprised at this rather unkind thought I'd had. I was the one who'd pored over so many texts concerning ordinary folk and I'd even written a study on sprites and phantoms in the folk tradition. Meanwhile, the man above in the open window was still pretending to be phoning. 'Damn it, you can't get any privacy any more even in your own room. Do those windows have to open into your face?'

I got up, resolved to get out of there as soon as possible, even if I'd paid for a whole month in advance. I angrily grabbed hold of the door handle and yanked open the door. At that moment, I remembered: the old man who had brought me the empty cup was the image of the old caretaker at the school I used to go to as a child. 'But how's that possible?' I wondered. He must have been about sixty then. And another thirty years have passed in the meantime. He should be dead.' I was very fond of that caretaker, with his eternally tearful eyes and the big bell that put an end to the teachers' endless gabbling. But why had he brought me an empty cup? 'Perhaps it's his son.' I'd settled on this as the most rational explanation when, there at my feet, close to the wall, I saw a large bell. 'It's becoming a joke,' I said, not a little affected, of course, by this unexpected find. I bent down and picked it up. I would have sworn it was that same old school bell, but I straightaway changed my mind: 'Don't be stupid. All bells look the same.' As I stared at it, I saw that the clapper was missing. 'Useless now,' I thought, 'that's why it's been left outside my door.' And without realising, I began ringing it. I was astonished at what I was doing and by the heavy, rather odd, feeling it gave me: a bell swinging back and forth without making any sound, as if all the air around me had been removed. I took a deep breath as if I were suffocating. I put the bell back in its place and, quickly crossing the corridor, I descended the wooden staircase. But instead of coming out onto the street, I found myself in a café. This was so unexpected that I was no longer surprised at anything.

The café would have been like any other café in the world if it hadn't been for the three beds at the back. Three patients, evidently, covered with khaki-coloured army blankets. I remembered the provinces, where I'd lived for a while, and that the same shop that sold hardware also provided First Aid – for fainting bouts, too much drink or the odd shooting for reasons of honour. But for heaven's sake, this was the capital! Or was something more terrible happening? My mind went to the wounded, in a bygone revolution, who, due to a lack of hospitals, were put in the most incredible places. We once put a wounded comrade of ours in a shop selling wedding goods. And because he was cold, just before he died, we covered him with piles of white bridal gowns.

At the farthest table, next to the exit, I saw my cousin, with whom I'd once been in love in my early adolescence. I knew that a year before the doctors had removed one of her breasts because of cancer. I wondered if she was ill again and felt worried. Standing beside her with that plump, smiling face of his, was her dead father.

'You've forgotten us,' he said, in a slightly jocular tone. 'You never come to see us at all.'

My uncle, of course, must have meant the cemetery. It was true that I hadn't gone even once to see the spot where he was buried. I tried to find some excuse:

'Uncle,' I started to say, 'you know how it is, so much to do that there's never enough time.'

He smiled good-naturedly, supposedly showing understanding, while my ailing cousin, trying to hide her movements, straightened her false right breast under her nightgown. At the other end of the café, two or three groups were playing cards; their joking and swearing could be clearly heard.

I looked at my watch. I had a date with my girl, who I'd been with for quite some time, but first I planned to go and see my mother who lived in one of the suburbs. I said goodbye to my uncle and cousin and went out. I stood at the bus stop and waited. It was Autumn and as the sun set, the rooftops kept taking on different hues – red, violet and golden.

I'd already been quite some time on the bus when, not without a little surprise, I noticed that it was only half a bus. Yes, only half – a bus cut in the middle. The wheel was to the rear, behind the passengers, and the bus was being driven by a woman with thick myopic glasses – no doubt a spinster. 'At last,' I thought, 'the authorities have found a clever way to reduce expenditure. And the woman at the wheel? We're becoming civilised. Women are at last taking their rightful place in society.' Nurtured as I was on sociological texts, my mind immediately had a ready answer for everything. And I was quite proud of this ability of mine.

The other passengers didn't appear to attach much importance to these innovations: a handsome young man, two girls and a few others, all of them nondescript. The young man, of an age that I once was, wanted to show off and not having enough imagination to find something original, he stood up and spouted something incoherent which, if put together coherently, was clearly most insulting to me. The girls giggled. I simply pretended not to hear. The evening was coming on and I stared outside at the grey scene. I thought a lot about the achievements of technology, the social role of women, etc. etc. – trying above all, of course, not to think of that impertinent young man who was becoming more and more direct in his offensive comments. Nevertheless, I didn't get off where I should have, but two stops further on. 'A victory in itself,' I was about to conclude, but I'd simply got confused and missed my stop.

I found myself in a neighbourhood that must have been close to the city abattoir as every so often there was the sound of plaintive bellowing and the briny smell of blood was everywhere. From afar, everything was quiet and picturesque like the tiny mountain villages you see when passing in a train. But as soon as I'd gone on a little, I was disappointed by the noise and the shouting. There were a lot of shops, all of them butchers' shops, and, as evening was falling, the shopkeepers were standing in their doorways gazing out into space. Their faces were fat and bloody.

A little further off, two women were having words and the servant boys from the nearby pothouses were staring open-mouthed. I tried to recall if I'd already passed by there – hoping to get my bearings. But it was no good. Of course, everything reminded me of something, but then again everything looks so much like everything else in the world. Just a few years before, for instance, I'd had this odd fixation of seeing an old friend, who'd committed suicide, in every passer-by who was outlined against the dusk or in the night's dim lights. Personally, I hadn't played any part in his suicide; I'd simply made fun of him whenever he'd confessed to me how unhappy he was. I'd made fun of him and laughed scornfully in his face. This went on for some time, I mean, I often saw people who looked like him. Till one day, he stopped appearing. It was that evening when I went up to someone and took hold of his arm.

'Kosmas,' I said, 'aren't you going to say hello to me?'

'But I did say hello to you,' he said, 'you couldn't have noticed.' And breaking free of my arm, he disappeared round the first corner.

From then on, he never bothered me again. Perhaps he left town, I thought. I recall that he always had some big trip in mind.

I walked through the narrow streets of the neighbourhood, looking for someone to ask. I stopped outside one of the butchers' shops. The man, who, almost with hate, was chopping up a lamb on a round wooden table, was tall with a huge, blank face, like the fat belly of a young peasant girl we once had as a servant and who I'd seen naked from the waist down while a doctor was examining her. She was pregnant by my elder brother and died in childbirth. My father, a wonderful man, gave a small amount to her father as a dowry for his other daughter.

'Excuse me, I'm looking for such and such a suburb,' I said, as politely as I could. 'Could you possibly help me?'

Without even raising his eyes, he went on chopping up the lamb. The blood ran from the table onto the dirty tiles, forming a trickle that reached as far as my feet. At that moment, I thought: why am I asking the way to this suburb? My mother had lived there ten years ago and we'd buried her in the local cemetery. But it was already two years since the cemetery had been moved. They had gathered up all the bones and built expensive houses on the site and at night you could hear lively music through the open windows. So, I decided to change my itinerary; I'd go to see my aunt, my mother's sister, in a district through which the train ran. I recall that, as a child, when my mother became ill through depression, this aunt had taken care of me for two years and, not having any children of her own, she worshipped me in a way I'll never forget. The house, of course, smelled of damp and, to my great misfortune, they made the fish soup with rice and egg and lemon sauce, but at night, in bed, I felt the floor shake every time the train went past, and it was sheer magic for me. It was the first time in my life that I hadn't been scared of the night – I even waited for it in order to feel that swaying in bed that sometimes, though not often, I feel again at some great moment of passion.

So, I summoned up my courage to once again ask the man, who was now hanging various parts of the bloody meat on large hooks.

'Excuse me, sir, I don't wish to be a nuisance, but it's almost night and I'm in a hurry. Could you tell me in which direction is such and such a suburb?'

His nostrils grew maliciously wide. I saw that he wanted to give me a rough time, but I became even more amiable.

'You don't know how grateful I'd be. I just need a little information and I'd be more than happy to pay for it. These days, I know, you can't be too open-handed. Just a little information, nothing at all to speak of. I'll do whatever you want. Don't pay any attention to my fine clothes. I could, for example, mop up all that blood for you . . .'

I waited for his reaction. But he had already turned his back on me. He went to the rear of the shop, opened the large fridge and took out a second lamb. The blood had by now soaked my shoes. 'He must be deaf,' I thought to myself and I was filled with compassion. So I went on, chancing my luck. Before long, I was outside the neighbourhood, in an empty space, on the slopes of a hill dotted with sparse bushes.

'Do you want us to go together?' I heard a voice beside me say. 'This path's a little difficult, but it's the shortest.'

I was quite alarmed, given that it was so quiet all around, but imagine my surprise when, on turning round, I saw the school caretaker standing beside me.

'Why did you bring me an empty cup?' I asked, angrily.

He shook his head in disapproval. The words coming out of his toothless mouth had a muffled sound, as if wrapped in cotton wool:

'So much learning, yet you still don't understand!'

I was about to repeat my question, but then I noticed how old he was – not like in the morning. There was nothing dislikeable or vulgar about him – but, no, I wouldn't go with him for anything in the world. He could go back to the school or to the hotel, I didn't care, all I wanted was for him to leave me alone. I couldn't roam the streets with a man who leaps like a locust from job to job and who, worst of all, ages in a day. These kinds of conjuring tricks are highly suspicious.

I turned left and found myself on a main road. It was now well and truly night. Every so often, some passer-by would hastily cross my path. The dim reflections from some tiny lights in the corners made the tramlines shine. 'They still haven't ripped them up,' I thought, smiling, when from afar I heard the familiar bell of the tram. It passed me by quickly, lit up and empty, I didn't even manage to see whether it had a driver. 'Where the hell am I? Have I lost my way again?' Over my head I was wearing a blanket, which, though protecting me from the drizzle, made me sweat and I found it difficult to breathe. Fortunately, in a large open space beside the road, a woman suddenly appeared. She was running. Before I could ask her whether I was going in the right direction, she was gone. Whereupon, a man, also running, appeared – evidently chasing her. I was watching them running one behind the other in an endless circle, when I saw that they were separated by a tall, iron railing, obviously impenetrable and without any gate. She was running inside the railing and he on the outside. Yet the woman was scared, though completely safe, and the man was chasing her, though completely in vain. 'Mad, should be locked up,' I reflected. Even if they were to go on running for an age, they'd never be able to catch one another.

The rain had become heavier. I decided not to ask anyone any more. I'd try on my own to find the street and I was sure that I'd succeed, even if it took me a bit longer. This thought somehow gave me new courage. And I continued all night, in the rain, searching for the neighbourhood where my aunt lived, my mother's younger sister, dead now for many years . . .

Original title: 'Mia mera san tis alles'. First published in Tassos Leivaditis, *To ekkremes* [The Pendulum] (1966). Translated here from the text anthologised in Makis Panorios (ed.), *To Elliniko Fantastiko Diiyima* [The Greek Fantasy Short Story] vol. 2, Athens: Aiolos, 1993, pp. 99–104.

The Rulers

Alexandros Schinas

It was the first time that Ilayia would spend a night with one of the rulers. He'd chosen her for that night from the catalogue of the rulers' pleasure preparation school, where she'd lived and studied since as long as she could remember, since the time, that is, that they'd taken her there from the biological station for the artificial reproduction of members of the higher servile classes. She was very young. A shining skin-tight suit in exactly the same colour as her blue-green eyes clung to her supple body, with its narrow hips and long legs, as it swayed to her light step. Her breasts were not yet full. Her fair hair reached down to her waist. Though she had been taught all the sexual procedures, she still felt a somewhat fearful curiosity as she had never been touched by a man. In the preparation school, the necessary knowledge was acquired through detailed descriptions in combination with depictions on screens and the exercises were carried out with other girl students and with male dolls. She was aware that the rulers, from the youngest ones to those who were over two hundred years old, had the same youthful faces, the same athletic bodies, were filled with insatiable lust and for hours on end vented their lust on the girls' bodies. How old, she wondered, was the man waiting for her now. One of her fellow-students had told her that you could tell their age, though not always with certainty, from their demands. The older they were, the more elaborate were the things they demanded, many of which were not foreseen by any of the preparation programmes. If she were fortunate enough to please this one tonight, perhaps he would book her again on other nights; she would become all the more closely linked to him as time passed and this would no doubt be good for her later, though she had no idea what to expect or what she should ask of him. In the preparation school, the lessons were almost exclusively about sex; the conditions of life in the community in which she found herself were known to her from information she obtained from some of the instructresses in the breaks and from rumours. She had heard in very general terms that the planet belonged to the rulers and that the whole of the rest of mankind was divided into two different categories of servants. She, herself, belonged to those who were reproduced artificially and who were intended to cater for the rulers' immediate needs, as was the case with the scientist-servants, the security-servants and some others. She lived in one of the city's better zones, consisting of relatively low buildings with only a few dozen floors, arranged in a circle around the centre where the towering skyscrapers of the rulers were situated. From the highest floors of her school, she had seen that behind a luscious green belt of woodland, the city spread out to all points of the horizon in a sea of smaller houses. From what she'd been told, this was where the millions of servants belonging to the other category lived. What purpose did they serve? What kind of services could they possibly offer the rulers from so far away? According to one rumour, energy was once scarce and life was primitive on the planet. The majority of people had to exert muscular strength, using tools and machines in order to live or in order to exterminate each other, in addition to which they were scourged by famine and disease. During the last few centuries, however, the scientist-servants had managed to harness the enormous quantities of energy from the nearest sun, which they channelled down to the planet by means of a network of space stations. In this way, mankind was freed for good from illness, famine, war and work; its muscular strength, particularly that of the lower classes, was used almost exclusively to fill the free time, and the rulers' lives were prolonged. In the past, so they said, the climate had been unpredictable, periods of drought and heat were followed by periods of cold, snow and rain, and now and again powerful winds would arise. How did the people at that time endure all this? However, the scientist-servants succeeded, through simultaneous reverse-directional explosions at the poles, to turn the axis of the planet so as to maintain the same agreeable temperature, without any meteorological fluctuations, throughout the year. And under these new climatic conditions, they developed a new flora and fauna, after having exterminated all undesirable plants and animals. The fresh grass, the tall trees swaying gently, the tame little animals that ran and jumped and scampered about, the colourful birds flying around her as she walked down the avenue, came, as she did, from biological stations for artificial reproduction. Far off at the end of the avenue, the centre's skyscrapers appeared like vertical needles. In one of these was the entire floor inhabited by the ruler with whom she would have her first night of sex. She had never been before to the area where the rulers lived and her joyful expectation was mixed with a certain apprehension. There was still some time before it would grow dark; she preferred to walk rather than take one of the moving walkways next to her in order to reach the nearest entrance to the underground transport network. A small communication and information device strapped to her left wrist like a bracelet was programmed with the stop where she would arrive at the centre, with the pass enabling her to get through the automatic control and with all the other information she would need to reach the skyscraper and the required floor. She got a call on the apparatus, brought her hand up to her eyes and, on a tiny screen the size of her thumbnail, saw the smiling face of one of her instructors. Her voice came across clearly without any mechanical distortion as if she were beside her: 'How are you feeling, Ilayia? Your heart rate has increased a little in the past few minutes.' 'I wasn't aware of it at all, I feel fine.' 'All right, I was just asking. Don't forget what we've talked about. Good luck.'

The centre was much more extensive than she had imagined. The glistening skyscrapers were so tall that they appeared to narrow at the top. Though they were built at quite large distances from each other, the wide, green avenues seemed like paths and the spacious squares like tiny clearings in a dense forest. She soon realized that none of the people moving around were rulers. They were all speaking in low voices and they all refrained from laughing loudly. Two security-servants in black leather suits quietly flew overhead in an upright position. She couldn't understand where the constant light all about her was coming from. The sky began to grow dark. Bright dots appeared like shooting stars, progressively reduced speed and landed on the tops of the skyscrapers. Others slowly took off and flew away at a constantly accelerating speed. These were the rulers' flying pods. As she got closer to the entrance to the skyscraper, she must have passed through an invisible beam as a small plaque at one side began flashing and a voice said: 'present your personal device'. She raised her left arm and held the device next to the plaque. A gap opened in the protective fence around the entrance, which was formed entirely of rays, and which closed immediately after she had passed through. Now, she, too, realized that her heart was beating faster. She found herself inside a vast area with shining walls which continually changed colour and on which strange patterns formed one after the other. Ahead of her were dozens of lifts. Her device led her to the right one. It must have shot up at a great speed, but she felt no discomfort. On emerging, she found herself before an opaque glass door, beside which another plaque was flashing, though without any voice coming out. Her heart felt as if it would burst. Trembling, she raised her left arm to the plaque and the door slid open. With one look, she realized who it was standing before her.

'So, you're Ilayia?' The familiar tone of his voice calmed her immediately. He was wearing a red costume, was much taller than her, of athletic build, with not a wrinkle on his face and with brown hair. Only his eyes revealed a deep weariness. He looked around thirty, she thought, but his gaze had lost its life a long time ago. 'You're a pretty girl,' he told her and stroked her hair. The door closed behind her. The reception area seemed endless to her and was divided into two unequal sections of shelves stacked with strange objects and crosspieces with rare climbing plants. Arranged on the floor were weird artistic sculptures and unusual figures that reached up to the ceiling. Everywhere there was furniture of various styles and low fluctuating lighting. From somewhere was coming the overwhelming sound of oboes and cymbals. Ilayia took a few steps forward, stopped and stared in amazement. He took hold of her by the shoulders and brought his face close to hers: 'How do you find it up here? Have you ever been up so high?' He led her to the nearest window. She felt dizzy. The nearby skyscrapers appeared to narrow at their bases, as if stuck like wedges in the ground. She had to lean over to see a section of the city's first zones between them. And beyond the woods around them, a sea of lights stretched as far as the horizon. 'I had no idea that the city was so vast,' she said in admiration. The ruler watched indifferently. 'It's just like all our other cities. They no longer have to be big. Beyond the wooded zone begins the megalopolis of the masses.' And with an enigmatic smile: 'now that's really vast.' Brief pause. 'Do you like the decoration I chose for this evening?' She looked puzzled. 'This evening?' 'But, of course, just for you. From your preferences in the catalogue, I thought you'd like it.' Ilayia remained silent. The ruler noticed her puzzlement and laughed. Then he immediately adopted a serious expression. 'How do you like this for instance?' he asked, pointing to a metal sculpture. 'Shall we keep it for tonight?' Ilayia didn't understand the question and continued to be silent. 'From what I see, you'd rather not. Let's have something else then.' He pressed a combination of tiny keys. The pieces of metal shook and the whole sculpture began to shrink as if it were being absorbed by its base, till it eventually disappeared. He pressed a different combination. Glittering bulges formed on the surface of the base, immediately grew larger and, intertwining themselves, shot up to the ceiling. Ilayia's mouth was hanging half-open. 'How do you like that?' 'Is it made of gold?' asked Ilayia, her mouth still half-open. 'Yes, but now that I see it, I think it would be better in some other material.' He pressed another combination. The sculpture started to shake and the gold was replaced from top to bottom by a crystalline material inside which colourful wavy lines flowed. 'Oh, how lovely!' Ilayia exclaimed. 'It's not bad. Look at how this branch resembles an arm. Wouldn't it be more appropriate it we made it out of flesh? Let's see.' He again pressed a combination of keys. The branch trembled, became flesh and the tips of its five shoots began moving like fingers. 'Touch it!' Ilayia hesitated. 'If I tell you it's all right, there's no need for you to be afraid!' She went up to it and touched it. The branch had the temperature of a human body; it bent and its fingers reached out to touch her hand. She pulled away. 'That base is magic,' she said, somewhat shaken. 'Where on earth did you hear that old-fashioned word? These amusing transformations can be performed on everything you see here.' 'Everything?' 'But, of course. Whatever appears to be made of metal, glass, wood or cloth can be immediately transformed into something else, in any shape, colour or size, for any use or amusement. Do you want me to fashion something especially for you?' He went over to a shelf whose front, like all the others, was covered in keys and he carefully pressed a particular combination. A small figurine shrank and disappeared into the shelf and in its place emerged a metallic pot with a fleshy plant whose calyx had the shape of human lips. 'Go on, put your ear up to it and listen!' He pressed a key. The flower trembled, stretched itself, spasmodically opened and closed its calyx, and let out a murmur from deep within that sounded like a voice from afar: 'I-laaa-yia- I-laaa-yia- I-laaa-yia . . .' and then immediately withered. Ilayia was fascinated. 'It's incredible how you do all that.' 'It's not only me. All the rulers' apartments are the same.' 'And how do you do it?' 'You ask too much,' he said, a little annoyed. 'How it's done is known to the scientist-servants who've succeeded in probing into all the secrets of matter.' And he added sarcastically: 'geniuses, all of them.' His look was icy: 'all we rulers need to know is the combination of keys.' Then, immediately, as if remembering something, his expression became tender again: 'with all this amusement, I forgot to ask you if I can get you something.' He went over to the wall between the two windows, touched a certain spot with his forefinger, creating an opening in the wall out of which emerged a cupboard with glasses of various sizes and decanters with variously coloured drinks. He concocted a mixture in a tall glass and handed it to her. A pleasant warm feeling spread throughout her body at the first sip. 'Do you like it?' 'It's wonderful,' Ilayia whispered and took another sip. She felt as if she were floating, as if all her hesitation were vanishing. Since touching the fleshy plant, she'd been wanting to ask him a question but something scared her. Resolved, she looked him in the eye: 'can the rulers fashion people in their apartments, too?' A grimace of annoyance clouded his face: 'I told you before, you ask too much.' Ilayia looked at him imploringly, forcing a smile out of him. 'Since you want to know that too; yes, they can. They can even refashion people.' It was clear that she didn't understand. That appeared to amuse him: 'what would you say if I were to make you something even better, just for you?' He took hold of her by the hand and led her to the other end of the apartment, through corridors consisting of shelves, partitions and curtains, passing before areas with a variety of styles and diverse objects, some of which moved, stirred and emitted barely perceptible sounds as if communicating with each other. They entered a laboratory area with various apparatuses and stopped in front of two semi-transparent glass cylinders, just big enough for a person to stand inside. His expression had become serious. He opened one of the cylinders and nodded to her to enter. Ilayia remained motionless. 'I told you not to be afraid if I've said it's all right. The copy rays are quite harmless; in a few minutes you'll be ready.' She stood somewhat perplexed inside the cylinder. He closed it and set the apparatus in motion. Coloured lights flashed; wavy lines raced across the screens. They soon stopped and he opened the door for her: 'come on, let's see how you've been refashioned.' He stood her in front of the other cylinder: 'open it yourself!' Ilayia opened it and let out a cry. Standing inside was an exact replica of herself. With the same shining blue-green suit and with the same perplexed expression that she had had before. Turning pale, she took a couple of steps backwards. The ruler asked her replica quite naturally: 'how do you feel?' The replica answered in Ilayia's voice: 'Fine.' 'Did you like the drink I gave you?' 'It was wonderful.' 'Do you know her?' The replica stared at Ilayia: 'it's Ilayia.' 'And who are you?' 'Ilayia.' 'You're mistaken, they're can't be two Ilayias. You're Ilayia's replica.' The replica began to cry. Then Ilayia began to cry too: 'please, I beg you, don't torment her any more.' The ruler's face darkened: 'she doesn't feel tormented. That's the replicas' only drawback.' He immediately realised that his words had upset her and he again adopted a tender expression: 'don't get the wrong idea; the rulers are not sadists.' And pointing to the replica: 'do you want to speak to it too?' Ilayia shook her head. The replica had taken a step out of the cylinder and continued to cry. The ruler took hold of it by the arm, put it back inside, closed the cylinder and went over to the apparatus. 'What are you doing over there?' Ilayia shouted. But the apparatus was already working. Ilayia rushed to the cylinder and tried to open it. 'Do you know what would have happened to you if there wasn't a safety system on it?' The apparatus stopped. 'Can I open it now?' 'If you want.' She opened it; the replica had been depersonalised.

The ruler sat next to one of the windows, Ilayia stood before him. 'It was so alive,' she said sorrowfully. 'Just like you. Its brain had as many billions of cells as yours and with the same things recorded in them. Except that it had no self-awareness. One of those things that the genius-servants still haven't succeeded in doing.' 'But it could speak and cry.' 'Just reflexes, without its being aware of anything.' And casting a glance outside: 'otherwise we would have filled the planet with replicas.' Ilayia showed that she wanted this explained to her, too. The ruler became angry: 'Listen, they haven't sent you here for further studies.' He pulled her to him with force and gripped her legs between his thighs. Ilayia understood that she would now begin to provide the services for which she had for years been preparing herself and immediately adopted one of the expressions she'd been taught that were suitable for every situation. But he paid no attention to her; he'd already pulled down her suit as far as her waist and was sucking her nipples and groaning. He relaxed his grip: 'take your suit off completely!' She was now totally naked. He opened the lower part of his own costume. Ilayia was shocked at his erection. But she did as she'd been taught: she looked longingly at him and bent to kiss him. 'I don't want a lot of tricks the first time,' he said. 'Open your legs!' He lifted her like a feather and sat her on top of him. Ilayia felt a terrible pain, which almost caused her to faint. He moved her up and down quicker and quicker. Inside her she had something much harder and longer than she had imagined; she felt as if it were beating against the bottom of her stomach. The speed of the continual ramming increased, reaching a climax; the ruler's eyes had turned up; his face was contorted and full of wrinkles. From out of his mouth came a groan that successively became a moan, a sigh, a rasping voice. Ilayia was able to make out a word unknown to her that he kept repeating: 'dolore, dolore, dolore, and more dolore, lots of dolore, oh so much dolore.' His ejaculation lasted much longer than she'd seen on the screens at her school, extending to minutes. Afterwards, the spasms grew less, his eyes returned to their normal position and his face grew calm.

Ilayia was standing dressed before him. Though pale from the pain, she again looked him in the eye with resolve: 'what's dolore?' His expression hardened: 'you keep asking about things that shouldn't concern you. How is it they didn't take note of that in your school? The rulers speak only when they want to and only about what they want to.' She looked at him again imploringly, but this time he didn't smile. 'I'm not going to spend tonight with you,' he said brusquely. 'You're beginning to displease me and a lot of dolore will be lost.' Ilayia realized that she'd suddenly fallen into disfavour with a ruler and she sensed a vague threat. 'Don't worry,' he said to her, 'nothing bad is going to happen to you. But you'll leave the school and you'll never be used again for the rulers' pleasure.' He saw her alarm and smiled: 'no, no you won't be sent beyond the wooded zone. You'll remain all your life in the city given that you were produced for this, and some other occupation will be found for you. After a short pause: 'and you'll be able to engage in as much pleasure as you want with your peers.' His smile became indiscernible. 'Except that you'll no longer play a part in the creation of any dolore.'

Ilayia sensed that now she no longer interested him sexually, he would find it amusing to answer her question. He, however, did not seem to want to say any more, his face had acquired a serious expression, he pressed some keys at the side of him and fixed his gaze on something behind her. She turned to see. On a screen was the face of a middle-aged woman: 'category for this evening's preference?' The ruler answered angrily: 'above all, some girl who won't ask useless questions.' The woman glanced at her disapprovingly. Ilayia realized that it was an instructress. The ruler's voice was heard again, calmer this time: 'whatever's immediately available from your school's catalogue!' And without addressing his words to anyone: 'let's see what's left for tonight.' 'Special features, age?' asked the woman. The ruler pointed to Ilayia: 'something like that.' The woman acknowledged him with a deep bow of her head and disappeared. In her place appeared a girl with a lithe body and long blond hair. She began to undress. Ilayia watched the same movements that she too had learned for the school's film catalogue. But she also heard the voice of the instructress giving information about the character, the preferences and the sexual performance of the girl being shown. The ruler pressed a key, the girl disappeared and another one, virtually identical, took her place. He half closed his eyes and watched her undressing. There must have been something he didn't like and he replaced her with another, much the same. 'What do you think of this one?' he asked, mockingly. 'She's prettier than I am,' Ilayia replied spontaneously. 'Not much prettier. But she's preferable now because she's never been used.' He replaced her with another, slightly different, one and froze her at the point where she was bending to remove her skin-tight suit, showing her buttocks. 'I'd certainly secure much more dolore with her than with you,' he said, lustfully. He went back to the point where she was removing her suit and again froze the picture at the point where she was bending: 'that look of hers is extremely arousing.' Nevertheless, he switched her off and, greedily watching the other samples, he said to Ilayia: 'you don't need to stand around here. Go and sit behind there while I choose something. You'll find whatever you want to eat and drink and pass your time.' And he pointed to a curtain at one side.

Ilayia sat at a table with drinks and delicacies that she'd never tasted before, watching a screen with cartoons, which would have seemed more amusing to her than the ones she watched during the endless breaks at the school if she hadn't been absorbed by the same thought: what was dolore? The ruler appeared with a look of satisfaction, sat down facing her and stared at her with a certain sympathy: 'your irritating questions turned out to my advantage; they've made me choose something different this time.' He mixed some of the drinks before him and after the first sip, said: 'I gave the order that your future be taken care of in the best way possible.' She stared into his eyes and he, understanding what she was thinking, laughed: 'I'm no longer annoyed by your insistence. Besides, the rulers have no need to conceal anything from anyone. It's just that there is no provision for certain knowledge in the lessons of a school like yours so that your performance is not diminished by thoughts like those you've begun to have now.' 'But I'm not having any thoughts; I simply don't know what dolore is.' 'Yet you have a strong predisposition for uncustomary thoughts and that's why I've had you transferred from the school for pleasure to another service. For your new peers there, in fact, for the majority of our workforce, dolore is a common secret. And for select servants, such as the scientists or the security force, it is essential knowledge.' He adopted a playfully severe expression: 'you see what you've done? Here I am sitting in my apartment with a girl at this time of night and talking.' Ilayia adopted a feigned expression of dismay. He took no notice of her and looked elsewhere: 'we know,' he said in earnest, 'that some members of our workforce occasionally engage in mistaken and undesirable thoughts concerning the significance of dolore.' And, as if talking to himself: 'it is, it seems, an unavoidable consequence of our wish to be served by beings with self-awareness.' He stared into her eyes with kindness: 'I wouldn't like anything like that ever to happen to you because they are all discovered by means of the psychological monitoring carried out by the scientist-servants and spend a large part of their lives in correction centres. If we have a few minutes left, I'll try to protect you from dangerous thoughts like that. As a gift for your visit.' Ilayia felt her heart leap; she sensed she was going to acquire some useful knowledge. 'You've heard how the world was in previous ages?' Ilayia wondered whether she should mention the rumours she'd heard: 'I know that the rulers always took care of mankind.' He looked at her distrustfully: 'The rulers' mission from the very beginning was to take care of themselves. However, they still hadn't become united then and even competed against each other. And what's worse, because they had only primitive means at their disposal, they all had to motivate their own masses to support their competitiveness. So each one of them was obliged to deceive the masses by not declaring his rule openly and by assuring them, through his cultural agents, that what he did was in their own best interests.' He smiled condescendingly: 'besides, the nature of the rulers' interests had not then been clarified. Most of them were simply satisfied by obtaining and maintaining as much power as possible. But power is only a means for achieving the ultimate goal.' Ilayia was hanging on his every word and the ruler appeared to be amused by her enlightenment: 'and do you know how they measured power then?' He adopted an expression as if about to tell an incredible joke: 'by amassing the metal that you saw before in one of the variations of that sculpture; a metal known as gold.' 'Did they make weapons out of it?' The ruler smiled: 'your question shows such innocence that I'd use you once again if I weren't expecting something better soon.' And then, seriously again: 'this metal was very rare then and that's why they had established it as a measure for evaluating everything.' Ilayia didn't understand, but he went on, carried away by his own account: 'the situation changed radically when the scientist-servants succeeded, by means of a simple transmutation, to produce the metal artificially, just like everything else that was rare and, for this reason, considered valuable. Now we could pave all the roads on the planet with gold and decorate them with diamonds, but these would be neither the most suitable nor the best materials. But you realize what this means?' He wasn't expecting her to reply. 'The disappearance of every unit of evaluation, together with the acquisition of huge amounts of energy, put an end to all forms of competitiveness and brought about the union of the rulers. They established themselves at the centre of cities that developed like this one, with circular zones to accommodate their servants and with a protective system around a green zone on the outer edges to prevent any possible disturbance from the masses. Our predecessors realized then that the ultimate goal was their own pleasure. The security-servants would keep them from being disturbed and the scientist-servants would see to their longevity. But how were they to achieve the highest possible quality of pleasure?' Ilayia, who was waiting for the opportunity to arouse again his desire for her, answered straight out: 'With me and my fellow girl students.' His gaze froze her: 'I am trying till the next one comes to help you, but I see that you are not paying attention to me.' 'I'm doing my best,' Ilayia murmured, letting out a sob. 'Don't cry, because you won't understand exactly what it is you need to know in order never to be put at risk by your thoughts.' He went on as if talking to himself again: 'at that stage, some rulers proposed that the planet's useless masses be completely exterminated. Some even went so far as to propose that the servant workforce be replaced by replicas. In this way, the ruling oligarchy could give itself to its pleasure without any distraction.' Ilayia's eyes popped out. The ruler noticed: 'don't worry, such proposals were made a long time ago and they'll never be brought up again. You and our entire workforce, together with the masses between our cities, owe your lives to a simple and pertinent question: what measure would there be for comparing the highest possible quality of pleasure if the rulers were left in absolute universal solitude? They all recognized the need to preserve some forms of self-awareness other than their own. And an ideal unit of value was established: the dolore.' Ilayia jumped on hearing this word again: 'does it glitter like gold?' The ruler stared at her with pity: 'the dolore is invisible.' A wrinkle lined her brow. 'It is a precisely calculated quantity of pain. It roughly corresponds to having a red-hot needle stuck several centimeters under your nail.' Her face contorted; his remained calm: 'now you understand just how essential the masses are.' Ilayia sensed something and turned pale. His voice became flat: 'microscopic emitters have been implanted in the centers of pleasure inside the rulers' brains. These are activated with the first sexual contact, function more and more intensely during intercourse and reach the highest peak of their performance at the moment of ejaculation, continually conveying the aetheric equivalences of the various sexual pleasures to special installations on the roofs of the skyscrapers.' 'And from there?' Ilayia barely managed to utter the words. The ruler now received her question with pleasure: 'from there, after an instantaneous calculation of the corresponding dolore and the selection of the type of goal on each occasion, signals are transmitted on different frequencies causing pain in microscopic receivers which are implanted at birth in the corresponding centers inside the brains of the masses.' His eyes sparkled: 'those billions of lesser servants living between our cities every so often experience sensations of scourging, cauterization, stabbing, flaying, mutilation, of every suffering possible, and so secure for us the highest possible quality of pleasure.' Ilayia was ready to burst into tears, but she held herself back, aware that this would be dangerous, and she asked as naturally as she could: 'how do these people manage to endure all this; why don't they commit suicide?' The ruler appeared to like this question, too: 'the means for committing suicide are almost non-existent and in the rare cases that it is attempted, it is severely punished. The would-be suicides are discovered immediately by the scientist-servants and are sentenced to multiple pains for the rest of their natural lives. Besides, they are reported by their fellow-humans as every departure from life means an increase in the pain corresponding to each.' And following a brief pause: 'the only hope for relief lies in the creation of as many children as possible.' In the silence that followed, Ilayia tried hard to keep an expressionless look on her face and then resolved to risk one more question: 'and what would happen if . . .' She was cut short by the doorbell. The ruler's face lit up: 'come, let's go now!' They again walked along various corridors and when they reached the reception area, Ilayia saw that it was completely different. The tall artistic sculptures on the floor and the weird objects on the shelves had been replaced by fairies and dwarves and all kinds of fairytale figures. The door opened to reveal a security-servant in his black leather suit standing beside a frightened little girl who only came up to his shoulders. Pointing to Ilayia, the ruler said to the servant: 'you'll take her to her new service in keeping with my orders!' And turning to Ilayia: 'I've done enough I think to help you. Good luck.' As she walked towards the lift, Ilayia heard the ruler's voice behind her, unrecognizably tender: 'so you're Vanisa?' Through a window she saw, for the last time from such a height, the outlying megalopolis of the masses shining and stretching as far as the horizon.

Original title: 'To antikrysma tis kyriarchias'. Published in Alexandros Schinas, *Anaphora periptoseon* [Case Reports] (1966/1989). Translated here from the text anthologised in Makis Panorios (ed.), *To Elliniko Fantastiko Diiyima* [The Greek Fantasy Short Story] vol. 2, Athens: Aiolos, 1993, pp. 207–216.

The Swans

E.H. Gonatas

The snails were feeding in the vast garden. They could be heard greedily searching for the soft leaves. From out of the darkness of the cage – just as every evening at the same time – appeared the lily-white, provocative necks of a pair of swans. Tiny frogs, whole swarms of them, trooped one behind the other and their gleaming eyes steeped the violets in a wet glow.

The tall lotus stood out among the other trees; a cloth was flapping from its top and at its root a young girl was sound asleep. She had gone there for just a moment, so she thought, but after calmly and enjoyably watering the thick grass, she'd forgotten herself, enchanted as she was by the beautiful evening, and fallen asleep.

An old woman, partly a servant and partly a nanny, with a linen ruff round her neck, with a bottle of milk in one hand and a lamp in the other, was brushing through the bracken and the rosemary.

'Mersini, stop playing games. Where are you hiding?' she called out anxiously.

The girl didn't reply; it was only natural as she was fast asleep.

Suddenly, the old woman stumbled against me; I was next to the cage and was preparing to grab the second swan by the neck. She flung down the bottle and lamp, took me by the ears, held a big handkerchief up to my nostrils and said:

'Smell it, you mangy hound. Open wide those nostrils of yours. Go on!'

The pungent smell almost suffocated me.

'Don't get snot all over it and dirty it,' she cried. Then, rubbing my nose in the ground, she snapped: 'Have you smelled it long enough? Off with you and find her.'

I tried to go but I was unable to move. She was holding me by the ears like a hare.

'Not so fast, not so fast. Who said you could go? Swear to me first that you're not going to trick me. Or I'll make mincemeat of you.'

'Old lady,' I said to her, trembling, 'on my grandmother's bones, I'll do whatever you want. But doesn't the handkerchief smell of garlic to you too?'

What was I thinking of to come out with such a thing? A heavy cuff to my head knocked it back, forcing me, though I wasn't at all in the mood, to look up at the sky.

'Did you say garlic? You damnable dog, you've got me confused. I must have given you my own handkerchief. Seems I didn't look in the right pocket,' she said, using one hand to search through the endless pockets in her apron (I quickly counted at least ten), while with the other she was pulling so hard at my right ear that she almost tore it off. In due course, she took out another handkerchief, a lace one, and after smelling it herself she thrust it under my nose.

'There, that's the one. At last, I've found it. And don't pull your neck away. Bring it here so I can get a leash on it. I'm not so soft in the head as to believe in oaths, despite what you might think. You'll see what a fine walk the two of us will have together. You in front and me behind.'

I realised I was done for. At that moment, the church clock from Saint Marina's began striking the hour, and the pigeons sleeping in the clock tower fluttered up.

One, two, three, four, five . . .

'Blessed Marina, you're trying to help me,' I said to myself and I almost burst into tears. 'I can hear your tender voice talking to me in the striking of the clock. If you only knew; my remorse is tearing at my heart like a wild beast. No, I can no longer bear to leave you in the darkness of your guileless ignorance. It's as if I were deceiving you for a second time. It was I who snatched the huge ruby adorning your hand; the one shining like a red star and admired for years by the church commissioners, who swelled with pride as if it were adorning their own hands. No one noticed me taking it. They all had their attention turned to the deceased and were praying, half-blinded by their tears and the smoke from the incense. And how could you possibly have seen me as I pretended to bend over to kiss your icon and covered your face with a bouquet of roses. How could you possibly have felt my hand, lighter than feather-down, as I removed the precious stone. I have it hidden beneath my goldfish bowl in a cobwebbed henhouse. No one ever sets foot in there. Early in the morning I'll bring it back to heal the horrid wound that I, a wretched sinner, dared to open on your holy hand.'

The clock went on striking the hour. With her mouth open, the old woman counted the number of strokes, which came slowly and constantly like huge droplets of water, and with every stroke, she let out a small grunt of joy.

'Six, seven, eight, nine . . . twelve!'

My confession was over. I came out of my ecstasy with a purified soul and a clear mind. I regained my courage.

'Did you hear the clock?' I shouted. 'Midnight! What are you waiting for with your mouth hanging open? It won't strike again.'

'No, I want it to strike, to go on without stopping. I want to hear it again. I like it so much,' said the old woman, almost bursting into tears.

'Why are you carrying on like that? I can't bear to see you cry. It hurts me. You remind me of my grandmother who, in the period before she died, had got into the habit of calling me to her bedside every evening. She would beg me in tears to tell her a fairytale.'

'And did you?' asked the old woman, curious.

'I'd frighten her first of all by telling her that if she went on wetting her bed, I wouldn't go again. And then I'd begin the story. Otherwise, she couldn't get to sleep.'

The old woman gazed at me as if she were dreaming. 'Undoubtedly, she's imagining the scene that I've just related to her,' I reflected. 'She's completely forgotten about the clock.'

If I wasn't so certain that I hadn't opened my mouth, I'd have said that I was the one who reminded her of it.

'I don't want fairytales. I want it to strike. I want to hear it again,' she said, screeching.

'What you really want to do is to turn the clock back! And perhaps there's a way. I'll try if you let me, but only for you, because you're so like my grandmother. So listen. I'll run over to the church, climb up the clock tower and, though I'm not promising anything, I think I can manage to turn the hands of the clock back and make it strike again. But on one condition, that this will be for the first and last time. You mustn't get drawn into this game and draw me into it as well. Don't forget how much work is waiting for us as soon as I get back. In the meantime, sit down here and be good till I return.'

'Wonderful idea!' the old woman shouted enthusiastically and she kissed me, tugging at my ears that she hadn't let go of for a moment all this time. 'So, you're really going to put yourself at risk for me by going up the winding staircase in the clock tower. The steps are all mossy and as slippery as if they were covered with seaweed.'

'I always come straight out with what I think,' I replied seriously, 'that's how I was brought up. "You," my mother would say to me when I was still young, "you can't hide anything even if you wanted to, unlike my other children, because your thoughts are written on your forehead and everybody can read them even before you speak." '

Her face suddenly grew dark.

'Should I agree? I need to think about it.'

'My plan is simple,' I explained to her. 'The whole question is for me to manage to move the hands. If I'm unable to turn them back, then I'll push them forward. If I see that it's too difficult, I'll have a look in the clock's works; there's bound to be a lever or something that sets them in motion.'

'You don't understand. That's not what I meant. The thing is whether it's right for me to send you to risk your life up there while I wait down here with folded arms?'

I stared at her, completely at a loss. As she spoke to me, I felt her tightening her grip on my ears, which were now burning and hurting me.

'Put yourself in my position,' she said, 'and you'll see what

I mean. I'd go crazy at the thought that at any moment I might see you slipping on a step without a rail, while I was far off, unable to catch hold of you, unable to do anything to save you. No, don't ask it of me, I wouldn't be able to bear it. Put your neck here, please, so I can tie this leash to you. You'll see how much more confident, how much more comfortable you'll feel like that, when you know that I'm right behind you, ready to catch you in my arms, ready to prevent you falling.'

'Ah! That's it then. So let's not split up, if it's for my own good,' I said to her, disappointed.

But before I surrendered my neck into her hands, a thought suddenly flashed through my mind.

'Heavens, what's that I see there?' I murmured in terror, looking opposite. 'They've locked us in. Now what's going to happen? We're prisoners.'

'Who's locked us in?' the old woman asked anxiously. 'I can't see anything.'

'Can you read? Look!' I replied and pointed to the sign fixed on a tree.

Before she'd had time to pick up the lamp and shine it on the sign, which said:

NO ADMITTANCE TO THE PUBLIC
AFTER SUNSET

I'd already got away from her.

Barking, I ran and leapt into the cistern. The marsh-mallows and night flowers closed over me.

'But I'm the warden's wife. My house is in here,' I heard the old woman screaming from afar.

I swam and swam for a long time (I was hindered by the fact that I was holding my one hand out of the water so as not to wet the head of the swan that I'd strangled; it was still warm and its eyelids fluttered every so often in my palm), till I reached the rock. There, I found the key, turned on the tap and the water gushed out unstoppably, roaring like a lion that had just been set free. The cistern overflowed, the flower-beds flooded, the water swept away whatever it found in its path. The little girl, still fast asleep, was carried outside the garden, beneath the cypresses. The surge of water also deposited the old woman, half-drowned, next to her. I watched her from the rock, wriggling like a fish. Her forehead was covered in big bumps.

'Saint Marina,' I prayed with all my might, 'let me see her breathe her last and I'll go straight to the henhouse, wet as I am, and I'll bring you your ruby this very instant.'

I don't know what I was thinking of just previously when I'd made the same promise, but this time I was determined and I had no doubt that I would keep my word. However, the old woman slowly came round and I felt angry at this . . . injustice. Presently, when she had completely recovered, she took the girl by the hand and they left together, stumbling along the road.

Suddenly, the young girl cried out: 'I've left them on top of the leaves; I haven't got my panties,' and leaving the old woman where she stood, she jumped over the fence and disappeared into the garden.

The water had receded. In the mud left behind, a different sky now shone: the eyes of the frogs scattered here and there.

The girl ran to her tree and, while I was swimming to get out of the cistern, I watched her circling it again and again. Then she raised her head and fixed her eyes on the top of the lotus, where the cloth was still flapping back and forth. She was angry like a little fox whose prey has escaped high into the branches. I went up to her without saying anything and, dripping water, I climbed up the tree with one hand; I got to the top, unhooked the garment, then, wrapping my legs round the trunk, I slid to the ground. The young girl looked at me in astonishment and admiration.

As soon as I had my feet on the ground, I bowed before her, hiding my hands behind my back.

'Before I give it to you, I want to ask you something,' I whispered in her ear. 'I have a question that's bothering me. How did you manage to get it up there so high?'

The girl moved her eyes up close to me and I felt scared.

'I put it next to me on the leaves of a bush. You're wrong if you think I hung it up there where you found it. Here, not long ago,' she said, pointing to the tall tree, 'was a small lotus that barely reached up to my neck. I've read that sometimes these trees can shoot up to their full height overnight. Are you happy now?'

I was; but her eyes were moving so quickly before me that I felt dizzy. Flustered, I held out my hand to her.

'Take it,' I said, 'so you don't catch cold.'

She let out a stifled groan and collapsed at my feet.

I'd made the fatal mistake. I'd offered her the swan's head.

Original title: 'I kykni'. First published in 1963. Translated here from the text published in E.H. Gonatas, *I Ayelades* [The Cows], Athens: Stigmi, 1992, pp. 23–36.

Dracula

Petros Ambatzoglou

It had indeed been a difficult year for Baron Gudermachter and his famous castle. With his hawk, bow and snares, this wonderful hunter returned one fine spring afternoon to his castle – with a rich harvest of assorted animals – somewhat earlier it must be said than usual, to find the beautiful Baroness Adelaïs in the bedchamber, naked on her back with her legs wide open and wrapped round the waist of a naked man with a beard – the knight De Flirt – who was holding her by the buttocks and tenaciously and rhythmically thrusting something inside her. Without seeking an explanation, Baron Gudermachter bared his sword and slew the couple. Such was his fury that he went on striking the lifeless bodies until he had sliced them into a pile of sexless pieces. Only their heads remained intact – though without eyes – like two bloody footballs. Then, in his desperation, the Baron ran down to the secret underground crypt and hanged himself. His suffering lasted no more than a few seconds. When he finally came round, he was literally taken aback. And quite rightly so, given that he was dangling two feet above the floor. So he waited to die, but nothing happened. Eventually, the noose round his neck began to irritate him, so he untied it and jumped down. He nervously felt his neck and his body, both of which were as right as rain. He immediately recalled the reason for his – so he believed – unsuccessful suicide, and found that he felt no pity whatsoever for his beloved and unfaithful Adelaïs. He carefully emerged from the crypt and it was then that he noticed it was the middle of the night. Through the huge window in the hall, he was able to see the full moon and the mist rising from the ground. A deathly hush filled the castle. The servants, the Baron supposed, must have been terrified at the sight of the lovers' mutilated bodies and fled from the castle. However, one question plagued his troubled mind. Given that he had hanged himself at 2.30 in the afternoon, how could it now be night-time? How was it that he was still alive after having been hanging for so many hours? Yet he felt sleepy and noticed that his steps were mechanically taking him to the castle graveyard. Unconsciously, he took up a pick and shovel. He arrived before the stone tomb of his hateful father – Baron Gudermachter. He worked with great care. He buried the dead man's bones in the tomb of his grandmother. He cleaned and scrubbed the tomb, fitted it with a mattress and covered this with silk sheets. But then, rosy-fingered dawn appeared so he lay down inside and, with his right hand, drew the marble slab over him and sank into a sweet and innocent sleep.

All this took place in April 1517 and now it's June 1986. Baron Gudermachter spent many happy but also frightful years, many difficult and hungry hours. At first, the region around his castle provided him with a comfortable life. With the setting of the sun, he would rise from his tomb and go for a nice walk inside the dusty and deserted castle. He took pleasure in breathing the damp and musty air; he went down to the secret chamber and hung there for about half an hour just for practice. This practice helped the muscles in his neck and sent the little blood he had to his head. Hyperaemia brought him a sense of well-being.

Then it was time for supper. He put on his gold-embroidered outfit and his velvet cap with its silver clasp and set off for the neighbouring village. He arrived late into the night. He walked like a shadow in the dim and narrow lanes and as soon as he found himself alone with some passer-by, he pinned him down in a judo hold and sank his teeth into his neck. The man squirmed and fainted. Later when he came round, he remembered nothing. He was somewhat numb and terribly irritable for no apparent reason. He immediately made for a tavern, drank in an effort to remember something and eventually returned home after midnight and, drunk as he was, beat his wife and children. This was how life was in the village following Gudermachter's visits. However, these years of unbroken happiness for the Baron did not last forever. And this was because the Baron could not die naturally. Someone or some group of people had to rise against him and plunge a stake through his heart. Nature passed through him without touching him. Gudermachter was ageless; he lugged his great bulk about irrespective of the environment. Nature, from the tiniest mosquito to the largest seal, had no effect on him. Everything passed as if at high speed while he remained fixed to the earth like a tree. Yet, though indestructible, the Baron could cause great destruction with his teeth. Naturally, his immortality had a serious drawback. He suffered as much as mortals suffer, but he could not be liberated by death. So for centuries this fiend ravaged the surrounding villages, even the towns, infecting people and creating other fiends. He had turned them into jugs filled with blood and he enjoyed his life, or rather his death, until the time came when he literally died of hunger. Of course, it was his own fault because, without his realising it, a new era had begun and he was still going around in his velvet attire and his feathered cap. Even at night, the villagers took him for a madman, for a so-called crank, and laughed at him. And so, as he was no longer able to get close to his victims, instead of drinking fresh blood, he eventually ended up frequenting the town's slaughter-house and swallowing the animals' revolting blood as it flowed through the gutter and into the sewers. He would kneel in the gutter and drink greedily, but no matter how much he drank he was never satisfied, since animals' blood is not particularly nourishing; you simply become bloated without consuming very many calories. Even a young vampire of two hundred years knows that. So, disappointed, he returned to his castle and wondered why people were no longer mesmerised by him as in the good old times and why they no longer offered their necks for biting. And thus the Baron might very well have died of hunger – scientifically speaking, an impossibility – if, one evening, he hadn't dropped his cap.

The moment he saw his funny, feathered cap, he cried out in delight: 'Eureka, that's it! I was dying of hunger because I'm démodé.' So he immediately had some cards printed introducing him as Doctor Alten Gudermachter OBE, BDE, MGC and changed into a nice tweed suit with a silk tie and handkerchief, a disguise that would make anyone trust him. It was a period of great contentment. He had never had such an abundance of necks. He almost became perverse about it. He preferred biting young girls in the belly or breast, young men in the neck and older men in the back of the neck. In general, he no longer drank blood to satiate himself but simply for pleasure. And perhaps Gudermachter would have gone on living for hundreds of years in this idyllic situation had it not been for the Second World War.

There was no food left any more. People had no blood. At the beginning of the war, the Baron basically got by on victims he encountered at the railway stations, where the soldiers said their farewells to their loved ones. Later, however, he found it impossible to lure even a born idiot. People were full of hate and there appeared on the scene some blood-suckers called 'black-marketeers', who made Dracula seem like an innocent schoolboy. In appearance, they were even worse than garlic and the sign of the cross. The Baron was terrified of them. In fact once, a black-marketeer, disguised as a nurse, offered to sell him blood from transfusions. The Baron had no money, so he was forced to give the black-marketeer all his silverware, his curtains and whatever else was of value in his castle. He remained alone in the empty rooms and felt angry. 'Dracula or no Dracula,' he said, 'I can't take any more. The black-marketeers have bled me dry, I hope the sky caves in on them.'

So he lay down in his ancestral tomb and waited to die. On the twenty-fifth day, he was woken by frightful explosions. The ground shook and, exhausted as he was, the Baron thought it was the Second Coming. 'As if everything else wasn't enough,' he murmured, 'now we're going to have to deal with God in person. You get what you deserve . . .'

Yet before he had time to finish his sentence, the stone slab was suddenly drawn back and a crazed soldier in a green uniform tumbled inside. The Baron grabbed him under the arms, squeezed him close and greedily sank his teeth into his neck, gulping down his blood as if he were a soft drink.

When he climbed outside to get rid of the body, he was amazed. There were fires all around, as far as the eye could see. Shells of 35, 60 and 180 millimetres together with rockets of all kinds were furrowing the air, which smelled of sulphur, smoke and burnt flesh. Baron Gudermachter felt a new sense of euphoria. He felt like an innocent young vampire again. He wanted to run, to embrace whoever he found before him, to bite and be bitten, to roll in the fires, to sing. And he began to dance around his tomb and sing in the voice of a mezzo-soprano:

It's a long way to Tipperary
It's a long way to go . . .

Suddenly, a brilliant idea flashed through his mind. He would leave his tomb half-open: a refuge for the frightened soldiers. 'If I only catch two a week,' he thought, 'I'll live like a king.' And so he got through the war quite comfortably. Of course, he ended up as something of a commercial traveller, running from one battlefield to the next, but he survived.

At the end of the war, as a veteran, the Baron returned to his ancestral castle in the hope that he would go back to living his previous carefree life. Though without his realising it, his idealism concerning innocent youth led him into new adventures.

One night, Baron Gudermachter emerged from his tomb for his daily constitutional. Lightly and noiselessly as befitted a vampire, he walked through the cobwebbed rooms, inhaling the dust and mustiness and eventually came to the dining-room.

Fortunately for him, he stopped just in time, because the room was lit by five or six storm lamps and around the huge table were seated eight gentlemen dressed for an outing. One was wearing a Tyrolean costume with leather shorts but with a captain's cap; another was wearing jeans and running shoes. In short, they were all dressed casually and in a youthful style, though they were over forty. The Baron noticed that they were eating something out of tins. They stuck their fingers inside and pulled out brown slimy cubes or dark green vegetables. Also, they were drinking some kind of liquid out of tin mugs, which certainly wasn't blood – yet they took great pleasure in it judging from the endless aaaaaah they all came out with. Hidden behind the huge curtain, the Baron heard the Tyrolean saying:

'No, there's nothing to be done. We'll demolish the whole of the interior and keep only the exterior. We can't bring tourists willing to pay two hundred dollars a night to freeze in this pigsty. Americans want European finesse outside and something resembling the Hilton inside.'

'You're right, I agree,' said one of the others. 'The castle's no good to us without bathrooms and toilets. We'll demolish the other rooms, but let's keep this dining-room. We'll keep the portraits of the Barons. And candles everywhere.'

'I suggest we also do something with the family graveyard,' said another. 'We can plant more ivy and bushes. Make it look wild and menacing. There's a legend about the castle being haunted. Baron Gudermachter murdered his wife and hanged himself. Now he's a vampire, they say.'

'That's marvellous,' shouted the Tyrolean. 'We'll seal off a room and we'll put it about that it's the room where he hanged himself.'

'Perhaps once a week, we could even hold a vigil,' added another. 'We could all carry candles and wait for the vampire to appear. And while we're waiting, we could play cards.'

'We could organise a kind of vampire safari,' said one of them.

Baron Gudermachter went straight back to his tomb, dug up the last gold coins that he'd been saving for an hour of need and took the train to the capital. 'I'm not going to become a laughing-stock,' he muttered, 'I won't let those rogues turn me into a tourist attraction . . .'

On arriving at the central station in the capital, he phoned his old friend doctor Desefenko, one of the first immigrants to the city. Desefenko had once written to him, telling him to leave the countryside and the vulgar peasants. 'The life of the vampire,' he stressed, 'is in the cities. Just think of the necks in the subways at night. What more need I say? Just think that you can move in the subways even during the day.' Now, however, doctor Desefenko was rather cool over the telephone.

'These are difficult times for us all,' he said. 'You should have stayed in your castle, albeit as a tourist attraction.'

'But they were going to turn me into a "Son et Lumière" performance,' replied the Baron. 'And how am I to drink the blood of some rich old American? It's enough to make your flesh creep.'

In the end, Desefenko found him a small but pleasant room. It was in the basement, was dingy and overlooked a dim light well. And it had a pleasant smell: something between stale food and a public lavatory.

The following night, when he woke up, he learned from the caretaker that doctor Desefenko had committed suicide and in an exceedingly strange way. He had plunged a broken wooden stake through his heart.

'Good man,' said the caretaker, 'though it seems that all his night work recently had taken its toll on his nerves.'

The Baron heaved a sigh of dismay.

'I must do something for furniture,' he said. 'You know what they say, the dead are dead and you have to take care of the living.'

Two blocks away there was a funeral parlour.

'My condolences,' said the assistant as soon as he saw him entering. 'What sort of funeral were we looking for?'

'I'm not interested in any funeral,' explained Baron Gudermachter. 'What I want is a comfortable and elegant coffin. I'll send one of my relatives to bury him in Transylvania. I'll take it with me.'

He chose an extremely charming coffin with simple classic lines, which showed its quality without being ostentatious. That same night, he installed it in the middle of his room and slept like a human-being.

His next visit was to the dentist on the following day.

'Excuse me,' the Baron said, covering his mouth with his

hand in order to hide his fangs. 'I have a slight aesthetic problem. You were recommended to me by the late doctor Desefenko.'

'Don't worry yourself about it,' the surgeon said. 'I know just what you want. Besides, that's my job. I'll remove your fangs and I'll fit you with two, shall we say, more discreet ones.'

'And how will I bite into . . . forgive me, I trust you understand,' Gudermachter replied.

'It's very simple,' the surgeon explained. 'When it's time to eat, you'll go into the toilets and fit your own teeth. All it takes is a minute. But afterwards remember to keep your mouth closed. Not even a smile, is that clear?'

'I am most grateful to you for showing such understanding in my case,' the Baron said, feeling moved. 'You are a man with a capital M.'

The surgeon laughed.

'I'm like you,' he said. 'What did you think? Today, you can't find "normal" types any more. These are difficult times. Hunger and loneliness. You'd be better off going back to your village.'

'But how can I go back to my castle,' said the Baron, 'now that they've turned it into a luxury hotel. Where will I find the money to rent even the cheapest room?'

'There's no longer any idealism,' said the doctor sadly. 'There's no fantasy. We're a condemned species.'

For Baron Gudermachter, all form of human contact was dead and gone. There was none at all; either in the subway, or at concerts, or at the cinema, or in congregations. Each time he made a furtive attempt to bite someone, he was greeted with a sad smile from the stranger and a phrase that said it all. 'My dear colleague.'

He again visited the dentist in case it had to do with the dentures.

'No, my dear sir,' the dentist informed him. 'The dentures aren't to blame. Technology is to blame. There are so many of us. Imagine, they've discovered a lotion for vampires to rub on themselves so they don't have to be afraid of the sun anymore.

They can even go sunbathing on the beach. It makes me shudder just to think of it.'

'Lord have mercy,' exclaimed Gudermachter. 'Sodom and Gomorrah. And what's going to become of us if we go on like that? Tell me.'

'I don't know,' answered the surgeon. 'I don't know. I've simply accepted it. Après moi le déluge.'

Baron Gudermachter took his silver-handled walking stick and went round the parks. He walked idly and purposelessly. He made no attempts to approach anyone. He knew what response he'd receive. Once he tried with a student. Unfortunately, in the morning he found the marks on his own neck and the student long gone. Baron Gudermachter got fed up and shut himself in his basement room. He bought a television and lies in his casket every night from eight o'clock watching it. As soon as he sees anything resembling a human face, he feels so moved that he bites his bare arm and drinks his own blood . . .

Original title: 'O drakoulas'. First published in Petros Ambatzoglou, Yannis Vatzias, Thanassis Mafounis, *Fantastika Diiyimata* [Fantasy Short Stories], Athens: Hestia 1990, pp. 23–33.

The Last Alchemist

Tassos Roussos

Hieronymus was orphaned at an early age. His parents were killed in an accident. But, thanks to the loving care of an elderly aunt, he grew up in the best possible way, among books and foreign-language teachers. When the old aunt died, he found himself in a position of relative ease – he was twenty years old then – which allowed him to live, albeit modestly, without having to work. This had a decisive influence on his life. It made him into a collector.

Even as a child, he'd had this inclination, which in time turned into a passion or rather something deeper and more substantial. Without any exaggeration, it became second nature to him. His penchant for collecting, somewhat vague and unconscious at first, gradually took on a particular form and direction. An overpowering force drove him to collect and study old yellowed manuscripts and rare books on alchemy, the mysterious science of the middle-ages. And so he filled his home – a solitary house surrounded by a garden – with piles of volumes that lay everywhere.

He spent his youth unproductively. As he did his maturity. Now he was approaching sixty and he realised, but without sorrow or hope, that he had still not found his purpose in life. This sober conclusion didn't dismay him. It was just a plain thought, without any emotional involvement. A thought of the type 'that tree needs pruning', or 'the wind's getting up'.

He sat in his study that was filled with books and papers. The light of the sunset fell aslant through the window, making the dust of time that covered the old furniture and curtains in the room look even more yellowed. He could just about make out his reflection in the glass of the half-open balcony door. He straightened up and looked again 'I'm starting to get a hump,' he thought. And immediately, 'When you don't sprout wings, it's then that you get a hump'. He again took hold of the small, black box. It had taken him three weeks of craft to buy it. He'd seen it cast aside in an old junk shop, amidst books and papers. He noticed it immediately. But he simply gave it a glance of feigned indifference and leafed through the book beside it. His practised eye discerned something that looked like a monogram engraved on the dark, seasoned wood. He touched it just for a moment and then left it. He moved away, picked up another book and leafed through it. The owner, who was watching him through his spectacles, came over to him. 'It's an extremely old box, sir. Quite rare, take a look.'

Hieronymus picked it up and examined it. It did, indeed, bear a monogram that was faded and hard to make out. He touched it lightly. He felt something like a burning in his fingertips. He touched it again and again felt the slight burning sensation. He hurriedly put the box down. 'I'm not interested in it,' he said dryly. 'Perhaps this old book,' he murmured and took hold of a worn edition. The owner then began extolling the dusty volume that Hieronymus was holding.

The same thing happened on several occasions. The owner was always strangely insistent. 'It's an extremely old box, sir. A rare item.' Hieronymus silently refused, playing his own game. As the experienced collector that he was, he pretended to be indifferent till, in the end, he bought the box at a much lower price, supposedly giving in to the owner's overwhelming insistence.

Now he had it in his hands and was examining it. It was old, perhaps dating back to the 16th century. The wood, blackened with age – it looked like linden – had no decoration other than that tiny, half-faded monogram. He took a magnifying glass to examine it. It was Latin. The main letter looked like a P. The other was perhaps an M. He touched the monogram. A warm current ran through his fingers. He tried it again, three or four times, and the warmth spread through his hand as soon as he touched the monogram. 'Just like the first time,' he thought. 'Strange, it's as if by magic.'

The sun had sunk behind the hills. His tiny study grew dark. He turned on the light and opened the box. It was lined with shining crimson leather. 'Like a parchment,' he thought to himself. He examined it closely under the lens. Low down in the left corner, on the very edge, he could just make out some faded letters. Again, it was a P and an M, together with some others that disappeared on the other, non-visible, side of the leather lining. He tried to loosen it to pull it further out, but he saw that it was firmly fastened. 'I have to see what it says. Something's written, what though?' he thought. From one of the drawers in his desk, he took out various small instruments: blades, levers, a pair of curved scissors, and got down to work. When midnight came, he still hadn't been at all successful. The box remained intact. Naturally, he didn't want to break it by force. He knew from experience that in such cases, you have to discover the secret. The bottom with the red covering didn't appear to be concealing anything. Yet, there had to be something. At least the rest of the letters. Then there was that burning in his fingers as soon as he touched the mysterious monogram. Rubbing his eyes that were heavy with tiredness, he went to bed with the thought that perhaps the box was *hermetically* sealed.

The next morning he woke up late. It was almost noon. He quickly made himself a coffee and returned to his study. He took out the box and placed it in front of him. He fondled the monogram. He felt the warmth in his hand. He pressed it – quite accidentally – with his thumb and he felt it give way slightly. He pressed it harder. The burning in his finger was almost painful. At the same moment, however, he heard a faint creaking in the box. He quickly opened it and stood there aghast. The bottom with the red leather covering had risen at least two inches. It now seemed to be loose. He searched it impatiently and saw that it was a kind of lid. He lifted it. Beneath it were several yellowed parchments, like narrow strips, and the last thing was a flattened, square leather pouch. It was sewn and sealed on all sides. Nothing else. Just the crimson leather that went all the way round.

Hieronymus took the magnifying glass and examined it.

'There's some kind of inscription here,' he muttered. He'd guessed correctly. He read the Latin words – they could be seen clearly: THEOPHRASTUS PARACELSUS, MEDICUS. His surprise was beyond words. He closed his eyes and tossed his head back. Theophrastus Paracelsus, Physician. The renowned alchemist. He leaned over the desk and picked up the yellowed manuscripts with trembling hands. These too were in Latin. Paracelsus' notes. He stared at the various alchemical symbols and an idea flashed through his mind. 'Notes on the preparation of the **panacea**,' he whispered. 'So,' he continued his babbling, 'that pouch, *hermetically* sealed, must have . . . must have . . . but of course, it must have a sample of the miraculous potion.' With not a little effort, he stopped himself from opening the pouch. 'Not now,' he said to himself. 'When the time's right.' He closed his eyes again. It was beyond all imagining. 'It can't be,' he thought. 'It can't be.' He was overcome by a feverish excitement. He took down countless volumes of books and dictionaries that referred to the **Magnum Opus**. Word by word, he began to translate the narrow Latin manuscripts, at the same time noting down the various symbols in order to give special study to their meanings. He soon realised that, despite his wide-ranging knowledge, the work was going to be laborious and difficult. He decided to keep a journal in which he'd note down everything relating to Paracelsus' manuscripts.

8 March
In the manuscripts, Paracelsus sets forth a theory, a most peculiar one, 'de natura'.

11 March
The last part of the manuscripts refers to something obscure. Most likely to the **Magnum Opus** of the Alchemists. If this really is the case, then I have before me the greatest secret. The **'drinkable gold'**, the panacea. Just as I'd supposed all along.

18 March
I'm working hard. The text is quite easy. But only superficially

so. It requires decoding as it's full of symbols . . . The weather's changing. It's drizzling. I've started getting those old stomach pains again. Just like that, without any cause.

27 March
Now the work's going more slowly. It's also the pain in my stomach. Almost every day. I must see the doctor.

5 April
The doctor didn't tell me anything new. He recommended some tests and rest. For the time being, he's given me some pills.

7 April
I haven't worked for the last two days. The pains have stopped. I'm sleeping all the time.

14 April
I've finished the first part of the manuscripts that are to do with Nature. It's a theory based for the most part on theology. I wonder what connection it can have with the rest . . . Despite the pills, the pains have started again.

18 April
The deeper I go into Paracelsus' theory – is it a theory? – the more fascinating I find it. No, no. I won't skimp my words. It's not a theory. It's a revelation. Yes, I'm dealing with a tremendous secret. I have to understand this. From now on, it will be the goal of my hitherto unproductive life. As I reflect on this, I can sense an invisible force all around, an unfathomable presence.

24 April
NATURA NATURANS. This phrase contains the meaning. Nature is an autonomous, self-willed Being. It bears no relation to God. Perhaps it was once a creative thought of His. It exists inside and outside Time. It conquers Time, though Time conquers it too . . . The stomach pains are unbearable. Yesterday, I almost fainted.

29 April
The doctor's seen my test results. He told me outright – how cynical doctors are – that I have an advanced case of cancer of the intestines. My time is short. But I must finish with the manuscripts and their secret. I must finish . . . I will finish.

3 May
I feel an inner power. The work is going more quickly now. The symbols are almost decoding themselves.

5 May
I've arrived at the pouch. Yes, it's what I'd thought. It contains a sample of the panacea and there are instructions for its preparation and use. The instructions end with the following strange phrase: **'But this must be Allowed'**. Be allowed! . . . What? By whom?

8 May
I have to go on living long enough . . .

So, I've made up my mind. The excruciating pains warn me that I don't have much time left. I'm opening the hermetically-sealed leather pouch . . . It contains extremely fine gold dust, as fine as flour. **Drinkable Gold.** In keeping with the instructions, I dissolved a little in pure spring water and I've just drunk the solution . . . Almost no taste. Yet, as I'm thinking about it – it's incredible – on the tip of my tongue I can sense all kinds of tastes including many that are unknown to me. My head is growing heavy . . . My eyes are closing. I feel sleepy . . . sleee . . . pyyy!

14 May
I still haven't fully recovered. My limbs feel heavy. It seems I fell into a stupor. I slept solidly for forty-eight hours. I drank a little milk and fell asleep again. But this time it was a strange sort of sleep. Full of dreams. Or rather, as if I were swimming in something huge, in something that resembled sleep. At times, I was deep inside the earth and passing freely through its rocks, I saw volcanic lava rising from the earth's

depths and gushing forth in fiery rivers, becoming mountains or silent subterranean layers. At other times, I found myself sinking in water, in rivers and seas. Sometimes I felt that I was a small fish or an enormous sea monster. There were times when, through the eyes of a beast, I saw the unsuspecting mammal just prior to its being pounced upon and torn to pieces. And then immediately I became the death throes of the vegetarians as they expired in the jaws of the carnivores. And afterwards I watched the fire of the stars above, a white blazing light, alive, growing larger and smaller, breathing and crying out. And then the microcosm. The systems of atoms, the worlds of molecular structure and among them, lit with a strange glow, the endless multitude of infinitesimal organisms. And all these rotated like planets around a dark centre. They lived and died on account of this. It swallowed and spewed them out like a huge heart pulsating with enormous beats . . .

15 May
The pains have stopped. I feel strong, full of health. The panacea has worked its miracle. Or am I being too hasty?

20 May
I went to the doctor's and asked him to examine me. I've never in all my life seen a man more surprised. He examined me carefully three times. He took my file, looked again and again at his diagnosis and the results of my previous tests. 'It's impossible,' he kept muttering to himself. I asked him what the matter was. In a faltering, distorted voice, he said '*you had cancer* of the intestines. In the final stages.'

'*Had*? You mean, now I don't have?'

'Exactly, your intestines are those of a young man. I don't understand it. It's incredible.'

I left him mumbling to himself in a daze.

28 May
I've finished the manuscripts. They contain all the instructions on how to prepare the panacea. But I also need the

Athanoras, the special furnace used by the alchemists. I'm going to construct one in the basement.

10 June
The **Athanoras** was constructed to the proper specifications. I've secured the appropriate alchemical tools and I'm about to begin. I intend to produce **'drinkable gold'** in huge quantities. I'll eradicate all illness from the world. This will be my life's work.

12 June
The doctor has submitted me to more tests. The results are conclusive. I'm more than healthy.

17 June
I'm proceeding slowly but surely. I'm very close to the first **sublimation**. A profuse itching has suddenly started. My hands are all red. Perhaps it's irritation caused by some liquid or the caustic fumes emitted by the **Athanoras**.

18 June
I've stopped work in the basement, temporarily I hope. My hands are the reason. Yesterday, the itching in my palms and between my fingers produced an unpleasant development. In a few hours, I was covered in blisters full of pus that hurt horribly. They burst and are running. They've turned into sores. I went to the doctor's. He told me it was a form of allergy. He gave me some ointments and creams. He examined my sores very carefully and his look was, I thought, rather pensive.

23 June
I haven't worked at all these last few days. It's the business with my hands. They look, however, as if they're getting a little better. The doctor's medicines seem to have had some effect.

25 June
I still haven't gone back down to the basement. My sores are healing. I'm rereading the manuscripts and my notes.

30 June

The sores have almost healed up. The doctor, who saw me today, told me smilingly: 'You know, Hieronymus, what you had was neither an allergy nor an infection.'

'Then what was it?' I asked.

'Don't think it strange,' he went on, smiling. 'It was a kind of leprosy. Yes, leprosy. It's the first time it's appeared in such a form. Over the last few days, I've been studying medical journals, conference proceedings, academic papers, I've talked to distinguished colleagues. Well, nowhere did I come across such symptoms. No one was able to tell me anything. It's a case of a *new illness*. I'm preparing a paper on it.'

'But is it leprosy?' I whispered in terror.

'It *was* leprosy. What I'm telling you is most certain. A new form of leprosy. And I stress again: It *was*. Because now it's been cured . . .'

'How? With your ointments, doctor?'

'Yes, er, that is, to be honest, no. Just like that, by itself, mysteriously, I'd say. Anyhow, every cloud has a silver lining. You'll make medical history as the first person to produce such symptoms. And I too, as the first doctor to study and announce it.' His voice had a tone of triumph in it.

With the thought that doctors are not always entirely rational, I said goodbye and left.

5 July

Today, I again began work in the basement. I can say that I'm proceeding satisfactorily. There's been nothing of any note except, that is, for one rather strange thing. As soon as I touched the product of the first **sublimation**, I felt the itching in my hands just like the first time, for no more than a moment, yet intensely. I didn't have time to be alarmed, because it went away immediately. It didn't bother me again. I wonder if this has some connection with the work I'm doing. I'll study the manuscripts again.

12 July

I'm beginning to understand. Paracelsus maintains that

Nature functions, exists, acts and behaves independently. As an Entity that regulates its life as it pleases. Consequently, any natural manifestation expresses one part of its life or rather one of its aims. What these aims are, no one knows or can discover. All we know, that is, all we can hypothesize from what we see, is that Nature's life or organism is distinguished by its wonderful equilibrium. And this equilibrium is achieved, must be achieved, through continual effort and conscious acts on the part of this autonomous Entity. If such a theory is true, then the preservation of its equilibrium will perhaps be one of its most vital aims. So when some danger to this equilibrium arises, then Nature defends itself. But what might this danger be and, in such a case, how does the NATURA NATURANS react? I can't come up with any satisfactory answer. Perhaps because I still haven't managed to discover what relation there is between this theory and the instructions for making the **panacea**.

26 July

I've arrived at the final **sublimation**. Everything is going as it should. I'm overcome by impatience. I hardly eat or sleep. My eyes are smarting, my ears buzzing. Occasionally, I have the feeling that I'm sinking into a blind chaos, that the noises too are sinking. As if I were losing my hearing. It must be from the weariness and exertions of the last few days.

3 August

I'm extremely tired. My memory deserts me quite often. I forget even the simplest things. I make mistakes. Yesterday, without thinking, I mixed together unsuitable elements and there was very nearly an explosion. In addition, I don't see well and I can't hear clearly.

5 August

I went to the doctor's. He seemed not to know me. He said, 'what can I do for you Mr . . . Mr . . .?'

'It's Hieronymus,' I replied.

'What!' he exclaimed in surprise. 'Are you the same Hieronymus that had leprosy?'

'The very same, doctor. Don't you recognise me?'

Yes, yes,' he muttered in embarrassment. 'It's the beard you've grown that confused me.' He continued, however, to examine me carefully with his eyes. 'You also had cancer before that. It was cured, isn't that so?'

I nodded my head affirmatively.

'Well, what can I do for you? What's wrong with you?' He'd again adopted his disinterested professional air.

'Something's wrong with my eyes and ears. I can't see clearly and I can hardly hear at all.'

He examined me. Then he said somewhat pensively: 'You'll have to see a specialist. He'll be able to tell you what you have with certainty. I'm only a general practitioner. In any case, it's serious.'

An hour later.

Fear. A sense of menace all around me, invisible yet real and almost tangible. I try to stay calm, to think calmly. This indescribable fear is not without cause. On my way back from the doctor's, a persistent thought flitted through my mind. *Why didn't he recognise me*? I'm certain that he didn't. I saw it in the embarrassment that he tried to conceal when I explained who I was. Have I changed so much simply because I've grown a beard? In the space of a month?

As soon as I got home, I ran to the mirror. The cold glass returned my image to me. Yes, it was me. I recognised Hieronymus. Though I sensed that there was some change, some alteration. No, it definitely wasn't the beard. There was something indefinable about the temples, the brow, the line of the nose . . . And suddenly, I saw my eyes. I saw two eyes staring at me from out of the mirror with *green* dilated pupils. It was then that I was overwhelmed by that inexpressible fear, because I *knew* that my eyes had always been *dark* . . . I looked at myself again to make sure. Yes, *now* they were *green* I jumped away. Beads of cold sweat ran down my brow. 'Lord, what's happening?' I mumbled. My mind went straight to the **drinkable gold**. Had the potion I'd taken brought about this inexplicable change? No. The **panacea** cures each illness for good. I knew that for certain. I'd read thousands of pages on Alchemy. Nowhere was there even the slightest hint of any distortion. On the contrary. My eyes again began to smart terribly. A new worry took hold of me. Perhaps before long I'd lose my sight and hearing? Yes, for sure. I could now see only dimly and I could barely hear. Exhausted, I collapsed into an armchair. My mind refused to help me.

I don't know how long I remained like that, in a strange sinking state. Suddenly, I jumped up like an automaton, went to my study, took the hermetically-sealed pouch with the panacea, emptied a little into a glass of water and drank it. The deep sleep came quickly. I only just managed to drag myself to bed.

7 *August*
I slept for two days. I awoke, it seems, because I was unbearably hungry. I ate whatever I could find in the kitchen . . . I feel like new again, rejuvenated. I'm as healthy as can be. It's the effect of the **panacea**. I can clearly hear even the faintest noise. My eyes too no longer hurt at all. Yet they're still green. I'm starting to reconcile myself to the idea. At least, I'm trying, postponing the explanation that must exist for later.

Absent-mindedly, I browse through the translation of the manuscripts. I look at the underlinings. Once again, I halt at the phrase: NATURA NATURANS and then immediately turn to the obscure warning: **'But this must be Allowed'**. My mind dwells continually on these two phrases that are separated by pages and pages. I look again at the manuscripts. What connection can they possibly have? None. Unless . . . I take the magnifying glass and examine them word by word. Feverishly, I isolate those phrases with one or two words whose initial letters are written in capitals (for some hidden reason, why hadn't I noticed this before?). I also notice that phrases like this are repeated at regular intervals. Every five or eight lines. I copy them out, the one under the other. There's some obscure, enigmatic meaning.

Life-giving Nature
(With)holds the Red Lion . . .
The Sage must Know . . .
The Forests will be burned . . .
The Dark Depths will open . . .
The Firmament and the Water . . .
The Invisible repugnant Races . . .
Then the Equilibrium . . .
But this must be Allowed.

In the language of the Alchemists, the Red Lion is the sought-after elixir, the philosopher's stone, and also the panacea. So, I reflected, whoever endeavours to arrive at the Red Lion, to concern himself with the making of the panacea, must *know*. Know what? Here, the verb 'know' is not in the sense of 'have the required knowledge'. What then? My eyes fell on the final phrase. **'But this must be Allowed'**. The 'This' can only mean the **'Magnum Opus'** and when someone achieves this, then he has in his hands one of Nature's terrible secrets . . . A secret, of course, that does not belong to him, nor is he allowed to know it, let alone to make it known. Yet, in such a case, who is it that forbids you, prevents you from using it for the good of mankind?

I stared intensely at the obscure phrases, striving to find the answer. Weary, I closed my eyes. My mind was spinning, it plunged over precipices. I felt dizzy, as if I were falling into a bottomless well, shouting 'help, help', and a hollow and unmoved Echo came back to me: heeelp, heeelp . . . Or perhaps not? I opened my eyes. I again stared at the paper with the strange phrases. The one that irresistibly kept on drawing my gaze was NATURA NATURANS. And then as if by divine inspiration, I **understood** and, realising what it was I'd understood, I fainted . . .

8 August
Everything is clear. And terrifying. But I've made my decision. I'll keep going. No matter how great the price. The good that I'll bring to the world is far greater. My life has this one

goal. I'll make a gift of the **panacea** to the world. I'll save people from illnesses once and for all. I'm not afraid of the consequences – if there are any – that I might suffer.

10 August
I'm again working feverishly in the basement. I've almost reached the final **sublimation**. In a few days, I'll be able to produce the **drinkable gold** in quantity. I've one last doubt. I'm not sure whether I've completely understood the enigmatic phrases I isolated three days ago. I've an idea. I'll start taking the newspapers each day.

12 August
Now I'm going more slowly. There's no reason to rush. I'm at the last stage of the **Magnum Opus** and it requires caution. The newspapers contain nothing of interest.

13 August
Today, there are two main news items in all the morning and evening papers.
The first:

> SUDDEN ACTIVITY BY THE SUN. THE OBSERVATORY AT NORTH CAROLINA HAS REGISTERED SUDDEN SOLAR ACTIVITY OF UNUSUAL INTENSITY. IN THE OPINION OF THE EXPERTS, IF THIS ACTIVITY CONTINUES WITH THE SAME INTENSITY, IT MAY VARIOUSLY AFFECT THE EARTH'S ATMOSPHERE, WITH UNFORESEEABLE EFFECTS ON THE PLANET'S CLIMATE.

The second:

> CENTRAL AFRICA. FROM OUR CORRESPONDENT IN ZAMBIA. THE APPEARANCE OF AN UNKNOWN DEADLY DISEASE. HUNDREDS DEAD. IT SEEMS A NEW ILLNESS HAS

STRUCK IN THE PROVINCES OF ZAMBIA AND THE NEIGHBOURING COUNTRY. SCIENTISTS BROUGHT IN FROM EUROPE AND AMERICA AGREE THAT IT IS A NEW FORM OF LEPROSY WHICH FIRST APPEARS AS A PAINFUL ITCHING AND THEN DEVELOPS AT AN AMAZING SPEED. THOSE AFFLICTED PRODUCE BLISTERS CONTAINING PUS ALL OVER THE BODY AND DIE IN GREAT PAIN WITHIN TWENTY-FOUR HOURS. THERE ARE FEARS THAT THE ILLNESS HAS ALREADY REACHED EPIDEMIC PROPORTIONS.

If these two reports are not simply a coincidence, then what I think is happening is, alas, true.

14 August
The newspapers carry reports of a new catastrophe:

VOLCANIC ERUPTION IN SOUTH AMERICA. FROM OUR CORRESPONDENT IN PERU. THE RAMON-JIMENEZ VOLCANO, DORMANT FOR TWO CENTURIES, HAS ERUPTED WITH UNPRECEDENTED FORCE. INCREDIBLE MASSES OF LAVA HAVE RAPIDLY ENGULFED EVERYTHING IN A RADIUS OF FIFTY KILOMETRES. ACCORDING TO THE MOST CONSERVATIVE ESTIMATES, THE NUMBER OF DEAD IS IN EXCESS OF TEN THOUSAND. THE POWERFUL QUAKE AT THE MOMENT OF THE ERUPTION CREATED A GIANT TIDAL WAVE THAT SWEPT THE COASTS OF THE NEIGHBOURING ISLANDS. THOUSANDS HAVE BEEN DROWNED. IT IS A BIBLICAL CATASTROPHE.

Now, there's no longer any doubt. These events are directly linked to the **Magnum Opus** I've undertaken. For what reason? Are they perhaps ominous warnings? From who? From the inconceivable Entity that Paracelsus calls the NATURA NATURANS? And why? I again asked myself. The answer came by itself. From elsewhere. As if it were not a product of my own brain. As if my mind had heard it from somewhere: 'Because in this way the Equilibrium is in danger.' Oh Lord.

I often think that all this doesn't exist, that it's not happening. That it's just a nightmare, a bad dream.

19 August

I've stopped working at the **Athanoras**. I'm at the end. A little more and it'll all be over. The **panacea** is in my hands, at mankind's disposal. The strange thing – not at all strange anymore – is that the newspapers have not reported any news of new catastrophes. In Central Africa, the new form of leprosy that just a few days ago was threatening the whole continent is now showing signs of receding. The activity of the Ramon-Jimenez Volcano in Peru abated just as suddenly as it had started.

Thousands of human lives have been lost though. This loss weighs heavily on me. It was I who provoked their horrible deaths. My sense of guilt is crushing me. How can I atone for it? How?

27 August

There is a way. I'll prepare the **panacea**. I'm going down to the basement.

30 August

A minor mistake has cost me time. I've corrected it and am going ahead.

3 September

The doctor telephoned. He asked me if I was all right. 'How are your ears? Can you hear clearly?'

'Why of course, I can hear perfectly,' I answered. 'I can hear you very clearly, even though the line isn't good.'

After a slight pause, he asked, 'And how are your eyes?'

'I told you. Everything's fine. And . . . doctor . . . I saw them too. They're green. They're still green. Strange, isn't it? You don't know the reason why, but I do. Yes, yes, I'll tell you. Come round here tomorrow morning. I have something sensational to show you. You know my address. Knock on the door. If I don't answer, push it open and come in. My study's at the back of the house. Goodbye, doctor. See you tomorrow morning.'

I'll have finished in an hour at most. I've taken a small sample. It's almost ready. A little more and it'll have the proper scarlet colour. I've regulated the burner and I'm waiting. Meanwhile, I'll glance over my notes.

Half an hour later.

Thankfully, the newspapers have no more news. Either about sun spots, or leprosy or volcanic eruptions. In a while, I'll go down to the basement to remove the amalgam from the fire and leave it to cool. Afterwards, it'll be ready . . .

Strange . . . Something's happening around me. As if the air in the room is moving. As if it's rustling. I can't hear it, but I can feel it on my skin. Perhaps it's the darkness that's to blame . . .

I've turned on all the lights . . . And yet, despite the abundant light, there's still a dull shadow, or am I mistaken? No, no, there's something. I gaze into the mirror facing me. It reflects the bare, white wall of my study and the glaring hundred-watt bulb in the electric lamp . . . An enormous sun, blazing, yellow . . . A mountain . . . Yes, it resembles a mountain, but . . . that's impossible. The mountain is moving. It's not a mountain. It's a huge being. Its dimensions are immeasurable, inconceivable. Yet it fits into a mirror . . .

It looks like I'm hallucinating. The fatigue and anxiety of the last few days have unnerved me. Yet I'm in my study. I'm sitting in my chair. I can hear it creaking as I shift around. I can also hear the distant horns of the cars passing by on the road outside. Feverishly, I rub my eyes . . .

It's still there. In the mirror. It's green and earthy. It's moving. Yes, it's moving. A strange movement like a pulse. And it's getting bigger – or was it like that all along? It still resembles a mountain. A round, living mountain. I can make out its sides that look like an animal's fur, wild beasts and forests, rivers and seas . . . The mirror . . . that too is getting bigger, becoming huge, infinitely deep like a universe. It's getting bigger and . . . advancing. It's coming towards me even though it's unmoving. Except that it's pulsating. It's alive. It's filled the room. It is the room . . .

The doctor halted in front of the old iron gate. He saw the address: 5 Saturn Street. He pushed open the gate and entered a thick, unkempt and silent garden. He walked along the narrow path smothered by wild grass. He went up to the front door and knocked. The hollow sound echoed in the house. The doctor knocked again and, on receiving no answer, he opened the door and went inside. Hesitantly, he proceeded along a corridor and stopped before a closed double-door. He knocked and pushed open the door. Yes, it was Hieronymus' study. Empty. The owner wasn't there. He'd left, it seemed, in a hurry because the electric light was still on. 'Hieronymus,' he shouted. No one answered. He quickly searched the house but didn't find him. The doctor returned to the study. There, he found various manuscripts scattered around. He glanced over them quickly. His gaze stopped at one particular phrase, underlined in red ink: **But this must be Allowed**.

Original title: 'O teleftaios alchemistis'. First published in the literary magazine *I Lexi* (June 1987). Translated here from the text anthologised in Makis Panorios (ed.), *To Elliniko Fantastiko Diiyima* [The Greek Fantasy Short Story], Athens: Aiolos, 1987, pp. 269–279.

Actor

Makis Panorios

For Brian Aldiss

He made the holy sign and went out onto the stage. Imposing scenery. Colourful lights. And behind their glare, the impersonal audience. For a moment, he stood there motionless, listening to his heartbeat. 'I can't do it,' he murmured under his breath, and he had the impression that everyone could hear him. But as soon as he uttered the first word, 'Gertrude', the sound grew faint and eventually faded away, and he found himself all alone on the stage. He felt a sudden panic. 'I won't be any good,' he thought, even though he had regained his composure. Gertrude stared at him inquisitively, as if she had heard him. He returned her gaze with a slight shrug of his shoulders. Then he wandered through the play's myth, like in that childhood dream in which he was being chased by a shapeless form and he was running ever so slowly to escape. That's just how it was now. Everything flowed like thick liquid. In fact, at one moment as he was watching the action, unmoving and without taking an active part, he got the impression that once the performance was over, he would go on acting ad infinitum on an empty stage, surrounded by dilapidated scenery, even when the Earth had become desolate, even after the end of the world.

He'd just finished one of the more important soliloquies when he suddenly sensed that someone was watching him, someone not in the wings, not even in the theatre; someone, a presence. 'Who?' She had gone; his folks had gone. They had long before departed for Absence, and he had remained alone with his roles. And tonight, in the theatre, he had no one. Not even a friend. 'So who then?' he wondered. 'No one,' he murmured. He thought that someone was staring at him precisely because there was no one. The sensation remained, however. He immediately noticed a change in his acting. Different tones and semi-tones, different notes and nuances in the sound of his voice. Something else was emerging from inside him, another actor. He saw the change in his colleagues' eyes, and he felt a different current, a different breath coming from the audience. And he himself felt that he was no longer living a role, a literary fabrication, but rather a live creation that he couldn't possibly have imagined when he first read the play. Now, he wasn't acting, wasn't interpreting; he had been transformed, having undergone a magical change, a mythical reincarnation. Someone else was residing inside him, and it was this someone else who was leading the play and the performance to its triumphant end. And only when the audience was applauding him on their feet and he was bowing with his hand over his heart did he become himself again.

Later in his dressing room, pleasantly tired, 'what happened?' he thought. 'You acted,' answered the other's voice. 'Really?' his former doubt, and when he removed the make-up, he felt empty for a moment. He lit a cigarette, but after a couple of puffs, he extinguished it. And then he heard the silence. It flooded the theatre and everything, the performance, the play, the actors, and he, too, sank into it. He'd known this from the very first. When the lights had gone out and everyone had left, nothing remained but silence, darkness and phantoms. 'Yes, but tonight . . .' he thought, '. . . tonight I acted.' 'Agreed,' replied another voice, 'but the performance is over and you have to leave.' He got up, put on his overcoat, lit another cigarette and, slowly walking through the empty theatre, went outside as if emerging from a splendid mausoleum with its beautiful dead, a petrified forest with fabulous trees and mythical creatures, the recollection of which no longer brought him any fragrance whatsoever.

He strolled in the calm night and the stars were high, distant and cold. The ancient darkness followed him, covering his footsteps, until he eventually arrived home. But even when he sank into his armchair, he still had the feeling that the house was empty as if he hadn't returned. Perhaps because he hadn't switched on the light and the darkness that had entered with him seemed dominant, omnipotent and solid. The real inhabitant of the house. He sighed and then the telephone rang. At the third ring, he picked up the receiver.

'Hello,' he said.

'Sorry to disturb you,' said a faint and reverberating voice at the other end. 'Perhaps it's not a good time, but it was impossible for me to calculate the time difference exactly. The distance . . .' There was a buzzing and the rest of the sentence was lost . . . 'It's late, isn't it? I mean, it must be night there now.'

'Dark and endless,' he replied with a certain sarcasm. 'Like night.'

'Oh,' said the voice, 'I'm bothering you! I'm sorry.'

'Not at all,' he replied. 'No, no! You're not bothering me. What is it you want?'

'I'm not interrupting anything?'

'Only the silence,' he replied just as before. But don't pay any attention to it. Ignore it. That's what I do.'

'I'll try, though . . . you're . . .'

'All ears. Go on.'

'Right! Well, it's about your performance tonight at the première.'

'Were you there?'

'I watched it. I've seen you in all the roles you've played until now.'

'Really?' He laughed, surprised but flattered. 'Are you a fan of the theatre?'

'A seeker of talent.'

'And have you found some in me? Are you from the Ministry of Culture?'

'We call it the House of Art. And we have indeed discovered, I've discovered, a major talent in you. You couldn't have put it better. I am phoning you, then, to tell you, first of all, that you didn't just act a part tonight; you created a work of art. That's my opinion. Of course it sounds a little pompous, but that's really what I believe.'

'The critics wouldn't agree, however. In the work of art that you saw, the critics will at best see another sound performance. That's what they usually write about me, Mr . . . What did you say your name was?'

'My name's Byan of Fox-Od,' the voice replied. 'That's how we're referred to in our community.'

'Pleased to meet you Mr Byan,' he replied somewhat perplexed now.

'I'd like to make you an offer,' the voice said quickly.

'Just a moment, please,' the actor broke in. 'What's Fox-Od? A district? A town?'

'Not exactly . . .'

'Ah, yes. A community I think you said.'

'Yes.'

'What's that? It's the first time I've heard of a . . . community. And where is it, whatever it means?'

'It's in my world,' the voice calmly replied.

'It's in my world,' the actor calmly repeated. He was silent for a moment and then said, 'I see,' and smiled.

'It's a planet in the Seventh Solar System,' explained the voice, as calmly as before. 'In relation to yours, I mean.'

'I see,' he said once more. 'And it's from there that you're phoning me now?'

'From there, yes!'

'I see. And it was from there that you watched my performance, right? With the aid of super advanced technology.'

'Precisely. Even though you don't believe me.'

'You're mistaken. I do believe you,' the actor replied. 'But, Mr Byan of Fox-Od, you've chosen the wrong person and the wrong time for your joke,' and he hung up, slamming the receiver down. Then he tilted his head back and, taking a deep breath, said 'No, it's too much! It's simply too much! For the love of . . .' He leapt up, went over to the bar, poured himself a drink and downed it in one go. Then he lit a cigarette and began puffing away at it non-stop while restlessly walking back and forth. Eventually, he sat down and turned on the Screen. There was a programme with old songs. His mind wandered while watching and listening, and he fell asleep.

Later, he got up and went out on stage. The theatre was dark and empty, but he had to act for some invisible person sitting in a secret box; he'd forgotten his lines, however, and so it was with some anxiety that he began quickly spreading white make-up over his face, before going out on centre-stage in a huge light and starting to speak in a strange language but without any sound; he acted his part wonderfully, and then someone called him and he descended from the stage and passed down the long aisle between the motionless spectators who, like stone, were staring at the stage; he too turned and stared at the stage and saw himself acting with pronounced gestures and the stage was a long way away; then he opened the door that appeared before him and went out onto the street and began walking, with the same anxiety, because he had to get to the theatre where he was due to act, but he couldn't walk, his feet were sinking into something thick, he took slow, very slow, steps, and then it began to rain and, in order to protect himself from the rain, he went out on stage, and the audience, which stretched far into the horizon, immediately leapt to its feet and began applauding as if it were one man.

He opened his eyes when it grew light. A faint, grey light was coming in through the window and the first, distant sounds of the coming day reached his ears. His mouth was tart and bitter; he had fallen asleep in the armchair and the Screen, still on, was now showing a cartoon programme. He turned it off and went into the kitchen. He made a coffee and drank it slowly while smoking a cigarette. Then, he got ready to go to the 'filming'. While tying his tie, he remembered the phone-call and smiled. 'Seventh Solar System,' he said out loud. 'No doubt the man was off his head!'

On the way to the studio, he stopped for a while at the cemetery. He always did this after every première. He'd promised her. Of course, she had long departed for Absence, but she'd hear him and he wanted to talk to her. Holding the funereal flowers, he walked among the tall trees of the cemetery and the sleep of the dead. When he arrived at her grave, he stood for a while and gazed at her photo, which even now was smiling. Even now. He put the flowers in the vase and said to her: 'I came. I came to tell you that the performance went well. And I . . . I had a few good moments.' She continued to stare at him with her enigmatic smile, and the silence rising up from the ground seemed to be the only presence there. Silence and the grave. Nothing else. And perhaps this was why he turned and left quicker than ever before.

At the studio, they greeted him with congratulations, and when he began to act, a hush spread all around. That other who had always been inside him had at last emerged, like last night, and he was now acting with a new air about him. And it was this other that they all saw, it was this other that they admired and he sensed it. He savoured it. And deep down inside, he felt a certain pride. 'So, you've finally managed it,' he said to himself and, without wanting to, he smiled and the camera slowly approached him in an impressive wide-angle take.

Late that afternoon when the filming was over and he left the studio, it was drizzling. 'It's already the Rainy Season,' he thought. 'How time flies,' and he got into his vehicle. By the time he arrived, the rain had got heavier. As always, his house welcomed him in silence. He stood at the window and stared at the city as it travelled in the rain. Darkness was falling and he felt a touch of melancholy. He switched on the light and the monsters withdrew to some other darkness. Together with the solace of the light came the mythical images of the previous day's fairytale. He was once again on stage, a god bathed in gold light, light from light, a creation within the eternal creation, and the people in the stalls, in the circle and in the boxes applauding him. Applauding his work. The work of art. Wasn't that how that madman had characterised his acting?

He smiled, opened the doors onto the veranda and went outside. The rain had stopped, and the damp night, a deep shiny mauve, greeted him with its bright stars, a colourful celestial forest, and down below, the people, as far as the non-existent depths of the horizon and of the universe. He felt that universal pulse, that cosmic breath, the deeply heart-rending music of mankind, a hymn and a dirge, and perhaps for the first time becoming aware of human destiny, he thought 'I too am part of that music', and it was as if he were reconciled with mankind's fate and with his own. A shooting star etched a silver line in the sky and just as it faded, the phone rang. He went inside and lifted up the receiver.

'Hello,' he said.

'How are you,' said the voice. 'It's Byan of Fox-Od.'

'Oh yes. From the Seventh Solar System. Right?'

'Right, but please don't hang up.'

'I won't hang up. I promise. I'm an open-minded sort, I'd say.'

'Thank you. Perhaps that will facilitate our conversation.'

'Perhaps. So, is it raining on your planet at the moment?'

'At this precise moment, no, it's not raining.'

'It was raining here, but now it's stopped. But I think you must know that. So, tell me about your planet. What is it there now? Night or day? Morning, afternoon or evening? Or midnight? What?'

'It's daybreak. It's getting light, in the same way that you characterise the coming of a new day.'

'So the sun's coming up?'

'Yes, the sun's coming up. Or rising. As you wish.'

'And how many suns do you have? Two? Three?'

'Just one.'

'And moons?'

'Also one.'

'You're not well-off, I see, Mr Byan. What about stars?'

'A multitude of stars. Our sky is full of them.'

'Mountains? Forests? Lakes? Rivers? Seas? Oceans?'

'Everything. Though my planet's natural environment is not like yours.'

'Of course not. Its appearance, as you've described it, is the work of science-fiction and the cinema. Anyway, how are you?'

'We have a few differences. Though no major ones. Major differences, enormous ones, I could say, exist only on the scientific-technological level.'

'You do have theatre I presume.'

'Of the highest quality.'

'Is it different from ours?'

'Generally speaking, no. Perhaps it's a little more inward-looking. But you could yourself assess any differences there may be if you were to agree to come and perform on my planet. My offer is an official one. That was the purpose of my phone-call right from the beginning.'

'I'm astounded. And . . . in what language would I perform? Given, of course, that I accept your invitation?'

'In your native language. But the audience will hear you talking in theirs. It's a matter of technology. I should also tell you – may I go on?'

'By all means.'

'Our audience is of a high intellectual level. Particularly cultivated on account of an age-old civilisation. It will see in you what I, too, saw.'

'A work of art!'

'And something more. The poetry contained within it.'

'I see,' said the actor, laughing. There was a silence. 'Yes? Hello?'

'No,' replied the voice slowly and with a vague sadness. 'Once again, you don't see. You think it's a joke. That I'm fantasizing. Or mad. Isn't that right?'

'Listen here. Let's be serious now. No, I am not implying that you're mad, no! But it's absolutely impossible for me to believe that you are phoning me from the Seventh Solar System. Nor can I accept all that about advanced technology. That's all.'

'I have to try to convince you, however.'

'I'll give you one more chance,' said the actor, again laughing.

' "I, too, am part of that music". You thought that just before I phoned you, and at that moment a shooting star appeared in your sky. Do you remember? Well, I agree with you. It's people who are the true music of the universe.'

And the line went dead. He remained rooted to the spot with a silly grin on his face, still holding the receiver and listening to its distant buzzing. Then he carefully replaced it.

'He read my thoughts,' he said, and he suddenly felt exposed to invisible eyes, just like on the night of the première at the theatre. Then, out of the corner of his eye, he saw, or thought he saw, a fleeting movement behind him. He quickly turned round. 'Who's there?' he shouted, and his voice echoed extremely loudly in the empty room. There was no answer save for the silence. Just like a child, he bent down and looked under the couch and then behind the curtains. 'The bogeyman,' he said, and forced a laugh. He lit a cigarette and his hands were trembling. 'Such things don't happen,' he said with an appearance of composure. 'They don't happen,' he repeated uncertainly. 'I'm simply imagining them.' But he felt agitated and worried. Daybreak found him still sitting there and smoking. He fell asleep just as the sun came up.

And then, much later, when some days had passed and the cycle of performances was at its end and he had finished his final performance and the curtain fell, he went to his dressing-room and, with that touch of melancholy that always came to him at that moment, he looked in the mirror at the face that in a short while he would never see again. 'Farewell,' he said to it, and spread the make-up remover over him. Afterwards, he once again dressed as himself and got ready to leave. It was then that he remembered Byan of Fox-Od. He hadn't contacted him again during all that time. But he had become entrenched inside him. He realised it now, strangely surprised. He smiled. A charming madman. He glanced round the dressing-room in case he'd forgotten something. No, nothing. 'You'd like it, though, wouldn't you?' He smiled again. 'Why not?' And louder, 'Yes, why not?' He went outside into the fog. A couple of vehicles disappeared into the depths of the street. It was chilly. He shivered and wrapped his cloak around him. He lit a cigarette and walked over to the theatre car park. There was only his car there and the desolation of the place made him feel despondent. His opened his car door and, as he did so, someone emerged from out of the fog and came over to him.

'Hello,' said the stranger, standing before him. He was

wearing a hat and a long overcoat and he had an ordinary face, as far as he could see in the dim light. His voice, however, reminded him of something.

'Hello,' he replied. 'What do you want?' and he stared at him, then almost immediately, 'You're . . .'

'Byan of Fox-Od,' said the stranger and smiled. 'I came to repeat my offer to you in person now that you've finished with your performances and you have no obligations, as far as I know. So then, do you want to discuss it?' The actor stared at him, speechless. 'No, it's no joke,' the stranger continued. 'It's time you started believing me. I suppose I have to convince you,' and he removed his mask. The actor simply let out an 'Ah!' 'I told you,' said the stranger, in his usual calm voice. 'We don't have any major differences, but back to the matter in hand. Do you want to discuss it now?'

'Yes,' replied the actor, refinding his voice. 'Let's go back to my place. We'll be able to talk more easily there. But I still can't believe it,' and he laughed as he opened the car door. 'And what's the name of your planet, Mr Byan?'

'Earth,' the stranger simply replied.

Original title: 'Ithopios'. First published in Makis Panorios (ed.) *Ellinika diiyimata epistimonikis fantasias* [Greek Science Fiction Stories], Athens: Aiolos, 1995, pp. 95–105.

A Strange Incident

Nikos Houliaras

I'd like to tell you about a strange incident that happened to me some time ago, without however being able to prove to you that it did actually happen.

Situations like the one I'm about to describe are like the ones I experienced in the dreams that recurrently tormented me at that time. And yet I'm certain that I was awake when I experienced them and that all my senses were functioning normally.

Everything began, then, from the middle. It was as if I already had a past in that situation; as if things had already happened to me that had led me there, but something had intervened and my previous life and actions were no longer necessary.

Suddenly, I sensed that I was at the far end of a long and deserted station. I say at the end because I had a vague feeling inside me that I had already covered the greater part of it, walking alongside the iron rails.

Behind me, however, there was no open space, nor had I any recollection of how I came to be there.

In front of me I could see a long passageway leading to a large door. It was closed in on all sides and the windows in it were covered by sheets of blue paper. A series of pins, closely arranged one beside the other, held the paper to the wood without leaving even the smallest chink.

Nevertheless, there was light in the passageway. It wasn't sunlight or electric light. I'm absolutely certain about that.

It was, if I may put it like this, a state of light, which, in a strange sort of way, concerned me personally. And this was the reason I felt a sense of security even though I had no idea why I was in that place.

So, as I was standing there, more perplexed than surprised or worried, I don't know how it happened but I suddenly felt that I could see myself, just a couple of feet away, as a child.

And so it was. There before me in the passageway was myself, aged five or, at most, six. I was wearing a soldier's tunic that was far too large for me and that reached down to my ankles.

Though the spectacle was undoubtedly comical, I didn't feel it to be so. On the contrary, I viewed the event rather indifferently at first and then, with a certain familiarity, I went up to my little self, just as if it were my brother Yorgos, and I gently took hold of myself by the sleeve.

He immediately turned towards me, and it may seem strange to you, but the only thing that made an impression on me at that moment was a small stain just below his left pocket.

So I set about cleaning the tunic at that spot, rubbing it with the end of my sleeve, and though during this time we never exchanged a word, I'm almost certain that he was saying something to me, but I couldn't understand.

At precisely the moment that I was about to repeat this action one more time, I felt someone's presence behind me.

It'll be a station attendant, I thought, and I turned round with the intention of asking him whether he knew the reason for my being there.

But behind me there was no one. The only thing I saw was a shadow at the end of the passageway, which gradually became smaller on the side of the wall and vanished.

Suddenly, my senses began to function with an unusual intensity. I understood that all around me there was a continual emptying, and this realisation took the form of something thick and unpleasant inside me.

There was no longer the image of myself before me and I was overcome by a sudden feeling of sickness. It was a contradictory feeling. A bit like a lack of gravity on the one hand and, on the other, the sensation that I was getting dangerously heavier. That I might fall, that is, and not be able to get up again, or if I did get up, that it might be with a vengeance, like a smoke-filled balloon that shoots up into the sky.

I eventually managed to reach the door and pushed against it.

It opened and two clumps of dark-green laurels appeared. Behind these, I saw a long dirt path. To the right and left of it, tall ferns were gently rustling and insects were buzzing in the air as though it were a summer's evening.

The atmosphere was filled with a strange intensity caused by the light. The whole place was lit only from below. A cold light ran through the roots of the ferns and gradually faded, leaving the upper part in darkness, where the tips of the branches – blown about as they were by the breeze – seemed as if they were constantly scratching against the roof of an invisible arcade.

I went outside and began to walk, making my way through the ferns, which were now being blown by such a strong wind that I felt as if I were going backwards rather than forwards.

At almost the same moment, the sound of voices reached my ear. Broken, rhythmic phrases like the persistent murmur of people getting further away. Then they returned again, louder this time. Their rhythm changed in my head and echoed irritatingly.

I put my hands to my face and, to my astonishment, discovered that where my thick beard had been until just a moment ago, there was now a child's smooth skin. Almost without thinking, I looked down. The soldier's tunic I was wearing reached down to my ankles, and my body ended in a pair of small, red pumps.

Inside them I could make out the pattern of my children's socks: the tiny grey-green rhombuses with the perforated yellow thread running all around them as if they were little lanterns.

Then, without any forewarning, the wind dropped. Not a sound could be heard, though the intensity remained. I started walking again, more quickly this time. I almost ran, at the same time watching my feet continually interchanging in a comical manner, till I started to believe that it was the path that was moving while I remained in the same place, playing the familiar game from my childhood.

When I lifted my eyes, I almost bumped into a small wooden door. I pushed it open and, without expecting to, I found myself in the dining-room of my aunt Hermione.

There was no one in the room. Everything was quiet in there and a pleasant rumbling in my stomach made me feel as if I'd never left that room and that I'd dreamt everything that had just happened to me previously.

So I went over and sat on the couch as always. Facing me, on the sideboard, were two photographs. In one of these, my cousin Merope – a grown-up woman now – was together with two of her friends, sitting in a field of camomile. She was holding a garland of flowers and offering it with a smile to whoever was taking the photograph.

Merope. A source of grief to my aunt Hermione. So many opportunities wasted through stubbornness. Gazing at her, I involuntarily went back to the time when people were just emerging from the Nazi Occupation.

To me then, the Occupation seemed in my mind like a trick played by the grown-ups. A bogey word that they used to put us in our place.

I recall how I saw Merope often then, and the image of Mother Greece came into my mind, just as I used to see her in the illustrations in books. Tall, with long, flowing hair and a perfect nose; a straight line from her broad forehead to her shapely mouth.

Perhaps also because she often wore that long blue taffeta dress that swished as she would walk back and forth in the room, laughing.

What had remained deeply ingrained in my mind, however, was one particular summer afternoon. I was outside on the street, just below my house, and I was playing at prisoners' base, I recall, with a few others, when I saw Merope pass by looking nervous and hurrying along the path leading to the vegetable garden. She was the image of Mother Greece, with that shine in the corner of her eye as she glanced at me hurriedly and then disappeared with big strides into the foliage.

For a moment, I remained there bewildered, staring after

her. But I soon came round and decided to run after her to see where she was going.

Two of the others came with me and we dived into the foliage without making a sound. We trod carefully between the tomato plants and searched the place. She was nowhere to be seen. So we followed a tiny path of flattened grass that led us to a thick clump of reeds. We dived in and more or less groped our way towards the edge of the lake.

We couldn't have gone more than a few paces when, in the darkness, I saw her long naked legs sticking up in the air and shining, then her clenched hands flailing among the reeds and, finally, holding my breath, I saw the captain on top of her, pounding up and down, pinning her to the steaming grass.

Her long hair ran over the grass as she flung her head this way and that, and from the corner of her open mouth a tiny trickle of saliva gleamed as it ran down to her neck.

They heard something, it seems, and in alarm turned their heads in our direction.

Merope fixed me with that look of Mother Greece and then, and only then, did I realise what the Occupation must have meant to all the others.

The captain leapt up, pulled up his trousers, and then the stones fell on us like rain.

Merope. A source of grief to my aunt Hermione. The years passed and she remained unmarried. On the shelf, as the neighbours put it.

I thought of the shelf and, unthinkingly, my eyes fell on the plate-rack. I began then to notice the various objects. I again looked at the sideboard, behind the glass doors, at the crystal and the antique dinner service. They suddenly seemed worthless and insignificant to me. And yet, years before, these same things had appeared different to me. They were huge and grand. Those cupboards concealed a colourful, magic world, full of mystical flashes and musical sounds.

My aunt's daily movements in this room acquired the dimensions in my mind of a complex and incomprehensible mechanism. Never mind, I thought. Better that way. Life in its true dimensions.

I slowly got up and went over to the window. I leaned against the rail and, looking outside, I saw with some surprise that my aunt Hermione's house was no longer in the place I knew! It was now perched at the top of a still unfinished neighbourhood that ran down to a seafront. The seafront was being formed at that moment with piles of rubble, which was noiselessly tumbling down towards the water, like someone pushing rice around in a baking pan.

I remembered very well that the house had never been in this neighbourhood that I saw before me. It was the third house in Angelon Aftokratoron Street, situated exactly in the middle of a large garden, and what you saw looking through this window were the climbers on the surrounding walls and the plum trees of the house next door.

I jumped at the sight before my eyes and, not knowing what was the proper thing to do at that moment, I remained at the window and fixed my gaze on a point in the neighbourhood, in the same way that we sometimes stare into the eyes of an animal threatening us so as to make it back down.

After I eventually realised that I was not getting anywhere this way, I decided to do something a little more rational. I would go and look round the other rooms.

So I stepped back from there and went over towards the door. As I got closer, I thought I could hear some whispering and I strained my ears to hear.

There were two women's voices. I could hear them clearly now. 'He married her,' they said, 'he married her and that was the end of it.' I slowly pushed open the door, and though I expected to emerge into the next room, I unexpectedly found myself before a dark and steep staircase.

It went down almost vertically to a gallery shut in on all sides by earth, wooden beams and stones, and only at the end of it was there any light. It was the light of the moon shining on the still waters of a sea.

It was then that I once again heard the whispering echoing inside that vault: 'He married her,' they said, 'he married her and that was the end of it,' and then I saw my aunt Hermione, an old woman now. She was sleeping on a soft, raggedy little bed and sliding as she snored; going together with her bed covers towards the sea, slowly and carefully dragging a little mound of earth down to the water, which began popping with tiny bubbles, as if it were drizzling.

Original title: 'Ena paraxeno peristatiko'. Published in Nikos Houliaras, *Bakakok* [Bakakok], Athens: Kedros 1981/Nefeli 2000, pp. 105–114.

Period of Grace

Yoryis Yatromanolakis

Grace was thirteen years and two months old when she came to know her angel one Saturday on the eve of the Veneration of the Cross in the year of Our Lord 19 . . . At the same time she saw and came to know her blood. More specifically, while she was incensing the icons and had become engrossed in the beauty of the archangel Gabriel, who, high up by the window, was handing a shining-white lily to the Virgin Mary and saying *Hail Mary, blessed art thou among women and blessed is the fruit of thy womb*, she felt a chill, white air moving around inside her. In less than a minute, no longer than it takes to say the *Our Father*, the chill air turned into a wicked pain that fixed itself in a deep part of her womb hitherto completely unknown to her. And this part of her womb was unknown to her because she had never felt it and, naturally, what you don't feel doesn't exist, even though it may be there, inside you.

It wasn't long before this strange pain, triggered by some unknown cause, spread and covered the whole of her womb. Then (so it seemed to her), it was as if it did the rounds of her pelvis – where, it's said, children live, swim and play prior to being born – before coming to rest on that mottled part of a woman which both laughs and cries and has a wisp of curly hair, and which stutters when it tries to speak, since it has the lips of a hare, and which opens slightly and pouts its tiny lips when it laughs and titters. Because, Grace, from the moment that women are born, they have two mouths: one above on their face, that can be seen and heard by anyone who wants, and another below, dark and hidden, deep down between their legs. And when the one smiles and titters, the other smiles and titters too, and when the one above cries, the one below cries too. Yet, whereas a woman's upper mouth is hairless and clean, there comes a time when the lower one becomes covered with soft hair, when it bulges and swells as it lives continually in darkness and chews on nothing but itself and nibbles unceasingly just like the mouth of a hare.

Grace liked cats and wanted to be one, as these animals sleep and laze all day and, what's more, have nine lives, so that if they lose one or two, they still have all the rest. So it would have been better if she'd had the lips of a cat rather than those of a hare, which is a tasty animal of course, but extremely fearful and nervous. However, since it was her lot to have the lips of a hare, she had to get used to them and to like them because they were hers. And Grace grew and flourished together with her hare's lips and the months passed by, round and full; only February was a little lame, though this was a fine month too. And so she reckoned the time and days and embroidered her dowry, little cushions with cats, birds and tiny hares. And at night, Grace, you liked to gently touch the hare's lips and you shut your eyes together and woke up together in the morning. And then you'd take the animal out into the garden to pass your water and you'd see your warm water gushing and splashing and becoming a river; a nice little river, not a wild one, just a little foamy on the earth. But you'd never met your own secret pain, your blood or your guiding and guardian angel of the Lord.

Yet now Grace was frightened by the unfamiliar pain in her body and, perplexed, put down the censer that was still burning. It was then that just beside her she heard a voice, one neither very familiar nor very unfamiliar, neither female nor entirely male, saying to her in Greek: 'Hail Grace. O Grace hail! Fear not, for the Lord is with thee.' And she immediately realised that standing beside her was her angel, about whom she had heard so much, though she had never actually met him.

And this, then, is what she saw amid her pain and the fumes from the incense. She saw her angel live and clear, sent from the celestial regiments in which he served. And from her very first look, she realised that it was indeed her angel. She was also completely certain that they were the same age, thirteen years and two months, because every person's angel reports and is enlisted in the celestial regiments at precisely the moment that their own person is born. This is why her angel was the same height as her, had the same manners, more or less, and spoke Greek, though the angel spoke it a little oddly like a stranger from Greece of old. But there was no doubt that it was Greek.

As for the rest, though, there were several differences. First of all, it was impossible for anyone to tell whether the angel standing there was a man or a woman, since one minute it appeared to be male and the next female. Without any doubt, however, Grace belonged to that gender called female – for she had the lips of a hare. Moreover, whereas she was dark-skinned, slender with black hair and eyebrows (the dark, furry part was black with a few reddish streaks), the angel was blonde and quite chubby. He was also dressed in pure white, whereas Grace was wearing a greenish dress and her apron was in a wretched state. Finally, the angel was also wearing soft, white shoes that gleamed, in contrast to Grace's clogs. Yet Grace had the fine posture of people who have learned to walk straight with their head held high in keeping with the example of the good months (not of February) and of the saints who never bow before their torments. Her ankles were tender and smooth like the Venetian glass from which the kings and rulers of the world drink their water, while her legs shone so exquisitely at her every step that they were hardly less beautiful than her angel's. It was also hard to say whether the angel's little breasts had yet filled out like hers. As for the hare's lips, she drove the thought from her mind, thinking it to be a great sin. Naturally, she didn't make a comparison with the wings as it's well known that there is no such thing as an angel without wings, whereas people only have arms, at least while they're still alive. What happens after death remains unknown and a great mystery.

Then the angel turned and said to her for a second time: 'Grace, O Grace, be not afraid of the pain in your *womb*. It is in your body that the pain must originate and in your womb that, for entire moons and curtailed months, it must remain, exist and end, my little, inexperienced girl. And from now on, you will have to measure your life (just as the Virgin Mary did at your age) in two sets of days: those of other people, known to all and evident from the calendar, and your own, secret ones that only you will know each month. And still more, Grace, I have to tell you that when women with their hare's lips go to bed, they are not permitted to touch and fondle these lips. These have to remain pure and unsullied, because it's from here that babies come out into the world and cry. And it is not right for women alone in bed to fondle themselves and, in the darkness, to clutch the hare because the animal may become afraid and be roused. And if it is roused, it may gnaw away at the woman's body so that she remains sick and pale. Only when the woman is married and the holy sacrament of marriage has been performed and the couple wed with all due honour is the husband permitted to touch the hare and fondle it. For then, even if the animal is roused and its lips redden inside, it doesn't matter. It will give out its own smell, will wriggle this way and that and foam, but it will eventually find contentment in company with the man. Yet this, too, Grace, must not happen continuously. But for now, since you have a pain in your womb, go and open the sugar tin and take a large spoonful, but no more. Then, go and change straightaway, put warm towels on your womb and don't go to church tomorrow, because you are with blood and unclean.'

And it was not before time. For, at that same moment, apart from the pain in her womb, Grace had a deep feeling of nausea inside her that almost caused her to faint and fall. And not only did she suddenly find herself with an overwhelming desire and craving for something sweet, but, as she dashed into the kitchen to take the sugar tin, she heard such a terrible voice coming from within her that both she and her angel were alarmed. In an instant, she opened the tin and swallowed not one but three spoonfuls. Saliva mixed with the unchewed sugar began trickling from her lips and down over her chin and white neck and, though her mouth was already crammed, she tried to swallow a fourth spoonful. But her angel was soon beside her and in a severe (though not angry) voice said to her: 'Grace, Grace, don't you know that greediness, and particularly greediness for sweet things, is a great and terrible sin? Oh Grace! The way you're carrying on, you'll succumb to the sweets temptation and not only will you be punished for falling into mortal sin, but you'll become fat and obsessed with sugar and syrup.'

Instead of feeling reassured, however, and realising the importance of that moment, Grace felt an even stronger craving for something sweet and believed that only by eating as much sugar as she possibly could would the pain in her womb perhaps stop. It was then that all the voices in her body again joined together, producing such a loud cry that her angel, being a celestial spirit and unused to loud noises, was taken aback and jumped up above the icons. Free to do what she wanted, Grace plunged her hand into the sugar tin and began licking her fingers, without being the slightest bit concerned as to whether she was giving in to temptation and would find herself eternally damned to Hell, where there is neither joy nor coolness. Yet her angel, who was there to protect her and guard her from evil, was afraid that if he let her eat sugar while she had the pain in her womb, she would succumb to the temptation for sweet things and then not only would she fry in hellfire, but he himself would have to answer to the one to whom angels generally report and give account.

Whereupon, he leapt lightly to the ground, stood beside Grace, and said: 'I'll allow you to eat one more spoonful of sugar, Grace. But no more, otherwise . . .,' and he shook his finger sternly, 'you'll succumb, my poor girl, to the powerful and irresistible sweets temptation and then nothing will be able to save you. Not to mention that it's Lent!' But Grace had already surrendered to her fate. Mad with pain, she pushed her angel aside and dug into the sugar with a will, trying to swallow it all to make the pain stop. And just as she was about to finish the sugar in the tin, Behold Grace! A wild wind, new and terrible, suddenly stirred. Everything shook and trembled. The burning candle shook and went out and the little black coals fell from the censer. Even your embroidery, Grace, a tiny white cat with a black patch on its forehead, was shaken like a leaf and turned into a rag that disappeared into the corner. And behold! There, amid the dense and powerful wind, mighty and irresistible, appeared the sweets temptation.

At first, Grace thought that another angel had entered the room, since the newcomer hardly differed from her angel. Almost immediately, however, she realised the difference. Whereas they were both wearing roughly the same clothes and had, more or less, the same build and features, her angel smelled of fragrant soap and rosemary, while the other was inundated in the smells of mint, cinnamon, vanilla, honey, treacle and chocolate, too. All these sweet smells created such a strong desire in Grace that all she could think of was to take the new angel into her arms and squeeze him tight (crush him, more like), smell him, lick him and eat him whole. And, as if understanding her desire, he not only went up closer to her – almost sticking to her – but he also smiled at her so sweetly (as they say) that Grace felt dizzy and would have fallen to the floor if the newcomer hadn't caught her. And, close together as they were, he immediately began to take from his clothes and wings and body all the sorts of sweets and syrups, of toffees and sweetmeats that Grace craved and desired.

First of all, he let her try the special sweet for those betrothed, a silver dish of honey with lashings of walnuts and a dash of powdered cinnamon to offset the sweetness. Although Grace knew that they were not betrothed nor did she have any connection with betrothals, not only did she not refuse the sweet from the hand of the temptation, but she ate three whole platefuls and felt very sweet herself. She then wanted a glass of cold lemonade, or at least a little water. The temptation (ready and willing as ever to oblige) clapped his hands and immediately there appeared before her a row of glass carafes filled with cold, delicious drinks. Some were filled with lemonade and orangeade, others with barley-sugar and cinnamon juice with powdered ice, others contained crystal-clear water. With all the water she drank, she began to think of vanilla. She immediately ate two spoonfuls of vanilla, licking the spoon clean and biting it. Once the drinks had offset the sweetness, Grace saw that spread over all the tables in the room, and even the chairs and floor, were countless jars containing the most wonderful preserves, cups of all sizes brimming over, coloured and painted plates all filled with strange and delicious sweetmeats, next to clean, silver spoons that shone in the half-light. First, she tried her favourite sweet, apricots with aromatic syrup and with a white peeled almond in the middle. Next, she ate all the jar of figs together with the clove, and smelled the fragrance from her mouth. After the bitter-orange came the grape, and after this the quince, both sliced and chopped. This was followed by the white pear, the whole of it, then slices of peach and, afterwards, plums and chestnuts dipped in sugary syrup. For the first time in her life, she ate sweet aubergine, but she preferred the cherry and the morello which was slightly tart. Then (having plainly succumbed to the temptation), she began running round the room and tasting the other sweets that she had never seen before and finally, when she had tasted them all and was used to them, she began mixing the contents of the various jars, smeared as she was in syrup and sugar. Tastes hitherto unknown and smells unfamiliar and intoxicating inundated her as she filled and emptied the spoons, and the plates, coloured cups and glass jars rang empty. Till the pain in her womb suddenly stopped. Or at least that's what she thought.

All this time, Grace's angel had been sitting greatly dismayed in one corner, with his lovely blue eyes filled with tears and with his face lowered, not wishing to see what she was doing and so become even more upset. On the contrary, the sweets temptation was skipping to left and right and, smiling and happy, brought everything that Grace desired. So when she asked him for a rose-coloured Turkish delight ('But plain, without any almond,' she told him), the temptation brought her three or four large boxes wrapped in coloured paper that must have cost a fortune. The thought that the temptation may have stolen them never even crossed her mind and, full of curiosity and anticipation, she began to open them. One was full of pink Turkish delight, another with green, and another with Turkish delight the colour of honey, all of them sprinkled with powdered and fragrant sugar. And together with the Turkish delight came halva, strips of nougat, bars of sesame and honey, bars of dark and crispy chocolate, chocolates filled with rum, mint, cherries, almonds and hazel nuts, together with truffles, cream buns and chocolate buns, macaroons, baklavas, kadayif and custard pies, all fresh, almost straight from the oven.

No one can say with certainty just how long Grace went on eating sweets and drinking chilled pop, orangeade and barely-sugar. Evidently having grown tired of watching, her angel had long since left the room, whereas, relaxed and attentive, the sweets temptation continually provided Grace with whatever she wanted. In fact, once when, completely covered in syrup, Grace had sat down on the bed, the temptation reached into an invisible and bottomless pocket and emptied onto the sheets thousands of toffees wrapped in shiny coloured paper, which, so the temptation said, had flavours for all the parts of the body. Flavours for the mouth, the tongue, the palate, flavours for the arms and legs, flavours for the eyes and ears and flavours, O Grace, for the lips of the hare!

Grace knew the flavour for the mouth, the tongue and the palate. But she knew nothing of, nor could she even imagine the other flavours, particularly those that delight the lips of the hare. So, she was about to ask, but the sweets temptation didn't seem at all willing to explain anything. Just the opposite. At that moment while she was stuffed with toffees and enjoying the flavours for the tongue, the temptation suddenly appeared to be in a hurry. 'Now,' he said, 'I have to be going, Grace, because there are other women with pains in their wombs and they are waiting for me, too. But before I leave,' he said to her, laughing, 'before I leave, I'll give you a sweet that you've never seen or tasted. You can't find it anywhere here in Crete. Neither in the town of Herakleion with its many confectioners', nor in the renowned town of Chania. Perhaps in Athens, or Greece of old – but it's not sure you'd find it there either.'

So he spoke. And, immediately, all the sweets, toffees and sweetmeats vanished. Grace's bed made itself and looked neater than she'd ever seen it and on its clean sheets shone a large, round (like an Easter bun) delectable sweet, completely unfamiliar and unknown to her. 'Cake,' the fragrant angel said. 'I've brought you a whole cake, Grace, the kind eaten and enjoyed by the rich and powerful in foreign lands. Eat now that you're unwell and your pain will cease.' And he took hold of a strange knife (where it came from no one knows) and cut an enormous triangular piece for her. 'Look,' he said again in his strange Greek, and pointed to the piece of cake. 'This here at the bottom is the first layer of the sweet and all its art and flavour rests on this. It is called sponge and is made from sugar, flour, cornflour and eggs and has been soaked in rum and brandy. On top of this is the second layer: thick, white cream made from full-milk and melted chocolate, mixed with caramelised almonds and slivers of dried figs and bergamot. Then we again put a thin layer of sponge to keep the filling in place, then another layer of cream with chocolate and almonds so as to make the cake rise like a tower. And where the layers end, here on the top (and he pointed to the top with the knife), those little white mounds that you see are of Chantilly, Grace. Which means that it comes from other, foreign lands. Go on and try it, and you'll never forget this sweet. Come, my child, try it, don't be afraid. For only if you eat of this sweet will you have knowledge of the difference between good and bad sweets.'

And abandoned as she was to the ecstasy of sugar and syrup, Grace couldn't resist, even though stuffed and sick of sweets and pastries. And she didn't simply eat one piece – that first one offered her by the temptation – but got stuck into the whole cake with a will and began tearing at it with her fingers, taking the mangled pieces and greedily and wildly wolfing them down. Nose, lips, chin, cheeks and neck were all smeared and her lovely face was distorted by cream, chocolate and Chantilly. Her bright eyes were shut, her eyelids sealed tight and her arched eyebrows sticky from the sugar. Her whole mouth was full of the cake's fresh flesh. Till the cake was finished and all gone. And then (though when exactly remains undetermined) everything suddenly stopped just as it had begun. Sweets, angels and temptations disappeared from the room; the candle shone with a steady flame and the censer was again burning in front of the demure and handsome archangel.

The blood lasted for four consecutive days, Saturday, Sunday, Monday and Tuesday, till Grace had learned to clean herself and change her towels. And all through those days, there was neither sight nor sound of any angel of the Lord or of any sweets temptation. There was nothing but the soft pain in her womb, which gradually died away and disappeared deep inside her body.

Twenty-six days passed between the Saturday of the Veneration of the Cross and Good Friday, the day of the Holy Passion, of the spear and the gall. In the afternoon and following the Service of the Hours, while, together with the other women, Grace was decorating Christ's bier, she suddenly felt a desire for something sweet. The smells from the roses, the lilies, the hyacinths, the lemon and orange blossom and from the half-opened lilacs became mixed with the smell of vanilla and caramel and the whole church smelled of roasted almonds and sugared buns, from the Sanctum to the women's pews at the back. At that same moment, Grace saw her angel fluttering high up on the altar screen, dressed just as he was the first time and watching her with his big bright eyes which were shaded slightly by his long eyelashes. And it was at that moment – while holding a big yellow rose, the colour of infidelity and jealousy – that Grace again felt the sharp pain deep in the depths of her body and felt the blood trickling, drop by drop, down to the lips of the hare with the black fur and the red streaks. And of all the women in the church, only she heard her angel speaking to her once again in a human voice: 'Grace,' he said to her sternly. 'Leave the church immediately, Grace, for you are with blood and unclean. Go home, change and put warm towels on your womb. And resist the sweets temptation, because today (and he stressed the word "today"), only vinegar and gall is drunk for love of Christ and His passion.'

Grace left with the yellow rose of infidelity and jealousy and, beside her, she could hear the rustling of the angel's wings. Weary and breathless, she arrived in her room with its icons and fell onto the bed, doubled-up with pain. And there, in the darkness and quiet, she sensed the triumphant and irresistible sweets temptation, sugar and sweetmeats coming from afar. Grace asked her angel to allow her to at least drink a glass of water with half a spoonful of sugar dissolved in it. But this time he was determined to protect her from temptation and infidelity. 'No sugar,' he said, 'or water. Just lie on the bed without speaking or moving,' and he began locking and bolting the doors and windows. And when she obeyed and snuggled into bed, he, too, took off all his clothes and, naked ('neither man nor woman,' Grace reflected), lay beside her and took her in his arms.

No sooner had the angel of the Lord done this than a terrible and terrifying banging was heard at the doors and windows. The house creaked to its very foundations and the walls shook and the floors moved this way and that and many glasses and plates fell from the shelves and shattered. And the sugar tin opened by itself and the white, powdery sugar spilled from the shelf to the floor, and the air filled with the smell of mint, cinnamon and chocolate. This was the last thing Grace was conscious of before swooning in the arms of her angel. And when (exactly when no one knows) she came round, she no longer had any pain from the blood nor any craving for sweets. No sound could be heard in the darkness. There was nothing but a barely perceptible light that seemed to start from the angel's body and inundate the room. And in this blue, celestial light, Grace, you saw that you had hold of your angel in your mouth and, like a baby, were licking him and sucking him. And like this the poor wretch was melting and had become almost transparent like paper. And you realised that during the entire period of your pain and blood, you had been doing nothing, Grace, but holding the angel in your mouth and licking his fingers, his wings, his fair hair, his lovely naked legs and, in fact, every part of him, whether heavenly or human.

Like this, you spent four days of sweetness and pain. Good Friday, Holy Saturday, Easter Sunday and Easter Monday. And all this time, Grace had hold of her lovely, transparent angel, ceaselessly tasting, licking and sucking at his tender limbs. And if she suddenly had a desire for preserves or pastries, she filled her mouth and her palate was pleased by that particular sweet. And if she wanted apricot with almond and syrup, she had it immediately. And if she longed for morello, chocolate, stewed apple or pear, plain or fancy chocolates, she had them all and ate her fill. But those strange sweets with the foreign names, with the unknown ingredients and wonderful combined tastes brought by the temptation were left unsampled by Grace. Nor did she eat any of the toffees with the flavours for arms and eyes and for the lips, both the visible and the hidden ones. Most likely she didn't want to. Or perhaps she felt shy before her angel and didn't dare ask him for such things. Besides, she wasn't all that sure that he could provide her with all these flavours. So she stayed with what was familiar to her.

At daybreak on the fifth day, the Tuesday after Easter, Grace woke up clean again and without any pain. Her angel was still sleeping beside her, pale and exhausted, almost unrecognisable, so much so that Grace felt sorry for him and decided that she should give him something to eat. When, however, he opened his lovely, blue eyes, his angelic beauty and the light of his heavenly body once again shone bright (even in his weakness and paleness). And he immediately got up out of bed and lightly went over to Grace, who was brushing her black hair in front of the window. Because the time had come for him to leave, for him, too, to go and celebrate the Lord's Resurrection, albeit belatedly. For him to go and wash and bathe and brush his hair and don new, clean garments and eat whatever angels are in the habit of eating at Easter and on the other major feast days. Besides, he had to gain weight again and form and reacquire all his limbs in full because, as he said, smiling coyly as he flew past Grace like a fair wind, 'For the last four days, Grace, I've been melting in your mouth. O my dear, sweet Grace.'

Original title: 'I periodos tis Eirinis'. First published in Michel Faïs (ed.), *Kimino ke kanela* [Caraway and Cinnamon], Athens: Patakis, 1998, pp. 29–40.

The Conquerors

Dimitris Kalokyris

I've been voyaging for ten lunar months. I can already feel my head growing, my limbs getting longer, so we must be getting near.

My place of origin was a droplet of flashes. I have no real memory of that realm, I simply reproduce certain data, like everyone else, concerning semi-astral bodies, gravitational lenses, black holes and dark matter; passions of the blood and paths of the tongue. A disturbance in the breathing forming nuclei. The sound of laughter disrupting the depths. Metallic fireworks in dream's flowering fields. What does all this mean? I don't know.

Over the network, I send thoughts, which are automatically recorded in the collective memory. As too the instructions, like a sensation of ocean in the arteries: looking at the eyelids in decay's dampness, smelling the silence's butterfly, grabbing the pockets of light from your chest, suckling the 'I' in sleep's lifeboat, eavesdropping on how the meteors come about. Existing even before you.

Inside here temperatures and definitions prevail. The liquid surround limits the vibrations for me and the warmth is agreeable. The vessel jolts continuously; it undulates, contorts, recoils and leaps. It is designed to choose its course by itself and to bring me safely to the destination ground. Night and day I can hear the monotonous sound of the main mechanism overhead. So I survive mechanically and coordinate myself with its beats.

Here and there I notice lights. To be precise, these are faint movements, shadows appearing outside the walls. Distinctive noises, momentary earthquakes, distant vibrations from the roots, dizzy, elliptical voices, in the obscure idioms of the unknown.

*

They say that as soon as you arrive, huge clamps seize hold of you and shake you; they promptly cut your respiratory tube and from then on you're obliged to inhale a cold gas. In general, what prevails outside is coldness, low frequencies and emotional outbursts. However, it seems that you quickly grow accustomed to it.

Theoretically, I know only too well what awaits me. First of all, I have to learn to live with more oxygen; on emerging, you are cut off from the internal feeding tube and are fed for some time by the vessel's external pumps. You also swallow various lukewarm substances that the locals persist in offering you. Later, you grow accustomed to food pleasantly altered by the temperature.

For several years, you remain inactive. You employ only a very few vowels, while secretly learning their language, their expressions, their silences. Initially, you are not permitted to speak; though you can cry freely. Forever. Because in their world we are regarded as the future. The more you learn about them, the more pleased they are. And the easier it is for you to move among them unnoticed.

(Warning: should they discover you, demand that you be treated as a prisoner of war. There are treaties, constitutions, blood protocols that we have signed, and it is worthwhile your becoming familiar with these in case of need.

The record of their administrative system's shortcomings is known as the law.)

Anyhow, it's amazing how quickly you become acclimatised and how easily you come to resemble them, so that sooner or later you begin to develop unhampered, without anyone realising the differences between us.

At the beginning, through signs and secret gestures, some of us meet regularly, supposedly by chance, in the open air or in enclosed areas, murmuring the words of our own language. We crawl on the ground, climb over artificial mountain ranges, roll in the sand, spin in colourful vehicles. Afterwards, we gather in special buildings where we are trained in the processes of profit and obedience. We gradually learn to forget our original language. We also learn about loneliness. We memorize the mechanisms for penetrating the countless systems and each of us eventually takes up a temporary position. All the positions are key positions, no matter how insignificant or humble they may seem.

There are no innocent professions. Nor is it of any significance whether you enlist in the ranks of the future leaders or evolve into a suckling vessel. For there is often a disturbance in the world order when the pilots temporarily unite with the vessels; this union takes place in conditions of red alert, which demand a great consumption of sensory organs, deep breathing spasms and abundant moisture. The internal hydraulic network is called after sensations; ideas are moistened south of arguments. When the vessel reaches critical union with the leader, then we begin vast journeys. Submersions through aquatic portals.

Care is required, therefore, when it comes to liquids! One of the most serious problems in these parts is water. They hold it in great regard and employ it abundantly in a variety of uses. It is, however, the main factor in decay. It gradually permeates everything; it inundates and destroys bodies, the ground, the entire planet. We avoid it at first as much as possible, but eventually, we grow accustomed to this too. Just as with everything.

Water has to do with the material part of their organism. Their software is influenced to a great degree by the process of covering the body with various materials. The most common of these are called 'fabrics'; these are responsible for every aspect of their behaviour. I am impatient to learn how exactly.

Our aim is to inconspicuously conquer every inch of this world. The lands, the allegories, the phenomena. We will undermine the fauna with unsteady flashes. We will press, we will advance, we will sacrifice ourselves if necessary, we will even turn on our own . . . The aim eradicates the means. In this is the message. You will crush their absence with tenderness.

The chief antidote for the liquids is light. I can't quite recall its definition.

Ah! Memory is a similar issue: whereas at the beginning you know everything, the water that we absorb erases the archives in the helixes, the past blurs and you live virtually in a stupor of information that you don't have time to process. Consequently, each one of us discovers everything from the beginning each time: the wheel, the fire of words, the hardness of labour and so on. Whatever era, whatever century we happen to arrive. As if nothing had existed before. They call this reconstruction of the world God.

Time is formed in a river that you attempt to cross by swimming in reverse. Sometimes fragmentary images from the past are illumined. This usually happens during periods of recharging, which last for several hours each day. It's then that the Others lie down in silence, close their eyes and temporarily disconnect themselves from their world. This process has a religious character and is seen as a way of practising for the Unbounded Darkness. While they are in this state, they don't come into contact with any water and so they regain their strength. We usually sink into this space in order to relive the visual anarchy of the past, though, over the years, the past too will be completely forgotten, so we simply see incoherent images from a future that we will one day imagine.

The Images of Sleep are like a kaleidoscope: by shaking slightly, the same materials are recycled, yet always produce a different visible result. You can't plunge twice into the moistness of the same dream. Each time you close your eyelids, you are with us. When you open them, you'll find yourself with them again.

That Unbounded Darkness is the place where we forget. The space that contains the infinite. It has many names, many genders, but no meaning. It is feared by all. Why? We'll find out.

⋆

You will live as a vehicle of death.
You will dream vaguely of ever-changing loves.

⋆

It looks to me as if everything is ready in the reception zone. The lights have been turned on. Instructions and voices can be heard. The capsule's placenta is reacting rhythmically. I wrap myself in the moist clouds of light. Is it raining? A flood of fluid exhalations. I dream of arcades with lightening speed. I feel palpitations. I am afraid and delighted. Everything is going according to the letter, in keeping with the plan. The machine is jolting rhythmically and screeching. Again and again. Am I waking now or being launched? Smiling faces are appearing. Blood. A slight panic. I'm choking! They hold out their hands to me. Sudden agitation. Exodus. As if I'm being born for the first time.

It makes me want to cry.

Original title: 'I kataktites'. First published in Dimitris Kalokyris, *To Mouseio ton arithmon* [The Museum of Numbers], Athens: Agra, 2001, pp. 96–101.

The Other Footpath

Demosthenes Kourtovik

The story I am about to relate is a true one. It happened to me personally in the summer before last. Otherwise, I have to admit that I wouldn't have believed it. I would have said that if it is not totally fabricated, then it is the creation of the mind of someone whose memory, through dream's subterranean logic, had linked together two entirely different things: something experienced by this person and something he had read or heard at some other time or under different circumstances. In this case, however, such a thing is out of the question. I recall only too well my amazement and anxiety when I experienced this event.

I was with an old girlfriend on the island of A. We had spent a week in a rather remote seaside village and we'd decided to move for the last two days to the island's port as we'd grown a bit tired of the quietness of the place. On the eve of our departure, we thought of going up the hill to visit the main village. But not by car, taking the road, but on foot, taking a footpath that our hotel-owner had suggested to us.

It was a little after midday. It was hot, but the footpath was smooth and reasonably shaded, and so we didn't find the climb too strenuous. My girlfriend was in front. She was wearing a long skirt in lovely combinations of earthy-colours and she had a delightful way of walking. I thought how much I loved her and how perhaps I hadn't shown it to her as much as I should have during the previous days. Our old passion had suddenly and wildly flared up again in the village, and between the moments of intimacy, I withdrew into myself, confused and not a little regretful, as I knew that it wasn't at all an easy relationship. But now, as I watched her gliding up the path, I felt overpoweringly in love with her and was sorry that we would have to part the next day.

At the top of the rise, the footpath crossed over a wide dirt road and then continued straight on through a large field of apricot-trees. Behind the field, the first houses of the village could be seen clinging to the slope of the steep hill.

We didn't spend very long in the village; we simply had a coffee and then made our way down the other side to have a swim in a lovely little cove. While we were sunning ourselves after our swim, something happened that upset me. My girlfriend said to me suddenly:

'I don't like the look of those two black moles under your arm. You ought to see a doctor.'

I'd had them just as they were for fifteen years, without any change. I told her as much and she didn't go on. But it seemed strange to me that she'd only just noticed them for the first time. She knew my body from way back and the previous week must have helped her remember whatever details she'd forgotten.

On the way back we hardly exchanged a word. It was already late afternoon when we reached the village. We roamed through the streets with their pots of basil and bougainvilleas, and my girlfriend took photos continually. At one moment, while we were standing and gazing at the view to the south from a vantage point, she turned, hugged me tightly and kissed me.

'I've had a wonderful week with you,' she said.

Evening had begun to fall when we set off for the port, going back the way we'd come. It was a walk of no more than three quarters of an hour. We crossed through the field of apricot-trees and when we started down the footpath, the light had already begun to fade.

After five minutes or so, I began wondering whether it was the same footpath that we'd come up by. It seemed quite different to me. The ground was softer, less flattened and somewhat damp. The vegetation to right and left seemed thicker. I couldn't recognize any of the places we'd passed on our way up. I confessed my anxiety to my girlfriend. She told me she had been having the same thoughts, but that it might just be our impression, because the light was now different, and in any case it wasn't so important since this footpath was also heading down towards the port.

We walked on for another ten minutes when I suddenly became convinced that this was not the same footpath. To the right appeared an old marble fountain. I saw some Arabic characters engraved on it, obviously something in Turkish. I was absolutely certain that we hadn't passed any such fountain as we were going up. Nor did my girlfriend recall having seen a fountain of any kind. We both halted in bewilderment. It was now almost completely dark and tall ferns sprang up all around us. The atmosphere had something foreboding about it; I don't know if it was the sudden coolness that made me shiver. I suggested to my girlfriend that we go back in order to find the right footpath. If this one didn't go to the port, it would be extremely difficult for us to find our way since it would soon be pitch dark. But actually it was something else that had alarmed me: it was quite improbable that we'd taken the wrong path. First, because the footpath crossing the field of apricot-trees was a straight extension of the other one and, consequently, anyone coming that way would continue, even if distracted, on the correct path. And second, we hadn't seen any other footpaths close by either going up or coming down.

I wanted to go back to solve this puzzle that had started to torment me. And I also wanted to get away from the unpleasant feeling I had in that place.

My girlfriend objected, however. She said that there was no point in our searching in the darkness. In her opinion, it was probably the same footpath, but because it was dark and we were walking more carefully, we noticed details that had escaped us on our way up. She also said that she was tired and was in no mood for any more adventures that day. Finally, she told me I could do what I wanted, but that she would continue going down and that she was sure she wouldn't get lost.

And so we separated at the marble fountain. My girlfriend was almost immediately hidden by the foliage. I turned round and started walking back up, almost running.

After a few metres, I began to feel as if someone or something was following me. I could hear a faint swishing behind the ferns to my right. At first, I thought it was the leaves rustling (though there was no breeze) or a large lizard, or even a snake scurrying away. However, the barely perceptible noise continued in parallel with my course. I suddenly halted and strained to hear. There was no sound. Alarmed as I was, I supposed that I'd attributed the noise I myself had made by running to some other cause. I took a few steps forward, still straining my ears.

And then, from the same direction, came another noise, equally faint, but very different from the previous one. It was a deep, gruff murmur, intermittent and strangely monotonous, as if mechanical. It was a bit like a frog's croaking, but I knew right away that it wasn't a frog. Between intermissions, there wasn't just one sound, but many confused ones. I broke into a cold sweat. I wanted to run away. However, I summoned up all my courage and shouted as loudly as I could to my girlfriend; I asked her if everything was all right. I heard her undulating voice coming back to me from far off, or so it seemed to me, that she was fine and that there was no problem. So then I set off running.

When, out of breath, I arrived at the edge of the field of apricot-trees, everything was clouded in darkness, yet there was more light than there had been down below. I looked back. I could see nothing moving. I hurriedly walked about fifty metres to the left and then to the right. There was no other footpath anywhere. I halted for a while, undecided, full of agonising emotions. Absolute silence prevailed all around. I started walking again along the dirt road and after about ten minutes I emerged onto the main asphalt road. Striding out, I made my way down to the port with my heart pounding.

As soon as I entered the hotel, to my great relief I saw my girlfriend sitting on the veranda and chatting unconcernedly with the hotel-owner. She told me that, as she had correctly foreseen, the footpath had led her straight to the port, roughly to the same place from where we had set out earlier that day, though she wasn't sure whether it was the *same* place.

I said nothing about the sounds I'd heard; I simply mentioned that I hadn't found any other footpath round about.

'But there is no other footpath going to the village,' said the hotel-owner.

'Well,' I said, 'we lost our way coming back and took another footpath.'

'Did you perhaps go off to the right towards M.?' he asked (mentioning the name of one of the island's beaches).

'No. We crossed the field of apricot-trees, just as we did when we were going.'

'Then there's no way you could have taken the wrong footpath,' said the hotel-owner. He was over seventy, but he was active and had all his wits about him. For anyone wanting to buy a plot of land on the island, he was, so we'd heard, the best source of information.

'Is there a marble fountain anywhere along that footpath?' I asked him.

'Marble fountain? No.'

'Well, on our way down, we saw one with Arabic characters.'

I saw him suddenly become alarmed. He looked at me as if he'd seen a ghost and then said, drawing out his voice and stressing the syllables one by one:

'You can't have seen any such thing.'

'No, it's true,' my girlfriend broke in. 'There was a fountain, though it seemed made of plain stone to me, rather than marble. And I don't recall seeing any Arabic characters.'

The hotel-owner remained pensive for some time and then, with an expression of distrustful resignation, he muttered 'anyway, perhaps I don't rightly recall.' We said nothing more about our adventure. The hotel-owner brought us some melon, told us a lot about his life and his activity during the Nazi Occupation, about his handicapped daughter, about the balance of political power on the island and, finally, he asked us whether we might be interested in a nice plot of land. A little after eleven, my girlfriend said that she was tired and was going to go up to the room. I felt like staying a little longer on the veranda or, even better, going for a walk alone. But it was our last night together and I got up to follow her.

'Stay a while longer, I've something to tell you.' The hotel-owner whispered to me, taking hold of my arm.

I told my girlfriend that I'd be up presently and I stood there, waiting on the veranda. The hotel-owner went into the reception and returned holding a small book. It was an old account of the island, published in 1938. The hotel-owner thumbed through the pages, stopped at one and showed it to me. It had a drawing.

'Is this the fountain you meant?' he asked.

It was the very same! I had no doubts at all. The caption said: 'The fountain of Khalil Bey'. I told the hotel-owner, who now looked alarmed and stared at me once again as if I were some kind of fiend.

'Come and sit down,' he said eventually.

He sat at the other side of the table as if wanting to keep some distance between us. He remained pensive for a while, so it seemed to me, looking straight ahead at the sea, and then he began. All the time he was talking, he never once turned his gaze towards me.

'That fountain no longer exists. It was destroyed by the locals during the Occupation or just before. Not even the footpath exists today. It's become buried beneath earth and bushes. You have to know where it is to make it out. When I came to the island in 1962, the old folk used to recount a tale: before the war, a young wife was having an affair with the son of a blacksmith and they would meet secretly at night by the fountain of Khalil Bey. There was a lot whispered about that affair. One day, a cashiered gendarme, a good-for-nothing in the eyes of the locals, was found murdered there. There were those who said he was watching them and that the blacksmith's son got wind of him and killed him during the argument that followed. Others said that the woman's husband, a merchant well on in years, but with money and influence, paid the rogue to ambush his wife's lover and do him in, or do them both in. But things turned out differently and he became the victim. Nothing was ever proven. Anyhow, shortly after the killing, the two illicit lovers left the island and never returned. It was said about the women that, after various adventures, she ended up in Athens in a brothel. How can anyone know what to believe, now? Nevertheless, after the rumours about the woman's demise, some old women started putting it around that when the two fornicators met, they became transformed into demons who tore to bits anyone who happened to be around the place. Stuff and nonsense. Yet even those who scoffed at the old women avoided going by the fountain of Khalil Bey, especially after sunset. They considered the place to be haunted. They preferred the other footpath, the present one, even though it was a rougher path at that time and a longer route. Later, it was rumoured that the water from the fountain of Khalil Bey was infested (naturally, the old women said that at night the fountain spouted blood not water). Well, after all that, it wasn't long before they demolished the fountain and the footpath fell into disuse . . .'

He slowly nodded his head as if pondering over what he had just recounted. Then, he at last turned to me and said with the wry smile of someone catching a rascal red-handed:

'Now tell me the truth. You've read this book, haven't you?'

'No,' I replied.

'Okay, then the story I've just told you is one I made up!'

'Now don't play tricks on me, Ilias!' I exclaimed. 'Was there another footpath or wasn't there? Did an illicit couple meet at the fountain or not? Did a murder take place there or not?'

'The footpath existed, but it doesn't exist any more. As for the rest, don't tire yourself. Folk here make up a whole bunch of tales to pass the time.'

'We're not talking about folk, we're talking about you,' I said.

'I wasn't here in those times. But what's it to you if what I said happened or didn't happen? Let's say it happened. How are you going to explain what you say you saw?'

I had no answer to that.

'Come on,' he said, again with a wry smile, 'go upstairs now, the girl's waiting for you. And tomorrow, when your head's clearer, think where you might have heard about that fountain.'

He said this with emphasis, almost as if exhorting me, so much so that I sensed that the whole business had affected him more than he was willing to let on.

I was and am certain that I hadn't heard about the fountain of Khalil Bey before. As certain as anyone can be about what he's seen or heard in forty years of living.

When I entered the room, my girlfriend was fast asleep.

The next morning, we left the island and in Athens went our separate ways. Since then, I've had no news from her, with the exception of one postcard.

Several months later, the hotel-owner wrote to me, telling me that he knew of a plot of land, the location and price of which would interest me. At the end of the letter, he asked me how my girlfriend was doing.

Original title: 'To allo monopati'. First published in Makis Panorios (ed.), *Ta prosopeia tou tromou* [The Masks of Fear], Athens: Nea Synora, 1998, pp. 111–124.

Nostalgic Clone

Aris Marangopoulos

To Anne and Patrick Poirier for the idea.
(*Le pouvoir des bibliothèques*, Albin Michel, Paris 1996, p. 299)

1

I am writing from a land that is distant and happy. I am writing in the words of a person who grew up in the Selves' Library. If I don't write the required *information*, I'll automatically die. So I write. Though I reserve the right to draw a little information too from the Others' Library. Just a little. So it's quite likely that you'll locate it. If you search you may detect foreign loans. But I proceed as I've learned and as I know how. As I learned from the very moment I was born and as I've known how for some time now. Let me speak and you'll understand. Don't jump to conclusions. Just keep your apparatus open.

Our Library, that of the Selves, is a star and at its centre is the Jukebox. It's from here that the Rooms with the laser books are determined. Laser books, each consisting of millions of gigas, are automatically read by means of the Information Jukebox. From here, the Information is channelled into any network providers: either into those in the main Reading Room, or into the personal ones at home or into the Biosphere's offices. Information from one laser book to the rest is passed at the speed of ten billion operations per second, providing the user, virtual or actual, with the possibility of multiple combinations for finding, linking and verifying the information in only a few seconds. There can be no Biosphere without the Jukebox.

All the above ('Our Library, that of the Selves, is a star,' etc. etc.) is always written automatically. The moment you begin writing to a non-authenticated recipient. It wasn't me who wrote this. I ought to add, too, that not a soul sets foot in these Rooms. (It was me who added this.) Apart from the slave-technicians, no one else visits the Rooms. This is why there are many who believe that the Rooms are completely virtual and that the Information comes from elsewhere, from some vague Unknown. I don't believe this. Whoever believes such nonsense hasn't *read* enough. (*Belief*: useless information; more useful: *Knowledge*.) Don't worry if you don't possess such systems. Provision for such systems had been made on Earth from as long ago as the end of the twentieth century. But if you don't possess them, it's not the end of the world. And that it's not the end of the world, I know only too well. There are some others here who live without a Jukebox. Whether they live better than us . . . I still don't know – bear in mind that everything I'm writing now is mine, totally mine – but what is absolutely certain is that there are others who live without a Jukebox.

The library classification system for laser books is of interest. Besides, it's the one thing that was preserved unchanged from the existing pan-American civilisation – at least until the moment of its disappearance in 2040. Our politicians, intellectuals and slaves, without exception, all agreed that this classification was the most important legacy from the former existing civilisation. It was also considered to be in keeping with our own vital Ideas concerning the preservation of our Selves' civilisation and this is why, with some minor corrections, we kept it unadulterated and didn't tamper with it.

The Others appear to have a much simpler classification system. But the Others don't live off the Information Library as we do. *The truth is that they maintain it so that they can say that they too have a library.* (I wasn't the one who wrote this. I might have written it some time ago).

Now, I'll give an example; I'll call up the word *propaganda*: you can find relevant entries by means of the Jukebox in almost all the library's laser books . . . such an entry doesn't exist among the Others. Not even a trace. And I'm in a position to know. They live in their own little world. At times, they seem no different to slaves. They read very little. *I was the one* who wrote this, even though it's like what the Library writes. I have my reasons.

Now I'll very quickly describe for you the famous pan-American classification (of the Jukebox type) that takes pride of place in our Library's Rooms.

01. Room for extinct peoples and civilisations
02. Room for extinct languages and dialects
03. Room for historic persons and events
04. Room for mythical persons and events
05. Room for mythologies and religions
06. Room for biographies and autobiographies
07. Room for mass desires and narcissism
08. Room for holocausts, national censuses and cenotaphs
09. Room for ethnic cleansing and genocide
10. Room for religious and political doctrines
11. Room for the instruments of doctrinal worship
12. Room for heresies and deviations of all kinds
13. Room for philosophical doctrines and non-implemented Law
14. Room for fanaticisms and political agreements
15. Room for the instruments of wielding power
16. Room for genealogies and apartheids
17. Room for futilities
18. Room for aesthetic rules in every age
19. Room for progresses
20. Room for regresses
21. Room for national literature and art
22. Room for erotic literature and art
23. Room for literature and art passa tempo
24. Room for classical literature and art
25. Room for useful literature and art
26. Room for widespread languages and idiolects
27. Room for metaphysical symbols and allegories
28. Room for travel and epic descriptions

29. Room for E.M. (= Essential Memory)
30. Room for developing theses in general
31. Room for developing antitheses in general
32. Room for burial rites and related customs
33. Room for erotic rites and related customs
34. Room for strategies of success
35. Room for terrorism and strategies of fear
36. Room for punishments
37. Room for objective illusions
38. Room for audio-visual illusions
39. Room for geographical maps and the drawing of boundaries
40. Room for idyllic spots
41. Room for deserted spots
42. Room for built-up spots
43. Room for scientific utopias
44. Room for political and social utopias

Information on everything. We've left nothing out. Try to find something that doesn't exist in these rooms. It doesn't exist. Everything is here. Everything that led the Earth of Information to its pan-American heyday. Everything that permitted and permits us to live in this viable Biosphere.

Ha, ha, ha. It's the first time I've done that. Don't think that *these* are the Rooms. That is, in a way, *these* are: the forty-four Rooms. They're not. Let me explain. Quickly. Before.

All right. I deceived you. I've just described to you the Rooms controlled by the Jukebox – but as they came to me. I myself don't know how they all came to me so amazingly, one after the other. It's at times like this that I astound myself. *That's literature, not information*, I might venture to add. Literature, information . . . six of one, half a dozen of the other, you'll tell me. And yet, for some, these slight differences mean a great many things; they do count.

Anyway, the Rooms turned out wonderful and, what's more, with amazing speed. Just like then with Ulma when I was young. I once again deceived, I played, I DIDN'T INFORM. You probably don't understand, but it doesn't bother me . . . These aren't the real names. I altered . . . I ALTERED MANY OF THE ROOMS' NAMES. Ha, ha, ha. It's the first time I've done that. Don't ever think that these are the Rooms. That is, in a way, they are. They're not. Let me explain. Quickly. Before. Soon the auto-regulation will start. I don't know. Perhaps, that is, I'll disappear before long. But I enjoyed playing with the names of the Rooms. I'm happy. Why? Like then when I was young. Because these aren't EXACTLY the names of the Rooms. They are and they aren't. I changed them somewhat. Not somewhat, *a lot*.

When I was young, I played at this with my sister. I know the game perfectly well. We always joked about the names of the Rooms. We changed them at random. And then we'd play with ourselves. It was a wonderful combination to be able to play with yourself and at the same time to play with the names of the Rooms. Ulma would say, for example, in a serious voice: 'Room for History,' and straightaway go down to her rosy fragrant labia with devotion and selflessness. I'd reply immediately, 'no, madam, the Room for Fear,' and as I watched her bending over and attentive to herself (as though I hadn't replied to her at all, as though she hadn't even heard me, as though I wasn't there), I too caressed and petted myself with corresponding devotion and selflessness, half-watching her and waiting for her to "call" another Room, gripped as I was with nervous excitement. The examples I just mentioned (History, Fear) were the first that came to mind and sound very pompous. Then, we used to give other names, more spontaneous, more amusing ones. But I have to hurry, THIS IS NOT THE POINT, I urgently wanted to tell you something. I have to hurry, you have to hurry. We grew up with this favourite game of ours. Together with some other kids. This game made us feel somehow different. But I can't go on with this topic . . . though I'd certainly like to . . . Time is against me. I'll tell you only of the important things. Any time now, it's certain, surely, the accursed auto-regulation is going to start.

2

I'm writing to you from a land that is distant and organised. My country is the Jukebox and my world is the Biosphere. Who might be out there? Who, in fact, is receiving this message? No one? Someone, surely. Before the auto-regulation gets underway, I must give you a little information about the Others. Ha, ha, ha. A *little* information . . . That's a laugh. As much as I can, at least.

The Others live like slaves. They do all the work themselves. They don't have slaves. The Others are few in number and know even fewer things; they're still using pre-war books. Whatever they do, they'll never become very many. Because they still use parents. The Others seem different. I mean: different from each other. They're not like us Selves. We Selves are Selves and we don't change; we don't have any such worries. That's good. Not to have to worry about this and that. Whatever you need, whatever you desire, you find it in the Library. You search, find, go on. It's not bad. All the information is suitable for all of us.

I recall, as an adolescent, going through the Rooms like a wild pony. How often I got lost in Rooms 22, 27 and 37. How often Ulma and I played hide and seek in Rooms 35 and 44. In Rooms 07 and 33, a woman gave me my first lessons concerning my body. Using my apparatus, I went back and forth for a whole age through the combination 01, 15, 17 and 44. It was a whole age it was; that's where it all began, in Rooms 01, 15, 17 and 44. Yes, now I know, that's where it all began; a small step before the Biosphere's Information was able to enfold me in its sweet elation, misfortune came unexpectedly. What I just wrote sounds like a silly little poem:

Before the Biosphere's information
was able to enfold me
in its sweet elation
misfortune came unexpectedly.

I'm going completely crazy. A little poem, indeed! Ha, ha,

ha! But I'll go on with my story as hurriedly as I can because the matter is now pressing. I was the most perfect Self. I looked through so many Rooms in the Library during those years; I consumed more Information than anyone before me had ever read. Who knows from what intercrossing such a Self as I was fashioned? Now it's too late for me to correct myself. I read, read, read. I filled to bursting. No other Self ever went through so many Rooms. None of us ever made such crazy combinations from Room to Room and from book to book. I've no idea how I became such a fanatical bookworm. What was I looking for? I don't know and I probably never will. It was as if not I but another self of mine was searching, some stranger, miles away from our viable civilisation. It was this stranger who directed me, calmly, silently but steadily . . . and I went along. This and only this has determined my life's direction ever since . . .

And so I eventually arrived very close to complete Information; and if I didn't embrace it, if I didn't acquire it, this was because (I've since learned that) its name is: Boredom. It's impossible to find peace if you pass into this. *It's impossible to cram any other information into boredom.* At this point, you eventually feel the interminable void enfolding you in its terrifying coldness. Death is not far away. It awaits you. There's no salvation. But, to my great good fortune, I managed to bury myself in the Library of the Others. Judith. It was then that I understood how the soul's astral void is filled. I wanted to go on living.

Now I can reveal this too: the 'game' with the Rooms that I'd previously been playing was not so spontaneous. I simply wanted to delay the Information's course towards auto-regulation. *Was it perhaps a game, though, because the Self that I am knows how to play from childhood? Did I simply play in the Rooms in order to focus your attention on our Jukebox?* These two questions were not mine. Notice how the second one is particularly suspicious. From the moment that the auto-regulation begins, the Information from the Library automatically enters the apparatus. Before long, when the auto-regulation has gone even further, my apparatus will flood with data, words, concepts, entries and information from the Library. Don't leave, however. If you're receiving this message, receive that one too. You never know. Perhaps. Never know. When my regulation begins, you'll understand. Because I won't resist. Because there's no *possibility* of my resisting. (*Resistance*: for information on this see Room 35 . . .). And, naturally, I'll die.

So I want to have time, before the situation becomes desperate, to describe to you the rooms in the Others' Library. Because you, my probable messengers out there, because you out there may, I don't know, but you may be able to judge. You can judge who lives the better life. Where am I sending this message? No one can say. Perhaps they live better in other Biospheres. Perhaps somewhere far from here, somewhere else, they haven't yet reached Biosphere 5. It's to all of them, to you, that is, that I'm talking.

I'll say it again; the Others are few in number. There are a hundred times fewer of them than us. But I'm wasting time. Quickly, I have to quickly record their Rooms now. How do I know them? Judith, she's an Other. We met at a Meeting and since then we've communicated through cybertime just as I'm communicating (?) with you now. In addition, we meet about ten times a year, at certain Meetings, when Selves and Others gather to arrange the common adjustments in the Biosphere. It's theirs too. A small part is entirely theirs. Yet, for some strange reason – that I haven't time to learn – without Others, life in the Biosphere is not possible.

We're linked together in this protected piece of earth. The Others also live in their Library, what else can they do, but more so they look at each other or do servile jobs rather than read. Yes. I have it from Judith. They try to read as little as possible! It sounds very strange. When it was in their texts (both laser ones and many pre-war ones) that I discovered my life. I discovered a better world. I found something useful to do. I found a goal that made me what I am today.

Suicide. I don't regard what I'm doing now as suicide. The apparatus lost no time in writing that it was plain suicide. If this word is repeated too often, you can be sure that it's not mine. I'm not committing suicide. I'm very happy to 'sacrifice myself' for an idea. In the past, this happened for a load of crazy ideas and millions of people gave some meaning to their lives. Why not now? I sense that the Others live a more interesting life in their Library. *Sense*: useless information? But how might I *know*? Quickly, the Rooms; I must hurry to record the Others' Rooms, I've committed them to memory. For a year now that I've known her, I recite them every night like a love song; they recall something of the pre-war Earth, when the Earth was not simply that dirty ark that looks like a vegetable greenhouse.

01. Room for vital instruments and techniques in general
02. Room for the senses
03. Room for silences
04. Room for fragments of memory
05. Room for inexhaustible readings
06. Room for classic desires
07. Room for untold desires
08. Room for poor days
09. Room for old days
10. Room for good days
11. Room for beloved objects
12. Room for ages
13. Room for pleasures
14. Room for coincidences and for déjà vu
15. Room for illusions
16. Room for real and dream places
17. Room for flora and fauna, water and seas, hills and air
18. Room for mental disturbances
19. Room for physical disturbances
20. Room for forgotten utopias
21. Room for death

There, I've recorded them, anyway there weren't so many. Now you understand what I was up to before with the Jukebox Rooms. I 'fashioned' them in the image and likeness of the

Others' Library. Can you spot the differences? Can you understand? I know these Rooms here so well. As if I'd visited them. As if I'd known them from my unknown mother's womb. To tell you the truth, I don't know why they should live better than us in this Library. It's just something I sense.

And then there's the look. Not only Judith's. Their look is 'richer', stronger, I don't know, it has something that makes you feel good, deep inside. And then they're different. The Others are different. They're better looking. Different. And yet they're the *same*, I mean they're not divided into intellectuals, politicians and slaves. We live divided and isolated. They all live the *same*. They all do the *same* things. They read so little. This is something in particular that I can't accept. 'One day you'll understand,' Judith replies meaningfully, whenever I ask her about it. 'You'll understand why we, who are the last and who love books more than anyone in history, read so little . . .'. But I don't really understand. And their Library is so small, so few gigas, so few Rooms, such indifference . . . They're certainly different people. Yet that impassioned look of theirs is after all reassuring; it calms your soul.

3

I'm writing to you from a land that's distant and wounded. On the one hand there are we Selves and on the other, from as long as I can remember myself, there are those Others. *From as long as I can remember myself, the Others have always been few, always enthusiastic for a few moments before falling into despondency again.* This was not mine. The apparatus wrote it *using my words.* The auto-regulation is proceeding wonderfully. Now it's certain. It's proceeding unexpectedly quickly. They're not despondent. They're nice and different. Their Rooms . . . The Rooms in their Library recall closed gardens from the pre-war years; they seem so happy, at least when you look at them through the apparatus . . .

Yet through the apparatus, everything in the Libraries seems different. We, too, probably don't look so revolting when you look at us from afar: so flawlessly identical, so clean, so consistently infallible and organised around our giant Jukebox. From outside, through the apparatus, it's different. *But real life is inside there. In the Library*. No, that wasn't mine. Though it could . . . While we're on the subject, I've no idea where real life is concealed. How could I?

Is it perhaps in *there*? I've used up my entire life reading in order to find out and I very nearly died in the darkness of the most frightful boredom. And I've no idea either if there's anything in their Library. And if *I* found something in there, is it simply that there's something wrong with *me* who found it? In other words, is there some intrinsic *flaw* in my construction? In which case, it's not worth the trouble of informing the others in cybertime about this something.

The only assuredness I have at this moment for this action of mine is that silly little poem that I accidentally fashioned a short while ago. Because no such thing has ever happened to me before. And because I thoroughly enjoyed it. Just as I really enjoyed the game with the names, of the Rooms, the real names of which you'll never learn from me. It's this unexpected pleasure that is guiding me now. I care nothing about auto-regulation and such like. Nothing.

It's me telling you that I succeeded in detaching myself from my like; that I succeeded in sacrificing myself for a vague idea. Maybe if I were more careful, I'd pass over safe and sound to the Others, without anyone noticing. Only God knows what I might have done to cross over to the Others. Since we've touched on the topic; another useful example, *God*: from what I know, the Selves, my few friends, my informants, and the women I mixed with in my classified life, all those without exception who accompanied me till now that I'm about to die, insist that they know everything about God (see, for example, Jukebox Rooms: 05, 07, 10, 11, 12, 15, 27, 32, 34, 35). I claimed the same, of course, until recently. On the contrary, the Others refuse to discuss the subject. *In general, they discuss very little and (here, in my view, lies their greatest flaw) think even less*. No, not even this was mine. The auto-regulation wrote it. No, the Others discuss everything *and* think. Imagine. What stupid nonsense that was.

My dearest Judith, I'm losing you. I'll enclose your sweet look inside me and . . . But what am I writing about . . . I got carried away. I'll get right back to the previous question; about real life. Let me formulate it in a more practical way: what does it mean when someone 'has a good time' in the Biosphere? A Self, an Other. It's no small matter. The Selves maintain that only those who have passed through all the laser Rooms are in a position to know the answer. But no one has ever been through all the Rooms. Take me, for example. I've been through infinite combinations and what have I understood? It's right what the older ones in here say: 'It's impossible to go through all the Rooms. You don't have enough time, death catches up with you.' It sounds like a little poem again:

It's impossible to go
Through all the Rooms, you know
Before you can say Jack Robinson
Your time's up son, you're dead.

Harmless twaddle. Though it does me good. Writing to you from a distant and desperate land, I've decided (now I realise) to *do as I please*; some will say that I behaved like a typical Other. These people, no doubt about it, continually *do as they please*. You can't control them, you can never be sure of their actions as you can with us. Nevertheless I didn't cross over to the Others. For the simple reason that I still have my reservations. Besides, I haven't managed to go through all the Rooms in their Library.

However, from the few that I have gone through, I managed to understand a little. I've no complaints. At first, Judith led me to the combination 03, 04, 07 and 09. You can't get enough there. When I first went in, as if by magic, the boredom fell apart like old paper. It was another world. I recalled something. My self found something ancient and pre-war.

Elation, that's the word. For a year now, I've been going back and forth through the combination 03, 04, 07 and 09. I could live with these books alone. What else could anyone wish for in life?

Judith says that there's a lot, a lot more still to be deleted. There are millions of bits of useless information that you can erase in order to give survival a few more chances. I got rid of quite a few laser books in 03, 04, 07 and 09. But I also read quite a few that were genuinely worth the effort. For a whole month we went through the combination 01, 18 and 19 together, just so that I might get an idea what crap the world contains, what unnecessary, monstrous information could be erased without leaving any trace behind . . . Of course, the combination 01, 18 and 19 will never be mine, just as the combination 03, 04, 07 and 09. But even so, I got something out of it, I understood something.

If I were a more patient type, if I were more cautious, I could go freely through the Rooms of the Others for a long time yet. I could do a load of things together with Judith. But given the kind of Self I am, I don't even know how to behave towards her. I keep feeling that something is escaping me, that I'm missing something. I can see the perplexity depicted in her eyes too.

I couldn't bear it any more. I betrayed myself. Listen well, all you out there: there's no worse thing in the world than boredom. There's no information that can alleviate it. None. And so I revealed myself. A fathomless, unknown *inside me*, came out. I almost became *someone else*. As I write to you now, I'm less of a Self than ever. And so I'm dying in peace. Just as once, through the Jukebox, I verged on complete Information, so now it seems to me that I'm verging on complete Knowledge. That's why I'm writing to you. Visit the Others' Library. As quickly as possible. Help so that the waste piled up by the surviving pre-war civilisation might be converted. Seek civilisations with hills not built on, ages with unpolluted water and air, go through the Rooms that I went through. There are so many useless books that we could destroy. Not a trace must be left. So few books that deserve to remain throughout eternity. A word to the wise. Why shouldn't a few souls be saved? *Resistance*: this old, useless information now acquires a fresh meaning. And as the meaning is being recreated, I'm leaving you.

4

And now it's I, Judith, who am writing to you. And not from any distant land. There's only us, the few who have remained. Together with the clones like poor Ulmo, who was writing in the apparatus just now. It's a known fact that there can be no Biosphere without the Library. Nor clones without the Jukebox. I know, it's inhuman, we fashioned it on the model of the American Library of Congress, as everyone knows. In addition to Ulmo, quite a few others have been self-regulated. Though not out of boredom. Out of nostalgia. But they don't know it. They never learn it. They just suffer. The poor wretch was looking for real mountains and seas like those he'd read about in the pre-war books. He was looking for small inconsequential things that have no connection at all with the Jukebox. He was searching in cookery books for dishes that it's impossible to make here, he studied handicraft books for clay, wood, iron, non-existent materials . . . Those who reach that point go on to develop a huge and insatiable desire for little inanities of the sort.

He went through our Rooms happily erasing; he erased thousands of *other* inanities on which he'd been fed over so many years – the ones we drive ourselves crazy trying to erase because there's no end to them. Those that we didn't erase at the right time and the result was what happened with the pan-American model and the clones. Those that condemned us to life in this miserable Biosphere.

Did I love him? If that's love. But it isn't. How could it be with a clone? You look into his blank eyes and try to find something in his irises that might distinguish him a little from the next one. There was that accident which obliged us to immediately enter Biosphere V. We were trapped in it. So we couldn't bring out others and we couldn't bring out varieties. Now it's too late. All the clones came out in the image and likeness of the pan-American. That was the one available during those difficult hours and that was the one we brought out. And then again, we couldn't risk being without clones. Very few of us had remained. If you don't know about the Biosphere, you won't understand a word of all this. If you don't know about the Biosphere, you're very lucky.

In any case, and to finish, there comes a time for certain clones like Ulmo when they start to feel *nostalgia.* Then, automatically, all the information concerning the surviving civilisation, with which they're fed in the Biosphere, crumbles and loses its meaning. In the deepest recesses of their beings, these clones, though programmed with the pan-American model of artificial intelligence, that is with all the pre-war information which allows them to survive in subservience, without resistance and demands, suddenly *lose their life-support centre.* They become nostalgic. Which means: they become mad, horrified, ill; they can't endure the fact that they're clones, that they stem from people, that these people fashioned them in the image and likeness of the pan-American nothingness. They want at all costs to return to the pre-war man. It's that simple.

Some begin to suspect something, even when still young. They simply accommodate themselves to the quiet and easy life we've secured for them through the Jukebox. They accommodate themselves with mathematical consistency in a tolerable trance. They have the necessary politicians, the necessary intellectuals, the necessary slaves. Nevertheless, if they come to realise (as in the case of Ulmo) that they have the *possibility of return*, the information concerning the suppression of human needs on which they had been previously fed, crumbles, sheds its leaves like trees in autumn used to – and they themselves immediately rush to bury themselves in our Library. This marks the beginning of the end. It goes without saying that we've taken care to make it virtually repulsive, impenetrable, useless for their measured and calculated lives. But once these Selves become nostalgic, nothing can stop them. They understand. In our Library, they find the warmth of Knowledge; what at any rate it's impossible, by definition, for the Congress' Jukebox to give them.

The outlet provided by auto-regulation didn't exist when we got trapped with them in the Biosphere. The possibility of nostalgia was unthinkable then. We introduced auto-regulation in the ninth year of the Biosphere a little after the first symptoms of deviance had appeared. So that the clones could at least choose 'freely' their own deaths. It sounds horrid, but as everyone knows that's how clones are. If you allow them to live like people, they go mad from raging nostalgia. For the time being, there's no better solution than auto-regulation.

For our part, we do whatever we can so that the Library gradually becomes limited to what's essential. We allow every clone suffering from nostalgia to 'play' as much as he wants in the Rooms. Their imminent death produces the same symptoms in all the Selves. That dizzy, unexpected knowledge of human folly gives them enormous, frenetic strength. In a very short time they are able to erase huge amounts of information. Every nostalgic clone is invaluable for survival. At the rate of nostalgia that we have at present, in a few years the Library will have been expurgated to a degree that will allow us to work on a new model of survival that will come close to the pre-war one at its best.

When the Library has been completely expurgated from the pan-American model of the past, when we arrive at the absolutely essential texts, when the information and narratives fashioning the suppression of needs have been disposed of and the lost knowledge returns, if nothing else at least we'll know where we're going, what possibilities remain. *This reversely progressing Library and those nostalgic clones are our only hope.* Ulmo was one of the lucky ones. He found me. I showed him something more than real life: a little tenderness. Though I don't know if he left happy.

Now after all this theorising, normally you ought to be suspicious of me. I too have burdened you with information. There was no other way. Many more Ulmos will be needed, many more clones will die, steeped in nostalgia and knowledge, before we . . . Having come this far, there's no other path open. In the Biosphere, no one has any doubts about that. There's no longer even one supporter of the pan-American model. Everyone knows. Life here doesn't allow much margin for choice. I'm not going to add anything else. But because there's always the possibility that you may be suspicious of me, I'm now going to join my voice with his final words. Ulmo's, that is. I deliberately kept them till the end. I began writing on the apparatus at the same time that he . . . Final words. Yes, it's better that you should be left with his image.

He kept our Library's Rooms in his broken memory like a prayer. I'll do the same, letting his final words fly through cybertime like a prayer – even if they're not: 'and yet I still have my doubts. I'll die with these doubts. I don't believe that the Others have found the Path. Otherwise, we'd know about it. Otherwise, we Selves wouldn't be so many and so identical. We wouldn't exist. We wouldn't be living in the Biosphere. We wouldn't . . . At least both they and we would have the strength to abandon this stupid Jukebox, which perhaps you might be envious of. We'd blow the wretched Biosphere to smithereens and, hand in hand, we would disintegrate into infinite space like astral dust.'

Original title: 'Nostalgiko klonari'. Published in Aris Marangopoulos, *Glykia epistrophi* [Sweet Return], Athens: Ellinika Grammata, 2003.

Dream Scholarship

Evyenios Aranitsis

The apartment where Frilos lived with his father was in the southern sector of Atlim, the new city, but the boy still remembered the time spent in Dithira, the hut on the shores of the lake, the palace of the little heaven and the face of the governor on the sole occasion that he had shaken his hand; finally, he recalled the spring evening when he'd walked with a spring in his step as far as the house in the wood. He also retained other images, fragmented by time, his mother for example, the two letters that she'd sent him from prison, as well as the dignified attitude she'd maintained when her very own husband had denounced her to the Horios for breaking the law concerning radioactive medicines. 'You were unfortunate,' the old man said looking first at Frilos and then beyond the horizon, where distant stars were being transformed into novas through noiseless explosions. After every dream he had, Frilos became even more beautiful, his skin was like ivory, his eyes were cold and deep, his hair formed waves of lace like the morning frost. Every now and again, he would close his eyes to think, and then the old man reminded him that he had to be careful each time he travelled in time, particularly if he did it in ways that were prohibited. The Horios maintained that it was only with the help of machines that you could travel in time, whereas these techniques seemed much simpler and much more enjoyable too. The old man also advised the boy to properly study the differences between times and to avoid the Horios, though discreetly. Something not so easy to do.

Very few historical cities were left now. Frilos knew that Atlim was one of the first image-cities and that this should be considered as something that strengthened its renown.

The locals referred to it ironically as the 'instant city', but the Horios said that its design corresponded to the design of the visible universe and that if anyone were to lose their orientation at night in the twisting corridors, they could easily find their way again by using the star-filled sky as a map. Most likely, however, this was simply propaganda. From the time that people were deprived of their ability to dream, sleep had become a state of temporary death, though to offset this, reality acquired a dream-like aspect and this was what the Horios were trying to exploit. The old man often spoke to Frilos about the experiments being carried out in the Centre on gifted individuals who were still able to dream. There was nothing they liked more than playing with electrodes. Apart from this, they were intrigued, almost tormented, by the idea of penetrating, through dreams, into the deeper nature of time, given that they had only managed so far to come up with a mechanistic model of it.

On the contrary, all that had remained of Dithira were the ruins and an even more extraordinary legend. This dead capital awaited the return of time. Built on transparent girders, it resembled, at first sight, a suspended system of scaffolding, with squares rising into the void above invisible bridges and buildings that hung between arches and slender columns. The forest had penetrated beneath the abandoned neighbourhoods, and among the creepers and bushes lived wing-wolves and sleepy, brawny lizards that lived on insects and garbage. Those silent ruins provided a truly ideal playground for the kids who escaped from Atlim's southern districts and who cut through the vegetation to get to Dithira, where the quest for adventures far from the eyes of the grown-ups was ten times more enjoyable. For their games, Frilos and Nidros preferred the old aqueduct, the central section of which recalled the Roman Colosseum. Around the arena ran a labyrinth of overhead conduits and piping, and it was here that strange rituals took place, together with invocations to spirits and dramatic representations resembling the Horios' weddings. Frilos didn't tell Nidros about the existence of the old man; it was a secret and keeping it made him feel strong. He initiated him, however, in the use of techniques that he had been taught in the forest at night and that made their games even more exciting. The master didn't always object to the pupil sharing certain skills with his friends, provided that he didn't reveal how he had acquired them. In one of these games, a somewhat dangerous one, they often ended up by swapping bodies, and Frilos would enjoy looking at himself in the mirrors of arcade 26, the only ones to have remained intact, and seeing Nidros. The former gave the appearance of being rather delicate, whereas the latter was more sturdy, yet they had been inseparable from the time that their parents had worked for the company, long before Frilos' mother was arrested by the Horios. They chased each other in the labyrinths, and Frilos, now running in his friend's body, always managed to catch up with Nidros and grab him. He found it funny to suddenly come into contact with the body that until just previously had been his own. Then each of them would assume their own bodies again and lie down under the glass mirrors of arcade 26 amidst the huge anemones. It was then that the wing-wolves, aroused by the smell of sweat, sprang anxiously from the thickets, whizzing across the surface of the water like purple arrows.

The old man had to keep on at him until Frilos realised that you can choose any time to go to. He explained to him that certain times existed only in books and that others got confused with each other in mistaken calculations when the Julian calendar was revised. Often, the lessons would acquire a somewhat poetic aspect, and one evening the old man described the gate of entry to 1780 as a form of curtain that opens onto a rough seascape, adding that this was one of the most spectacular voyages aboard a Portuguese sailing ship. The old man referred to all this, at the same time showing Frilos sketches in books written in Dithiric languages with complex ideograms, like the engravings on ancient tombs. Together, they leafed through the books and played with the significance of the page numbers. The number four, said the old man, is the number granted by Hephaestus to Apollo, the pagan equivalent of the creation of the Sun and Moon on the fourth day. And the number ten, that Pythagoras believed expressed the very arrangement of all the worlds, is the weapon of logic. Yet the truly fundamental expression is the number seven, the music of the heavenly spheres, the states of human existence, the scales and the senses. Then the lad got as far as the number fourteen, and the old man referred to the fourteen apocryphal texts, to the fact that Osiris' body was cut into fourteen parts, and to the fact that Frilos himself was fourteen years old, exactly at the age when his eyes were changing colour. 'Play on your own,' he told him gently, 'otherwise, you won't learn.' Frilos was hesitant at first, then he began to play. While searching for page twenty-one, he learned that the world's archetype is the almond, which matures twenty-one days after the blossom falls, and on page twenty-eight, he came across the division of the zodiac into twenty-eight Houses. During the course of discovering this apocryphal knowledge, the lad made no comment but, inside him, a hotch-potch of dim and fragmented impressions began acquiring some rudimentary order. 'That,' said the old man, 'means that you've already dreamt it all . . . And besides, that's the reason I chose you.'

The old man, of course, had unlimited opportunities to meet, even to associate with, any human being of his times or any other time, but he really wasn't interested in becoming familiar with narrow-minded and garrulous types who felt absolutely nothing other than fear and a morbid curiosity. Frilos was different, and the old man had liked him from the very first, because he had sensed that his extreme introversion would help him to understand that there are as many opportunities for journeys as there are worlds in every bundle of dreams. 'My job,' he explained that first evening when the lad had come to his house by chance, having taken the wrong path in the forest in order to escape a wing-wolf, 'is to make them dream of me.' And on another evening, he stroked his beard and openly confessed: 'the way you fall silent causes everything to stop, young man. . .'. This was the first time that the boy had smiled, and the old man looked away and stared into space. He himself never smiled, or laughed; he simply fell silent or spoke in whispers.

Frilos, who was extremely intelligent even when he didn't feel happy, usually reacted to what he heard with a fluctuation in the look in his eyes. Then, they would go for a stroll in the forest, and the old man would talk to him of the attributes of plants. One evening, they found a sacred mushroom close to the lair of a wing-wolf that Frilos put to flight with his thought, in order to show the old man that the lessons hadn't been wasted. The sun had begun to set and the treetops had disappeared into an ocean of pulsating purple. 'This here,' said the old man with an unhurried gesture, 'helps you to see the true dimensions of place, which are not the length and breadth, but rather the strength of the relationship between each individual thing and the rest . . .'. They went on even longer walks through the forest, going as far as the outskirts of Dithira, and the old man taught the lad the secrets of the use of herbs. He showed him vrithy, which only drugs women, and ringwort, which provokes nausea in the Horios, but which can, in other circumstances, save a pregnant woman in danger, along with the therapic carnation, which only flowered once, on the sixth night of the creation of the world. Finally, he explained to him which plant corresponds to which star and to which chemical element, and how you can learn everything about the past by observing the movements of the leaves when the wind is right. Frilos found all this very boring, but he liked the walks as the old man held him by the hand and he could feel magnetic waves passing into his own body, making him feel light and cheerful. At other times, however, he lowered his gaze and blushed, because he realised that the old man knew everything, even when he used his thought to oblige two wing-wolves to have sex, simply in order to impress Aoukin, a boy from the northern parts, who had come to the aqueduct for the first time and was looking all around in amazement. Yet the old man wasn't worried; he watched Frilos and saw a child in a mirror.

On the evening of their twenty-first meeting, the old man

reflected that he ought to initiate some form of systematic teaching which would correspond to an hourly programme, because with all these techniques and pleasantries, all they managed at best was to waste time, and time was not something they had a lot of anymore. So he once again turned his attention to the books. The Invocations began with the phrase:

FOR ME TO WAIT FOR YOU IS THE END,
NOT THE BEGINNING

And the old man, who had been waiting for Frilos for so many years, realised that he felt moved. This hint of happiness caused a rippling of the leaves in the moonlight coming in through the skylight. Frilos was standing opposite the old man in a silver abyss ribbed with green hues and seemed ready to hear anything. Then the old man said that it would be worthwhile for them to start from the astral bell, whose sound stops the entire universe for an indivisible moment of time and adjusts itself to the will of the magician. And he actually gave the lad just such a bell, made of an amalgam of seven metals, with a small clapper of human bone, and he explained to him how it worked. He revealed to him that this instrument both calls and awakens, and that it was this same instrument that once rang in the churches during the raising of the Holy Gifts. Frilos saw for himself that the sound of the bell, however melodic it may be, was most imperious and majestic, and that in the silence surrounding this uncommon sound no question's reasoning could endure and no spirit of doubt appeared genuine. The following day he said to Nidros: 'Have you ever heard anything extremely profound in the depths of your existence?' 'Oh, don't start all that again!' Nidros laughingly protested, while watching through infrared binoculars a newborn hydron changing scales in the channel's water while the current dragged it towards the moss. Then he put down the binoculars and got hold of Frilos by the arm. 'Let's go and run in the 26th,' he proposed. But Frilos was in low spirits as he was thinking of the old man and the slight movement of his lips at the moment when he pronounced the word 'failure'. In the end, they remained where they were, gazing at the vegetation and lost in thought.

Then there was the night that Frilos arrived late in the forest. Just as every night, he waited for his father to go to sleep before sneaking out, but his father was now sitting with a Horio officer in the large room, before the screen, and they were chatting about matters concerning the company's politics. They had drunk quite a lot and continued taking pills without any thought of going to bed. When the Horio finally left, it was four in the morning and the sun had set long before. Frilos wondered whether he should borrow his father's horocopter in order to arrive sooner at the old man's house, but the Horios forbid anyone under sixteen to fly horocopters, and the men patrolling at night were very strict in these matters. So he again covered the distance running between the creepers. It was the mating season for the hydrons, and Frilos was careful as hunters frequented the forest. When he got there, the old man was sitting beside the window, more serene than ever. 'Today,' he said, 'I'm going to teach you the last real thing . . .'. 'Why the last?' asked Frilos anxiously. In a low voice, the old man muttered something incomprehensible and, lying down, closed his eyes. Frilos now looked tranquilly at the sight, listening inside himself to the noise of the bell, like a hint of the forest's trills in the summer, long before the Horios, when Dithira was still full of life beneath God's gaze. Then the Horio officer got up from his chair and went over to the screen. 'It'll be over any moment,' he said to Frilos' father, who was called Natron. And then, 'Look! He's already dead . . .'.

'So soon?'

'Tests of this kind don't last very long.' The screen went blank. Then the Horio spoke about Frilos. 'If he continues to do so well,' he said, 'I'll propose him for a scholarship . . . in which case, he'll have to spend some time at the Centre.'

The other man nodded his head, which was heavy from the drink and the pills.

'Well, the company will compensate you,' added the Horio and his voice sounded sharper, perhaps because this time, he was touching on a more delicate matter.

Original title: 'Ypotrofia oneiron'. Published in Evyenios Aranitsis, *Istories pou aresan se merikous anthropous pou xero* [Stories Liked By Some People I Know], Athens: Nefeli, 1995/1999, pp. 257–266.

Theocles

Theodoros Grigoriadis

It was at that time that one more island was added to the dozens of other inhabited islands in my country. A small, secret and inaccessible island. Its existence was known only to the satellites and to a few select scientists. The secrecy had to do with the construction and operation on the island of an entire scientific research centre. No one paid any attention to the island concerned. It was barren and uninhabited; a rocky islet consisting of a few square kilometres, one of the thousands scattered throughout the North Aegean.

Yet the most amazing thing about all this was the announcement by my elder brother, Theocles, that he intended to live and work on that island. He was the one who told me of the existence of the island and of his intentions. My brother had just returned from America, where he had been doing research into ancient Mediterranean religions, having meanwhile graduated from the University of Thessaloniki with a degree in Archaeology. In due course, he would reveal more to me concerning the nature of his studies.

Our parents were no longer alive, and the ten-year difference between us meant that I thought of him not only as my elder brother but also, in a way, as my guardian. Naturally, this was the case while I was still an adolescent, because his university studies meant that we were suddenly drawn apart.

I lived in our family house, a large building close to the Byzantine Maximianopolis in Thrace. I farmed many acres of land, beside the dried-up lake at Bistonida: corn, wheat and a kind of mild cannabis used for pharmaceutical purposes. When we lost our parents, we were already fifteen and twenty-five years old respectively. He was already studying in Thessaloniki and I was at High School in Iasmos. An aged aunt of ours had undertaken to take care of us at home. (Even today, I still avoid referring to the tragic death of our parents in a plane crash, as it always fills me with deep despondency.)

I read a great deal, mainly general-knowledge books that Theocles stacked in my room, but I had no leaning towards academic study. As soon as I left High School, I began working with the crops and managing the family fortune. Through this tiring work I was able to forget my parents' cruel fate and my brother's absence. I lived in a house completely lacking in family warmth.

During the last summer that we spent together, Theocles, already a university graduate, told me of his intention to continue his studies in America. We were holidaying in Samothrace, the place he had chosen for our summer vacation. I saw how his character and interests had changed. There was nothing to recall that spirited lad who was my role-model while I was growing up. He had lost weight and his face had acquired a sobriety and sanctity which recalled an ascetic. Fortunately, he hadn't abandoned his exercise. He would get up early in the morning and go up the hill, in the afternoons we would go swimming, down by the pebbled beach, and in the evenings he would take me to the island's ancient city. There, he would study the prehistoric sanctuary, where the ancient inhabitants of the island sacrificed to their gods. We would sit on the highest point, on a level piece of ground used as the place of sacrifice, and from there he would gaze out and stare into nothingness. He always carried maps and diagrams with him and he spoke to me not only of Samothrace, but also of two other islands that he pointed out to me on an old map. He joined the three islands with dotted lines, forming a perfect triangle, and exactly in the middle of the diagram was a dot, the remains of an island.

Another ten years passed after those summer holidays before I made the connection between that dot and the barren island on which my brother was going to work.

This time, he had come from America for my wedding. A simple ceremony that took place at the Town Hall. He stayed with us for just two days, poring over his books, playing with my computer and going for walks to the familiar spots.

'You've got it made, little brother,' he said to me one evening, while gazing at the stars. 'You've got your feet firmly on the ground. I learned to observe the sky and to study its secrets. But the earth is essential to man. Those who look upwards are lost all the sooner. The stars wink at men, and sometimes they do so deceptively.'

Strange words, it's true . . . completely out of keeping with his old interests. It was then that he revealed to me his field of specialisation in America. Modern Astrology and Astronomy, but based on ancient sources. Arcane knowledge was never lost, he told me. And he reminded me of the sanctuary of the Cabeirians in Samothrace. He drew the three islands in the soil with his finger and once again sketched the triangle. In addition to Samothrace, he also pointed to and named the other islands: Limnos and Tenedos. All three, he said, had a similar sanctuary on the top of their mountains; a level space where they made sacrifice and came into contact with higher powers. But these sacrifices had another purpose. The people who went to sacrifice themselves there had pledged themselves for other things. But what exactly?

He smiled enigmatically. He alluded to something about chosen people who of their own free will consented to the journey to the summit and to their participation in the mysteries. I asked him again about the sacred triangle of islands. The secret, he said, was in the centre of the triangle. In that barren island, which was in total harmony with the power of the other sanctuaries. The other sanctuaries put into operation and prepared for the supreme sacrifice which took place on this island, the nameless island. He stuck a piece of wood in the ground, in the centre of the diagram.

'Here, today, a research laboratory has been set up. There's a huge library, a few computer disks that is, containing whatever's been written up until now and whatever our civilisation has produced.

He avoided going into detail about the ultimate aims of the research centre, though he did promise me that one day I would learn everything, 'when the time is right', he said and added:

'Consider yourself fortunate to know what you already know and keep the existence of the island a secret.'

Afterwards, I lost touch with him for a long time. Every so often, he would send me greetings by fax, a few words, compliments of the season and the wish that we might see each other soon. He always repeated without fail that we would see each other soon. One day. But when? I missed my brother. I may have had a wife who was already pregnant, but recalling him took me back to the peaceful and carefree years of my childhood, when I was in the process of discovering life and nature. I missed Theocles and as I grew older, my need to see him was immeasurable.

'Why don't we visit the island?' my wife would keep asking me. She knew vaguely that my brother was doing reconstruction work on a partially inhabited island.

I couldn't explain to her that the island was only to be found on shipping charts or that my brother wouldn't want me to visit him there. My wife didn't understand.

'Your brother's not a secret agent, is he?' she asked me, jokingly. I laughed at the characterisation, though deep inside me, I instinctively knew that my brother's mission had a much higher goal. I knew Theocles very well; he wouldn't devote himself to anything with such passion unless there was a serious reason.

With the child still in her womb, my wife and I went to Limnos on holiday. It wasn't far from where we lived. From Komotini airport, we took a flying-dolphin and within half an hour we were on the pale-hued island. We stayed in the main town. I immediately rushed to the museum and bought a volume on the history and maps of the island. I located the spot where the Cabeirians had had their ancient sanctuary. I rented a car and climbed the black hill, without taking my pregnant wife along. The road was so bad that it wouldn't have done her pregnancy any good at all. Luxury tourist complexes had been built at the bottom of the hill. The heliports stood out clearly. Up in the sanctuary, however, there was no one. Not even guards. The wind and the years had removed the earth and its precious finds. Who knows, perhaps some sleazy dealers in antiquities had also had a hand in the past.

I stood in the area of the sanctuary, perched as it was right on the edge of the cliff, and was overcome by awe at the altitude and the stunning location. The sea broke at the foot of the cliffs and the waves disappeared into the eroded caverns. I clearly recalled my brother's words. There, on the edge of the cliff, I looked in every direction, trying to make out an islet or mountain peak. Nothing on the horizon. Just endless blue, which merged with the clear blue of the sky. I may be a practical and down-to-earth person by nature, but I had the feeling that my brother was somewhere in the farthest reaches of this place and that he was watching me. I was sure.

In the suffocating heat of the afternoon, I was once again gripped by deep emotion and a sense of grievance. I was all alone in the world. Why wasn't my elder brother with me? Why couldn't he live normally with us, close by with his own family, so that I could see him regularly and we could talk and he could convey his boundless knowledge to me? Then I thought of the baby growing in my wife's womb and I felt calmer. I was consoled by the thought of the new life soon to appear, as it would add to the family and perhaps I would have something to make up for Theocles' absence. That same night, my wife realised how much I missed my brother. She may even have been slightly envious of the love I felt for him. But blood is blood and it's not easily replaced.

We went back home, to our jobs, and her womb went on swelling impressively. It wasn't long before she brought a sweet and bonny baby boy into the world. A lovely baby. Almost at once, Theocles sent his congratulations by fax. How had he found out? We hadn't been in touch for months. It was a pity, though, that I couldn't thank him, and my question as to how he knew about the birth remained unanswered at the back of my mind.

Unfortunately, the baby didn't bring the relief that I'd expected. My brother's absence became an obsessive and tormenting thought. I went to the harbour authorities at Porto Lagos, where an old schoolmate of mine was working as an officer. I asked him to get out all his charts and show me every rocky islet in the northern sea. He printed out the navigational chart from his computer and gave it to me. I went back home and pinned it up on the wall. I stared at it for hours. There was nothing in the centre of the Sacred Triangle and I vainly tried to link the islands with straight lines. As the time passed, the lines became bent and took on strange rhomboid shapes that made me dizzy. This went on for the whole of the following month. My wife began complaining every day, but fortunately the household responsibilities were many, and I eventually stopped drawing lines on the familiar chart.

One weekend, I returned to Porto Lagos and sought out my friend. I asked him to take me in the harbour patrol boat to a spot that I would show him. I would pay all the expenses and whatever else he wanted as a fee. He laughed and said he would do this favour for me, even though it meant contravening his duty. I lied to my wife, telling her that we were going out fishing, something I'd never before done.

We set out. For three hours we sailed on the clear and open sea, using my chart to guide us. Eventually, we spotted Limnos and I was disappointed at its familiar sight. Where was the secret island that Theocles had told me about? Why couldn't we see it? My friend laughed when I asked him if we had made a detour round an uninhabited islet. 'Quite a few reefs, without doubt,' he said, laughing at my obsession with looking down and seeing dolphins.

I returned home despondent. There was a new fax message waiting for me. 'Don't be in a hurry, little brother,' it said, 'soon we'll meet. You'll come to see me. Be patient.' That's how the message ended.

His ability to guess my actions and my intentions, together with the prospect of some future meeting, created a sense of anxiety in me that manifested itself at the expense of my work and my family. My wife continually complained and even the neighbours found my behaviour strange. All I did was smoke and, in the evening, look at my charts and my notes. Occasionally, I spoke out loud to Theocles, because I was certain that somewhere he was watching me and listening to me. Often, between the images on the television, I thought I discerned his image and then he would speak to me quite naturally. When I called my wife to point him out to her, she started screaming, grabbed the baby in a panic and went to stay at her mother's house in Olympiada in Halkidiki, which is where she was from. I went and brought her back, three days later.

Her threat of a permanent separation didn't daunt me. Nor was I interested any more in the fields and my work. I felt as if an extremely important moment in my life was approaching; one which would join our fates, mine and Theocles'. I was sure that he approved of my actions, otherwise he would have discouraged me through another fax message.

Three days later, my separation from my wife proved unavoidable. She made one last effort to make me see sense, and instead she found me smoking, dirty, unshaven and with a vacant expression. She took the child, two bank account books, and left for good this time. In spite of all the bad feelings and the dramatic scenes accompanying separation, I had a pleasant sense of relief now that I was alone in the house. I wandered round, smoking cigarettes from my own produce and anxiously watching the fax machine. His message was not long in coming. 'In three days, you'll be with me.'

From that moment, I was unable to get a wink of sleep. I closed my eyes and I saw Theocles on a jetty, embracing me and welcoming me. Sometimes I couldn't recall him as a person with a normal appearance. I saw him in a strange mist while his figure faded and dissolved into the horizon. How would I be with him? Who would take me to him?

It seems, though, that he had taken care of everything, down to the very last detail. In his next message, he instructed me to go the following night to the quayside in the harbour at

Porto Lagos. At midnight. And, of course, all this with the utmost secrecy.

I was trembling as I drove to the harbour in my jeep. Fortunately, it wasn't too windy because that would have meant a choppy sea. I avoided parking too close to the port authority building and I left the car behind the warehouses. I was carrying a small bag, as I had no idea what to take with me. At half-past eleven I was standing on the quayside wondering how a boat could possibly tie up inside the harbour without being seen by the officer on duty.

At precisely midnight, my question was answered. Speechless at the sight, I saw a vessel rather like a miniature electronic submarine rising from out of the sea. Its pointed hull drew up beside me. Its hatch opened silently.

No head emerged from inside. So I carefully placed my foot on the platform below the hatch. Then I stood on it firmly with both feet. The platform descended and I immediately found myself in a narrow chamber. There was no one else. The hatch closed automatically and I lay down horizontally in order to be able to fit inside. I waited in case some other door opened, but no. It was clear that I was to travel alone in this underwater capsule, which left at great speed without any vibrations whatsoever. Perhaps half an hour or an hour went by – it was too much for me to even try to reckon. The important thing is that it eventually moored. Everything was automatic.

I found myself on an iron jetty, which was lit by dim lamps attached to the floor. I walked up a slight incline. The buildings and the rock presented an indivisible appearance, a dark backdrop. Someone was waiting for me before the entrance which was dug into the rock. I discerned the figure of Theocles. We hugged each other for joy and, without our saying very much, he led me inside the installations.

I won't dwell on detailed descriptions of the place, because I'm still forbidden to do so even today. Let's just say that it recalled the control tower of an ultra-modern airport. Theocles took me down to his own quarters, to a second underground level. It was there that he slept and studied. Lord, how he'd changed . . . distant and withdrawn. Only his eyes recalled my brother. And he was thin, as if he'd been through some grave illness. With a look of pain in his eyes and a hint of resignation about something inevitable soon to take place. He told me how happy he was that we'd spend the whole night together. We'd talk over old times and he'd tell me about everything new that had happened. We both lay down on the only bed. Fortunately we were both thin and so there was room for us. I'd lost weight because of him but what was his reason?

As he talked, I became paralysed by his words, falling into a state of hopeless inertia, because everything he said was so very harsh for both our fates, particularly mine.

At first he spoke to me, as comprehensibly as possible, of our knowledge about ancient astronomy and modern astrophysics (some of this I'd heard before). He endeavoured to link the ancient doctrines with contemporary research concerning the universe and the search for other civilisations. Concerning the activating of earthly forces existing for thousands of years. Only to conclude that we are not alone. That there are many others who live far from us in this expanding universe and who are waiting for us. That this island constituted a point of contact with the infinite and that there were indications and references concerning its powerful cosmic location, as old as the first references to civilisation on earth. Because of its location, it was chosen by unknown civilisations. In the past, of course, it was bigger in area, but over the years the sea-level had risen, limiting it to no more than a mountain peak.

And now the time had come. A few thousand years before the rocky islet disappeared beneath a new ocean, it was to constitute the place for transporting an 'intelligent' being from earth into the universe. The initiated people on earth have been receiving the messages conveyed for years now. It's not known how they interpreted these messages in ancient times. Nevertheless, evidence exists. Nothing happens by chance. Our language has a universal structure and it can be read by other inhabitants of the universe.

Yes, the moment had come. For the past twenty years, discussions have been taking place about sending a man together with evidence of the civilisation on our planet. A great many countries are taking part in the programme and the man chosen must not only be a scientist, but also pledged to the programme of his own accord. By coincidence (really?) he would come from the country to which the apocalyptic islet belongs. And there is one. Only one. Theocles.

I wanted to wake up from this dream and embrace my wife and child, explaining to them what I'd seen. Unfortunately, everything I'd heard was true and my surprise was compounded not so much by the wealth of detailed information that Theocles had given me as by the outcome of the whole endeavour. He would leave. Where to? How? For how long? And why didn't he answer these three simple questions of mine directly?

He kept on telling me how close he felt to me and that he'd deliberately kept away from me because he'd known all along that I would lose him one day and he didn't want to hurt me by his irrevocable decision. He was living in a state of continual departure. Not that it didn't hurt him too, not that he too wasn't afraid. That's why he'd brought me there. In order to have someone close to him during those final moments.

'Why final?'

'Because you won't see me again . . .'

I wanted the earth to open up and swallow me.

'Why won't I see you again? What are you saying?'

'Because I'm going so far that I can't even describe it to you using your own mathematical data. The transfer will take place in a way hitherto impossible, given that a part will be played by those who have called us to their unknown civilisation. That's where I will be transported. And when I return, bringing back with me the fruits of their knowledge, maybe hundreds of earth years, perhaps even thousands, will have passed . . .'

Lord, why am I drowning in the sea's catacombs?

'What kind of talk is that? Do you want to die?'

'But you'll die too. I'll voyage beyond your natural time. My time is cosmic time. The endeavour will be an important moment in science and in the history of our planet. And an overwhelming justification of primeval knowledge . . .'

'Will you go for good?'

We slept all night arm in arm. When I came to, I realised that my brotherly tears could not get him to change his decision. I was far too down-to-earth for his aims. Theocles had been gone for a long time now and I hadn't been aware of it. He was already far from me and I had to accept his loss for good. With bravery and pain at the same time. He didn't want me to treat him as someone condemned, but to be proud of the uniqueness of his choice. He would still be living when we had gone, having ascended the pyramid of cosmic life; having fulfilled the humble goal on earth, simple survival in a universe that would increase its entropy.

Day broke. Nothing moved on the dry, rocky island. The sea had taken on a dark hue. I was led to the visitors' stand together with the foreign observers. The scientists from the base took up position behind the recording and control instruments. Exactly opposite our own stand was another platform: the island's natural platform. Another level piece of ground that recalled the corresponding sites on the islands in the Sacred Triangle. But on this piece of ground there was no trace of any ruins. Only twenty steps or so, that had been carved out naturally by the footsteps of time. This is where my brother's departure was to take place. So many studies, so much research so that he might stand up on this projecting tip of the island.

Theocles. I saw him emerging through the central door and I felt awe. He was naked. Tied round his waist with a metal belt was the box with the computer disks. His nakedness and his slenderness. And his eyes that looked at me meaningfully and that I saw momentarily filled with tears – or were the tears my own? What value can be attached to human sentiment at such a moment, when individuality and time are subverted? Was he perhaps regretting his decision?

He stood on the level ground, the last piece of earth on which he would ever tread. Who knows whether what he said about returning was simply by way of consolation. For him, there was only one certainty; others were waiting for him, intelligent beings with an undetermined shape and form.

Theocles looked upwards like the other observers. I was the only one to look straight at him, trying to imprint this final image of him in my mind and give him a last look of support.

At first, I thought something like a whirlwind or hurricane would descend and take him with it. But, as he had told me himself, the electromagnetic cloud that had been travelling towards earth since who knows when would arrive at a specific moment and would naturally not be seen as it was invisible to the human eye.

I was reeling. I was about to shout out, to try to dissuade him . . .

But in the wink of an eye, in no more than a fraction of a second, he was gone. Vanished. The invisible wave came, enfolded him and took him. Sending him There. We remained staring at that part of the horizon corresponding to his figure. It was accomplished. Nothing else. Nothing had changed in nature's setting. The visitors remained speechless, perhaps not believing what they had just witnessed and still looking up into the heavens.

An officer from the base came and escorted me as far as the jetty. I had to leave there. They handed me a small bag with my brother's personal papers, but no one ventured to tell me that he would need them on his return. From now on, there would be no question of 'his return' for us.

I again entered the underwater capsule as if in a trance, and I closed my eyes. For a moment, I thought that I was travelling together with Theocles to nowhere and to everywhere. My only consolation was that he was travelling in the chaotic universe, even though he would never have used such an adjective. In the universe there is only structure and order. I had my doubts. Inside me I had mixed and confused feelings, despite what's said about our being a microcosm of the universe.

It was night again when I got back to the harbour at Porto Lagos. The lights were on in the harbour master's office and there was an unusual commotion. When I'd left, just the previous night, I'd seen only a couple of boats there. I went to find my officer friend. Instead of him, I found another officer who informed me that my friend had been transferred to Maroneia the previous year. But we were together only recently, I whined. The officer laughed and pointed to the calendar on the wall. Alarmed, I saw that exactly one year had passed. There must have been some mistake. A year? In order for me to reach the island?

It was then that I recalled my brother's words. That on that island, earthly time doesn't exist. Because on that stretch of land, in the centre of the Sacred Triangle, the endless continuity of the World continued. This was the source of its uniqueness.

I looked at myself in the mirror. I was no different from how I was when I set out. But was I? I went home. Another surprise. My wife had returned and was waiting for me. She believed I would show up, because she'd received a fax message saying that they shouldn't worry, that I would be back in a year. The 'unknown sender' warmed my heart.

I embraced my son, who was already two years old and, with great emotion, I heard his name for the first time: Theocles. Whose idea was it? My wife looked at me with understanding. Could it be that her intuition had led her to understand everything?

The years passed, my son grew and I told him stories from the books I read, which I now did systematically. The boy asked me about his uncle. He asked me where he was and when he could meet him. And every time he uttered his uncle's name, his face lit up and took on an expression that made him look amazingly like Theocles.

One evening, beneath a starry sky, I couldn't help myself and I pointed to the stars.

'That's where your uncle is. A long way away, though he might be beside us. Here, right alongside us.'

And the boy seemed to understand. Though only ten years old, he jumped up and ran out of the garden and onto the street; there where the dried-up lake began and the night embraced the infinite. He ran, shouting 'Uncle Theocles. Don't hide. I can see you. Take me with you, uncle, don't hide . . .'.

Original title: 'Theoklis'. Published in Makis Panorios (ed.), *Ellinika diiyimata epistimonikis fantasias* [Greek Science Fiction Stories], Athens: Aiolos, 1995, pp. 135–148.

Mania from Heaven

Kostas Arkoudeas

Kenke could hardly swallow. Unconsciously, his hand went to the knife that he had in his belt. What was this before his eyes?

A gleaming oblong cube was flying over the forest. It had no wings, it wasn't a bird; it was too large to be any bird he'd ever seen. Afraid, he crouched behind the altar, praying for it to go away. The flying chest hovered above the temple and then gently settled on the huge stone of the main entrance. A door opened. Three men and a woman in linen robes jumped out.

That was all he needed now: to be caught red-handed. Kenke crawled on his belly and hid like a cockroach beneath an upturned pitcher that was used for libations in the sanctuary. He cursed the hour that he'd decided to climb up there. He'd been in too much of a hurry. He should have bided his time, stayed in his straw hut in the jungle, as he'd done on the day the Toreros' fleet had left. He hadn't been able to restrain himself. He'd heard that the plundered temples inside the pyramids contained fabulous treasures. The Spanish invaders had taken as much as they could, but this was chicken-feed compared to what they had left behind. The temptation was too much for a poor native like Kenke. Rumour had it that the sandstone statues of the gods were adorned with precious stones and solid gold trinkets. Kenke had once scorned gold, like his fellow-villagers. Now, the invaders had opened their eyes. They went crazy for it, so it must be something of great value. If he were able to snatch just a few pieces, he'd live like a lord for the rest of his life.

The strange visitors stood before the entrance. They seemed upset, and were flushed and jittery. Behind them, the sun rose over the forests of Ecuador, setting the sky on fire.

Kenke availed himself of the opportunity to examine them more closely. The first was a slant-eyed old man with a huge belly and skin the colour of sand. He heard the others calling him Milarepa. Beside him was a thin-faced woman with black hair and long dangling earrings. Milarepa kept her close to him and called her Serasvati. The third member of the group was tall, had his face covered by a veil and wore a turban. Hanging from his shoulders was a box that was connected to some strings going to his ears. The fourth one seemed to be their leader. His face was ringed by long, fair hair and a slightly darker beard. There was something serene and sacred about his movements. Kenke was unable to explain the awe he felt at his presence. He watched him quickly climbing the steps and entering the temple. Behind his beard, his face was pale. He was furious. He shouted:

'We're too late! We weren't able to prevent the destruction. I told you we had to hurry. Now there's nothing to be done.'

The language he spoke was foreign. Yet Kenke was able to understand what he meant. That surprised him. How could this be? His mind was unable to take it in. It was as if he were speaking into his heart rather than into his ear. Now he was really confused. He couldn't understand who they were or where they'd come from.

'They set fire to the temples, the irreverent wretches,' said the slant-eyed old man. He winced on seeing the charred manuscripts of bark, the ashes of what was once a library. 'The hieroglyphics and genetic calendars are all burned. The ancient astronomy charts turned to ash. Do you remember how hard they worked to come up with these texts?'

The four of them walked among the still-smoking remains, looking around them in horror. Kenke saw their leader going up to the altar and leaning over a mangled body. He covered it with a piece of cloth and stood beside it, unmoving.

'Thou shalt not make unto thee any graven image, or any likeness of any thing . . .,' he mumbled apologetically. 'We tried to inspire you with a higher moral principle. We taught you everything apart from war. We thought you would have no need of it, just as the lion in the jungle has no need of it. What a utopian world we wished to create for you!'

The man in the turban grimaced. He took the strings out of his ears and said:

'Commander, they've just informed me from base that conquistador frigates are sailing out to sea. They're about forty Ks away. They've massacred the tribes on the coast and have crucified their chieftains. Their ships are full of plunder. We're waiting for orders. Shall we destroy them?'

The fair-haired man stared at him with eyes glaring. He stood up, clenched his fists and said:

'Was that it, then? Have we committed a crime? Have we filled the Earth with dogs and vultures? And tomorrow, what will we do? Spread more monsters throughout the Universe?'

'No, commander!' the other protested. 'It's only here on Earth that we've come up against such savagery. I suggest that we make this the last time. We have to wipe them out before they spread and infect the neighbouring planets.'

'We don't have to do it ourselves, my dear Prophet. If they carry on like this, they'll create a hell for themselves. What happened here, exactly? Was the standard procedure adhered to? Give me the full report from base.'

'Certainly! Here it is. The branching and reproduction procedure was followed to the letter. First, we made sure that we created the suitable atmospheric conditions. Once the flora was formed, we scattered the frozen multi-cellular organisms, which in time formed the fauna. The procedure was completed with the creation of a human tribe. In other words, the animal forms that evolved normally entered the multiple-transformer and were changed into proto-humans, adapted to the climatic conditions of the environment in which they lived. All we did was to fashion replicas of ourselves. The levels of intelligence of the new beings were determined by robotic programmes. These human beings were imbued with three concepts: the concept of God, of light and of freedom. The next stage was the intermingling, the degeneration and the combinations of the different coloured tribes. Apart from some rare instances of mutants, our efforts were judged to be successful. In the same way, we have created humans throughout the finite universe. So, each time that we need to replenish our nickel, plutonium or uranium, these humans welcome us like gods, given that they preserve deep memories of their Creator. It's true that, recently, base has been somewhat worried about the antics of the Earthlings. Our envoys have reported that they have been developing rapidly and rather irregularly.'

'I was afraid of that. Accumulated knowledge often leads to holocausts,' said the slant-eyed old man, breaking in. 'We ourselves, the sons of Man, are the most tragic example. We've spread throughout the universe in order to fashion worlds in keeping with our own standards and yet we consider it a waste of time to vanquish our inner demons. We're only too familiar with what's happening here on Earth. The same things were done long ago by our ancestors, our own race, the sovereign people of Koite. Don't be fooled by the fact that it's all now been erased from the historical records. It's common knowledge, but it suits us not to remember it.'

'Don't be too hard, Milarepa,' said the woman, who had not spoken before. We've created wonderful beings, even on Earth. We were misled by the amazing abilities that we saw in this race. Do you remember the glory enjoyed by the red race of Atlanteans? Or the black race of Abyssinians? Or the joy bestowed on us by the Hyperboreans with their blue eyes? Their civilisation began fifty thousand years ago, much quicker than we'd estimated. The Earthlings could have gone far if it hadn't been for their egoistic instinct, which more often than not finds expression in war.'

'The Earthlings are but a handful of arrogant animals,' said the man in the turban, scornfully. He allowed the words to fall from his mouth as if he were spitting. 'They think they know everything, the conceited fools. What do they know about flights under the light of the stars? Have they ever heard the tales related by the moss and the soil? They're blind and dumb. They know nothing.'

'They vacillate between the mind and the body,' added the slant-eyed man. 'What do you expect of them? They're totally confused! Their minds are looking for one thing, their hearts another and their bodies another. The one gets satisfied and the other two remain empty. They don't function together. There's no equilibrium.'

'Enough!' said the turbaned man, in a broken voice.

'Yes, enough,' muttered the slant-eyed man.

Kenke heard all this and couldn't believe his ears. These people here were total crackpots. They passed themselves off as gods, yet they were no more than a pack of over-fed merchants! He was a man of faith, who didn't forget to honour his ancestors and who knew that the Creator was infallible. He never regretted anything. He was beyond all human passions. God doesn't let anything happen if he doesn't wish it. He would never sit and snivel like a little old woman.

'Tell them to send teams to empty the pyramids,' said the fair-haired one with resolve. 'I want them to be left empty. In Egypt, in Mesopotamia, everywhere. Not a trace is to be left inside them.'

He took a small metal box out of his robe, put it close to his mouth and began speaking feverishly.

'We're leaving everything on Earth half-finished. Full of mistakes and inaccuracies. It's a slow and painful punishment that will torment them all their lives. I call upon base to forbid any contact between Man and the Earthlings in the future. We must not let one ray of knowledge reach this planet. Let them live with ignorance and prejudice for their companions. Uncomprehending. Inexperienced. Crossbreeds. Outcasts.'

'There's someone in the temple,' the woman said suddenly, pointing to a flashing light on the metal box.

Kenke shrank back in his hiding place and held his breath. It was something he hadn't expected. He nervously clutched at the snake's rattle that he had hanging from his neck. He mumbled a wish.

'It'll be one of the natives,' the fair-haired one said wearily, heading towards the exit. He appeared to have aged in only a few minutes. 'They congregate from the surrounding villages like hyenas. I saw quite a few earlier crossing the river and coming this way.'

The others followed him. Kenke breathed a sigh of relief. Then he heard the fair-haired one say something that greatly surprised him.

'It is a characteristic of the intelligent being to recognise his mistake and to make sure that it doesn't happen again. We made a mistake, gentlemen, and we have to admit it. All of us, prophets and mystics alike. We all erred. We continued to cast water into the mill of Creation and we returned to find the most peace-loving of our children massacred.'

Kenke very nearly burst out laughing. What else would he hear? Fortunately, the strange visitors moved off. They descended the temple steps on their way to the chest that gleamed in the sun as it awaited them.

'Our next stop is the Second Pulsating Planet in the Great Asteroid Belt,' the fair-haired one went on. 'The Men there are doing everything possible to make it inhabitable. Reports speak of acid and alkaline rain, creating a landscape of sublime destruction.'

'No more destruction. We can't bear it,' said the man in the turban indignantly. 'It would be better for us to go somewhere to rest and forget the horror we've seen here. Let's voyage to the outer world of Zeo 17 with its four satellites. They say that the solar race there is developing marvellously. They're making the best possible use of their kinder instincts. An encounter with them will be like balsam after the spectacle here.'

'If that's the case, then I prefer the Bright Nebulas,' said the slant-eyed old man meekly. 'It's time we got away from the material levels. There are beings there that live by means of fragrances and a highly sensitive sense of smell. Their last mystic said that they have maintained their conscience intact. They're on the right path.'

'With all due respect, master, I should remind you that I am captain of this ship,' said the fair-haired one. 'I alone plot the course. My decisions carry weight in the judgement of the elders.'

'I disagree, commander. You can't choose to ignore our opinions,' said the man in the turban curtly. 'Your decisions concern all of us.'

'Please, gentlemen, control yourselves!' said the woman, trying to calm things down.

'There's one for you! Even repentant whores have an opinion now . . .'

'Now listen here, just keep that tongue of yours in check . . .'

They were arguing as they once again entered the strange chest. Kenke watched it rise up from the ground noiselessly and then disappear over the treetops. He emerged from his hiding place. At last! He'd got stiff after so long in there without moving. He'd no time to lose. He had to hurry. Others were on their way there. He made sure he was alone and ran over to a corner of the half-burnt temple. His eye had been fixed for some time on a gold bell in the shape of an upturned pyramid. He knew that it was a symbol of authority and this would increase its value when he went to the town to exchange it for barley. The bell gleamed in the sunlight, abandoned beneath a fresco of Virakotsa, the bird god of Creation.

Original title: 'Mania ton ouranon'. First published in 1986. Translated here from the text anthologised in Makis Panorios (ed.), *To Elliniko Fantastiko Diiyima* [The Greek Fantasy Short Story] vol. 4, Athens: Aiolos, 1997, pp. 25–29.

It Was Already Past Midnight

Aris Sfakianakis

It was already past midnight when I decided to turn off the lights and go to bed. Outside, the North wind was raging and the driving rain, which had shown no signs of stopping all evening, ran down the glass panes in the balcony door. I lost no time in diving under the covers and, shivering, I picked up a thick book that I was reading. I soon put it down, however, and turned over.

I'd hardly had time to get comfortable when the doorbell rang. I switched on the light somewhat surprised as neither the time nor, indeed, the weather was ideal for callers. When I heard the bell a second time, I decided to go and see who it was.

Standing at the door was that tall, pale girl who I'd seen that morning in town and whose beauty – and above all her glazed look from the heroin – had led me to follow her for quite a distance though without venturing to talk to her, which was due not only to my innate irresolution but also to her sudden decision to enter a chemist's and not come out again – at least for as long as I remained outside.

I beckoned to her to step inside and she followed me to the bed without speaking. She sat submissively on the edge of the bed while I lost no time in diving once again under the warm covers. Now that I got a better look at her, I saw that she was not at all wet; not one drop of rain – despite the deluge continuing outside – had smudged her black patent-leather shoes, while her stockings (impeccably stretched) showed no signs of a long walk, though the house where I lived was a good few miles from the nearest farm. I have to admit that my surprise was such that I didn't dare open my mouth lest this exquisite vision disappear from before my eyes.

After removing her long gloves and fixing her hair somewhat, she stared at me with a look that filled me with terror and said: 'I'm going to tell you the story of the young artist.' All I wanted at that moment was to put my hand on her knee or to take her slender fingers in my mouth, but as this would happen before long, I nodded to her to go on.

The story, which she began to relate with a breath smelling of mint, was as follows:

'The young artist lived on the fifth floor of an old apartment block, on the banks of the river. When, on returning home one day, he found his house demolished, he didn't give it much thought but went straightaway to the block across the way and rang a bell at random. A door opened on the ground floor and a girl beckoned to him to step inside. The young artist lost no time. He immediately accepted the offer and, smiling, found himself in the girl's apartment. The girl introduced herself as Esmé and sat him in an armchair. "I'm going out for a while," she said, "but you stay here and make yourself comfortable." The young artist replied "I'll wait for you," and sank back into the armchair.

Before long, however, he began to get bored and hoped the girl would return soon. To pass the time, he got up to take a look round the other rooms. He went first into the bedroom. The walls were bare and apart from an old wooden bed, there was nothing else in the room. The bed – which immediately attracted his attention – was covered by a thick duvet, which gave the impression that it was quivering as waves of ripples kept passing through it. Astonished, the young artist went over to it and pulled back the cover. The blue sheet was strewn with numerous snakes that, unable to rest, were squirming and continually making the duvet ripple. The snakes themselves seemed harmless, though they were quite big and thick. The young artist quickly covered them over again and hurried out of the room.

His investigations led him next into the kitchen. With a sudden, though completely justified, feeling of hunger, he opened the fridge door. But all he found was a tin of mussels. Again, he didn't think twice about it. He took the tin and sat down at the table. He had a little trouble opening it, but eventually managed it and leaned back in his chair, tired from the effort. When he then opened the lid of the tin, he got a shock. For, floating in the white sauce in place of mussels were human lips. Women's lips, as he subsequently determined, on recovering from his initial shock. Moreover, the lips were painted and appeared to be alive as they slowly opened and closed, emitting tiny indeterminate sounds, rather like sighs. The young artist jumped up and lost no time in getting out of the kitchen.

In the bathroom, he found a dagger stuck in the mirror. When he pulled at it, a groan shook the whole house, but the knife wouldn't come out. The young artist suddenly felt very tired and decided to go back to the bedroom.

Passing by the kitchen, he noticed that the lips had got out of the tin and were climbing up the walls like slugs and emitting a murmur that was growing louder as the time passed. The young artist locked the door and went towards the bedroom.

The bed was just as he'd left it except that the snakes must have calmed down because the duvet was no longer rippling. He got undressed, looked around in vain for a pair of pyjamas and, shrugging his bare shoulders, quickly got down between the sheets. The snakes jumped a little, turned over and went on sleeping, while the young artist, though having fallen asleep himself, could still hear the sound of the lips' whisperings, which gradually filled the whole house.

When Esmé returned, she found her guest fast asleep. The snakes had opened the kitchen door and were drinking milk from a large earthen bowl, while the strange lips had vanished, leaving behind a faint odour of unhealthy saliva.

Esmé stood for a moment in the bedroom doorway gazing at the young artist who was sleeping, then she slowly got undressed and slipped under the covers. It wasn't her intention to wake him, but his beautiful skin that smelled of vanilla made her snuggle up to him and she began licking his neck. But the young artist felt tired and didn't appear at all willing to sacrifice his sleep. So without even opening his eyes, he pushed her away and tried to get comfortable again. Esmé was furious at his action; she leapt out of bed and called her snakes in their secret language. They immediately obeyed and lined up before her, licking their lips that were still dripping milk. Esmé whispered something and the largest of them slid up into the bed and stopped beside the head of the young artist, who was again breathing soundly. The snake lowered its head to the young man's ear and put its tongue inside. Then, with a terrifying noise, it began sucking out the brain of the young artist, who suddenly felt his dreams shrinking and shrivelling like wrinkled skin.

When the snake withdrew, having sucked even the last ganglion from the young artist's brain, Esmé grabbed hold of it and thrust it between her legs.'

'Do you understand, now?' asked the unknown girl, still fixing me with that same dark look. She was finished with her story. I knew that I had no other choice. I lifted the covers and made room for her in the bed. She caressed my head and began to get undressed.

'Anyway, my name's not Esmé,' she said.

'And I'm no young artist,' I replied. 'There's just one thing I want you to do for me,' I added, 'don't take your stockings off right away.'

She went on getting undressed, however, without paying the slightest attention to what were, in her opinion, childish requests on my part.

Original title: 'Itan idi perasmena mesanychta'. First published in Aris Sfakianakis, *Oi paraxenes synitheies tis oikoyeneias Morfi* [The Strange Habits of the Morfis Family] (1984). Translated here from the text anthologised in Makis Panorios (ed.), *To Elliniko Fantastiko Diiyima* [The Greek Fantasy Short Story] vol. 2, Athens: Aiolos, 1993, pp. 203–205.

Sleeping Beauty and the Forty Pirates

Nikos Panayotopoulos

Once upon a time, long ago, when people still used aeroplanes to travel no further than the ends of the earth, when some still died from illnesses and others from hunger, when wars were still fought for oil, in other words long before the wars fought for water, in this dark age, then, in a corner of the Old World known as Europe, a baby girl was born to whom her parents gave the name Aurora.

The wagging tongues were quick to say that the name couldn't have been more apt for a girl with such a golden future – and this was no exaggeration or figure of speech; gold still had some value then and her father was one of the richest men of his times. His ships plied the seas and his planes split the skies, the same skies that his factories' chimneys polluted, though there were very few who protested about this as most people were employed in his businesses, the most renowned of which was the colossal media corporation he had created out of nothing, because, in addition to riches, he also desired fame. At the age of seventy-five, he had both, and it was only then that it occurred to him that he might share all this. So, he got married, and his wedding surpassed any other in splendour given that he, the king of power, took for his wife a queen of beauty, forty-five years his junior. It should be pointed out here that marriage was still the custom then and beauty was highly regarded, just like riches and fame.

So, it was only natural that the common mortals should envy Aurora for her good fortune, and if they were to hear that there was even one person in the whole world who was worried about her future, they would have called him mad, after first having had a good laugh. Nevertheless, there was someone who was worried about Aurora's future, and as one might easily guess, this was her own father. He was so concerned about his daughter's future – or, rather about the future of his dynasty some might say with not a little cynicism – that he decided not to leave anything to chance. Besides, he had both the money and the power – or so he thought – to prevent any mistakes or slip-ups which might jeopardise his plans, the most ambitious of which – even if he still hadn't admitted it even to himself – was her future marriage to the seven year-old son of his chief competitor.

Aurora's father was forward-looking; this was his greatest asset and it was because of this that he'd got where he was. From the very first, then, he'd seen that he himself was rather old to become a father; his health was shaky and he was not good-looking. And from the very first he'd realised that his wife may be extremely beautiful, but she was not particularly gifted mentally. So, in order to avoid any mishaps and in order not to be caught out when it would be too late for him to do anything about it, two weeks after learning that his wife was pregnant, he urgently summoned to his office three leading geneticists who also happened to work for him, holding as they did managerial posts in the research department of the largest pharmaceutical company in the New World and his flagship company in the health field. He summoned them and told them to drop their research projects and concern themselves exclusively with the still unborn Aurora. His request was as follows: her intelligence should be such as to allow her to manage the fabulous inheritance wisely and dynamically, at the same time promoting her father's name; her beauty should be such as to automatically bring her mother's name to everyone's lips; her health should be such as to allow her to live to a ripe old age, without any problems.

'Can it be done?' he asked them sharply, confirming the legend that had him saying little and doing a lot.

The three geneticists looked at each other, delighted by the challenge and, though science had still not proved that it was able to overcome fate, they answered, equally laconically, that it could!

And the truth is that they worked miracles in order to keep their promise. For a good many months they worked night and day, without any thought for their pains, sparing no expense, surpassing themselves in resourcefulness in order to carry out the difficult task they had been assigned.

The first addressed the thorny problem of intelligence. Using the research findings by a team of Greek scientists who had recently succeeded in transferring a section of genetic matter from one chromosome to another, he managed to increase the intelligence quotient of the precious heiress by fifty points! In fact, at one stage, it occurred to him that he may have overdone it. In a rare burst of philosophical reflection – which might well be attributed to his tiredness after so many hours over the microscope – he wondered whether he may, in this way, have condemned her to total solitude, given that an IQ of 180 would drive everyone around her away. But then he thought of how grateful his boss would be and dreamt – closing his tired eyes for a moment – of the likely rewards, so he decided to leave things as they were.

The second addressed the burning question of beauty. After having first decided on the ideal physical proportions and those features determining beauty, he made his boss's daughter ten whole centimetres taller, removed her obvious predisposition for body fat, slightly darkened the colour of her hair, at the same time lightening that of her eyes and skin, removed a little of the roundness of her face, reversed the curve in her nose and – one final touch – added a couple of centimetres to the size of her breasts, straying no more than a suggestion from the ideal, for no other reason than that he himself liked women with full breasts. And, with the help of a friend who specialised in three-dimensional computer graphics, he fashioned Aurora's future image in order to present it to his employer, counting, without doubt, on his generosity.

The third addressed the major question of health. And he very quickly realised that he would have his work cut out. Aurora was condemned to inherit from her father not only his fabulous wealth but also a problematical cardiovascular system, several troublesome allergies and a vulnerability to respiratory problems, which, in combination with the rest, could prove fatal. All this from her father. Her predisposition for cancer of the womb came straight from her mother's genes. Seeing that things were tricky, the sensible scientist turned to his assistants. He told them what it was all about so as to overawe them and then appealed to their sense of pride. They swore that they would do their best. And they did. All except one.

Among those called upon to lend a hand was a talented but arrogant young man, who, for reasons unknown, believed that his supervisor was holding him back; he believed that his position in the company, and consequently his salary and prospects, was far below that befitting his skill and ability. He had appealed to the company management, but his grievance had been ignored. He had tried to come into contact with the owner himself and was incredibly upset when his request was rejected, though even he had thought it unlikely. It was then that he decided to sound out the competitors and he had already scheduled his move. He thought that fate was offering him an excellent opportunity: he would leave, as he had planned, but first he would deliver a telling blow to his supervisor's prestige, to his department, and, consequently, to the company itself and the person who owned it.

And that's what he did. While his colleagues were doing everything they could to reformulate the laws of nature, he was opening the back door to a hormonal storm, which, of course, would not break immediately, but, when the time came, would sweep everything in its path. He calculated that the storm would break after twelve or thirteen years; in that crucial period when the girl would emerge from her protective cocoon and, a woman at last, would open her wings and stretch them, before flying off to a life strewn with flowers.

Except that Aurora would not get as far as flying, for, even before she was born, an imperceptible discrepancy in her genetic code had accelerated the time-bomb that would kill her. The ambitious young geneticist calculated, and correctly so, that no one would tumble to his intervention in time; he calculated that his supervisors, having located all likely problems from the very beginning, would, quite reasonably, have their attention focused on the results of their endeavours. He even imagined them gloating and celebrating and congratulating each other and secretly making plans for how they would make the best use of their reward. Just for a moment, he wondered whether thirteen years was too long a time. Just for a moment he toyed with the idea of a more immediate blow. But then he reflected that if he was going to demolish something, he should wait for it to be built first; so with this comforting thought that remained with him night and day, he continued his work as planned, and he carried it out with determination and diligence.

To some extent, however, he failed. His predictions did not prove correct, either in terms of the time when the symptoms would appear or in terms of the final outcome. Even so, however, the damage had been done.

*

Aurora was born without anyone spotting the problem. On the contrary, the first tests showed that she was a healthy, happy and beautiful baby. After only four months, she uttered her first word, 'daddy', sending her father into raptures. Two months later, she was easily able to run through the huge hall in the house, or rather in the palace, where the happy family lived, articulating words such as 'statistics', a development which brought tears to her father's eyes.

The problem began to become apparent at around her fourth birthday. And, again, not immediately. Anyhow, it was around then that they began to realise that Aurora exhibited an interest in men that was open to misinterpretation; at least, that is, when she decided to raise her angelic face from the thick volumes of Numerical Theory, or when she considered that she no longer needed to practise Schubert's piano sonatas, given that she played them perfectly.

One day, the estate's head-gardener, a good-natured sixty-year-old, came up to Aurora's father, shaking with fear and shame at what he was obliged to relate. Sweating profusely and mincing his words, he described how Aurora had enticed him into the elm grove, had convinced him using the most elaborate arguments that he was obliged to play with her, first coaxing him, then threatening him, and how, finally, she had almost had his trousers off, imploring him, in his turn, to fondle her with his callused hands. The head-gardener couldn't bear it; he broke into tears and, sobbing loudly, added that his assistants had had to confront the same problem. It goes without saying that he and his assistants were dismissed, though the amount of compensation they received testified to their employer's regret.

Aurora's father, who was now approaching eighty, rushed to the doctors. Aurora spent the following years surrounded by the best endocrinologists in the world – mostly women, as the presence of men often led to explosive situations. Her problem was located, analysed, discussed, studied and investigated. But to no avail. No one was able to provide a convincing solution to the problem.

Eventually, in desperation, Aurora's father summoned the three geneticists – the girl's godfathers – if not to give account, then at least to give their opinion. Astonished, not to say terrified, they expressed their inability to understand what had happened and their inability to determine what would happen. Aurora's father dismissed them curtly and the legend has it that they died penniless and forgotten.

Before Aurora was seven, her mother died as a result of complications following an operation to remove her womb, though everyone knew that she died of grief and not cancer, which, in any case, could be more or less successfully treated at that time.

Aurora's father, this forward-looking man, found himself facing an impasse. He shut himself up in his palace with his daughter and an army of servants, whose task it was to prevent the fair and foxy little girl from chasing after the only man around – her ageing and ailing father. They didn't always succeed. Aurora's resourcefulness was inexhaustible and her desire so intense that nothing could restrain her. The old man, now virtually bed-ridden, ended up by managing his empire bolted inside a room, the walls of which were lined with dozens of tele-conferencing screens. It took him some time to come up with a solution or, rather, to postpone the solution for the distant future, as it was impossible for him to accept defeat. It took him some time to decide who he could trust with the fate of his daughter and of his fortune. It took him some time to set up a foundation – bearing her name – and, through its constitution, to bind the board of directors so that it would carry out its complex mission. It also took him some time to consult the leading experts in the field of cryogenics and to commission the construction of the Ark that would save his kind. Finally, it took him some time to accept that he had done the right thing and that the time had come for him to part from his daughter for good, and to send her where no con man would be able to exploit her misfortune.

The legend says that at the last, not even he dared remain alone with her. The legend also says that the twelve-year-old Aurora understood that something was going on and tried to escape. She didn't manage it. She was taken in chains, like a schizophrenic convict, to the nearest launch pad, was immersed, without delay, in liquid nitrogen by the special team which had undertaken the task, was carefully placed in her glass bed – some called it a glass 'coffin', but they were mistaken – and this was taken, in its turn, to the area specially designed for the space shuttle, which had the name of the most famous vessel in history written in golden letters on its side. It's said that, grief-stricken, her father watched the launch from the screens in his room and died a few hours later, murmuring her name, under the illusion that he had done the best he could.

★

As might be expected, the story of the unfortunate Aurora did not remain secret for very long. And for a long time afterwards, it was the main topic not only of the news reports, but also of the conversations by ordinary people, who would often raise their eyes to the skies, as if it were possible for them to spot the spaceship rotating in a fixed orbit around the earth. Meanwhile, the members of the board of directors of the AURORA Foundation were obliged to give dozens of interviews, in which they explained her dead father's intentions and the reasons that led him to this decision. The scientists who had taken part in the various stages of the *Sleeping Beauty* project, as it was called, gave hundreds of interviews, in which they explained the method, the process and the likelihood of success. Those who happened to know the girl at first hand gave, in their turn, thousands of interviews, in which they praised her surpassing intelligence and beauty, but also explained her problem, though not without some excess, which only inflated the issue so that it took on mythical proportions.

However, as the years passed, Aurora was forgotten not only by most people but also by the few who were responsible for her fate. And as often happens with stories that grow old, so, too, Aurora's story faded, so much so that it seemed more like a fairytale once thought up by someone in order to get his grandchildren to sleep a bit sooner.

In time, the original members of the board of directors retired, making way for younger ones, who, perhaps justifiably, concerned themselves more with the tangible and visible part of their mission, namely the fortune, rather than with the frozen daughter. And, as is only natural in such cases, it wasn't long before disputes and conflicts broke out among them, resulting in the split and fragmentation of the empire into small kingdoms that fought over which one would prevail. They were so absorbed by their earthly war that, when they received the ominous message 'We are holding Aurora', they didn't attach any importance to it, believing that it was some stupid hoax.

The forty pirates who were indeed holding Aurora were

surprised. At first, they thought that they were dealing with some kind of regular negotiating trick. But they quickly realised that there was a serious possibility that the time, the toil and the money that they had invested in kidnapping Aurora might have been to no avail. It would indeed be a shame, as their plan was brilliant, both in conception and in execution; and original, since it was the first space kidnapping in history. They had snatched the discarded *Challenger IV*, literally from under the noses of the guards at the vast, open-air Space Museum at Cape Canaveral, put it into orbit, docked with the *Ark*, which they had boarded, only to land a few hours later at the abandoned Baikonur spaceport, where they were met by lorries, one of which had been suitably re-fitted in order to carry the valuable cargo. Everything had gone according to plan.

What they hadn't taken into account was human greed. And it was ironic, to say the least, that they should have to face the very thing that had motivated them. Not one of the members of the board of directors of the AURORA Foundation was prepared to spend even one dollar to save a frozen girl who had been forgotten by everyone. Not one of them had any wish to suddenly find himself working under a twelve-year-old girl employer with serious hormonal disorders. It should be pointed out that no cure for her problem yet existed, given that, with the Board's tacit consent, the relevant research had long ago been abandoned. So the members decided, and unanimously for the first time in many years, to completely ignore the pirates' demands. They, in their turn, threatened to publicise the matter, but the Board of directors knew that if they had a grain of sense, they wouldn't do it; all they would succeed in doing would be to draw world attention to themselves and bring the powerful Interpol down on them.

The members judged correctly. The forty pirates grew desperate. One after the other, they saw their threats come to nothing. They saw their plans crumbling like sand castles. They saw all this and decided, therefore, to put into operation the only alternative solution left to them: they would revive

Aurora in the hope that her reawakening would bring her ungrateful employees to their senses. They'd heard something about a rare disease from which the girl was suffering, but they thought that this would most likely help make the board members change their attitude.

So they approached a low-paid employee in the same company who had been responsible for freezing Aurora and he willingly went over to them, taking her file with him. This was the first person that Aurora set eyes on when she awoke after more than sixty years. He was a rather dishy though shy young man, by the name of Grim, who was taken aback by her forwardness and took to his heels screaming. On hearing his screams, the pirates ran to rescue him and when he recounted to them what had happened, they began to wonder, for the first time, whether they had made the right choice. It was Aurora who solved the problem for them a little later when they were obliged to explain the situation to her, before sitting her in front of the videophone in order for her to speak to the board members.

Aurora realised that her father had died and this must have shaken her as, for the next two hours, she appeared to keep control of herself without any effort. Instead of grabbing and groping the pirates, she sat quietly in her chair and discussed the situation with them with a maturity and discernment that surprised them. After first asking for the facts, Aurora informed them that they would get nothing out of the Board in this way. It took a great deal of time and effort on her part to explain to them – slowly and patiently, like a teacher with young pupils – that they had to change their plan, which, naturally, she herself would draw up.

Over the next days, it was leaked to the press that one of the board members – who remained unnamed – had organised Aurora's kidnapping with the aim of blackmailing his colleagues and acquiring complete control of the board of directors. The report, which was accompanied by an old photo of Aurora, caused an incredible stir in the ranks of the board of directors. The suspicion that existed among the members helped to maintain the stir for quite some time. And the suspicion was cleverly maintained thanks to various reports that focused the suspicion first in one direction then in the other. All this resulted in a significant fall in the share-prices of all those companies connected with the Foundation. Aurora spent many laborious hours trying to teach her unreceptive pirates the secrets of profiteering; particularly how to exploit the *time-gap* – in other words, that small time-margin between the order to buy and the actual payment – so as to profit without having to lay out any money. And if this caused her difficulties, it's not hard to imagine what she went through in order to get into their thick heads the concept of hostile take-overs.

Fortunately, there was that rather dishy young man, who still avoided her, but who, thanks be to God, at least had some idea concerning the stock-market. With his help, and thanks to the initial capital begrudgingly provided by the pirates, Aurora managed in the space of a few weeks to get control of a small, though not insignificant, percentage of her companies. She then once again leaked it to the press that the business of her kidnapping was nothing but a fabrication thought up by some fanciful reporter. The author of the report ended by appealing to common sense and asking the more rational readers to look for the proof in the skies.

When it finally occurred to them to look up, they were all relieved to see the *Ark* tracing its endless orbit in the sky. The members of the board of directors immediately called a cease-fire. Share prices again began to rise. The media again remembered little Aurora, though the nostalgia didn't last very long.

Meanwhile, little Aurora had some real fun with her forty pirates in zero-gravity conditions. Of course, at first, these roughnecks were hesitant. They had committed more than a few atrocities in their lives, but this went beyond all limits. What they had before them was just a twelve-year-old girl – hot, but still only twelve years old. When Aurora asked them how they reckoned her age, they became confused and, scratching their heads, looked puzzled at each other. Aurora immediately explained to them that she may, in actual terms, have only lived twelve years, but she had been born long before they had and, consequently, there was no legal or moral issue involved. There was only one problem: that *she* was much older than them. The pirates didn't take a lot of convincing. They looked at each other again and saw that they had before them a girl with more brains than all of them put together, a girl who was willing and, above all, a girl who was so beautiful that she could seduce even a saint.

★

Within a few years, Aurora regained control of her father's crumbling empire. Her pirates became experts in hostile take-overs. The legend has it that the *Ark* landed a number of times at the forgotten Baikonur base. Each time, one of the forty pirates, in a state of exhaustion, disembarked from the space-ship and unwillingly went into retirement – which means that he took over the management of one of the dozens of companies controlled by the Foundation. His place in the harem was taken by some young and ambitious astronaut, in the belief that he was participating in an experiment to do with improving the chances of conception in zero-gravity conditions. The recruitment of the young astronauts was the responsibility of Grim, the dishy and shy young man who had revived Aurora.

Legend has it that the three geneticists had done a very good job. As to the first two, here was no doubt whatsoever. But it also seems that the third succeeded in accomplishing the impossible. Despite the criminal intervention by the malicious assistant – who, it should be noted, died young, having been bitten by a genetically modified mouse – Aurora lived a long, long time without any particular problems and reached a ripe old age, enjoying herself with her pirates.

In fact, many say that, even today, if you raise your gaze to the skies after dusk and look towards the West, you may see the gleaming *Ark* passing by, a bright, flaming circumflex above the omega of Cassiopeia, and if your heart is as pure as that of a little girl, you may even hear Aurora's groaning, which some take to be thunder even when the skies are clear . . . They also say that if you're not taken aback and manage to say her name three times, then you will enjoy a full love life just like hers . . . There are some, of course, who believe that all this happens only in fairytales, and in this way they may live happily ever after, but we live happier still.

Original title: 'I oraia kimomeni ke oi saranda pirates'. Published in Michel Faïs (ed.), *Paramythia apo to mellon* [Fairytales from the Future], Athens: Minoas, 2001, pp. 117ff.

About the Authors

(Listed according to year of birth)

Andreas Lascaratos (1811–1901) was born in Cephalonia. His work reflects the literary tradition of the Ionian Islands and was undoubtedly influenced by the two major poets of these islands, Dionysios Solomos and Andreas Kalvos, with whom he was personally acquainted. His own verses were collected in a single volume, *Various Poems*, published in 1872. His prose works include: *The Mysteries of Cephalonia* (1856), *Ecce Homo* (1886) and the posthumous *Morals, Customs and Beliefs of Cephalonia, Thoughts*, and *The Art of Public Speaking and Writing*. His satire was often directed against the Orthodox Church and, like Roïdis (see below), he was excommunicated as a result of his writings.

Emmanouil Roïdis (1836–1904) was born on the island of Syra, though he spent much of his early life travelling and studying abroad. He returned to Greece at the age of twenty-one and established himself in Athens, where, later in life, he worked as director of the National Library. He first appeared in Greek letters in 1860 as a translator of Chateaubriand. He wrote mainly literary criticism and short stories, though is perhaps best known for his one novel, *Pope Joan* (1866), which caused a sensation at the time because of its scandalous theme, and resulted in his being excommunicated. This novel has been translated several times into English, most notably by Lawrence Durrell.

Achilleus Paraschos (1838–1895) was born in Nauplion in the Peloponnese. He published his collected poems in three volumes in 1881 and his work is generally regarded as being representative of the final phase of Greek Romanticism. It is interesting that Roïdis, writing in 1877, singled him out as one of only two contemporary Greek poets worthy of praise.

Alexandros Papadiamantis (1851–1911). 'I was born in Skiathos on 4 March 1851. I finished Primary School in 1863, but it was not until 1867 that I was sent to Secondary School in Chalkis, where I attended the first and second years. I attended the third year in Pireaus, before cutting short my studies and returning to my hometown. In June 1872, I went on pilgrimage to Mount Athos, where I stayed a few months. In 1873, I came to Athens and attended the fourth year at the Varvakeio High School. In 1874, I registered in the Philosophy Faculty, where I attended a few literature courses, while privately studying foreign languages. In my youth, I painted icons of Saints, then I wrote verses and endeavoured to compose comedies. In 1868, I attempted to write a novel. In 1879, my work, the "Emigrant Woman", was published in "Neologos" in Constantinople. In 1881, a religious poem of mine was published in the magazine "Sotiras". In 1882, the "Traffickers in Nations" was published in "Mi Hanesai". Later, I wrote some one hundred stories, published in various magazines and newspapers.' (Alexandros Papadiamantis).

Constantine Cavafy (1863–1933) was born and lived most of his life in Alexandria. Though the first collected edition of his poetry was not published until after his death, he is now generally regarded as the most important figure in twentieth-century Greek poetry and has become the most widely-known Greek poet abroad, having influenced many major poets such as W.H. Auden and Joseph Brodsky. His work continues to be translated and read and to stimulate scholarly discussion. He is less well-known for his prose works, which were published in Athens by Ikaros in 2003.

Andreas Karkavitsas (1866–1922) was born in Lechaina in the Peloponnese. By profession he was a doctor, first in the navy and later in the army, giving him the opportunity to witness life at sea and in the village. He would return continually to both these themes in his short stories. His first works were collected in a single volume entitled *Tales* (1892). His subsequent stories were collected in *Tales From the Prow* (1899) and *Former Loves* (1900). He also wrote several novellas, the most notable of which is *The Beggar* (1896).

Menos Philintas (1870–1934). A writer and philologist, his works include: *From the Legends of the Centuries* (1901); *In the Hills of Halkidiki* (1916); *A Child's Loves* (1922); *Taormina* (1922); *Stories of the Orient* (1936); a poetry collection, *Octaves* (1921), and a number of scholarly works on Linguistics and the Greek language.

Demosthenes Voutyras (1871–1958) was born in Constantinople and grew up in Piraeus. A prolific writer, he started writing short stories and novellas that first appeared in literary periodicals around the turn of the century. In 1903, he published his novel *Lagka*, which established him on the literary scene, and he went on to publish thirty-five collections of short stories and novels. His writings were particularly popular and influential following the end of the First World War, due perhaps to their focus on the plight of the urban poor and the growing interest in the social themes he dealt with.

Nikolaos Episkopopoulos (1874–1944) was born in Zakynthos. He worked for a short time as an assistant in a pharmacist's before moving to Athens at the age of eighteen. He became a regular contributor to the newspaper *Asty*, in which he published a series of short stories, entitled *Mad Tales*, together with regular columns, features, theatre reviews, even articles on popularised medicine. He was the first translator into Greek of Baudelaire's *Prose Poems* (1895), but published only one book of his own in Greek, *Twilight Tales* (1899). In 1902, he left for Paris, where he began a second literary career as a French critic, essayist and novelist under the pseudonym of Nicolas Segur.

Napoleon Lapathiotis (1889–1944) was born in Athens. His

father was a Cypriot from the village of Lapatho (hence the name) and his mother came from the island of Hydra. At University, he studied law. His poetry was influenced by the aestheticism of his age (particularly by Wilde) and is noted for its despairing and melancholy tone. His first collection, *Poems*, was published in 1939.

Fotis Kontoglou (1895–1965) was born in Ayvalik in Asia Minor. He studied art in Paris and travelled extensively in France and Spain. His first book, *Pedro Cazas* (1923) marked an important break with the exclusively Greek settings and preoccupations of his contemporary writers. Despite a large output (mainly of short stories), his subsequent development was limited. He is best known and was more influential as a painter, who drew on Byzantine and Orthodox traditions.

Andreas Embiricos (1901–1975) was born in Braila, Romania. Between 1926 and 1931 he lived in Paris, where he associated with André Breton and the French Surrealists and began psychoanalysis with René Laforgue. He became one of the pioneers of psychoanalysis in Greece and practised the profession for sixteen years (1935–1951). In 1935, in Athens, he gave his famous lecture 'On Surrealism', which introduced and established the movement in Greece. He published several collections of surrealist poetry, an eight-volume novel, prose works and translations.

Yorgos Theotokas (1905–1966) was born in Constantinople and studied in Athens, Paris and London. He belongs to the group of Greek writers known collectively as the 'generation of the thirties' and his essay *The Free Spirit* (1929) is regarded as the manifesto of that generation. His work as novelist, short story writer, essayist, dramatist and founder and editor of literary journals has secured his place in modern Greek letters. Of his better-known novels, *Argo* (1933–6) and *Leonis* (1940) have both been translated into English.

Nanos Valaoritis (1921–) was born in Lausanne, Switzerland.

He studied Literature and Law at the universities of Athens, London and the Sorbonne. In London, he was the first to present and translate Greek poets of the '30s Generation (Seferis, Elytis, Embiricos, Engonopoulos, Gatsos). Between 1944 and 1953 he lived in England and associated with T.S. Eliot and his circle. From 1954 to 1960, he was resident in Paris and associated with André Breton and his circle. He returned to Greece in 1960 and edited the literary magazine *Pali* (1963–1967). Since 1968, he has been teaching comparative literature and writing at San Francisco State University. He has written numerous books of poetry, prose works, novels and studies. He has twice been awarded the Greek State Prize for Poetry (1959 and 1983) and has also received the American National Poetry Association Award (1996).

Tassos Leivaditis (1922–1989) was born in Athens. He studied Law at Athens University, but left without taking his degree. He was active in the Greek resistance in World War II and a member of the Greek Communist Party. He subsequently spent over four years in detention camps for his left-wing allegiances. In 1954, he became poetry critic for the newspaper *Avyi*, a position he held until the advent of the military dictatorship in 1967. He published over twenty collections of poetry and his poems have been translated into numerous languages.

Alexandros Schinas (1924–). A writer and journalist, his works include *Case Studies* (1966/1989); *The Chess Game* (1991) and a collection of journalistic texts. Two of his novellas, *With Red Light* and *Before the Machine Gunner*, were published in 1969 in German translation.

E.H. Gonatas (1924–) was born in Athens where he made his living as a lawyer. As a writer, he has particularly cultivated the short prose piece and has published six slim volumes: *The Traveller* (1945), *The Crypt* (1959), *The Chasm* (1963), *The Cows* (1963), *The Hospitable Cardinal* (1986) and *The Preparation* (1991). He has translated, among others, Ivan Goll,

Antonio Porchia and Pierre Bettencourt and was awarded the Greek State Translation Prize. His own works have been translated into English, French and German.

Petros Ambatzoglou (1931–) was born in Athens. He has worked for the Greek Electricity Board, as a writer in an advertising agency and as a newspaper and radio journalist. Since 1962, he has published eleven books comprising novels and collections of short stories, and in 1988 he received the Greek State Short Story Prize. He is himself a translator and his own novels have been translated into English and French.

Tassos Roussos (1934–) is a poet, prose-writer, critic and translator. He is the author of numerous poetry collections, novellas and collections of short stories. He has translated Roman and Greek tragedians, Shakespeare, Webster and modern fantasy writers, including H.P. Lovecraft, Abraham Merit, Isaac Asimov and Arthur Clarke.

Makis Panorios (1935–) is an actor and author of novels, short stories and plays. He has translated, among others, H.G. Wells, Horace Walpole and H.P. Lovecraft. He has done more than anyone for the cause of fantasy literature in Greece, having written numerous fantasy works himself and having edited several anthologies of fantasy, science-fiction and horror stories. In 1993, he received an award from the World Science Fiction Association for his contribution to science fiction in Greece.

Nikos Houliaras (1940–) was born in Ioannina. He is a graduate of the Athens School of Fine Arts and is well-known as both an artist and songwriter. He began writing in 1962 and published poems, prose works and art criticism in various magazines. He has subsequently published books on art criticism, several novels and a number of collections of short stories. His novel *In My Enemy's House* (Nefeli 1995) was proposed by Greece for the 1996 Aristeion European Literature Prize. A number of his short stories have been translated into French, Italian, English, Swedish and German, while his collection of stories *Bakakok* (Kedros 1981) and his novels *Lousias* (Kedros 1979), *Life Next Time* (Nefeli 1985) and *In My Enemy's House* have been published in French by Hatier. Several of his short stories have been adapted for television and his novel, *Lousias*, was made into a TV series broadcast by Greek Television (ET-1) in 1989.

Yoryis Yatromanolakis (1940–) was born in Crete and is a professor of ancient Greek at the University of Athens. He is a novelist, poet, essayist and critic. His third novel, *The History of a Vendetta* (Kedros 1982) was awarded the Greek State Prize and the Nikos Kazantzakis Prize. Four of his novels: *The Spiritual Meadow, The History of a Vendetta, A Report of a Murder* and *Eroticon* have been published in English translation by Dedalus.

Dimitris Kalokyris (1948–) was born in Rethymnon in Crete. He studied modern Greek literature in Thessaloniki, where he founded the literary periodical *Tram* (1971–1978). In Athens, he published the art and literature magazine *Hartis* (1982–1987) and also served as managing editor and art editor of the cultural magazine *To Tetarto* (1985–1987). He works as a graphic designer and an illustrator of books, and has staged four exhibitions of his collages. He has published numerous books of poetry, prose and translations and has twice been awarded the Greek State Short Story Prize (1996 and 2001).

Demosthenes Kourtovik (1948–) was born in Athens. He studied biology in Athens and Stuttgart and wrote his doctoral thesis in Poland on the evolution of human sexuality. He has published twelve books (novels, short stories, studies, aphorisms, etc.) and has translated sixty-two books from eight different languages. Today, he works as a literary critic for the Greek newspaper, *Ta Nea*.

Aris Marangopoulos (1948–) was born in Athens. He is a graduate of the University of Athens (History and

Archaeology) and has a post-graduate degree from the Sorbonne (History of Art and Archaeology). He has published over ten books, including novels and short stories and, as a Joyce expert, has written three studies of Joyce's work. He writes regularly on literary topics for Greek national newspapers and translates from English and French, having translated, in particular, works by Irish writers (Swift, Joyce). At present, he is General Secretary of the Hellenic Authors' Society.

Evyenios Aranitsis (1955–) was born in Corfu and is a poet, prose writer, essayist and critic. He founded and is the managing editor of Akman Press and, since 1978, has worked regularly for the Greek newspaper, *Elefherotypia*. He was awarded the 1999 Greek State Prize for his work *To Whom Does Corfu Belong?*

Theodoros Grigoriadis (1956–) was born in Palaiochori, Kavala. He studied English Literature at the University of Thessaloniki and has taught English in state schools in Thrace and Athens. Between 1999 and 2001, he was responsible for organising a series of seminars on Greek and foreign literature in public libraries in Northern Greece. He regularly writes articles for newspapers and periodicals. He has so far published six novels and a collection of short stories. His novel *Partali* (2001) has been translated into French.

Kostas Arkoudeas (1958–) was born in Athens. Since 1986, he has published nine books, including novels and collections of short stories. He works as a journalist and critic.

Aris Sfakianakis (1958–) was born in Heracleion, Crete. He studied Law at the University of Athens and works as an air-traffic controller. Since 1981, he has published six novels and collections of short stories. He has translated extensively from English and French, including works by H.G. Wells and Edgar Allan Poe.

Nikos Panayotopoulos (1963–) was born in Athens. He studied Technical Engineering. Between 1989 and 1992, he worked as an arts correspondent for newspapers, magazines and television. Since 1992, he has made his living writing screenplays for television and the cinema. He has published a collection of short stories, *The Materials' Guilt* (Polis 1997) and two novels, *Ziggy from Marfan: The Diary of an Extraterrestrial* (Polis 1998) and *Benefit of the Doubt* (Polis 1999).

Dedalus Literary Fantasy Anthologies

The Dedalus Book of Greek Fantasy – edited by David Connolly £9.99
The Dedalus Book of Spanish Fantasy – edited by Margaret Jull Costa & Annella McDermott £10.99
The Dedalus Book of Roman Decadence – edited by Geoffrey Farrington £8.99
The Dedalus Book of German Decadence – edited by Ray Furness £9.99
The Dedalus Book of French Horror – edited by Terry Hale £10.99
The Dedalus Book of Dutch Fantasy – edited by Richard Huijing £10.99
The Dedalus Book of Portuguese Fantasy – edited by Eugenio Lisboa & Helder Macedo £10.99
The Dedalus Book of Austrian Fantasy – edited by Mike Mitchell £11.99
The Dedalus Book of Medieval Literature – edited by Brian Murdoch £10.99
The Dedalus Book of Polish Fantasy – edited by Wiesiek Powaga £10.99
The Dedalus Book of Surrealism – edited by Michael Richardson £9.99
The Myth of the World: Surrealism 2 – edited by Michael Richardson £9.99
The Dedalus Book of Decadence – edited by Brian Stableford £7.99
The Dedalus Book of British Fantasy – edited by Brian Stableford £9.99
Tales of the Wandering Jew – edited by Brian Stableford £9.99
The Dedalus Book of Sexual Ambiguity – edited by Emma Wilson £9.99

For full descriptions of these titles visit our website dedalusbooks.com, click on catalogue and then anthologies and decadence/empire of the senses . . . All Dedalus titles can be ordered from your local bookshop, bought online or can be obtained from Dedalus directly by writing to:

Cash sales, Dedalus Limited, Langford Lodge,
St Judith's Lane, Sawtry, Cambs, PE28 5XE